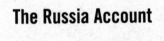

The Russia Account

FROM NATIONAL BESTSELLING AUTHOR

# STEPHEN COONTS

# THE RUSSIA ACCOUNT

REGNERY
FICTION
www.RegneryFiction.com

Regnery Fiction™ is a trademark of Salem Communications Holding Cor-poration; Regnery® is a registered trademark of Salem Communications Holding Corporation

Cataloging-in-Publication data on file with the Library of Congress

ISBN 978-1-62157-660-0
ebook ISBN 978-1-62157-717-1

Published in the United States by
Regnery Fiction
An Imprint of Regnery Publishing
A Division of Salem Media Group
300 New Jersey Ave NW
Washington, DC 20001
www.Regnery.com

Manufactured in the United States of America

10 9 8 7 6 5 4 3 2 1

Books are available in quantity for promotional or premium use. For infor-mation on discounts and terms, please visit our website: www.Regnery.com.

## With Jim DeFelice

*Deep Black: Conspiracy*
*Deep Black: Jihad*
*Deep Black: Payback*
*Deep Black: Dark Zone*
*Deep Black: Biowar*
*Deep Black*

## Nonfiction

*The Cannibal Queen*
*Dragon's Jaw*, with Barrett Tillman

## Anthologies

*The Sea Witch*
*On Glorious Wings*
*Victory*
*Combat*
*War in the Air*

## Writing as Eve Adams

*The Garden of Eden*

# DISCLAIMER

This is a work of fiction, peopled by and involving foreign and domestic companies, institutions, organizations, and activities—private, public, and government—that are products of the author's imagination. Where actual names appear, they are used fictitiously and do not necessarily depict their actual conduct or purpose.

# Chapter One

**"W**hat's that noise?" Bill Leitz whispered.

I heard it too. We killed the miner's head lamps we wore on our heads and sat in the darkness listening. Tiny noises, like a mouse playing with something metal. Low, just barely audible.

It was two in the morning in Tallinn, Estonia, and Bill Leitz and I were inside a branch of the Bank of Scandinavia working on their server. This little branch only had the one. We were modifying it so that a copy of every transaction that went through it also went via internet to Langley, Virginia, back in the good ol' USA.

But that noise! *There it was again.*

"Maybe we had better get the hell outta here," Leitz whispered. The darn guy just couldn't keep his cool. And the front door was the only way in and out of this office.

"Stay out of sight," I told him and rose from my sitting position. Why these servers have to be mounted so low is a question that I'll never figure out.

I stayed low and moved from the little equipment room where we had been working to the main part of the branch. It only had four small rooms and a toilet; one of the rooms was a little break room with a small refrigerator. The natural light in the room came from a light in the hallway through a frosted glass transom, and from two windows. This being Europe, the branch was on the first floor of a fairly new modern building only two blocks from the train station. In Europe, the first floor is the floor above the ground floor.

Yep, someone was working on the door lock. If they managed to get in, they had about ten seconds to punch in the code to the alarm panel on the wall near the door so that it wouldn't wake the nearly dead at the local police station. We had used that code earlier when we entered, so the alarm was now off. Getting that code had been a trick, but that's another story, one I may include in my autobiography when I get around to writing it.

Whoever was working on that lock just now didn't know the alarm was off. I wondered what their plan was. If they had one.

Oh, of course they did. You don't just zip off to rob a bank without a plan.

Still, two sets of trespassers inside one bank in the middle of the night was probably one set too many.

They were working on the lock with something inserted in the key hole, picking it. Open the door, run in and grab... not the cash in the vault, which was locked as tight as Hillary's heart... but the server. These guys wanted the server!

That didn't seem fair. We were here first, and we wanted the server to stay right where it was, doing the business of the branch and faithfully sending the CIA copies of all the transactions.

The little noises seeped through the door. This wouldn't take long. I had to do something!

What?

I reached for the wall switch and turned on a light in the office. The noises stopped instantly. I put my ear against the door. They were whispering just on the other side... couldn't make out the words... or even discern the language.

They were worried, though.

I snapped the light off, then back on.

Silence now.

I slithered back toward the break room. There was an upright vacuum cleaner there. I unwrapped the cord as quickly as I could, plugged it in, and pushed the "on" switch. It started sucking... not too loudly, but I was sure they could hear it.

I thought, *What the heck,* and started vacuuming the office, moving that little thing around. Bill Leitz watched me from behind a counter.

After ten minutes, I turned the vacuum sweeper off and returned it to the break room. Wound up the cord.

"Think they're gone?" Bill asked nervously.

"They'd better be. Let's finish up and get the hell outta here."

We did. Took another twenty minutes. I was weighing our options as Bill completed our installation and sent a message over the new line to Langley, testing it. If those guys outside came back and stole the server, our work tonight was for nothing. Perhaps we should steal the server.

Then we would learn history, not what was going to happen, which was what the company really wanted to know. *Eeny, minie, miny, moe... Choices, choices...* I decided to do what we were sent here to do, and if someone stole the damn server, we could always come back and do our magic again.

"They might be waiting for us," Bill said softly, pointing out the obvious. He wasn't a covert warrior, but a tech support guy. Stealing information from computer systems was his profession, and he was good at it. He should have been better than average since he had been hacking into computer systems all over the earth for at least twenty years.

I pressed my ear to the door.

"Wish we had been bright enough to bring guns."

In for a penny, in for a pound. Getting caught inside a bank in Estonia in the middle of the night with guns on us would have created a serious international incident. Before Uncle Sam popped us out, we might have spent some unhappy weeks or months in an Estonian lock-up—not a cheerful prospect. We finished tinkering with the server and cleaned up our tools and trash. When I was sure we had everything we had carried in, I turned off the lights, punched in the code to the alarm pad, arming it, and opened the door. The hallway was empty. Phew!

I inspected the lock on the door as well as I could, squinting in that light. It seemed intact. We stepped into the hallway, and I pulled the door shut behind us. Pulled until the lock clicked, then I double-checked it. Locked up tight.

As we went along the hallway, we stripped off our surgical gloves and stuffed them in our pockets. There was a chance the frustrated lock mechanics were waiting for us to leave the building, so we took the stairs to the top floor, found a men's room, and made ourselves at home.

I got out my cell phone and checked my messages. Nothing urgent. Leitz had a porno mag in his backpack; he got it out and settled in for some sexual fantasy. I dialed a number that I had pre-loaded into my cell. Got Joe Kittredge, also known as Joe Kitty, who was outside with Armanti Hall. Both were covert agency operators. I explained the problem. Summed it up by saying, "Leitz and I don't want to get caught, arrested, or shot."

"Couple of lightweights."

"Well, Joe, is anyone out there waiting for us or not?"

"Give me a half hour to look around. I'll call you back."

I put my cell on vibrate so when he called I would get a cheap thrill, and settled down with my back against the men's room door.

Five days ago I had no idea Estonia was in my future. Jake Grafton, the director of the agency, called me into his office one morning, said a senator was coming over for a chat, and maybe I should be there. Listening to senators sure beat reading and writing memos and directives for Grafton to sign, so I took a seat and got comfortable with my notebook, just in case Grafton wanted notes.

"What's this all about?" I asked, idly curious.

"I don't know," he said. "We'll find out together."

Now you may believe that BS if you wish, but after a few years of observation, I was of the opinion that Grafton knew everything about everything, so I concluded he wanted me to get it from the horse's mouth—or rear end, as the case might be.

The senator was only ten minutes late, which was remarkable for a senator, and doubly so since the exalted one was a female. Grafton nodded at me and said, "Tommy Carmellini, my aide."

The senator wasted a small fraction of a second glancing at me, didn't nod, and took a chair that Grafton gestured toward. I resumed my seat on a couch where I could hear both sides of the conversation clearly. The senator ignored me.

"Thank you for taking the time to see me," she said to Grafton. This was just oil she was spreading around. She was on her third term in the senate representing a Midwestern state. After sixteen years in the senate, there wasn't a door in Washington that wouldn't open to her knock.

"My brother's daughter is a branch bank manager for the Bank of Scandinavia in Estonia," she said. "Three days ago, her nine-year-old daughter was kidnapped on her way home from school. She usually walks the five blocks home to her parents' flat. She left the school—the teachers saw her go—and never got home."

"A ransom note?" Grafton asked.

"None yet," the senator replied.

"Other kids getting snatched around there?" the admiral asked calmly, watching her face.

"Not that we know about. Tallinn, the capital, doesn't have much of that, to the best of my brother's knowledge. It's actually a pretty safe place to raise children."

Grafton didn't say anything. Merely played with a pencil on his desk. A retired U.S. Navy two-star rear admiral, he had learned long ago that he got more information by letting people tell it their way rather than asking questions.

The senator decided she had to fill the silence. "The daughter, Penny, has been sending memos and queries to her bosses in Copenhagen about the sheer volume of money going through the bank. This is the busiest branch the bank owns."

"How much?"

"Lately, over a billion dollars a week."

Jake Grafton just stared. I looked up from my notepad.

"A *billion* a week," he repeated softly, his eyes on the senator.

"That's what my niece Penny said," the senator told us. "Maybe more."

"Perhaps you should give me all the particulars—names, addresses, telephone numbers, all of it."

When the senator left a half hour later, my notebook was brimming with facts. Jake Grafton had ushered the senator out, merely promising that the company would look into it, and thanked her for bringing this matter to our attention.

The senator paused by the door. "My niece and her husband want their daughter back."

"We'll see what we can do."

"A personal favor to me..." the senator muttered, then walked out. Grafton closed the door behind her and dropped onto the couch beside me.

"You don't think that number is anywhere near accurate, do you?" I asked.

Jake Grafton looked skeptical. His thinning hair was combed straight back, his nose was a bit large for his face, and he had a strong, square jaw. Six or so feet tall, he hadn't porked up like many men his age stuck in sedentary jobs. Maybe it was exercise, maybe he didn't eat much, maybe it was nervous energy, or a combination of all three.

Grafton called Sarah Houston, his data guru and hacking expert. She said she could be there in five minutes. Sarah is also my off-again, on-again girlfriend. Just then we were on.

"Call it fifty billion a year," Grafton said while we were waiting. "Apple had a net income of forty-eight billion dollars in 2017, and that is probably the most profitable corporation in America. It's more now, yet... fifty billion a year would be more than the net profit of every business in Russia. All of them. It's impossible."

"So what the heck is going on in Estonia?" I wondered aloud.

We were still noodling when Sarah came in, closing the door behind her. She flashed me a smile, which was nice, then took a seat. Grafton briefed her with a summary of the senator's tale.

"Someone is lying," was Sarah's verdict. Diplomacy isn't one of her skill sets.

"You need to hack into the Bank of Scandinavia, find out what's going on. See if you can get into the reports they file with the Swedish government. If someone is lying, let's find out who it is."

"Their systems are undoubtedly encrypted."

"Do the best you can."

Having received her orders, she left.

Grafton turned back to me. "I'll have our man in the embassy there make inquiries," the admiral said. "Draft a message for me to sign. Then get busy planning on how you are going to get into that branch bank. You know what we want."

"Everything."

"Or as near to it as we can get. Plus the encryption codes. They should be on their server." He sighed, then stood. That was my cue to get on with the program.

I popped up, said "Yessir," and made for the door. Sure enough, in the reception room were two people waiting for appointments with the boss. After they went in to the director's office and the door was closed, I asked Robin, the receptionist, "Where's Estonia?"

She gave me a warm smile, batted her long lashes, and said in her sexiest, Let's-Do-It-Tonight voice, "Google it."

Google knew precisely where Estonia was and so did the folks in the company transportation office: in the Baltic, right next to Russia. A great big bird flew four of us guys from the company across the pond to Berlin—flying all night—where we changed planes. Then a turboprop flew us to Tallinn, the capitol and biggest city in the country. We arrived late in the afternoon, tired, dirty, and jet-lagged. Why I do this crap for a living I'll never know.

Tallinn is a medieval city, full of cobbled streets, old buildings, and here and there, a castle or museum. I checked into a hotel, then went over to the American embassy to visit with the senior spook, the station chief. Turned out that our man in Estonia was a woman named Dulcie Del Rio. I had never met her before.

"Penny Rogers," she said. "Her husband teaches at the American school where the daughter, Audra, is a student. Penny isn't talking to us, nor to the police. She says she knows nothing, has had no ransom demand, doesn't have any money to pay ransom, and claims she is completely baffled."

"The husband—Frank Rogers, I believe his name is—what's he saying?"

"He's talked to the police and been to the embassy twice; nothing of much use. He's trying to keep his wife from freaking out. He gave us a photo of Audra. It's a school photo; the police have one too and are looking. Not a trace, so far. Here's a report the embassy staff filed with the State Department."

She handed me a copy and I read it carefully. Then I looked at the school photo. Well, Audra looked like a nice kid. She wore glasses and had teeth that were going to need an orthodontist.

"What do you think, Ms. Del Rio? Is Audra alive?"

"I don't know."

"Any other kids snatched lately?"

"Not foreign kids. The usual messy divorces among the locals, but this is a small country. You can't grab your son or daughter and disappear in the direction of Texas."

"I suppose not. What do you know about this branch bank where Penny Rogers works?"

Del Rio shrugged. "Five employees. Quite unremarkable."

"Do they do much foreign business?"

"Oh, of course. Russia is right next door. Five trains a day roll in from St. Petersburg and three from Moscow. Then there are all the countries around the Baltic. Commerce and money move all over this area every day."

I just nodded. I had to give the station chief a heads-up on our plan to go into the branch and tap the server, but I didn't say when. Didn't ask for her help. She had to know in case anything went wrong—such as the local police busting us for burglary—yet the less anyone in Estonia knew of our plans, the safer we were. Anyone who thinks intelligence agencies can keep their secrets is living in Oz. Half of what intelligence agencies do is try to learn other intelligence agencies' secrets, by any and all means at their disposal. But I digress.

Del Rio took me upstairs to meet the ambassador, a career diplomat. This was another woman in her fifties, with salt and pepper hair and not a smile in sight. While I was supposed to be a State Department investigator, of course she knew I was CIA. She never mentioned it, though.

She talked, I made noises, then followed Del Rio back to the SCIF in the basement. This being a little embassy in a little country, the SCIF, a secure compartmented information center, was also little, about the size of my hotel room.

The next morning, my fellow burglar, Bill Leitz, and I got busy casing our target, the local branch of the Bank of Scandinavia. We took turns watching the doors for a day and counted just seven customers walking in. *A billion a week* through that little office? I didn't believe it.

Of course, Grafton wanted this op done yesterday, so we didn't have the luxury of spending a week or so sizing up the place, checking on alarms, photographing everyone going in and out, checking out the employees. I did see Penny Rogers enter the building in the morning and leave it in the evening, and I took her photo. I thought she looked stressed to the max. Well, if I had a kid—and I don't—and my kid got snatched, I would be beyond stressed: I'd be in a strait jacket.

On the third day we were in Estonia, I dropped by the American School to see Frank Rogers, the father. I met him in the break room during the lunch hour. "My name is James Wilson, Mr. Rogers. Jim." I gave him a hint of a grin and we shook hands. When lying, always look them in the eyes and smile sincerely.

"I'm with the government, Mr. Rogers. State Department."

For the first time, he gave me serious scrutiny. He was about forty, at least eight years older than I was, and losing hair. His ears stuck out. His skin was that pale white of a man who rarely gets out in the sun.

"Got credentials?"

I seated myself at the table where he had his sandwich spread out and gave him my fake diplomatic passport and my fake State Department credentials, complete with photo ID. He actually examined the photo on the passport, then the one on the State ID, then scrutinized my handsome visage. We were alone in the break room.

As he handed the stuff back, he said, "Audra was kidnapped a week ago. Where in hell have you people been?"

"I got here as soon as I could, Mr. Rogers."

"The people at the embassy said they were sending a good man. I thought you would be older."

"I was the only one in the office," I said, to take some of the starch out of him. "Why don't you tell me about it?"

"I've been all over it with the local police. Talked to the embassy people twice."

"Apparently your daughter is still missing. Maybe it wouldn't hurt to go over it again with me."

"They snatched her a week ago yesterday on her way home from school. This school. I had to stay late. She never got home. That's it. That's all there is to tell." He set his jaw defiantly. I thought I saw tears in his eyes.

I nodded.

"Have you talked to my wife yet?" he asked.

"Uh, not yet."

"Better not. She's taking this really hard."

"Have you had a ransom note?"

"Nothing at all. Not a whisper. And it's not like we're rich. My wife works in that piss-ant branch bank and I teach school. We pay taxes here. We live in a flat and are lucky to own a four-year-old car. Little piece of Italian shit."

"Why are you two here and not back in the States? Seems you might do better there."

He swallowed, set his jaw. Broke eye contact to control himself, then came back to my face. "My wife makes twice what I do. They told her she had a bright future at the bank, and next year we'd be moving to Stockholm. Big promotion. She's worked hard for this."

I nodded to show I understood.

His sandwich lay there untouched.

"Mr. Rogers, whom do you suspect?"

He simply stared at me.

I tried to look sympathetic. "Sir, someone snatched your daughter. Was it someone here at school, one of your colleagues, someone in your neighborhood, a drug gang, a rapist? A pedophile? What do you think?"

He broke eye contact again. Didn't say anything.

"Or was it someone from the bank? Something to do with the bank?"

His face was cracking under the strain.

I waited.

"My wife has been writing letters to bank management in Sweden." He had to force the words out. "Way too much money has been going through the bank. Huge transfers in, huge transfers out. The bank charges a fee for these. It is so much money... It is very profitable—for the bank."

"I see."

"This is the bank's most profitable branch."

I nodded.

"I'm not accusing anyone, Mr. Wilson. It's Wilson, right? Not accusing anybody. You understand that? All we want is Audra back. Alive. Do you understand?"

"How much money are we talking about at the bank, Mr. Rogers?"

He got up and walked out of the room. Left his sandwich right where it lay, unwrapped.

I stopped by the office, thanked them, and went off to find Leitz.

Twenty-seven minutes after I'd called Joe Kitty, he called me back. I was still in the men's room. "Tommy?"

"Yeah."

"Two guys out here. Only two. One in front of the building, one in back."

"They armed?"

"I didn't ask."

"Do they look like cops?"

"Ahh, might be, but I doubt it. Dressed too well. Nice ankle-length coats, leather shoes. Cops are on their feet too much for shoes like that."

"How old?"

"Mid-thirties would be my guess. Fit."

"So, what do you think, Joe?"

Joe Kitty took his time answering. "I think they are wearing ear pieces and talking. We can take out one, and you can run out and hop in the car."

"Don't want him or his pal seeing us."

"Okay. Okay. Armanti will take care of the guy in front. Give us five minutes, then come out the door."

"Tell Armanti to be careful."

"Yeah."

"And tell him not to kill the guy."

Joe Kitty broke the connection.

Leitz and I hustled out of the men's room and took the elevator down to the first floor. Right outside the branch bank's office was an atrium, so we could stand there in front of the bank's office and see through the large window over the main entrance. Yes, there was the watcher, on the other side of the street standing inside the entrance to another building. He was against the west wall of the entrance, almost out of sight. If the dawn hadn't been breaking—the spring days are long at this latitude—I wouldn't have seen him. But he moved occasionally, and there he was.

I waited. Beside me, Leitz stood motionless.

In less than a minute I saw a big guy coming from the west, along the sidewalk. He was obviously drunk, swaying, staggering, and he was the only person in sight. At this hour of the morning the streets were still empty. The big guy put his hand against a wall and paused to retch. Then he resumed his journey toward the watcher, who may not have seen him yet.

The guy heard Armanti Hall coming, I think, because he stuck his head out in time to see the big man staggering along. Armanti was as tall as I am, but bigger through the chest and shoulders. A black man, he never cut his hair or beard, so all that hair added to his imposing presence. I was glad he was on our side, because if he just scowled he scared the crap outta me—and I'm fearless.

He didn't scowl at the watcher, who tried to back off a step or so as Armanti passed. He wasn't expecting what happened next. In one swift motion, Armanti grabbed the man's head and smashed it against the wall. I saw him go limp. He would have collapsed if Armanti hadn't lowered him gently to the concrete.

Leitz and I shot down the stairs and out the door and were on the sidewalk when Joe Kitty stopped to pick us up. As we jumped in the car, Armanti was still bent over the watcher.

"Come on, Goddamnit," Leitz muttered. He was worried about the guy behind the building, or any other guys he might have missed.

Then Armanti was trotting across the street. I threw open the back door, he climbed in beside me, and we were rolling. He handed me a wallet, a pistol, a cell phone, a passport, and a headset.

As we rolled, Hall gave the door a good hard pull and it latched.

I looked at the passport. Swedish.

"Nice job," I said to Armanti and Joe.

"I may have cracked his skull," Armanti said, stripping off a pair of medical gloves.

"It's a tough business," Joe Kitty observed.

# Chapter Two

I used the secure satellite communication system in the SCIF at the embassy to call Sarah Houston in Virginia. She answered warmly. After a few delightful boy-girl moments on Uncle Sam's dime, I got down to it.

I gave her the information on the passport and from the documents Armanti Hall had stolen from the watcher. "Anything you can tell me."

"When do you need this?"

"We've been up all night doing that branch bank. I'm going to bed. By the way, are you getting anything from their server?"

"Oh, yes. We've been working it for a couple of hours. A river of money flows through that bank, mostly from Russia. It doesn't stay long. Then it flows all over the world. About half goes to South America and a big chunk comes to the States. Another nice chunk goes to the UK. We'll be trying to figure out where it comes from and where it goes."

I grunted, trying to fit these revelations into what I knew of the world of finance and money laundering. We said our goodbyes and I walked the old streets to my hotel.

I kept thinking about the kidnapped little girl, wondering where she was, why she was snatched. Since there had been no ransom note, I wasn't optimistic.

I examined the pistol Armanti had taken from the guy outside the bank. A Walther in 9 mm, loaded. I took out the magazine, thumbed out the cartridges, cocked the pistol and dry fired it, then wiped off each cartridge with a hanky and reloaded the magazine. Kidnapping, loaded guns, a billion dollars a week through a branch bank in Estonia... I pocketed the piece and decided it was time for food and bed.

The city was alive, bustling, a tourist magnet. My hotel was on the edge of the Old Town. I ate a continental breakfast while watching my fellow diners. I noted two men, sitting apart but both in their thirties, dressed in similar business attire. I committed their features to memory, ensuring I would recognize them if I saw them again. Then I went upstairs and crashed.

Two hours later, I was wide awake. Got to thinking about the kid, Audra, and about the interview with the father, Frank Rogers, and how he had suppressed his emotion. He obviously knew something.

But why had there been no ransom note? That had me stumped. Only perverts grabbed kids without ransom notes. Kidnapping is a business. It's done for money. Or revenge. Or something.

I kept coming back to the bank. A river of money. There was the cash, right there, Tommy, you twit.

That interview with Frank Rogers. Had he been lying? Fact is, I am a professional liar. I know all the tells. Recalling Frank Rogers' face, I suspected that the emotion had covered up some of the tells. On purpose. Perhaps.

Maybe I should find out.

I gave the watcher's documents, wallet, and cell phone to the station chief at the embassy to put in the diplomatic bag for delivery to the company in Langley. I kept the pistol. Dulcie Del Rio wanted a debrief, so I told her how it went down.

She said, "Isn't it an interesting coincidence that they tried to get into the bank the same night you did?"

I didn't believe in coincidences. Oh sure, random chance rules the world, but always bet on cause and effect. A little paranoia will take you a long way... and keep you alive.

The Rogers lived in a two-bedroom flat on the second story of a five-story building in a new section of town. At least the plumbing was modern, and they had electricity. The place had no doorman and a self-service elevator. No security cameras. With Armanti Hall and Joe Kitty standing guard front and back, I went in during the afternoon and took a look around.

The first things I found were wireless electronic bugs. The tiny microphones were transmitting, according to my hand-held receiver. Uh-oh.

I went out twice as fast as I came in and started searching for the booster. There had to be one someplace nearby, but I didn't see it.

The three of us held a huddle by the embassy car and I told Joe and Armanti about the bugs.

Armanti whistled softly. "Oh, man."

"It isn't just the snatched kid," Joe Kitty said. "These people are in trouble to their eyes."

"And they've been lying to State and to me," I said. "Let's get the dad first when he gets out of school, and intercept the mom coming home from work. Then we can have a quiet little prayer meeting, just the five of us."

"Not together," Joe Kitty said.

"Oh, no," I agreed. "One at a time."

We went back to the embassy to check out another car, and while we were there I again visited with Dulcie Del Rio. "I need three guns and shoulder holsters."

"Who is the opposition?" she asked flatly, just like that.

"Don't know yet, but I kinda doubt it's Estonians."

"Check their identity papers before you shoot them."

"Of course. And we need a safe house."

"For Christ's sake, this is *Estonia*."

"So I'm told, but we need a secure place to have some interviews."

She didn't ask who we planned to interview, which was a credit to her. She dug in her purse and gave me the key to her flat. "Check for bugs, don't mess the place up, stay out of the liquor, and don't let the cat out. Her name is Oreo."

"We may need it all evening."

"I'll spend the night with a friend. Feed the cat."

"Thanks," I said.

We ended up with old Baretta Nines. The U.S. government bought them by the millions. I gave Dulcie my liberated Walther for her collection. We loaded the Barettas, put them in holsters and went to get the other car.

I sent Bill Leitz to check Dulcie's apartment for bugs. As a tech support guy, this was his area of expertise. "We'll meet you there," I told him, and repeated Dulcie's instructions about the liquor and the cat. "Make sure you aren't followed," I added, "and that there aren't any eyes on the place."

"Got it," he said, took the keys, and went back into the embassy to get his gear.

I was waiting beside one of the cars when Frank Rogers came walking along. He was going home. This was probably near the place where someone snatched his daughter.

I was friendly. "Mr. Rogers, Jim Wilson. We met the other day."

He looked me over, obviously was not glad to see me. He edged around as if he wanted to walk on.

"I was hoping that you and I could spend another few minutes together." I opened the car door and held it.

"I don't think—" he began.

"You haven't been thinking—that's the problem. Now if you want to ever see Audra again, get in the car."

He got in the passenger seat. I went around and settled myself behind the wheel, snapped my seatbelt. "Put on your seat belt," I told him as I inserted the key in the ignition and fired up the tiny motor.

"What—"

"Save it."

I put the car in motion and pulled into traffic. I was paying attention to the mirrors and saw another car pull out as we passed. I made the second turn and it followed. Terrific.

Two turns later and I was sure: we had a follower. I stopped at a light and checked the rearview mirror. He had hung back, but I could see that there were two guys in the car and one was on his cell phone. When the light changed I headed for Old Town, with its traffic and narrow streets. We crossed a few bridges, then we were there. I didn't know the street pattern, but apparently neither did they, because they followed me into a narrow street where only one of us could turn around—and that was me—before getting wedged in by traffic.

I worked the car around as the guy behind me laid on his horn, then drove back the other way. As I went by our pursuers, I looked them over; they didn't look at me. The passenger was glued to his phone and the driver stared straight ahead. But there was a car in front of him and a delivery truck behind, and it was going to take him a while to get turned around. Tough luck for him.

Out on the boulevard, I headed out of the district. Four turns later, I was sure I was clean. I used the map feature on my phone to direct me to Dulcie Del Rio's apartment.

Frank Rogers started talking as we left Old Town. He was chattering as we crossed the bridge and chattering as we entered Dulcie's neighborhood.

"I've told you everything I know. Told the people at the embassy. We're Americans… for God's sake, you can't treat us like this." There was more, a lot more, about his wife knowing a senator and the fact they had written their Congresswoman.

"Can it," I said and concentrated on my cell phone.

At one stoplight, he popped the buckle on his seat belt and reached for the door handle. I backhanded him gently across the chops. "Put the damn belt back on," I said harshly. If I had had any doubts that he had lied in our previous interview, they would have evaporated then. But I didn't. He was frightened. Scared. Whatever he and his wife had gotten themselves into, he knew the stakes were blood. His, his wife's, and his daughter's. He knew it and now I did.

Leitz let us into Dulcie's pad. He handed me the keys, glanced at Rogers, and walked out, pulling the door shut behind him.

I took Rogers by the elbow and guided him into the little living room. "Sit." He did, in a little couch just big enough for two bottoms.

I checked out the apartment. Two bedrooms, one bath, a kitchen with a dining area that doubled for a home office. As if Dulcie Del Rio had stuff she could work on at home. She had a little laptop, however, probably to send emails to the family back in the States. Maybe check on how the investments in her IRA were doing. I hoped she was getting rich.

I opened the refrigerator. Dulcie had beer.

"You want a beer?" I asked Frank Rogers. He shook his head.

I sat down opposite him in a stuffed chair and made myself comfortable. Dulcie's cat climbed up on the couch beside Frank and presented itself to be petted. He stroked it once, mechanically, and eventually it wandered away.

"Frank, we have a problem. You've been lying to the folks at the embassy, and perhaps the local police. You haven't given us a damned thing that will get us to Audra. How are you going to feel if Audra shows up dead? If the local cops find her corpse in some alley? Knowing that you told a bunch of lies when the truth might have saved her, knowing you didn't tell all you know? How are you going to feel?"

Big tears leaked from both eyes. He began sobbing and finally buried his face in his hands. I felt like a jerk. Still, if he ever wanted to see his kid again, we were his main chance. In fact, probably his only chance.

"I've never had to deal with anything like this. I don't know what to do."

"You *have* heard from the kidnappers, haven't you? What did they say?"

"That if we made any more noise about that bank they'd kill her. Told us to shut up and Penny was to keep doing her job."

"Un-huh."

"It was those letters to the big honchos in Stockholm that Penny wrote. The bank is making a lot of money from the deposits and withdrawals flowing though the bank. The fees are a fraction of one percent, but the amounts are so large…"

"How large?" I instantly regretted that question. His wife knew, but Frank would only know what Penny told him. Hearsay. And Sarah Houston was going to have it chapter and verse very soon.

"Some days it's more, some less. Never less than a hundred million U.S. dollars. Sometimes three or four times that."

"A day?" I was incredulous. It was as if the bank were a depository of the Treasury Department, collecting tax checks after the 15th of April.

He nodded. After a bit he stopped sobbing. I went to find Dulcie's liquor cabinet. She liked vodka and bourbon. I poured some vodka on the rocks and brought him a tumbler full.

"Let's go back to after Audra was snatched. Did they call you?"

"They called my wife. Penny told me what they said."

"Tell me."

He did. Going over it took half an hour. The threat was the kid would get killed or maimed if Penny Rogers didn't shut up and behave. If she did, the kid would come home alive and well. If she didn't, they would start mailing her parts.

He had finished the vodka and I thought I knew most of it when I heard a knock on the door. I went and checked with my gun in my hand.

It was Joe Kitty and Armanti Hall, and they had Penny Rogers with them.

"We were followed," Armanti said. "We managed to ditch them."

Penny Rogers was a sight. She was not a large woman, never pretty, and the last few days, or perhaps the ride with Armanti and Joe as they ditched her tail, had wrung her out.

"She didn't say a word," Joe Kitty said. He went outside to keep an eye on the cars.

I nodded towards Frank and whispered to Armanti, "Take him into the bedroom and keep him quiet."

Penny watched them go in silence, then sat on the little couch.

"A glass of wine, or perhaps water?" I suggested.

She thought wine, so I poured her a glass from a bottle of red that Dulcie had corked in a cabinet, then sat down across from her.

"Who are you men?" she asked.

I showed her my fake passport and State ID. She scrutinized the documents, then handed them back.

"Frank said you talked to him at school."

"I did. And again this afternoon, right here."

"Whose apartment is this?"

"A friend's."

"Why here? Why not the embassy or our place?"

"Your apartment is bugged and I didn't want anyone to see you entering the embassy."

She stared at me. "How do you know our apartment is bugged."

"We went in and looked."

"The door was locked."

"We picked the lock, Mrs. Rogers. Just like the men did who bugged the place."

She sipped at the wine, remained silent, and looked around. The cat sniffed her feet, then wandered off. It was black, with one splotch of white on its face. Oreo. Looked like a nice cat.

"They'll kill Audra if we talk."

"Not if we get to her first. And there is no way on earth for that to happen unless you tell us the truth."

"She doesn't deserve this."

She lost control of her face. The refrigerator hummed and somewhere in the building a door slammed. I could faintly hear traffic down on the street below the windows. She wiped at her eyes, and finally her eyes dried up.

Penny Rogers began talking. All that money flowing through that tiny little branch bank aroused her curiosity. Her employees, all Estonians who had worked there for years, told her the branch had always been profitable. More than ninety percent of the accounts were Russian, and they were always opened over the internet. The only people who came into the branch were locals. Their accounts were small and legitimate, with paychecks deposited into savings or checking accounts. But the Russians...

Big deposits, in the tens of millions. Day in and day out. The money didn't stay long, but was wire transferred on to America, the UK, South America, southern Europe. All over the world.

"How much money?"

"It varies. The deposits have averaged a billion a week during the last year."

"Fifty billion dollars in the past year?"

"Yes."

She finished her glass of wine and put it on the little table to her right.

"They're laundering money," I suggested.

"Obviously," Penny Rogers said, as if I needed a dozen more IQ points. "All the businesses in Russia don't generate fifty billion dollars of profit in a year."

"So what did you do?"

She began to talk. As she spoke the words poured out, faster and faster. She tried to check on the accounts where the money was being transferred. Used the internet to track down the accounts, which were all corporations. She finally realized they were all shell corporations, without assets. She wrote emails and memos to her superiors in Stockholm. She was told to remember the bank's business was the bank's business, and not to discuss it with anyone. Her emails became more strident. Then Audra was kidnapped.

"And someone came to talk with you…" I suggested.

She nodded. "At the bank. It was a man I didn't know. He was blunt. Told me to keep my mouth shut and run the branch. If I discussed the bank's business with anyone we would never see Audra again. In one piece. He said that. 'In one piece.' I told him we had already reported the kidnapping to the police. He sneered at that."

"Tell me about this man."

"In his forties, I thought. Spoke with a heavy accent. Not Swedish. Russian, perhaps. Terrible teeth, stained yellow from cigarettes." She made a face. "A horrible man. Evil. Pure, unadulterated evil."

"Did he demand money, anything like that?"

"No."

"Did you ask for proof that they had Audra, that she was still alive?"

She nodded and sniffled. Dug in her purse. Produced a photo. A snapshot. It was Audra all right, against a white wall, with a welt across her face. No glasses.

"May I keep this?"

She said yes, so I put it in my inside jacket pocket.

"She's all we have," Penny said, so softly I almost missed the comment.

What do you say to that? I couldn't think of anything.

"How are you going to get her back?"

That was an excellent question. "Who did you write to at the bank in Stockholm?"

"I sent emails to Arne Soderman, who supervises the branches, and then finally a letter to the president, Isak Dahlberg. Three letters, actually. A scandal like this could wreck the bank."

"We'll talk to them," I said.

I went to the bedroom door and told Armanti and Frank to come out. I said to Armanti, "You and Joe take the cars back to the embassy. Get some new wheels, rental cars. Then come back here."

Armanti left. The Rogers sat beside each other on the couch and held hands.

Jake Grafton came by invitation to Sarah Houston's office in Langley. When he was seated with the door shut, she turned a computer monitor so he could see it. "The branch bank server gave us the encryption codes. This is what we have so far from that branch. Money in, money out. Euros, dollars, pounds, yen, Swiss francs, you name it. It'll take a few more days to get into the main servers in Stockholm."

As Grafton scrolled through the transactions, Sarah said, "I didn't believe it, but the size of these transactions is awe-inspiring. It could easily go a billion dollars' worth a week. It's money-laundering on a massive scale. They must be washing money for Iran, North Korea, Syria, and every drug syndicate on the planet."

"Get all the information you can as fast as you can. I'll have a department head meeting and get you some help. Someone at the bank knows there is a leak or Audra Rogers wouldn't have been kidnapped. This river of money is going to stop flowing soon. We want to know where it comes from before it goes into the bank and where it goes from there. Let's find out before the river stops flowing."

They discussed the logistics of the operation. "If I can get into the bank's main computers, the sheer volume of data could take man-years to unravel," Sarah noted. "And we are just seeing a tiny piece of the operation."

Grafton didn't look up from the screen. "We need to see the entire watershed."

Sarah said, almost as an afterthought, "We happen to have a full plate already. I don't think you understand how labor-intensive it will be to dig into records at other banks, assuming we can get in by hook or crook or even—God forbid—invitation. It will be like trying to sort plates of spaghetti. The whole reason washers transfer money hither and yon is to make it difficult to trace. Sometimes tracing becomes impossible."

"This is priority One," Jake Grafton shot back. "We'll get the people and equipment you need as soon as we can. We don't have man-years."

"Okay."

"I need your help to figure this out, Sarah."

After Grafton left, Sarah made a face at the door, then began drafting a memo for him to sign.

Back in his office, Jake Grafton ignored the pile of paper in his in-basket. He looked at the paintings, at the flags, thought about the river of money. And he thought about Audra Rogers.

He was sitting at his desk doodling on a pad when the phone rang. The receptionist. "Tommy Camellini on the secure link from Estonia."

"I'll take that."

Two button pushes later he heard Tommy's voice.

After Tommy had brought the admiral up to date, he continued, "Seems to me, boss, that the first priority is Audra Rogers. Truth is, she may be dead, and the trail is what, thirteen days old now? To get to her, we're going to have to go to Stockholm and sweat the people at the bank. One or more of them is dirty. They won't want to talk to us and we don't have the horsepower to put serious pressure on unless you're willing to create an international incident with an American friend."

Jake Grafton took a deep breath and exhaled slowly. He too thought Audra was probably dead. Why would the kidnappers keep her alive? "You need to get that branch server. Go in and get it before the bad guys do."

"I've got a guy watching the bank to make sure it doesn't walk out the front door," Tommy said. "We'll snatch it ASAP."

"What time is it there?"

"Ten p.m."

Grafton looked at the clock on the wall. Seven hours difference. "Get it tonight."

"Yes, sir."

Grafton hung up and pushed the intercom, summoning his executive assistants.

"I want to go to Stockholm as fast as possible," he told them. "Get me a plane, an executive jet out of Andrews. And I need more people." He named them. "They can come with me. Make it happen."

# Chapter Three

M y telephone rang. It was Joe Kitty.

"Tommy, two guys just entered the bank building. There's a car and driver waiting out front. They might be after that server. What should I do?"

"I'll be there as fast as I can."

I tore out of the embassy, jumped into my rental car, and headed for the bank. Eight minutes later, I pulled up behind the suspect car parked in front of the bank. The engine was running. I hopped out with my shooter in my hand and walked toward the driver's door. The driver didn't wait to see what was going to happen next: he gunned his ride and tore off down the street.

Joe Kitty came running over. "Now what?"

"Watch the door in back of the building. We want the server."

He hotfooted it for the nearest alley. That's what I like about Joe Kitty—no stupid questions. As if I had any answers.

The interior of the building was dark except for a few night lights on the stairs. The guys in the building, if they were indeed in the bank's branch office, would come out and look for their ride. And it was gone.

If the driver of the getaway car was on the phone to them, Lord only knows what they would decide to do. Maybe hunker down like Bill Leitz and I did the other night.

The door to the building was unlocked, so I went in. I eased up the stairs and checked the door to the branch office. Unlocked. Should I go in?

Not feeling suicidal, I decided not to.

Were they still in there? No more than a minute had passed since the getaway car made its quick departure.

I retreated to the top of the stairs, faced the branch office door, and waited for it to open. They were coming through that door or they weren't coming out. Two guys, Joe said.

I stretched out on the floor with the pistol at arm's length. The light wasn't very good—I'd be almost invisible to them—but I could see the sights well enough to shoot. I waited.

Wished I had a silencer on the pistol. Oh, well. Next time.

How do you say "Stop" in Russian? Or Swedish?

No more than sixty seconds had passed when the door opened quickly and two men came out. One of them was carrying something. They paused and looked over the transom that gave them a view of the main entrance. Looking for their ride. So the driver hadn't called them, or they had their cell phones off.

"Halt," I said loudly. One of them, the guy without the server, turned my way and I saw the flash of a pistol in his hand. He shot from the hip without aiming, and I heard just a muffled pop. The bullet must have gone over my head.

I pulled the trigger of my shooter and the report filled the hall. The guy staggered and fell.

The other guy decided he wasn't a hero. He froze.

I sprang from the floor and walked toward them. The guy on the floor wasn't moving. The man holding the server watched me come. I kept the gun on him.

"Put it down," I said.

He was looking at the pistol and trying to decide. I motioned at the server. "Down slowly."

He got the idea. After he put the box down, I motioned back against the wall. He turned around, spread his arms, and leaned on the wall. He'd done this before. I hit him in the head with the pistol, as hard as I could. He collapsed.

He had a gun on him too. No wallet. No phone. No passport. Nothing but the gun.

I checked the guy I had shot. He was still alive but out of it with a hole in the chest. Blood frothing out. A lung shot. No wallet, phone, or passport, but a pack of Marlboros and some matches.

I picked up the server and trotted down the stairs. Joe Kitty was already behind the wheel of our car and had the engine running. I climbed in, slammed the door, and he put us in motion.

"I heard the shot."

"He shot first. Had a silencer."

"What do you think this is, Tommy, a fucking cowboy movie? Man, never give the assholes the first shot."

"Sarah Houston on Line Two, Admiral." That was the receptionist.

Jake answered it. "Grafton."

"The server in Tallinn is off line."

"Maybe Tommy got it."

"Someone did, or turned it off."

"I'm going to Sweden in a couple of hours. I'll need a printout of everything you can give me from that server."

"Yes, sir."

When Sarah was gone, Jake called Tommy on his cell. Tommy answered.

"Unsecure line. Do you have the box?"

"We got it."

"Great. Call me on a secure line."

"You should have marched that dude you hit into the car," Joe Kitty said, "and sweated him to see what he knows about that kid."

"Then what?" I said. "Let him loose to tell his boss all about us, or should we shoot him and dump him somewhere?"

"I keep thinking about that kid," Joe Kitty said.

"Yeah, I do too."

"If she isn't dead she soon will be."

That was my thought too, and it sat like a rock. Nine years old. Probably scared out of her mind. Damn!

I said, "Let's go back and see if we can follow that guy when he leaves the building. He'll go somewhere. He doesn't have a cell phone or wallet on him."

"Someone will come for him," Joe said. He made a U-turn on the wet empty street. He parked the car around the corner from the bank building. There were three other cars parked on the street—none of them occupied. I stepped to the corner and peered around. It was raining gently and I didn't have a hat. Temp in the mid-fifties. I checked my watch. In five minutes I was damp all over. After ten I was wet. I hugged the building, trying to stay out of most of the rain. The wind came up, a gentle breeze, and I began to chill. Say what you will, this spook business was for the dogs.

I had been standing in the rain for seventeen minutes when a dark sedan came slowly from the other direction and stopped immediately in front of the bank. Two men got out, adjusted their clothes and weapons, looked around, then tried the door to the building. It was still unlocked. They went in. The driver stayed in the car and kept it running.

In three minutes they came out with the guy I had slugged. His legs were working, but not very well—no doubt he had a concussion—and the two men supported him. They put him in the back seat of the sedan, then went back inside for the man I had shot. They carried him out. I zipped over to my ride and hopped in the passenger seat just before the car passed us, going to the left.

"That's them. Lay back all you can."

"I know how to do this, Tommy."

"Yeah, but I feel better giving you orders. It's a power thing."

"You get off on it, I know."

Joe pulled out and stayed a block or so behind the sedan, which was obviously going somewhere. That somewhere turned out to be a hospital. They took him into the emergency room while we sat watching from nearly two hundred yards away. Hospital people rolled out a gurney for the gunshot victim.

Well, at least they were decent to their friends. That was something. Maybe there was some hope for Audra Rogers after all.

A *billion* dollars a week! Think about it. Talk about a score! Man, this was like winning the Power Ball Lottery.

And yet, all that money belonged to someone, or an army of someones, and they would be very unhappy if even a significant percentage happened to disappear. Like, poof, off into cyberspace. If that happened, the boys in Stockholm were going to need to find a way off this planet, fast.

I looked around at the server lying on the back seat. Wondered what secrets it held. Well, Sarah Houston and her colleagues would tell us, book, chapter and verse. Just put it in the diplomatic bag, and *voila*, it would magically appear at the CIA campus.

When the dudes had been in the hospital for a half hour, Joe Kitty said aloud, "Wonder how long they are going to be in there."

"Until they come out."

"They could have called someone, Tommy. If they spotted us tailing them, help could be on the way with a lot more firepower than we have."

"Let's move the car. Park it near the exit to that parking lot."

Joe did. While we were sitting there, an ambulance came and the crew took someone into the hospital on a gurney. After it left, a private car rolled up, parked behind the sedan that had brought our guys, and an elderly man helped a woman into the hospital.

The rain continued to fall. A gentle breeze off the Baltic stirred the leaves of the trees, which were enjoying the spring after a miserable Baltic winter. I watched the entrance to the emergency room in my side mirror. The bad guys' ride was still where they left it, with a man at the wheel. We kept our heads on a swivel, watching for cars. Sitting still like this in Indian country made me nervous.

I called Armanti Hall on his cell. "Hey."

"Hey."

"How's things?"

"Quiet."

"Folks asleep?"

"Yeah."

"We're parked outside the emergency entrance to a hospital"—I named it, and since my command of the local lingo wasn't great, spelled it—"and need your help. Come find us. Call when you get close."

"Okay."

"We'll give him the server, just in case," I told Joe.

Another ten minutes went by. The rain was steady. The sea wind caressed the trees.

Twelve minutes. Fourteen.

"Let's get the hell outta here," Joe said.

I had the willys terribly bad too. "Go," I said.

He fired up the engine and put the car in gear. As we started to move, a van pulled in front of us, facing us, blocking the exit lane. Two men piled out, one on each side. Men with submachine guns.

"Oh, fuck," Joe said, and aimed the car for the guy on the passenger side and stood on the gas. As we jumped the curb the windshield exploded. Little pebbles of glass flew everywhere and I slammed my eyes shut. Somehow Joe kept his foot on the gas pedal and the car was accelerating. I opened my eyes in time to see the guy who was in front of us going over the top of the car.

Joe's head was a mass of blood. He was leaning back against the headrest and still had the accelerator floored, his lifeless hands on the wheel. The engine was howling.

The car shot across the street and slammed into a parked vehicle. The air bag deployed; I felt it smack me a good one. I was conscious and miraculously alive. I could hear the engine winding at full screech, tortured metal screaming a banshee wail. Then the little four-banger quit dead. The air bag lay there like a deflated balloon.

I didn't have my seat belt on, so in the great silence I shoved hard against the door and was out onto the pavement. On my face. Got the pistol out and started shooting at the guy who was still standing beside the van across the street. He jumped back into the van as I emptied the pistol at it. The van driver shot straight ahead, past the entrance to the hospital and on out into the street. I could see the shooter we had smacked lying flat on the glistening pavement.

I looked back into our ride. Joe Kitty had stopped four or five bullets with his head. Blood and brains were blasted everywhere. Both shooters had been aiming for the driver, which was the only reason I was still alive.

The rear door was buckled and wouldn't open. I leaned in over the passenger seat and grabbed that damned server—it was on the floor—and set off down the sidewalk. The car that had brought the other guys to the hospital was gone. How the driver got that thing out of there I had no idea, nor did I care.

I was having my troubles walking. Staggering. I had glass pebbles in my hair and clothes and maybe in my eyes. I was trying to clear my vision when a car pulled alongside with Armanti Hall at the wheel.

I stared at him.

"*Get in*, you damn fool."

I opened the door, tossed the server in, and managed to cram myself in. I was still trying to get the door closed a block later.

"Holster that fucking gun."

To my amazement, I found that I still had the Beretta in my hand. I managed to jam it under my armpit.

"What happened?" Armanti Hall demanded.

"Fuckers killed Joe."

"Oh, man..."

I could hear sirens wailing. I put my head down on Armanti's shoulder and went to sleep.

A doctor came to the embassy, wiped Joe Kitty's blood off my face, and rooted around in my left eye for a little glass shard. With the glass out, I wrote a message for Jake Grafton which Dulcie Del Rio sent over the secure com system, and Armanti Hall took me back to my hotel. My clothes were wet and splotched with Joe's blood. I took them off and threw them in the trash. Then I showered and fell into bed. Armanti stayed in the hallway, just in case.

Lying in bed, I felt as if I had really screwed up this assignment. Joe Kitty was dead, which wouldn't have happened if we hadn't sat outside that hospital for way over an hour while the bad guys summoned help. How stupid can you get? Then there was Audra Rogers... imprisoned... somewhere.

Tired as I was, I still couldn't let it go enough to fall asleep. I wandered back and forth around the room, looked out the window... the rain was now a misty fog.

What should I have done? Sure, the Rogers had lied. If they had told the truth immediately, would that have gotten us to Audra? There was no way to know.

I laid down on the bed and thrashed around, going over and over it. The kid was dead; I knew it in my bones. Finally, I must have dozed off. When I awoke, the sun was out and the sky had cleared. My left eye bothered me. Felt as if something was still in there, although I wasn't stupid enough to rub it. It was slightly blurred, but since I had two eyes, I was good to go.

I showered again, shaved, got dressed, and packed my bag. No doubt the Estonian authorities wanted to talk to me. One had to assume the authorities had been back to see the Rogers after the robbery at the branch bank, and the Rogers had probably told them all about Jim Wilson, U. S. State Department investigator. Then there was Joe Kitty, sitting in a smashed, shot-up car with his head blown off. Any way you looked at it, we had worn out our welcome in lovely Estonia.

Armanti was indeed waiting in the hall, sitting on stairs coming down from the floor above. He looked as tired as I felt, even with my nap. We rode over to the embassy, were admitted by the gate guard, and went to the basement to see Dulcie.

She had news. The Estonians said the man outside the bank branch—he had bled out—was a Russian, as was the man who had flown over our car in front of the hospital. "Go to the cafeteria," she said, "get something to eat. You two are leaving on a plane at noon." She produced two diplomatic passports. "These will get you through immigration and on to the plane."

"Where are we going?" Armanti asked.

"Berlin. You change planes there for Stockholm." She produced folders with tickets.

"What about the Rogers?" I asked Dulcie.

"They left Estonia this morning on their way to the States."

"And the kidnapped kid?"

"Sit down, Tommy. Armanti." Dulcie reminded me of my grandmother, plump, with salt-and pepper hair.

"A body of a child was found last night floating in a canal. The Estonians think it is Audra Rogers. It will take a while to be sure. The child has been dead about ten days, according to the forensic examiner, and in the water for much of that time."

"Shit," Armanti Hall said.

*They killed her after they took the picture to give to her folks,* I thought.

"Have the Rogers been told?" I asked.

"The ambassador broke the news to them."

After some silence, Armanti and I gave her our guns and wandered down to the cafeteria. I wasn't hungry, but I ate something anyway, and drank some American coffee. Nursing it, I asked Armanti, "Was Joe married?"

"Once," he said. "For awhile. He never said much about it." He shrugged. "It just didn't work out, I guess."

"Damn," I said. "I liked him."

"Served with him in Syria and Afghanistan," Armanti Hall said slowly. "He saved my life once. If he hadn't been there, I'd be dead now." He growled. "But, shit, Tommy, we all gotta go sometime, and one place is as good as another."

Embassy staffers had already been to Armani's hotel. They brought his suitcase, a carry-on, which was now in Dulcie's office, and they brought Joe's stuff too. No doubt the Estonians had Joe's gun, which meant Dulcie had some paperwork to do for the company to explain why a pistol from her inventory was missing. Maybe the local police would eventually give the gun back, but I doubted State would allow the American government to claim it. Maybe the local cops or the Estonian spooks would slip it to Dulcie under the table; they had their troubles with the Russians too. Or maybe not. The bureaucracies keep grinding along, sure as death and taxes.

Armanti found an empty couch and stretched out on it.

We were going to have to move on. Help find the Russian muscle and the mastermind behind the river of money. I was going to need to get my head clear and on straight and do a hell of a lot better job than I had been doing the last few days.

I said a little prayer for Audra Rogers and her parents, then added one for Joe Kitty. Then one for myself and Armanti Hall. We were going to need all the help we could get. Perhaps we too had an appointment in Samarra.

# Chapter Four

Sweden's head spook was a clean-shaven guy in his late fifties with blond, close-cropped hair and a fit build. The Swedish Military Intelligence and Security Service is a division of the Swedish military. They do everything from providing security to the armed forces to spying. I can't even pronounce the Swedish name for the service, but it goes by the acronym of MUST.

I wasn't sure whether this guy, who was introduced as Hakan Rossander, was the director of MUST or just in charge of espionage and clandestine activities. I didn't think it mattered.

He treated Jake Grafton as a professional colleague, but the chill came pretty quickly when Grafton began talking about the Bank of Scandinavia and produced a ream of paper from his leather case. He explained that this was a printout of transactions from the bank's branch in Estonia for the last two months.

"What it boils down to is that billions of dollars in a variety of currencies have been passing though that branch every day for at least a year, perhaps longer. This printout is only two-month's worth. As you can see, most of the inflow is from Russia. Money is transferred all over

41

the world from the branch. A lot of it goes to the United States, the U.K., Europe…"

He fell silent while Rossander perused the pile, sifting through it.

I yawned. Armanti and I both slept on the plane, but I was still exhausted. Sleeping on airplanes is not something I would recommend for guys as big as we are. We both woke up feeling like we had recently been in a car wreck, which I had. Jake Grafton was waiting at the airport in Stockholm when Armanti, Bill Leitz, and I came out of customs with our carry-ons. He didn't say anything, just shook our hands and led the way out of the terminal to a big Chevy SUV parked by the curb with a driver standing by.

"Any trouble with immigration or customs?" he asked.

"None."

Grafton just nodded. He had other things on his mind. The driver, a black woman, took us straight to the embassy. I didn't catch her name, although she was young, fit, and well put together. Probably had a great education and a good career in the State Department in her future. "She'll get you guys checked into a hotel," Grafton said. "Bill, you and Armanti go with her. Tommy, you come with me."

He and I got out and walked into the embassy.

That evening we were in the MUST stronghold.

Hakan Rossander cleared his throat. "We will have to take this under advisement, talk to the people at the bank." He had an excellent command of English, with only a slight accent. Since I didn't know any Swedish, I was impressed.

Grafton went into the saga of the Rogers: the kidnapping and the recovery of their Audra's body yesterday from a canal in Tallinn. "After the kidnapping, Mrs. Rogers said a man who she thought was Russian came into the branch and told her to stop sending memos and letters to the people at the head bank office here in Stockholm if she ever wanted to see her daughter again. It was that kidnapping that caused my agency to be involved."

Hakan Rossander looked as if he were constipated.

Old Mr. Smooth, our very own Jake Grafton, continued without missing a beat. "Our banking and law enforcement agencies are very interested in this branch bank's activities. I assume the authorities of other nations will be equally interested." That was probably a gross understatement. If the U.S., British, and European Union banking honchos leaned on Sweden, the pressure would be excruciating. A mess like this could cause seismic tremors throughout Sweden, which is not a big country. If they tried to minimize it, it could blow the government sky high.

Rossander abandoned the paper pile and looked Grafton in the eyes. "So you came all the way to Stockholm to discuss this matter." It wasn't a question.

Grafton nodded. "I came to you as a matter of professional courtesy. And to possibly sit in when you or your government officials interview the officers of the bank. Our ambassador will visit the foreign ministry in the morning.

"You see the problem, sir. Many of the American corporations listed as recipients of wire transfers from the branch bank in Estonia are merely paper shells. If these are not legitimate transactions, we are talking about money laundering on a grand scale. Tax evasion. At the very least, repeated, numerous violations of American law. An average of a *billion* American dollars-worth a week went through that branch. *Fifty billion dollars a year.* Our guess at first blush, looking at just the last two months-worth of branch records, is that fifty to sixty percent of that amount made its first stop in America. Where it went from there, and where it ultimately came to rest is, at this point, anyone's guess."

Hakan Rossander looked as tired as I felt. "May I ask how the United States' Central Intelligence Agency came by transaction records for a Swedish bank?"

"You may certainly ask, sir, but I must reserve that. I assure you we believe those records are legitimate and accurate, as far as they go."

Rossander knew a closed door when he saw one. He dropped that subject with good grace and said, "I'll have to talk to the banking people in the government. No doubt they will want to interview the bank officers as soon as possible. I can reach you at your embassy? I'll keep you advised."

Grafton picked up his leather briefcase and stood. "Thank you," he said. He motioned toward the pile of paper on Rossander's desk. "You may keep those."

The spook didn't thank him. He pushed a button, a man appeared, and we were ushered out.

The embassy car we had arrived in was waiting, with the driver leaning nonchalantly on a fender. "Shouldn't he be wiping the car or something," I muttered.

"Let's go get a decent dinner and a drink," Jake Grafton said. "Maybe this guy knows a place."

As we munched our dinner and swilled a couple of drinks each at a white-tablecloth restaurant, the president of the Bank of Scandinavia, Isak Dahlberg, was busy dying. Apparently, he got into his car in his garage with a bottle of Aquavit and started the engine as he sipped. He didn't raise the garage door. They found him the following morning.

I found out about Dahlberg from Grafton when I strolled into the embassy at 10 o'clock, after a wonderful night's sleep. The admiral was in the SCIF and broke the news to me. "It's all over the television," he said.

"Anything about the bank?"

"Not a peep."

"Heard anything from MUST?"

"No."

"So the Swedes are sitting on the dynamite, hoping it doesn't explode."

"Probably trying to figure out the size of the mess before they go public," Grafton said. Then he got busy on messages.

I sat for a while, in case the boss needed me to break into the Swedish capitol and plant bugs, but apparently he hadn't gotten that far. I left the SCIF and called Armanti and Bill Leitz. They were having breakfast with three covert operators Grafton had brought with him. I knew a couple of them: we had been in trouble together before.

When I got back around noon, Grafton said, "Get lost, Tommy. Find something to amuse yourself."

So I did. Ate lunch at a nice little spot in the downtown, and bought a new raincoat and a brimmed hat that I thought I might need in these climes. Then I bought a ticket on the Hop-On Hop-Off bus, where I mixed and mingled with the passengers of a cruise ship. A couple from Iowa said they were doing all the Baltic ports. St. Petersburg and Tallinn were next.

Fortunately, I was not on the open top of the bus, so when it started raining I was homesteading a dry seat. In front of the Abba Museum, two guys I knew, Armanti Hall and Doc Gordon, climbed on the bus. They ignored me and I ignored them. However, I decided to brave the weather at the *Vasa* Museum, and queued up to get off. Out on the sidewalk, I found them behind me.

Pretending we didn't know each other, we went into the museum. The *Vasa* was a huge wooden man-of-war that overturned and sank in the Stockholm harbor on its maiden voyage in 1628: a tip-top, first-rate naval disaster. It was a good thing the old sailor Grafton wasn't with us. We three spooks wandered around, watched the tourists snap photos.

We'd been in there about an hour when Doc said, "We have friends following us."

"Swedes, you think?"

"How the hell would I know?"

"Let's get back on the bus and see if they come along."

There were two of them, and they jumped in a car that followed the bus.

"Should we make their day and split up?" I asked.

"Okay."

"Rendezvous for dinner at the hotel," Armanti said. He and Doc got off at the next stop. The car stayed behind the bus. It was me they were tailing.

It was still drizzling when the bus got back to its starting place. I got off and walked to the embassy. So that Swede spook, Rossander, had put a tail on me—or someone had. It was a thing to think about.

Back in the SCIF, Grafton was finishing up a long day sending and receiving messages. I told him about my tail, and suggested that it would be nice to have a gun under my armpit.

"Stay out of trouble," was his response.

"Aye aye, sir."

Truthfully—and I am truthful in these reports, even though I tell a lot of lies to people I meet in my trade—I was a bit peeved. I don't go looking for trouble. I have a strong sense of self-preservation and I try to avoid it. Can I help it if trouble finds me occasionally, especially when I'm doing something nefarious, that Grafton told me to do? Shit happens, man—ask Joe Kitty. Fact is, I feel kinda undressed without a pistol. Screw Michael Bloomberg.

The news about the bank broke on the fourth day we were in Stockholm. I had caught up on my sleep, been out for a couple of morning runs, and maybe gained a couple of pounds. The Swedes are good eaters. I was feeling like myself again.

Grafton was invited to a briefing at some government office, so I went along as his aide. I carried the briefcase with my notebook and a couple of pens, just in case, so that Grafton had his hands free.

The briefing was held in a small auditorium, and delegations from the U.S., U.K., and European Central Bank were there. They had either gotten the word or been invited. As I surveyed the crowd, I saw a small knot of Russians. The only reason I knew they were Russians was because I recognized one of them: a tall, cadaverous man whom I knew as Janos Ilin. He was the second or third banana in the SVR, the Russian Foreign Intelligence Service, the bureaucratic successor to the foreign intelligence directorate of the old KGB. He and Grafton had crossed paths in the past, and I had once had a one-on-one rendezvous with him. He was a nicotine fiend and ran his own private intelligence service, so it was a wonder he was still alive. One of these days they would put him against a wall and shoot him, if cancer didn't get him first.

I nudged Grafton and whispered, "Ilin." The admiral didn't appear to hear, but I knew he had.

So the Russians had sent a delegation to see how much the West knew about Russian money laundering. Maybe those guys who tailed me weren't Swedes. I vowed to renew my request to the admiral for a pistol as soon as this meeting was over.

The briefing was a real production. The Swedish finance minister ate some crow and told the international audience that one of the branches of the Bank of Scandinavia had a large amount of suspicious transactions in the last few months. That was a lie: according to Penny Rogers, it was at least a year—probably more, perhaps as many as four years. After the minister made a statement, a translator repeated the gist in English, then in French, then in Russian. Same translator, all three languages. This thing was going to drag.

Grafton whispered, "If Ilin goes to the men's room, you go too."

I passed him my briefcase and went to the back of the room. The minister was explaining how the government's routine bank oversight uncovered the suspicious transactions when I faded into the hallway. Only a few Swedish security guys were there, obviously packing heat, wearing little earphones and lapel mikes. Not a reporter in sight. I supposed the press briefing was going to happen later, after the Swedes tried out their story on the international banking community.

I wandered around until I found both the men's rooms on that floor. I was pleased to find you didn't need a coin to use a toilet stall, as you did in France. Apparently that French contribution to civilization hadn't worked its way this far north. Maybe next year.

No one kept an eye on me. Since this was a huge government building, I was tempted to break into an office just for grins and steal some pens, but decided against it.

Twenty-seven minutes after my exit, Ilin came out of the conference hall. He had another Russian with him. They walked toward the east men's room and went inside. I was right behind and saw Ilin enter a stall while the other Russian unzipped at the urinal. I went into the stall beside Ilin's, dropped my pants and sat down.

In less than a minute, I saw a matchbook visible under the partition. I took it and pocketed it. Made some grunting noises, peed since this was a good opportunity, used some Swedish government toilet paper, pulled up my trousers, and left the stall. Took the time to scrub my hands and dry them on a paper towel, then left after a glance at Ilin's Russian escort drying his hands so I would recognize him if I ran into him again.

I went back to the conference room and stood against the wall. Three minutes later, Ilin and his escort came in and took their seats with their delegation. No one paid any attention to me. Officials from the various governments were taking turns grilling the Swedish banking official, who was trying to stick to the script. Things were tense. I stood there thinking about Audra Rogers.

Back at the embassy, I gave Grafton the matchbook and told him how I got it. He opened it carefully. Wedged under the matches was a tiny piece of paper with two words typed upon it, in Cyrillic. Russian isn't one of my languages, so I left it to Grafton to enlighten me. He didn't. He merely grunted and headed for the SCIF, carrying his treasure in a fist. I decided to postpone my request for a gun—Grafton had other things on his mind.

I went to dinner. There's something missing when you're eating at a nice restaurant, with background music and white tablecloths, good dishes, a glass of excellent wine, and you're all by yourself. I wished Sarah Houston were sitting across the table, listening to my repartee and smiling occasionally because she liked me. Really, I needed to think about another career. Something that meant I could come home every evening and find her there.

But was it Sarah I wanted? I sat there toying with my food, sipping wine and thinking about that woman.

After dinner, I was strolling across a bridge toward my hotel when a car pulled up in front of me. The driver and passenger got out: I was on the sidewalk when the passenger got in front of me and the driver got out of the car to get behind me.

They were not big dudes, but they were fit.

The rain had stopped so I was carrying my new raincoat over my left arm. I let it slide to the pavement as I walked toward the passenger. I could feel the driver coming up behind me, and got a glimpse of him out of the corner of my eye. Looked like he was planning to give me a kidney punch.

I turned, blocked the punch, and staggered him with a right to the chin. I damn near broke my hand, but I grabbed him and threw him toward the guy in front of me. That guy sidestepped his oncoming buddy and leaped for a kick to my head.

I managed to grab his ankle and lift. The kicker slammed down on the sidewalk pavement. The other guy was on his face. As the kicker tried to rise, I kicked him a good one in the ribs. That settled him.

No one was watching the fight, which hadn't lasted more than eight seconds, if that. I bent over, rifled the pockets of the kicker. Got his ID. It was all in Swedish. He was packing a gun. Looked to me as if some MUST guys decided to even the score for the Swede in Estonia whose head Armanti had cracked.

He didn't look to weigh more than a hundred and eighty, and was *hors de combat* for a few more seconds. I put his ID back in his coat, picked him up by a leg and ankle, twirled him and threw him over the railing into the water.

The driver had a broken jaw, a broken, bleeding nose, and a badly skinned forehead from his face plant on the sidewalk. Another tough day at the office. I decided he didn't need to go swimming.

The car was still running, so I grabbed my coat, got behind the wheel, and drove away. Went to the train station and parked the car, a Saab. Nice car. I wiped the steering wheel, gear shift lever, and door latches. Locked the car and dropped the keys in a nearby storm drain. Massaging my sore hand, I walked back to my hotel feeling pretty good. Exercise will do that for you. That night I slept like a baby.

The next day, a Saturday, I was summoned to the SCIF. Jake Grafton had a pile of paper spread out on a folding table. He was the only person there. A folding chair was next to his, so I parked my behind and looked at the stuff with him. I told him about the Swedish security guys last night. He listened, had no comment.

"The name," he said, changing the subject, "on the paper in the matchbook is Yegan Korjev, one of Vladimir Putin's cronies, and a multi-billionaire. Ilin gave us nothing but the name, but that hint speaks volumes. All that money pouring from Russia into the branch bank in Tallinn couldn't have gotten through the country without Putin's knowledge and tacit approval."

"Okay," I acknowledged. That wasn't news. I had already gotten that far myself. Putin ran a tight ship.

"We know only the accounts in the banks that sent the money and the accounts around the world it went to. The recipients that we have checked so far are all shell corporations, with few or no assets. And to the extent we have been able to check, the money went on from those shells—call them Layer A—to other accounts at other banks, Layer B. What we would like to know is where the money *really* came from and its ultimate destinations."

"It didn't come from one source," I speculated, "but multiple sources that the Russians would like to be friends with."

"So one suspects. If Yegan Korjev put this laundry scheme together, or was told by Putin to make it happen, he must have records that show

the sources and the final destinations. That is information we want."
Jake Grafton sighed. "However, given enough time and investigative
resources, the police and banking authorities will come up with payors
and payees. The golden nugget of this scheme is the identity of the person
or persons who thought this up. Did this brainstorm originate in the
Kremlin or elsewhere?"

I took a deep breath and let it out slowly. "And how do you propose
to get this information?"

Grafton shuffled through the papers. He pulled out a sheet, pointed
to it, and said, "Korjev owns a dacha in the Moscow hills, not far from
Putin's, but he likes to hang out on a mega-yacht that he keeps in the
Med, *Catherine the Great*. She's six years old, 560 feet long, has a
65-foot beam, and a top speed of 30 knots. Has a helicopter on board
and several boats for ferrying people and supplies to and fro. The damn
thing is too large for most of the traditional Mediterranean yachting
ports of call, so must anchor out and be refueled from fuel barges."

"I wish I had been born rich."

"This tub is the size of a destroyer, has a crew of at least fifty, and
can accommodate forty or so guests in the lap of luxury. There are twelve
staterooms plus an owner's suite, a swimming pool, gymnasium and
steam bath."

"Where is it now?"

"Capri."

"Is Korjev aboard?"

"We think so. You're going to find out."

Why did I know this was coming? "Why do *we* think so?"

"This yacht has more communications gear than NASA. We've had
an E-2 Hawkeye in range for the last twenty-four hours to capture every
electronic beep she emits. *Catherine* has been lighting up the ether. If
Korjev was in Russia, *Catherine* wouldn't be transmitting like she is.
Everything is encrypted, of course, but NSA is trying to crack the codes.
It's just a matter of time."

"How much time?"

"I don't know, Tommy." Jake Grafton wasn't one for pumping up the troops with hot air.

Still, I was beginning to lose my temper. "So what do you want me to do? Hang out in Monaco until *Catherine* comes steaming in, bankrupt Korjev at Baccarat, then swim out and take over the yacht?"

Grafton eyed me frostily. "No."

Smarting off to Jake Grafton is never a good idea, but I didn't like the sound of any of this. "That's good. I don't own a white dinner jacket, a bow tie, or a Walther PPK. And you aren't M."

He didn't say anything, just turned back to his stacks of paper. I kneaded my right hand, which was aching.

"This sounds like a job for the SEALs or Marines, not little ol' me. I'm just a thief, for Christ's sake."

Jake Grafton ignored my comments—he's good at that. After some silence, he focused his eyes on me and said, "Here is what you're going to do and how you're going to do it." Then he told me.

# Chapter Five

C apri is an island in the Gulf of Naples, rocky, with a peak about two thousand feet above the ocean. I suspect it's an old volcano, but I'm not a geologist. The ferry from Naples was a nice ride, with day trippers and the yachting crowd. I didn't think I had been followed from the airport, but I kept a wary eye on my fellow passengers: in this business, it gets to be a habit.

The little village in the harbor of Capri came into view, picturesque with the big mountain behind it. As soon as the ferry entered the old harbor, I saw *Catherine the Great* anchored on one side of the roadstead. I looked her over as we slid by. The helicopter was on the helo-pad, chained down. People in uniform were on deck doing sailor things, and a couple of voluptuous young women in bikinis were strolling near the rail, showing off their assets. They were tan and gorgeous. Apparently Yegan Korjev liked some light diversions in the evening—perhaps in the morning and afternoon, too.

I watched the ferry dock and joined the crowd going ashore. Pulling my little wheeled carry-on, I wandered along the quay taking in the scene. There were boats of every size and description, yachts moored stern-first to the quay, the so-called Mediterranean moor, and a holiday crowd, even though this was the end of the weekend. Some of the boats looked like they belonged to working fishermen, getting fresh fish ready for the restaurants.

The thought occurred to me that dinner would be nice, so as the shadows lengthened, I entered a sidewalk café and scored a seat on the sidewalk at a little table. I ordered a local red wine and a fish dinner. The scene looked like something from a post card: splotches of blues, yellows, and reds, the little cafés, the picturesque quay. I had to pinch myself. It was too good to be true. I work for the CIA, and with only a few exceptions, the places I spend my working life aren't anything like this. To top it off, the sunset was spectacular, the air superb, the zephyr of a breeze perfect. I envied the locals.

As I sipped wine and stretched my meal to make it last, I kept an eye on *Catherine*. Indeed, that was a ship, not a yacht. When I had drunk a couple of glasses of the vino, which had a real body, and finished my excellent repast, I paid for my meal with euros and left a nice tip, courtesy of the American taxpayers. Ah, the simple pleasures of a civil servant on per diem.

I walked along until I found the stepped path that led to the peak, Mount Solaro. I started up, keeping an eye out for street signs. When I found the street I wanted, it led off to the left on a level grade along the slope. The house that Grafton had told me about was on the downslope side of the street. There was a peephole in the door, so after I knocked I arranged my handsome mug to show my best side, and smiled benignly.

I knew the guy who opened the door. His name was Rod or Robert— I don't know which—but his last name was O'Shea, so everyone called him Rick. I had done some operations with him over the years; he was competent and pleasant to be around.

"Hey, Tommy," he said. "Come on in."

He closed the door behind me. That's when I realized he had a pistol in his hand. He put the pistol in his pocket. I left my little suitcase in the hallway and followed him into the living area. A wall of windows looked out on Capri harbor; we were at least three hundred feet above the harbor on the side of the mountain. In the middle of the room was a platform, and on the platform was a large telescope and a chair. It was far enough back in the room that no one in the town or harbor could see that this was an observatory.

After we caught up, I asked Rick how long he had been here. "Three weeks," he said.

"When did *Catherine the Great* come into the harbor?"

"Two weeks ago."

"Why did they send you here?"

"The powers that be have had us keeping an eye on *Catherine* and some other yachts, some of the big ones the Saudi princes own. Keeping tabs on who comes and goes from them. I'm an eye. We have others up and down the north side of the Mediterranean, from Gibraltar to Istanbul."

"Uh-huh."

"It's a job, Tommy," Rick said. "Nice work if you can get it. Beats the hell outta Syria, Afghanistan, Iraq, and a few other shitholes I could name."

"I'll put in for this when I do my next dream sheet."

"Anyway, you get the little bedroom. There are three of us in here working shifts, so it's a little tight. The other guys are eating dinner somewhere. That's one of the perks."

"I suppose."

I climbed onto the platform and inspected the telescope, which was a big one. No doubt if you pointed it skyward you could see the American flag waving on the moon. There was a digital camera mounted to the thing, so the operator could snap a photo at any time.

I climbed back down. "So you take photos of people coming and going?"

"Yeah, when they come in on one of the yacht's tenders. But the gold is photos of people getting into or out of that helicopter she carries. The distance is a bit over a mile, so sometimes the atmospherics interfere."

"Atmospherics… Got any pics I can see?"

"Got an assortment."

He led the way to a table in the dining room, which was covered with computer printouts of photos. He held up one, and I gave it a look. It was me, getting off the ferry. I gave it back and took my time inspecting the ones spread on the table. I pointed at one of a guy with a gut, in his sixties, maybe, balding, wearing a sport shirt and shorts. "Who is that?"

"Yegan Korjev."

"I can pick 'em, can't I?"

"That was taken last week when he came in on the tender to meet a couple of whores he had flown in to Naples. They came over on the ferry. The girls couldn't have been a day over sixteen. From the Ukraine, I think, but the company can't identify them, so they said." He pointed to their pictures. Yep. Future super models.

I inspected every photo. Many of the crew guys looked like they were military age, and suspiciously buff. The yacht guests were older and rounder. I wondered if there was a gym on *Catherine*. Of course, I told myself. I studied each picture, trying to ensure I would recognize them if I met them ashore.

"How about these blurry photos? Looks like you shot people getting on and off the chopper."

"Yep. Amazingly, computers can resolve these most of the time if we get a good facial shot at a decent angle. We send them encrypted via the satellite. See that guy there? Iranian oil guy would be my guess. We got him coming and going, eight photos total. And that one there? Obviously a Korean. We got six of him. The company doesn't give us their names."

"So how long has the company been watching Korjev?"

"Like I said, he got there a couple of weeks—"

"No. Weeks, months, years. How long?"

"Oh, I dunno. Here and other places, like Cannes, Majorca, Monaco, maybe Corfu, and some other places, I'd be guessing. We keep an eye on this crowd. This set-up has been here quite a while. Years, maybe."

"But we're not in every port?"

"Of course not. We only have so big a budget and so many people. For Christ's sake, this is the fuckin' government, Tommy."

"Yeah. Got any booze here?"

"All the comforts... If you like bourbon or Scotch."

"I do." My right hand was aching, so I decided to self-medicate. I should know better than to hit some bozo in the jaw. I thought I was lucky I didn't break some bones, but the way my hand was aching, I may have cracked one or two.

A car picked Jake Grafton up at Joint Base Andrews, the old Andrews Air Force Base, and took him to Langley. The early morning was squishy, the lights of the city making the low clouds glow. At his request, Sarah Houston was waiting in his office.

The admiral didn't even say hello. "Okay, what do you have?" he said as he closed the door behind them.

"We have ten people working around the clock, trying to trace the money that came from that branch bank. Five each on twelve-hour shifts. That server Tommy stole in Tallinn arrived yesterday and we're mining it. We think it has two years-worth of transactions on it. The codes for the Bank of Scandinavia in Stockholm are worthless. They changed them the moment they found out the server was stolen."

"Uh-huh."

"A lot of the money apparently came to the United States."

"Why do you think so?"

"So far as we have been able to determine, downstream many of the foreign currencies seem to have been exchanged for dollars."

"That doesn't prove anything," Grafton grumped. "The American dollar is the world's reserve currency."

Grafton fell onto the couch and ran his hand through his hair.

"How long before you can give me some kind of a spreadsheet on this?"

Sarah Houston was tired and sank into a chair. "There's more. The shell corporations that we have looked at here in the States didn't just start receiving money in the last few months. This has been going on for years. Oh, and some of the shells dropped out and some more started receiving money. It's a mess."

"*Years...*"

"At least four would be my guess, based on the state records of when these shell corporations were created. The FBI is already visiting state capitols. All we told them was that we're interested in these corporations—not why. Here at Langley, we've only sampled the river. Assuming the worst case, we think over two hundred billion dollars has been going though that branch bank in Tallinn in the last four years."

Grafton merely stared.

Finally, he whispered, "Where in hell is all this money coming from?"

"More to the point," Sarah said, "Where is it going?"

"Yes," Jake mused. His eyes widened. "Some people are getting filthy rich."

"Remember the Panama Papers?" Sarah asked.

Indeed, Jake did. Records from a Panamanian law firm were leaked to the press in 2016. It then soon appeared that a branch of Deutsche Bank in the British Virgin Islands had more than 900 customer accounts that had run 311 million euros—about $353 million U.S.—through it in the year 2016 alone. Two of the bankers were accused of helping set up accounts for criminals in tax havens. A couple of Swedish banks were also involved, and they paid fines and had their wrists slapped. But the Germans authorities went after Deutsche Bank with a vengeance two years later. It took that long to merely sort out the records.

"Deutsche Bank was accused of laundering drug money," Jake said. "After that wash operation was shut down, that money had to go someplace. The drug syndicates are still in business peddling their poisons. Maybe the money went to Estonia, with the help of some Russian banks."

Sarah Houston brushed her hair back from her face. "This is about eight or ten times as much money as the Deutsche Bank's rogue branch in the Virgin Islands laundered. Drugs are profitable, but not this profitable. Why are you assuming the money that went through Estonia was real?"

"Banks don't—" Jake Grafton was galvanized. He stood up and strode around the room several times. Finally he settled into his chair behind his desk.

"Banks are only supposed to take real money," Sarah said, completing the sentence. "Real banks have to balance the accounts, income versus out-go, every single day. The banking authorities are sticklers on that. But what if some Russian banks making the transfers are just... shells? What if some of these banks making transfers to Tallinn are creating money out of thin air?"

"Counterfeiting?"

"Why not? Some bank somewhere in Russia electronically transfers money to an account at the branch bank in Estonia. It doesn't stay there long. The account holder, a Russian, sends the money along on its merry way to... wherever. You only assume that there was money in Russia to back up the original transfer. What if there wasn't?"

"Then the Russian bank collapses."

"Or doesn't."

Grafton pulled out a lower drawer and propped his feet up on it. Then he kicked off his shoes. "Two hundred billion dollars in four years."

"Maybe," Sarah said. "Maybe more, maybe less. Right now, only God knows, and He isn't telling."

Grafton muttered a cuss word.

"Anyway, it may have been fake money when it started its journey," Sarah said with a sigh, "but it's real money now."

Grafton sat thinking about that. "It's not enough money to destabilize the money supply," he said.

"Lord, no," Sarah agreed. She looked exhausted. "The American economy has a GDP of twenty *trillion* dollars a year. Fifty billion is a mere quarter of one percent of the American economy. It's a pittance compared to the money the Fed creates every year, a tiny drop in a vast bucket, a rounding error."

"It's big money if you got some of it," Jake Grafton said, his voice flinty.

Sarah nodded. "For wine, women, and song, if you are bent that way. Or enough money to fund a serious drug import business, take over some businesses, build skyscrapers, fund immigrant caravans, buy elections, make movies... manufacture cars, computer chips, pharmaceuticals, cell phones, booze, toilet paper... Enough money to build an empire."

"*Enough*," the old attack pilot echoed.

A minute later he said, "Thanks, Sarah. See you tomorrow."

"I have no proof that it's funny money," the master hacker said. "Just a gut feeling. This isn't a million here, a million there. It's hundreds of millions every day, billions every month."

She stood. Jake Grafton was lost in thought as she left the room and closed the door behind her. After a moment, he said to the four walls, "It's real money now."

He was still sitting behind his desk when the dawn came.

The receptionist brought him a breakfast tray from the cafeteria, complete with a small pot of coffee. "I want to see all the department heads and the deputy director at eight o'clock," he told her. "Call them at home."

"Yes, sir. The morning summary is on the tray."

He poured some coffee and looked at it. The first story leaped at him. The chairman of the Bank of Scandinavia drowned in his bathtub last night. Grafton looked at his watch. While he was somewhere over the Atlantic.

"Yegan Korjev, Russian billionaire and Putin pal," Jake told the CIA brass. "And the chairman of the board and the president of the Bank of Scandinavia, both recently deceased. I want complete dossiers on all three on my desk as soon as possible. Everything we know, everything the FBI knows, everything the State Department and NSA know—everything."

Grafton summarized what he knew about the river of money flowing through the Estonian branch bank. "It's been going on for years—we don't know how many. Billions of dollars every month. A lot of it has been coming to the States."

"Money laundering?" one department head asked.

"We don't know," Grafton said. He wasn't about to repeat Sarah's speculations, although he had decided she was probably right. Real money didn't flow like this, except perhaps from government treasuries in the third or fourth world. And not this much. That, he thought, was the real problem—there was simply too much money.

They discussed housekeeping details, priorities—because the world was in its usual turmoil and the agency had limited resources—then Grafton turned to the deputy director, Jack Norris. "You are our liaison with the FBI. They are going to have to investigate the American money trail. No way around that."

"I'll get briefed and go downtown to talk to Levy." Robert Levy was the director.

"As soon as possible," Jake said, then shooed everyone out. The whole meeting took about ten minutes. Grafton didn't like long meetings.

After the big honchos had scattered, Grafton called the White House on a secure line, identified himself and was soon talking to Reem Kiddus, the president's chief of staff. "I need to see you this morning, if possible."

"Is this about Sweden, by chance?"

"Yes. Why do you ask?"

"The Swedish ambassador has been making noises to the State Department. Your name came up. Something about the CIA rooting in confidential Swedish bank records. Then there's the bank mess over there that's on the news—the president will be asked about that."

"I was in Stockholm over the weekend. Just got back early this morning. I'll brief you."

"This afternoon after lunch, Jake. That's the best I can do."

"See you then."

Since he had the wheels turning, Jake Grafton went home to shower, shave, and visit with his wife. He took along a locked briefcase with another two months-worth of printouts from Sarah Houston's shop of the Estonian branch bank's transactions to show to Kiddus.

When he had his tie knotted, Jake went to the breakfast nook to have coffee with Callie and watch her eat a poached egg.

Reem Kiddus was a lawyer and political operative. He was smart, loyal to the president, had a low tolerance for fools, and by reputation was absolutely ruthless. He and Grafton knew and trusted each other. He listened to Grafton's summary of what had happened in Estonia and Stockholm, asked a few questions, looked at the printouts, then sat staring at the admiral. "This is going to be a major shit storm," he said.

"Yes."

"The Democrats in Congress are investigating the president for everything he and his businesses have done since he got out of diapers. They'll go nuts with this."

"I suppose."

Kiddus leaned back in his chair and scratched his chin. "A major FBI investigation… the politicians will hear about this soon, if they haven't already."

Grafton closed his empty briefcase. Kiddus could have the paper.

"Is it real money?"

"One of my staff pointed out that if it wasn't when it went into the branch bank, it is now. It's in accounts God knows where, and people are undoubtedly spending it, paying bills and taxes, buying securities or whatever."

"How long before you and the FBI can create a money trail?"

Grafton shrugged. "Months, maybe years. Whoever got some of this money had to explain it somehow to their colleagues, boards of directors, accountants, and the tax authorities. They'll hide behind their facades and demand that we prove they lied. You're a lawyer: you know how it is. Innocent until proven guilty. And if they've done a good enough job creating explanations, we may never crack the walls. Oh, we'll catch some incompetent crooks, but the smart ones…" He let it hang.

"It doesn't work that way in politics," Reem Kiddus said with a frown. "In politics, the rule is guilty until proven innocent. If the Democrats can ever show that the president's businesses or enterprises ever got a dime of this money, for any reason, they'll try to impeach him."

Jake wasn't going to argue with that assessment. He knew the state of domestic political warfare as well as anyone who read newspapers or watched television. *Thank God this isn't my problem*, he thought.

What he did say was, "If Putin was looking for a way to destabilize the United States, emasculate it politically for years to come, he couldn't have dreamed up a better scheme."

Kiddus made no comment. Played with the stack of paper. No doubt he was trying to think of the best way to handle this problem in Washington before it became a self-sustaining chain reaction. Grafton knew without being told that Kiddus merely advised the president, Vaughn Conyers, who had his own survival instincts well-honed. The president would make the decisions on how to proceed. Or if.

"The fact is," Grafton continued, "at this stage of the game no one knows where that money went or who ended up with it. It could be anyone. Could be a lot of people. Probably was a lot. Even the vampires who want the president's blood will realize that going off half-cocked could backfire dramatically when the revelations start hitting the press, as they will sooner or later. There's always another election coming."

Kiddus shook his head as if to clear his thoughts. "So what is your next step?"

"Yegan Korjev. He left tracks. We'll find them."

"He may die suddenly," Kiddus remarked.

"Indeed," Grafton agreed. "That thought must have occurred to him."

"If he does, make damn sure none of the blood splatters on the CIA."

"I'll do my best, Reem."

The chief of staff called the president, asked for some time. An hour later, Kiddus and Jake were in the Oval Office.

President Vaughn Conyers listened to both men as they laid out what they knew. Didn't ask a single question.

When Kiddus had run down and Grafton had nothing more to say, the president remarked, "Boiled down, we don't know anything for a proven fact."

"Anything about where the money went," Kiddus said.

"The Russians…" the president mused. He ruffled the stack of computer printouts that Kiddus had brought with him. "These Russian banks… the Kremlin is in this, to the roots of their hair."

He paused. "Until we know more," he said after a moment, "I don't know what we can do except let the FBI investigate here and the CIA abroad." He eyed the two men sitting across his desk. "Keep me advised. And take this stuff with you. Don't leave it lying around, Reem."

Back in the chief of staff's office, Kiddus handed the stack to Grafton. "I don't want this paper in the building. Take it back to Langley with you."

They shook hands and Grafton left.

Back at Langley, Grafton called in his vice-director, Jack Norris. Norris was the consummate intelligence pro, and no doubt he thought he should be the director of the agency; he might even make it when Grafton retired or got fired. He still had most of his hair and large, sleepy eyes.

"We need to find a way to get a peek into these Russian banks that sent wire transfers to Estonia," Grafton told him. "We can't do it alone—we don't have the assets. We're going to have to get NSA involved." NSA was the National Security Agency, which had the largest collection of main-frame computers and cryptographers on the planet located in their facility at Fort Meade, Maryland, between Washington and Baltimore.

"I'll talk to them," Norris said. "I've already been downtown to see Robert Levy. I gave him what we have. He looked at me as if I had brought him a dead skunk to decorate his office."

"I'll bet."

"He got a call from someone at Justice while I was sitting in his office. I figured out he was talking to Justice from what he said—he didn't enlighten me."

"Not Levy," Grafton muttered.

"Jake, don't expect big news from Levy any time soon. You know how the Hooverites operate: they hold their cards close to their shirts. Given their druthers they won't tell anyone anything until they have some cases ready for Justice, then Levy will hold a press conference."

Grafton thought that if Levy thought he could sit on this stinking mess while the bureau did business as usual, he was in for some unpleasant surprises, probably very soon. "We live in a deep, dark swamp," he said to Norris. "The people the FBI talk to will talk—they all have congressmen and senators. And the FBI will leak. The story will be on the street by tomorrow morning." He waved a hand. "But all that's beyond our control. We'll leave the FBI to the tender mercies of the Attorney General, the White House, the press, and the Congress. Go stimulate the guys and gals at Fort Meade. If you get any pushback, have the director call me."

"I'm on my way."

When Norris left, Jake asked the department head for Southern Europe to come see him. Tommy Carmellini was going to need a lot of help, and soon.

# Chapter Six

The story was on the street in America the following day, as Jake Grafton predicted, yet there wasn't much to it. A Swedish branch bank in Estonia had had a lot of Russian money pass through it. The Swedish banking authorities had decided on a line: Rogue Russians had tried to manipulate a small branch bank in Estonia, which was being shut down. Oversight would prevent future occurrences of this nature.

Of course the Russians would deny everything when they were asked, though no government on the planet had yet asked. One reason for this was that the amounts involved were still Swedish secrets. Another reason was that the governments of Europe, the U.K., and the United States suspected they needed to know more—a lot more—before they lit fuses in their own bailiwicks or bearded the Russian bear. The FBI cited its well-known rule that it would not comment upon ongoing investigations, or even admit it was investigating. The White House Press Secretary said she had nothing to add. The media cycled on to other, juicer topics, such as illegal immigration and the antics of the elected ones. After all, the media had cars, beer, and pharmaceuticals to sell.

A thin dossier on Yegan Korjev dropped onto Jake Grafton's desk. There would be more later, Jake knew. He opened it and began reading.

Korjev was a 1983 graduate of the Higher School of the KGB, the elite training school for Russian intelligence officers, and a KGB colleague of Vladimir Putin. After the collapse of the old Soviet Union in December, 1991, Korjev had gone on a mission to get rich, grabbed everything in sight, and turned it into money. Somehow he stayed on Putin's list of valued colleagues: When Putin needed help putting together a banking network to evade Western sanctions, he turned to Yegan Korjev.

Since Russia grabbed Crimea, invaded two breakaway provinces in Ukraine, and squabbled with Georgia over breakaway provinces South Ossetia and Abkhazia, they had been fighting sanctions from the European Union and the United States. A sophisticated system of shuffling money to and fro had allowed Russia to evade the sanctions and fund commerce between the rebels in Ukraine and Georgia—and Mother Russia. Money, money, money. Korjev had helped engineer the money pipeline. He performed well and got even richer.

The dossier went on, but Jake merely scanned it and tossed it on the desk. Putin and money.

The public was largely unaware that Russia had an economy merely seven and a half percent the size of the United States' economy, and twelve point three percent the size of the Chinese economy. It ranked a distant twelfth on the list of the world's national economies. Russia's GDP, Gross Domestic Product, was smaller than Canada's or South Korea's, and just a smidgen larger than the economies of Australia, Spain, or Mexico. Although it contained 144 million people, its economy would rank fourth if it were a state in the U.S., behind California, Texas, and New York. There were a lot of reasons for that, including Russia's vast size and terrible winters, its abysmal history of czars, Communist stupidities and mismanagement, the horrific carnage of World Wars I and II, an aging population, and pervasive, systemic corruption.

Yet the Russians had huge ambitions and visions of past glory, some real and the rest—the majority—mostly imagined. Russians wanted their country to be a world power, not a regional one. Perhaps Vladimir Putin, with the aid of Yegan Korjev, had found a way to magically increase Russian access to hard currency.

Maybe. Perhaps.

Jake Grafton picked up Yegan Korjev's dossier and slammed it down on his desk.

I was enjoying Capri. I could settle right into the scene here if I had some real money or was married to some. Alas, neither was the case. I was a civil servant on per diem, and neither my salary nor the per diem was princely. I didn't have a yacht, a boat, or even a skiff.

What I could do was wander around in vacation attire keeping an eye out for folks who might be keeping an eye on me. I hiked up Mount Solano, took in the view, and hiked back down. Didn't see a soul who thought I should be followed or watched. Even the hot young women, of whom there were many, paid me no mind. I was the invisible, anonymous man.

If there were people watching the crowds on behalf of Yegan Korjev, we needed to know. I told Rick O'Shea, Doc Gordon, Armanti Hall, and the other company guys that. Time was short. Things were going to happen, I said. I didn't tell them what.

Doc and Armanti went to find a hotel. Rick's pals, Fred and Tom, were nice guys, not covert operators but young studs in the company working their way up the food chain. Capri was a nice break from stations in embassies around the world, sort of a working vacation.

I took my turn at the telescope, and even got to photograph a few of the young lovelies that decorated *Catherine the Great*. The people I was really interested in were the Russians aboard, but they seldom came out on deck. I studied the photos Rick had again and again. I asked Rick, "How many of these guys are there?"

"Six guys who look like they could handle a situation. I don't know if they are really sailors or SVR or just Korjev's personal thugs." He gestured at the pictures. "We sent these photos to Langley but haven't heard anything."

I set up the satellite telephone, got the code for the day keyed in, wondered how secure it really was, and gave Grafton a call. An executive assistant whom I had worked with before answered, a brilliant black woman named Anastasia Roberts. "'Tasia, I need to know anything you found out about those people in the photos Rick sent you recently."

"The ones from the *Catherine*?"

"Anything they sent you. Everyone. Dirt and all."

"As soon as possible," she promised. "We'll have to send it by courier, which will take a few days."

"And I want to see any photos you have of previous port calls of *Catherine* in the Med. Everything as far back as you can go."

"I'll see what I can do, Tommy."

I sent Bill Leitz out on the streets with his equipment to find any sources of radiation that we couldn't account for, specifically radios. "Anything radiating," I told him.

"I can make you a map that shows every microwave oven in town," he said without enthusiasm.

"Be a tourist," I told him. "Stroll every street in town."

"This would be a lot easier if we had a van or something."

"I can get you a goat to ride. That's my best offer. Get after it."

The third morning I was in Capri, Rick O'Shea said to me, "You're going aboard that yacht, aren't you?"

He had no business asking questions like that. I smiled at him.

"What is it about that yacht that brings all you guys here?"

"Ask me no questions and I'll tell you no lies."

"I've heard that shit before."

"It's still true. Keep your mouth shut, your bowels open, and do your job."

He went back to his lonely telescope. I went outside on the patio overlooking the harbor and wondered why he asked. Maybe he was just curious. And he *did* know better than to ask. I reminded myself that there were literally billions of dollars floating around somewhere, enough filthy lucre to turn some feet from the straight and narrow path.

Maybe even mine. If I did decide to betray my country, how much money would they have to tempt me with? I sat in the sun watching people and boats come and go, waiting for the next ferry. I could just see it out on the ocean in the direction of Naples. It was at least a half hour out, I thought. The surface of the sea glistened in the sun.

After awhile, I went inside and closed the door to the house behind me, making sure it locked. Then I set off along the street for the harbor.

There was only one unattached American male on the ferry, and I had seen his photo before—although in the photo he had been in a naval uniform. Lieutenant Wilton Cogsworth, USN. Since he was only about five feet, eight inches tall, no doubt they called him Wilt the Stilt. I would have to ask.

He was wearing jeans, a tee shirt, a windbreaker, and tennis shoes. He glanced at me and walked by with a backpack over his shoulder. I hung back, made sure he wasn't being followed as he wandered the quay. He wasn't. Then I headed off up the hill toward the company observatory.

Rick was looking through the telescope when Wilt let me in.

Wilt smiled at me. "Tommy?"

"Yep. Let's go for a walk."

Walking along, we got acquainted. Wilt was a Navy SEAL. "I hear you want aboard that yacht down there in the harbor," he said.

"Yep."

"Any reason you don't want to talk in the house?"

"Let's just say a little itch between my shoulder blades."

"The place bugged?"

"My expert says no."

Cogsworth merely nodded. He got the picture.

"You want to do it while that yacht is there in the harbor?"

"I want to do it as quickly as possible, wherever it is."

"If it's underway, we have more options. Just anchored there…"

"Do you have anyone to help us?" I asked hopefully.

"Four guys and some equipment. They are coming in tonight on a small yacht that will tie up to the quay if there's room, anchor if there isn't."

So wheels were turning.

"Where did you get your equipment?" One doesn't carry wet suits, scuba gear, weapons, and explosives through Italian customs.

"The yacht rendezvoused with a Navy LHD last night. USS *Hornet*. Man, we're ready for whatever."

"Let's talk how you want to do it," I said.

"Do you care if they later learn you've been there?"

"No. They know the shit has hit the fan."

"That will make it easier." He grinned, showing white, even teeth. "This is gonna be fun."

"We'll see." I had this sneaking suspicion that this SEAL's idea of fun and mine were two entirely different things.

Sarah Houston reported to Jake Grafton in his office. "We've made a little progress, but not much. It will take years to follow the money trail if we can get into bank records, which will be very difficult. If they catch us at it…"

Grafton nodded. Sometimes you have to accept an expert's opinion, even if it isn't what you want to hear. "We'll have to leave it to the FBI. I expect we'll be reading their findings in about ten years."

Sarah nodded glumly.

"Let's work the other end," he said. "Those photos the guys in the Med are sending you. Let's assume anyone who solicited Korjev's help to get some serious cash didn't go to Moscow to see him. They or a middleman talked to him somewhere else."

"He's been back and forth on the yacht coast for years," Sarah acknowledged. "Attended conferences in Europe and Middle East. He owns a couple of companies that manufacture arms and ammunition. He exports arms... and is into banking."

Grafton thought the irony delicious. *Banking*!

The admiral leaned forward in his chair. "Have your team research our photo archives. I want every photo you can find of Korjev. Make up a spreadsheet of where he spent his time the last four or five years, check on the people he was with. Everything you can find.

"And he wasn't shoveling money through Estonia for his health—he was getting a serious cut. See if you can trace that through foreign banks."

"Follow the money," Sarah said, nodding.

"That damn yacht of his—see how he paid for it, if you can. Find the shipyard that built it, get into their bank records. Wouldn't surprise me to find that he paid for the yacht with his first big score. That may have gone so well he decided to expand the game."

"We're going to run into serious opposition on this one, Admiral." Sarah brushed the hair back from her forehead. "These people—whoever they are—made a lot of easy money with Korjev's help. They won't want any of this to come out. Even if they don't get convicted, just being suspected or investigated could ruin them."

Grafton merely nodded. There was going to be a war, and in war there are usually bodies.

That night in the shower, Jake Grafton turned the water on as hot as he could stand it. As the warmth cascaded over him, he stood thinking about who might have profited from Korjev's activities. He usually had some of his biggest insights in the shower.

Perhaps the money was drug money. That would be a nice, comfortable solution. If it wasn't money from international drug dealers, it was someone else, or a group of someone elses, people who could slip big money into their companies or operations and explain it away. That last qualification was crucial, he realized. Accountants, lawyers, staff... all would have to be satisfied that the money was legit or they would have to be paid off. Who, he wondered, fit that description?

The man who instantly came to mind was Bernie Madoff, the financier now serving a life sentence in a federal prison for masterminding a massive Ponzi scheme. Bernie would have been the perfect co-conspirator for Yegan Korjev. But Bernie did his thing before Korjev got his operation fully underway...so it was extremely doubtful that he could have ever been a beneficiary.

Other Ponzi schemers trying to expand their bubble... or people who needed new investors or donors in the worst way? People who needed serious money...tens or hundreds of millions, perhaps a billion, or two or three...or even more.

Grafton mulled the problem over with his eyes closed and let the water run.

The yacht was old and wooden, about sixty or so feet long, with two masts and a jib on the bowsprit. She was schooner-rigged and the sails certainly weren't new. Looking though the telescope in our observatory, I saw at least two sail patches that were slightly off-color. On high magnification I could see that she needed some serious work on her varnish and paint, which was blistering in places.

The two guys I could see on deck were in loose trousers and sweatshirts that fine morning. There were also two young women, also wearing sweats. They knew which rope was which, pulling or loosening them at the appropriate times.

The captain was in the cockpit manning the helm and giving orders. I focused on him, which was difficult as the yacht was moving, and caught my breath.

The captain was a woman, one I recognized. She was wearing a faded blue windbreaker and her long dark hair was tied back. The image jittered, but I was certain. Clarinda Day, the most dangerous woman alive.

I leaned back from the telescope and wiped my eyes.

"What do you see?" Rick O'Shea asked.

"A boat."

I put my eye back to the eyepiece and got busy focusing. Clarinda Day was a spook, and her specialty was recruiting human assets—spies—and running them. She was damned good at it. A few hours of gazing into those brown orbs and listening to her would make even the most honorable married men forget the seventh commandment and betray their country. Clarinda didn't take them to bed because she didn't have to. Maybe after her recruits were up to their eyeballs in treason she... but I don't know that she ever did. Perhaps her fellow spooks were just envious and spread vicious whispers.

Clarinda Day had a femininity that had to be seen to be believed. It wasn't that she was beautiful; she was certainly good-looking but no cover girl. Neither was it her figure, which was good but not great. It was just *her*. She radiated, *I am woman*. Any heterosexual male between twelve and ninety-two could feel the attraction, like the heat of an erupting volcano. She might have been the reincarnation of Helen of Troy for all I know. Perhaps Bathsheba or Cleopatra.

There was a time when Clarinda and I... but perhaps I should also save that for my autobiography.

The yacht glided into the harbor and the sailors expertly maneuvered it to the quay, where a line was passed to a man waiting on the dock.

They turned the boat, which was still moving, dropped the anchor and the jib, which was the only sail still up, then used a winch to pull the stern into the quay. It looked to my unprofessional eyes as if they had done this a couple hundred times.

I turned the scope and focused on the Russian yacht. If anyone was watching the arrival, he or she was on the bridge and hidden by the reflections on the bridge windows.

I turned my attention back to the sailing yacht, which was being snugged up by muscle power. The name on the stern was *Agamemnon*, and under that her home port, "Argos." A Greek flag flapped bravely from the masthead.

I wondered if Jake Grafton had sicced Clarinda Day onto Yegan Korjev. If he did, that Russian was about to have the experience of a lifetime.

Oh, well. I had my orders. Aye aye, sir, and all that.

When I finally rolled the stool back from the scope and looked around, Wilt was sitting in a stuffed chair eating something and drinking coffee.

"They're here," I told him.

# Chapter Seven

Wilt and I were eating dinner at a café on the quay that evening as the sun eased into the sea. We were wearing our windbreakers against the chilly breeze off the ocean. I was trying to concentrate on what he was saying, but Clarinda Day was in the back of my mind. Maybe it's my hormones. I asked Wilt about her. He eyed me suspiciously. "She's something, huh?"

"How did she get on your boat?"

"We needed someone who could actually sail a schooner, and somehow she showed up with two other women. Our guys have a lot of skills, but sailing isn't one of them." He shrugged. "I have no idea where she got the boat. I don't think its hers and I doubt if Uncle Sugar owns it. Maybe she borrowed it."

"Probably," I said. I could readily believe that there were a dozen guys with yachts willing to lend theirs to Clarinda Day. Maybe it belonged to the pope, or, more likely, the president of Greece.

We were sitting where we could watch *Catherine*. The Russian yacht was lit up with bulbs along every rail and up to the top of the mast from bow and stern. She was ready to get her photo taken for the cover of a yachting magazine.

We poured more wine and sipped.

Automatically, I looked around at the folks eating nearby, at the strollers on the quay... then it registered. I recognized a guy who was three tables down. It was one of the Russians from the yacht that Rick O'Shea had photographed. In his mid-thirties, close-cropped haircut, clean-shaven. Yep, that was him. He was arranging his backpack in his lap.

"Do you have a gun on you?" I asked Wilt while keeping my eye on the Russian.

"No. Should I?"

Now the guy had both hands in his backpack. One of his hands was making a twisting motion.

"Let's get the hell outta here," I said, and jumped up.

Wilt Cogsworth didn't need a brief. He was right with me. I shoved him out onto the quay as I looked back over my shoulder. The Russian had pulled a submachine gun out of the backpack, and it looked like it had a suppressor on the muzzle.

We crossed the quay at a dead run. Bullets spanged on the concrete and snapped past as people screamed. The only thing that saved us was that the quay wasn't more than twenty feet wide, a distance I made in three strides.

We both swan dived into the water and surfaced alongside a fishing boat, then paddled toward the harbor. We were nearing the front of the Med-moored boat when the Russian ran into view on the quay to hose off a burst in our direction. Wilt and I both went under.

Four minutes later, three boats along, we inched our dripping heads up and surveyed the quay. People were lying on the concrete, women were still screaming, and the Russian was nowhere in sight.

The sun had set. *Catherine* was creeping up on her anchor. Lots of people on deck. Then the anchor came free of the water and she swung, turning the bow toward the harbor entrance. On our left, *Agamemnon* was still tied to the quay. Everyone was on deck, watching.

Wilt and I heaved ourselves out of the water and onto the quay. We stood, dirty water pouring off us.

Wilt started toward *Agamemnon*, but I held his arm. "Later. The observatory. Let's check."

We began to trot. Some Italian cops were moving along the quay with their pistols out, searching the crowd for the guy with a gun. Wilt and I went in the other direction, leaving wet footprints with every step.

Off the quay, we ran up the hill. Along our street. Slowed as we approached the house. The door was open.

"This ain't good," I said, stopped and took a good look around. Without a gun, I felt absolutely naked. This would be a bad time to blunder into an ambush. I didn't want to meet that Russian or his submachine gun again.

Working along close to the wall, trying to see everything, we approached the house. I went in first. Rick O'Shea was lying just inside the door. He had been shot three or four times. Spent cartridges littered the floor. He still had his pistol in his hand, so I picked it up, checking to ensure it was loaded. It was. I clicked off the safety and crept into the house.

Someone had shot the shit out of the telescope and computer. The windows were full of holes. A dozen spent cartridges under foot. Fred and Tom were in the kitchen on the floor, dead as Rick O'Shea. One of them had a gun in his pocket, so I took it and passed it to Wilt, who was behind me taking it all in. I rescued my carry-on from the guest bedroom; I was going to need clean dry clothes. Then I checked out the satellite phone, which was undamaged. Somewhere here was book with the daily encryption codes. If they got that...

But they didn't. I grabbed the book and unplugged the phone.

"Let's get back to the boat," Wilt said. There was nothing we could do for the three dead company guys, so I followed him outside and passed him the phone and code book.

"I gotta get my other guys," I said. "They're at a hotel. Meet you there."

Armanti Hall and Doc Gordon were on the hotel restaurant patio lingering over dinner when they saw me come up the street. Taking in the sodden clothes and the carry-on, Armanti asked, "What happened?"

"Went for a swim. Let's go up to your room. I'll change while you get your stuff together. We gotta get out of here."

In the room I stripped and threw my wet clothes into the shower stall. As I did I told the two covert operators about Wilt's and my adventure on the quay, and about the hit on Rick, Fred, and Tom.

"Apparently Rick opened the door and the shooter started blasting, probably with a silenced submachine gun. Rick got it first, then the other two in the kitchen. Not a lot of blood—they died quickly. I got the code book and satellite phone. Get packed and let's get out of here."

We did. I stood watch in front of the building in my damp windbreaker while my guys paid their hotel bills with credit cards. Getting arrested for stiffing a hotel next time they were in Italy would be embarrassing, definitely not career enhancing.

We hoofed it down the hill and out the quay to *Agamemnon*. The night was clear, the sky full of stars. *Catherine the Great* was no longer in sight. Wilt was standing in the cockpit with Clarinda Day.

"Hey, trifle," I said as I stepped aboard. Okay, I was nervous, and not about the shootings. This was too much woman.

"Hey, Tommy," she said.

As Armanti and Doc got aboard, Clarinda began issuing orders. From somewhere below I heard the rumble of a diesel. As the lines came off she used the engine to inch ahead while the guys and gals on the bow raised the anchor. She spun the wheel, and in less time than it takes to tell, we were underway toward the entrance of the harbor, which was to the west, or perhaps slightly northwest.

"Which way did *Catherine* go?" I asked Wilt.

"South around the point."

"Help me set up the sat phone."

Grafton came on the line two minutes after I got through to Langley. It was morning there. "Yes, Tommy."

I told him about the events of the evening. "We're underway on this yacht, but we'll never catch *Catherine the Great*."

"I'll get the Navy on it. Have Mr. Cogsworth take you to the LHD. We'll get you some other transportation. And stay by the phone. I'll call you back when I know something."

"Yes, sir." I hung up.

Sat on deck with my back to the little cabin and looked at the night. My hand ached, so I massaged it. I was sure I had at least one green-twig fracture.

Of course, the question of the hour was how Korjev's thugs found out about the company observation house. Maybe Rick O'Shea and his guys did bad tradecraft. Or perhaps there was a watcher watching them that they never spotted. Or maybe someone sold us out. Maybe that someone was curious Rick.

I pulled out his pistol and checked it. A Beretta. Yep, magazine loaded and one in the chamber. Nice shooter, and it hadn't done him any good at all. Why did he open the door to a dude with a burp gun? There was a peephole in the door. Why didn't he look?

Treachery is so tacky, but man, the money that was floating around! Do one dirty little deal and get set up for life. Korjev would be appreciative. Buy that yacht, live on the Riviera, fuck hot young women until your dick wears out. Yeah, that would tempt a lot of guys. Maybe Rick, or Fred, or Tom. Maybe, maybe, maybe.

Any way you cut it, that Russian on the quay with the bullet hose knew exactly who Wilt and I were, and someone had decided precisely what they wanted done about us. Wilt and I were damned lucky we were still breathing and not leaking blood. Yeah, that's me, ol' Lucky Carmellini.

The guys and gals rigged the sails and the engine died. I sat there thinking about billions of dollars... and the sight of Rick, Fred and Tom lying on the floor, full of holes, dead as men can get.

Jake Grafton had a full plate. The *Washington Post* had broken the real story that morning: Billions of dollars had been deposited in the Bank of Scandinavia branch in Tallinn, Estonia, and the depositors had wire-transferred the money all over the earth, according to the *Post*. An unknown amount had come to the United States. This banking scandal, according to the *Post* writers, was much larger than the Panama Papers scandal of 2016, which had involved apparent drug syndicates laundering their profits. That breach in banking ethics had involved millions—this one involved billions.

Jake Grafton read the story before he left his condo in Roslyn. He had even watched a little of the commentary from the talking heads on television, who apparently had no source but the *Post*. Yet.

In the office, he had a pile of telephone messages to answer. He called Reem Kiddus at the White House back first. "Where did that *Post* story come from?" Kiddus snapped.

"Not from here," Grafton said. "My guess is someone at the FBI called a reporter friend and dumped the load. Does it matter?"

"Two opposition senators are already on television accusing the administration of a cover-up. They want the attorney general to send this to the special counsel to add to his Russian-influence investigation."

Grafton took a deep breath before he spoke. "Reem, you knew this was coming. The only question was when. The appropriate arms of the government are investigating. When they have some facts, not rumors, they will be announced at the proper time. Call Levy and give him hell for leaks from his organization."

Kiddus broke the connection without saying goodbye. A few minutes later, Tommy Carmellini called on a secure satellite link and Grafton learned about the shootings in Capri and the sailing of Korjev's yacht, *Catherine the Great*. After he finished talking to Tommy, he called the agency op center and learned that they were already talking with the Navy, which knew immediately of *Catherine*'s departure from Capri. Other departments reported. The State Department was talking to the Italian authorities about the murder of American nationals in Capri. Their police had just discovered the bodies. The *Catherine*'s encrypted messages were being attacked by both Navy and NRA crypto-analysts. Dossiers of Korjev's contacts for the last few years, and people photographed in his company or coming and going from his yacht, were being compiled. Already intelligence analysts had a tentative list of names that was growing by the hour.

A staff meeting in the director's conference room brainstormed about stopping *Catherine* on the high seas. "Korjev probably knew or could guess that we intended to make a surprise raid on his yacht in Capri harbor," Grafton told them. "If he has tossed his computer and all his records overboard, there is nothing there now to be found."

A senior woman shook her head. "He's using that computer to encrypt messages and burping out a steady stream of them. If we grab the boat while that computer is still aboard, we might be able to snatch it."

Grafton wasn't so sure. "The computers we really want are at the Russian banks that sent money to Estonia. Have we identified them?"

"Yes. The server at the branch bank in Estonia had those."

"So can we or NSA hack into those bank records, or do we need to think about a surprise raid?"

"The National Command Authority will have to approve of any operations in Russia," someone pointed out. Superfluously, Jake thought, although he didn't say it. He suspected that the mood at the White House this morning meant that he could get authorization for anything short of nuclear war. The real question was, did he want it?

He wondered aloud about how the Russians were responding to this morning's *Post* revelations, and the specialists in the Op Center soon gave him an answer. The Russian government denied it had any role whatsoever in bank fraud. If any governments thought some Russians did, international agencies should give the Russian government their evidence, and decisions would be made about whether the evidence was sufficient to prosecute.

"Putin's a hoot, isn't he?" Jack Norris, the vice director, remarked.

When the department heads left, Jake and Norris put their heads together. "If Yegan Korjev is our guy," Jake said, "we have to tie him to this some way. Just knowing who he has been talking to won't get us anywhere."

"We can sweat anyone we can identify, or the FBI can."

Grafton didn't want to wait. He wanted to seize the offensive and make Korjev play defense. And he wanted to put the fear in anyone who had purchased Korjev's brand of financial shenanigans. He said as much to Jack Norris.

"Stop the yacht on the high seas on some pretext or other and search it from stem to stern," Norris suggested. "The Russian government will squawk, but so what?"

"Will they? They've been capturing Ukranian ships on the high seas. Maybe they have a full plate."

"If they don't squawk," Norris shot back, "we can leak it. Make damn sure the press gets it. Get rumors started. If your source is right, Korjev is dirty, and the fact that we are after him will cause things to happen."

"What if he's being set up?"

"By whom?"

"The Russian government, possibly. Korjev could be a dangle."

"Jake, this bank thing is going thermonuclear. There's no way on earth to put a cork in it."

"What will happen when it does?" Grafton mused.

"Man, if we knew that we wouldn't have to snatch Korjev."

If Reem Kiddus thought he had big troubles this morning, Jake thought, wait until tomorrow's troubles come bursting through the White House door.

The director mulled it for at least a minute, weighing the pros and cons. Then he called Reem Kiddus and explained what he wanted to do. Kiddus said he would get back to him.

Grafton and Norris went to the Op Center and looked at the position of *Catherine the Great*. She was steaming southeast toward the Strait of Messina at eighteen knots. The position of the LPH and its task force was also there on the map, south of Capri. *Catherine* and the LPH were only a hundred miles apart now.

"If she gets through the Strait of Messina before we get authorization, we will need our Navy near the tip of Greece. Get them there before *Catherine* gets there. Find out how long it will take."

That answer he soon had. Thirty hours, unless *Catherine* sped up, then less. There was a carrier task force in the eastern Med. Helicopters and Ospreys could transfer people back and forth.

Jake took one last look at the positions on the map. There was no doubt in his mind that if the Americans dithered, *Catherine* was going through the Strait of Messina, around the Peloponnesus into the Aegean, then north through the Dardanelles into the Sea of Marmara, through the Bosporus into the Black Sea, and on to a Russian port.

Jake Grafton could feel Korjev's panic. Only a panicked man would have shot those Americans on Capri. He should have pulled *Catherine*'s hook and sailed away without a word. Maybe the shootings were Korjev's first mistake.

Yet perhaps Korjev had been as surprised as Tommy Carmellini. Perhaps he was being set up. After all, Ilin had merely pointed at an obvious suspect, Putin's money wizard. The Americans would have gotten around to Korjev before long. If Korjev was being set up, he was skedaddling in the wrong direction—that is, if he were still alive.

Grafton asked the Op Center staff how much fuel *Catherine* had aboard. When and where did she last fill her bunkers? Could she make a Russian port without a port call? He had the answers in twenty minutes. *Catherine* had topped her tanks in Naples before calling at Capri, and yes, with full tanks she could sail half-way around the world at thirteen knots. At eighteen knots, any port in the Mediterranean or Black Sea was within range.

He and Norris went back to the office to write messages to the Navy authorities in the Med: "Get ready to stop *Catherine*."

The television was on. After the executive assistants had departed with the messages, he flipped channels. All the news shows were concentrating on the *Post* story, politicians were in front of cameras, and ignorant experts were pontificating.

Grafton killed the sound, then called Reem Kiddus on the secure line.

He quickly briefed the White House chief of staff on the shooting in Capri. "I want to stop that yacht and search it. Interrogate Korjev."

Kiddus said, "You're going too fast."

"We're not going fast enough," Jake shot back. "We are either going to get ahead and stay ahead of this story or we'll be road kill. Why do you think that kid was snatched in Estonia?"

"To shut the parents up."

"No. The kidnappers took a photo of the little girl, killed her, and *threw her body in a canal*. They knew it was just a matter of time before someone found the body, then the parents would talk. *That is what they wanted to happen*."

Kiddus sounded puzzled. "You're saying that someone wanted the branch bank's money river uncovered."

"Someone."

"Who?" Kiddus was plainly puzzled.

"Guesses are three for a quarter. Probably the same someone who killed three CIA officers a few hours ago in Capri and took some shots at another on the quay at the harbor, in full view of Korjev's yacht. Korjev immediately weighed anchor and cleared out. One possible reason is that he realized he was being made a fall guy. Every tale needs a villain."

"Maybe Korjev ordered the Capri hits."

"If he did he's a fool. He may be a lot of things, but I doubt that description applies."

Kiddus took an audible deep breath. "So you want to talk to Korjev."

"I think he's panicked. He knows the game is getting bloody and he may be next. He might just talk. I want to be there to talk to him."

"So how do we do this?"

"We need a request from the Italian government to stop that yacht, and we need it as quickly as we can get it. Like within a few hours."

"I'll get on it," Reem Kiddus said.

About an hour after I talked to Grafton, Clarinda Day came forward and sat down on the deck beside me, with our backs to the cabin. I confess, I had been thinking about her, and had put off going below to pee so I wouldn't have to pass her and converse. Isn't that a hell of a way to be?

"Nice boat," I said to her.

"I borrowed it from a Greek friend of mine."

"He needs to spend some money on maintenance."

"He's not rich. He inherited it."

I couldn't think of anything else to say. I could feel her presence, her feminine essence. I thought maybe she was a witch.

She inspected the sails as the breeze played with her hair. "So how is your life going, Tommy?"

"They keep me busy."

We sat in silence watching the jib pull. There was just enough light from the masthead and running lights to see the sails, taut and rigid against the sky full of stars. My windbreaker was dry now and felt good. The Beretta in my hip pocket was lumpy, but I liked the feel of it.

"I once thought," she began, "that you and I..."

"I did too," I said. "Years ago."

We sat there for another five minutes in silence. I could feel the heat of her presence. Finally, she arose and went back to the cockpit. I followed her, peed in the little marine head, then went back on deck and sat down beside the satellite phone.

The *Agamemnon* ran on under the stars, pitching gently, riding the back of the sea.

# Chapter Eight

Richard Philbrick was the chairman and CEO of the most successful private investment firm in Atlanta, Georgia. This morning he stood at the window of a glass tower office downtown. From where he stood, he could see Peach Tree Creek, the shopping emporiums, and storm clouds beyond, which he thought somehow apropos. Behind him the television was on CNBC, which was giving the Bank of Scandinavia scandal a big play.

Philbrick's standing in the Atlanta investment community was spotless and he had a growing reputation as a financial wizard. It hadn't always been so. He got his start about ten years ago running a little Ponzi scheme. His office manager and accountant were in on the scheme, and they knew the truth. Bernie Madoff's fall was an object lesson that no tree grows to the sky. All three of them had been sweating that reality and making plans to disappear to South America with all the money they could grab when one fine day he got a visitor in his office — which was in a suburban shopping center back then. A European dressed in an Armani suit and wearing a handsome tie walked in.

The man had a proposition. It took him forty-five minutes to get around to it, while he flattered Philbrick as a financial genius and told him a bunch of lies about his principals. Once Philbrick began to suspect this guy was an SEC investigator, the European got around to it. He represented a group that wished to invest money in Philbrick's mutual funds. The money would be transferred from an account here in the States. Of course, there would be a fee to him and his associates for arranging this financing.

Philbrick knew a skunk when he smelled it. "How big a fee?" he asked.

"Before I answer that," the European said, "We need to discuss how much money my friends wish to invest."

Philbrick smiled. The European smiled.

"A hundred million dollars every two months," the European said.

Richard Philbrick almost fell out of his chair. He tried to control his face. His own bubble had only expanded to $25 million.

"As I said, there is a fee for bringing you this investment." The European smiled, smooth as old whiskey. "It's half."

Philbrick had to turn his face away. Of course this guy was some kind of crook, scamming somebody. But if this guy did indeed net Philbrick $300 million a year, Philbrick didn't give a damn if he was scamming the pope. Hell, maybe he was.

When he had gotten himself more or less under control, Philbrick smiled at his visitor. "Perhaps we can make a deal," he said.

That conversation was twenty-six months ago. Listening to CNBC as he looked out of his corner office windows at Atlanta lying below him, Richard Philbrick knew in his gut that he had probably seen his last deposit from "the syndicate," as he and his two co-conspirators called their mystery investors. And they had made their last "fee" payment. Oh well. Nothing lasts forever.

Richard Philbrick looked around the office at his expensive trophies. He was going to miss all this. They still had a couple hundred million in the bank. Soon it would be time to fade into his next life as a rich retiree.

He wondered if he could transfer the money and scram before his two partners figured out what was happening. Why share?

Another businessman who had an epiphany as he watched CNBC was a money lender... well, a loan shark. Sal "Big Tuna" Pizzolli had a very specialized business. He loaned money to guys importing heroin, cocaine, meth, pot, ecstasy, and anything else addicts would pay for. The importers needed huge wads of cash to fund their deals and were willing to pay his interest rate: twenty percent a *week*. Big Tuna had access to money, but he had to split the interest income fifty-fifty, and he had to make sure he collected the interest and the principal. Since his customers were all criminals who would kill at the drop of a hat—and they would drop the hat—Big Tuna had to fund a small private army of collectors. That was a necessary expense, but he was making serious jack, so his business remained profitable. You just gotta deal with problems when they arise, iron 'em out. He also needed a small army of personal body-guards since his customers had been known to cancel their debts with bullets.

When he needed more cash, he talked to a Palestinian who lived in South Boston, Hany Khalidi, and swear to God, that raghead always had whatever amount of non-traceable currency Big Tuna asked for. "You need two million next week? Sure."

Big Tuna always wondered where the Palestinian got it. Listening to the television idiots describe the Russian money river flowing though Estonia, the light dawned for Big Tuna. The fucking Russians!

But Big Tuna wasn't worried. The feds could never trace the money Khalidi loaned him. There was no paper anywhere. The only possible source of trouble was if the Palestinian was arrested and fingered him as a recipient of loans in order to save himself.

That problem was solvable. He would send a couple of guys to attend to the Palestinian. Big Tuna couldn't borrow any more money from the

raghead if he was dead, but his demise would cancel Big Tuna's outstand-
ing loans. It wasn't as if the raghead's wife would sue him.

Business is business, Big Tuna told himself, and switched the channel
on the television to a rerun of the New England Patriots' last Superbowl
game. That had been a hell of a football game. And Tom Brady was a
hell of a quarterback.

Zeke Rossen was in the Southside Mall trying to figure out what to
do with an empty storefront of a tenant who left the day before. Zeke
had been in the mall business for thirty years and had developed four of
them. The Southside Mall was the last one he owned, and it was struggling because the tenants were struggling. Two of his anchors had left—
one had gone bankrupt—and the small retailers were getting eaten alive
by internet giants. They could only carry a limited inventory, and yet the
internet merchants, large and small, had access to every item made by
man in every color and size and at every price point imaginable. The mall
merchants had to pay rent for their space and hire clerks to sit there even
when business was so slow they were losing money on the clerk's salary;
their competitors were shipping from giant mechanized warehouses, a
make-on-demand factory in China, or somebody's garage. How do you
compete with that?

The only reason Zeke Rossen still owned this mall was that a private
investor had approached him with an offer. The investor and his friends
would pump fifty million into this mall in return for a twenty-five percent
interest. But there was a catch. They wanted a thirty percent kickback
up front. Fifteen million dollars.

Of course the deal stunk. They were telling their investors they were
investing fifty million, yet skimming fifteen right off the top. They were
thieves. Zeke knew that. But without the deal he was going to lose the
mall, which would bankrupt him. Everything he owned was tied up in
the Southside Mall. So he said yes. That was about a year ago.

He was thinking about that deal when he got home. His wife was waiting for him. "I've been watching the news," she said, and sat him down in front of the television. Fifteen minutes was enough. The Russians were pumping money through a little branch bank in Estonia and it was leaking out all over the world.

"That deal last year..." his wife said. Her face was a study. She knew the agony Zeke had gone through before he agreed to the investment and kickback.

"We should call the FBI," she said.

He stared at her. "We don't know if that investment was any of that money."

"Zeke. That was dirty money. We both know that."

"Maybe. But it wasn't Russian money."

She rose and left the room, leaving Zeke Rossen alone with the television and his conscience. And a half-empty mall.

An hour before dawn *Agamemnon* rendezvoused with USS *Hornet*, a huge gray U.S. Navy assault ship. I had fallen asleep on the deck and Clarinda Day woke me. I gathered up the satellite telephone and my airline carry-on and went aft to the cockpit. We were tied to a makeshift float that rode between us and the big ship. The SEALs helped me with my stuff. I was so shaky I had trouble stepping from the pitching yacht to the float. Wilt grabbed my arm. Doc Gordon took the carry-on from a SEAL.

"Goodbye, Tommy," Clarinda said. I couldn't see her face very well.

"Goodbye, trifle," I said, and staggered across the float to the ladder. I didn't look back.

The Navy fed us, then escorted my colleagues and me to an eight-man bunkroom. I dumped my stuff on the floor and fell into a bottom rack. I was asleep in less than a minute.

Armanti Hall shook me awake. "Tommy, they want you in the Operations Center. Wake up, shipmate."

I blinked mightily at the glare of the overhead light and looked at my watch. It was nearly noon. I rolled out. I felt grubby and needed a restroom.

I got myself up and asked Armanti, "Where's the head?"

"Follow me."

My business done, I told Armanti I wanted food. "Chow first." He led me along endless passageways to a mess hall, and we went through a serving line with metal trays, helping ourselves to good, wholesome American grub. I took two slices of pizza, a naked hamburger patty, and some beans. There was a container full of salad but I skipped it. Armanti heaped his tray with junk food too.

As we ate Armanti filled me in, talking softly. "Looks like the Navy is going to stop that yacht. Maybe tomorrow. Maybe off Greece. They're in the Ops Center figuring it out now."

"Why do they want me?"

"You're going aboard it with Jake Grafton when they get it stopped."

"He's coming?"

"So they say."

"Fucking wonderful."

I went back and got more beans. The Swedes and Italians don't do beans like the U.S. Navy does. I was going to fart my way across the Mediterranean.

When we got to the Ops Center the balding captain who looked like he was running things scowled at me. "Took you long enough," he grumped.

Although the beans were great, I thanked my stars I wasn't in the Navy. I didn't even bother answering him. Found a chair and parked my bottom. Armanti sat down beside me.

The captain frowned at Armanti's hirsute splendor. "Eat your heart out," Armanti told him.

The captain briefed us. All we had to do was ride a helicopter over to *Catherine* with Jake Grafton after she stopped. If she stopped. "What are you going to do about that helicopter on her deck?" I asked. "Our guy could just get into it when he sees these big gray ships coming over the horizon and chopper away."

The captain looked at me as if I were simple. "We're going to disable it on her deck."

"How are you going to do that?"

"With bullets."

I nodded sagely. "Why didn't I think of that?"

We left shortly thereafter. I went to the eight-man bunkroom and stripped off my clothes. Doc Gordon was sitting on a bunk cleaning his pistol. I headed down the passageway with my towel, took a long shower, ignoring the water conservation signs. The ship was wallowing in the sea. I wasn't used to this. Water in the commodes slopped around.

Back in the bunkroom I changed into my last clean outfit. If we stayed out here on this tub for more than a day or two I was going to have to get my clothes washed or borrow some duds. Maybe I could get a cool sailor outfit.

I went up on deck to watch Marines work on their helicopters. It was misting rain out of a low overcast and the wind was brisk, so I didn't stay long. Visibility was only a mile or two across the surface of the gray ocean. I could see one destroyer with a white bone in her teeth keeping station on our port beam. She seemed to be going swiftly, as I suppose we were. I went back into the ship and wandered along the passageways looking at hatches, hoses, and shoring timber, dodging sailors and Marines all going somewhere in a big hurry, thinking about Audra Rogers. And Clarinda Day.

I felt a little seasick.

# Chapter Nine

The following morning in the hours before dawn, a helicopter settled onto the flight deck. The weather had cleared a little and the misty rain had stopped. I could see the running lights of a destroyer running parallel on the port side, but except for those lights, the night sea and sky were as dark as Hitler's heart.

As the rotors wound down, Jake Grafton got out of the Marine machine. He was wearing jeans, tennis shoes, and a brown leather flight jacket that had seen better days. I was standing in a little office full of windows that jutted out over the deck, so I had a good view. There were three officers standing on deck to greet him: an admiral, the captain of the ship, and a Marine colonel. All three saluted. Grafton shook their hands, then they went inside the island though a door that was apparently right under my aerie.

I thought I had better go say hi to my boss, maybe take him to breakfast. I said goodbye to my host, the Air Boss, and wandered out of his office and down the ladder. Grafton was at the foot of the ladder on the flight deck level talking to the brass. I made sure he saw me and stayed out of the way.

After a bit, we all trooped down another ladder, a little procession led by a couple of enlisted Marines in blue trousers and khaki shirts, to the Flag Ops Center. By that time I was the proud possessor of a tag that dangled from a chain around my neck, so the Marine sentry accoutered with a sidearm gave the tag a good look and admitted me behind the heavies. Then he closed the door, with him on the outside.

"Gentlemen, you've probably met my aide, Tommy Carmellini," Grafton said and gestured at me. I nodded, although the big kahunas didn't bother to look at me.

The admiral went to a table that was really a computer screen. This morning the thing showed the ocean around Greece. "The *Catherine* is here," the admiral said, pointing with a finger, "and we are here, on the eastern side of the island of Cythera. She can pass north or south of Cythera, and we'll meet her in international waters on the eastern side. We hope to intercept her at dawn."

They got into the mechanics of how they were going to do it. It sounded to me as if they intended to wait for *Catherine* to come to them. "We have an E-2 watching her, recording all her encrypted transmissions," the admiral said. "On this presentation you can see the other ships in the area, fishing boats, yachts, freighters, and so on."

"It's a crowded ocean," Grafton remarked, surveying the table.

"No doubt we will appear on *Catherine*'s radar when she comes through one of the straits, but she won't know what kind of ship we are. We intend to launch two helos to intercept her just after dawn. The lead will make a low pass and shoot into the engine of the helicopter on *Catherine*'s deck. That should anchor that chopper right there."

"You're sure that helicopter didn't fly off during the night?" Grafton glanced at the admiral.

"The E-2 would have seen it if it did."

"You've got the message from State?" Jake Grafton asked.

The admiral nodded. "The Italians have requested our aid to stop that yacht and if possible, detain Yegan Korjev for questioning about a shooting night before last in Capri."

"We're going to need a translator," Jake Grafton said.

"We have a couple. The woman who volunteered speaks Russian like a native. The man is an enlisted Marine linguist."

"Please brief me on how you are going to stop this yacht," Grafton said.

So they got into that. I found a stool in a corner and parked myself on it. One of the sailors offered me a cup of black coffee, for which I was grateful.

When the heavies were through, Grafton came over to me and shook my hand. "Sorry about the guys in Capri, Tommy."

"Yeah."

"You and Bill Leitz are going aboard *Catherine* with me."

"Why didn't Korjev fly off that yacht in his helicopter during the night?"

Grafton gave me an appraising glance. Then he said, "Maybe he thinks he's safe, or maybe because he's dead."

"You think?"

"We'll see. I'll be surprised if we find him aboard."

"Sleeping with the fishes..."

"He's the fall guy, I think." Grafton shrugged. "That shootout in Capri may have surprised him as much as it did you. We'll find out in a few hours, won't we?"

"I suppose," I said. Then I decided to voice my doubt. "This whole thing about stopping this yacht sounds damned iffy to me. All the captain of *Catherine* has to do is run her in close to some island or other, into Greek waters, and we can't touch her."

"That's right," Grafton said.

We made a head call and went to breakfast. Joined the company operators at a long table. Grafton told them it was good to see them again. He's a born politician.

I shouldn't have worried. *Catherine the Great* had transited the strait between the island of Cythera and the mainland of the Peloponnesus in the hours before dawn and was well out into international waters. A helicopter loomed out of the sea haze from astern, paralleled her track, and slowing, opened fire with a door gun on the chained-down helicopter on deck. One long burst, then another for insurance. A small plume of smoke came out of that shot-up chopper and trailed off downwind. Since the helicopter platform was aft of the bridge, I wondered how much of this action the officer of the deck saw.

More choppers came up from astern and went into a hover over the deck while destroyers came out of the haze from either side on a collision course. The idea, the admiral had said in the briefing, was to overwhelm *Catherine*'s crew before they had time to decide on a course of action. That goal was achieved.

From the chopper that also contained Jake Grafton, Bill Leitz, and the male translator, I watched the SEALs rappel down ropes to the deck. The SEALs went down those ropes like they were fire poles. Once they were on deck, they jerked out their assault rifles and cleared the area, running for the bridge, the radio room, and then the engine room. Five SEALs each from two choppers. In less than a minute, the radio squawked. The copilot of our machine turned and gave Grafton a thumbs-up.

Shortly thereafter we were approaching the ship. The shot-up helicopter took up most of the space topside, but our guy hovered over the fantail and we got to try our hand at rappelling down a rope. The crewman in the door made sure we were hooked up right and that there was a SEAL holding the bottom of the rope. Then we each took a deep breath and stepped out into space.

The beat and downwash of the rotors made it almost impossible to breathe. I went down slowly, careful to not let the rope run too fast. Leitz lost control about six feet above the deck and would have broken something if a SEAL hadn't been there to break his fall. I was slow. Grafton slid down faster and walked away with a SEAL beside him. I shucked the rappelling harness and trotted to catch up. We passed the pool, which was not large and too shallow for diving. The hot tub gave off steam.

"No guns in sight anywhere, sir," the SEAL beside Grafton said in a familiar voice. I took a good look... yep, the SEAL was Wilt the Stilt.

The interior of the yacht reminded me of a high-end cruise ship, only more so. Overdone, with a garish color scheme that would be hard to take with a hangover. The passageways and compartments were empty. I figured the passengers and crew were still asleep in their staterooms. There was a circular staircase in the center of the ship that gave access to every deck—and guaranteed that the ship would sink quickly if the hull were ever pierced. The bulkheads—walls to you—were decorated with original oil paintings, with sculptures scattered around, all accented by subdued light.

Grafton walked forward until he found the door to the bridge and entered without knocking. Wilt and I were right behind him. Three officers were on duty there, two men and a woman who looked like a Russian babushka, with a lot of lumps and gray hair. All were wearing uniforms with an Italian style and cut. Wilt was the only guy on the bridge with a visible gun, decked out in combat gear and helmet. He certainly impressed these civilians. They kept a wary eye on him.

Grafton walked over to the helm, looked things over, then pulled the engine telegraph or throttles to idle. The deck vibration changed and the yacht began losing speed.

"Mr. Cogsworth, we think you should come look. Dead man in the master suite."

As Jake and Cogsworth departed behind the SEAL, I pulled my pistol from under my windbreaker and herded the three officers off the bridge at gunpoint. I made them sit in the lounge behind the bridge and deputized a SEAL to watch them. He had a submachine gun in his hands and looked fierce, although his was a pale imitation of the presence of Armanti Hall. We should have brought that great one along to control the crowd.

I trotted along behind the disappearing admiral. Down a ladder, across another lounge into a passageway that ran amidships, with staterooms on both sides. The owner's cabin, or master suite, was at the stern of the ship. The double door was open. Sure enough, in the large lounge there was a man sprawled out before another double-door, this one closed. He had soaked up some lead, bled some and looked dead. A pistol lay on the deck beside him. Spent cartridges lay scattered around. I looked at the guy's face: he was not Yegan Korjev. The double-doors had bullet holes in them.

Grafton tried the knob on the doors. Locked. He rattled it, and bang, a bullet punched another hole in the door, missing Grafton by barely an inch.

Cogsworth and I sprawled on the floor beside the dead man. Grafton threw himself to one side and shouted, "Korjev, we are Americans. We are not here to kill you."

He said to the SEAL, who was also on the floor, "Bring a translator down here. Quickly now."

The SEAL hotfooted it back the way we had come.

Grafton addressed the door in a loud voice. "Mr. Korjev, we are Americans. This man in the lounge is dead. Please open the door."

Someone inside said something, unintelligible to me. Grafton repeated, "He's dead."

A noise at the lock, then the door opened. It was Yegan Korjev, sure enough, and his shoulder and side were covered in blood. Looked like at least two bullets had nailed him. He swayed, then sank to the deck. Grafton grabbed him and took the pistol from his hand and passed it to me.

"Mr. Cogsworth, we are going to need medical help to stabilize this man and get him to the hospital aboard ship."

"Aye aye, sir." Cogsworth headed topside.

With my pistol in hand, I went into the compartment, which was the master bedroom. The big round bed was very impressive. The paintings on the walls were of naked women, very well-done, I thought. The large flat-screen television on the bulkhead was running a fuck movie without sound, just humping, licking, and sucking. Two naked teenage whores were huddled against a wall, apparently uninjured. I could see where several bullets had torn sheets and at least one punctured the circular headboard. The large windows that looked out onto the ship's wake had a couple of bullet holes in them.

I had the whores put on their nighties, then ran them out. The translator met them coming in the lounge and was impressed, I could tell.

Korjev had lost a lot of blood. It was all over the bed, the rug, and him. He was semi-conscious at best. One of the SEALs was a corpsman, and he worked on the Russian, checking his vitals and slapping some bandages on to stop the bleeding, until a medical team with a wire basket arrived. They fussed over Korjev some more, plugged an IV into him, then loaded him into the basket and carted him out. All this time he didn't say anything for the translator to translate.

When they were all gone, Grafton and I got busy on the corpse. He was wearing a suit and had stopped two bullets—one in the chest and one in the leg—but two more had gone through. From the cut of his clothes, he looked as if he bought his duds in Europe. The metal in his teeth said he was a Russian. We emptied his pockets. He had a cell phone, a wallet, passport and some keys that he wouldn't need anymore, so we helped ourselves. The passport agreed with his dental work: it too said he was a Russian, so I was beginning to believe it. The pistol was a Beretta, with only one round left in it.

"It looks like this dude shot Korjev," I said, "who was standing in the doorway of the master suite, or was outside going in. Korjev got inside, locked the door, and then they traded shots through the door."

"I'll buy that," Jake Grafton said.

"Korjev got the best of it."

"Well, he's still alive," Graton mused. "And whoever told this guy to kill him presumably still wants him dead."

"You just can't trust the help these days."

"Get a SEAL in here to stand guard until we can search this compartment."

The radio room seemed intact. Several computers were still wired up: they would give us the crypto codes and a history of messages sent and received. There was a printer, a couple of radios that one could have used to listen to taxi drivers in Moscow and Cape Town, and a couple of file cabinets. The radio operator was a Russian, and the female translator was working on him when I got there. The Russian was smoking a cigarette that stunk up the place. Bill Leitz was engrossed with the computers and a SEAL was unloading the contents of the file cabinets into boxes.

After a bit, the translator said, "The dead man's name is Pavlychev. He spent two hours in here early this morning, before dawn. He used an encrypted voice radio." She pointed at the equipment.

The SEALS herded passengers and crew into the main lounge, which gave us free run of the ship to search. We had more helpers now, more SEALs and a bunch of Marines. Two of the passengers, a man and woman, were Americans, by the sound of their accents, and they weren't happy. Their Congressman would hear about this, heads would roll, piracy on the high seas, CNN would eat us alive, and so on.

Two Englishmen, a German couple, and one from somewhere in Eastern Europe. An American naval officer was inspecting passports which he had arranged in a pile.

The deck crew seemed to be all Russians. These were the military-age, buff guys. They huddled in one corner, smoking and staring. The chefs, however, were French, and they too were unhappy. There were also several Italian maids sitting together with their mouths shut. The Ukranian girls were huddled together in one stuffed chair with blankets around them. Their eyes looked the size of saucers.

"Every compartment," I told Wilt Cogsworth, who seemed to be in charge here. "Take them apart. We're looking for computers, cell phones, diaries, anything you can find. And search all these people to the skin. Get some female sailors to do the women."

The ship's head chef or purser had a small office that was accessed through the kitchen of the dining room. The wardroom for the passengers looked like a high-class restaurant, with tables that seated four. Indirect lighting, subdued colors, thick carpets. In one corner of the room was a well-stocked bar. The wine and liquor pantry was a sight to behold. Stuffed chairs, big windows, uniformed waiters and waitresses hovering to satisfy your every whim... all in all, going to sea on *Catherine the Great* looked like a nice break from a Russian apartment or your McMansion in Connecticut.

Grafton and the female translator questioned the captain on the bridge. The captain, as it turned out, was the Russian grandmother. I listened in. She spoke some English, so the translator only had to help with unfamiliar words. She had a low, deep voice that carried and an air of command. It was obvious the two men on the bridge took their orders from her, and she took no nonsense from anyone. I decided I liked her.

Under questioning, it became clear that the decision to leave Capri had been made suddenly. Korjev had been on the bridge, scanning with binoculars, and it was he who suddenly told the captain to raise the anchor and get underway. She protested—two crewmen were still ashore. Korjev insisted, giving no reasons. He was obeyed; after all, he was the owner. He paid the crews' salaries, which were at least twice what they could earn in Russia.

The dead man in the passageway, Arkady Pavlychev, had come rushing to the bridge when he felt the ship moving. He and Korjev had held a heated discussion that the captain, Olga Something, claimed she did not overhear. Korjev's orders stood. Captain Olga was to take the yacht to Sevastopol after dropping the passengers who wished to disembark in Istanbul.

Korjev went below. The yacht steamed through the night, all the next day, and into the night. An hour before the Americans stopped the vessel, Captain Olga claimed that a crewman had rushed to the bridge, claiming that he had heard shots. She had investigated, found Arkady Pavlychev sprawled dead in the owner's lounge and Korjev barricaded in the suite's bedroom.

Unsure of what to do, she reported the situation to the authorities in Sevastopol, *Catherine*'s home port, and was awaiting a message from them when the Americans stopped the ship. She reported the boarding to Sevastopol.

Grafton went back to the conversation between Korjev and Pavlychev.

"I did not hear it," Olga said flatly.

"This bridge is not that large," Grafton said, the soul of reason. "Surely you could make out part of what was said."

"I heard enough to know that it was owner's business, and maybe political, and I don't hear owner's business or political things."

And that, by golly, was that, as Grafton found out.

I wandered on, inspecting the ship. Yegan Korjev had an office with a computer, printer and drawers full of stuff. The door had been locked, but I picked it. I wasn't optimistic about our chances of finding anything in the office that gave a clue about his activities: after all, with all these crewmen aboard, he shouldn't have even bothered locking the door.

I went to the engine room to eyeball it up. Ran into a naval officer there who obviously knew a lot more about ships' engines and fuel systems than I ever would.

The crew compartments were bunk rooms without portholes, just above the waterline, I thought. And they were not very neat. I doubted if the Italian maids ever got this far down in the ship—nor, I suspected, did Korjev. The crew head hadn't been cleaned since the ship was launched, apparently.

The crew's messhall was composed of two long tables just off the galley where the grub was prepared. There were large, well-stocked walk-in refrigerators and a pantry the size of my apartment in Virginia. Two chefs were busy preparing food in a kitchen that would have done credit to a New York restaurant. They glanced at me and went on with their work. A third person, a baker, was working on a cake. No one was going hungry on *Catherine the Great.*

Prepared food was lifted on dumbwaiters the two decks to the main dining room. I looked in the dumbwaiters and pushed the buttons to run them up and down. Every multistory house should have one of these.

I ran into Jake Grafton in one of the passenger staterooms. He was searching. He was taking luggage from under the bed and dumping it on the bed to paw through the contents. "The Americans were in this stateroom."

"What kind of folks go cruising with Yegan Korjev?" I asked.

"People who are on his Christmas card list, or want to be. The FBI will check them out."

His handheld radio squawked and he listened a moment. I couldn't understand the words.

When that conversation was over, he put the radio back on its belt-holder and turned to the pile on the bed.

"Korjev is sedated," he told me over his shoulder. "Over on the *Hornet* they're giving him whole blood. Still has one bullet in him that will have to come out when his vitals stabilize. The SEALs will finish up the staterooms. You supervise the transfer of every computer on this ship—all of them, regardless of whom they belong to." He pointed at a laptop on a stand by the bed. "That one too. All of them."

He went up to the main lounge to interrogate each of the passengers. I picked up the laptop and its charging cable and took them up to Wilt Cogsworth, who was making a pile. I borrowed a magic marker and wrote the owner's name on the lid. The Stilt and I discussed the computers—in true executive fashion, I relayed Grafton's orders on down the line for the little people to execute—then went up on deck to commune with nature.

Visibility was five or six miles and there was a long, gentle, low swell. Three U.S. Navy ships were in sight lying dead in the water or moving very slowly, just enough to maintain steerageway. The sun shone down on the glistening sea from that misty sky. It was a nice morning.

# Chapter Ten

The Americans onboard were Mr. and Mrs. Ricardo Silva, from West-chester, New York. I knew that from glancing at their passports before I sat down with them in a little reading nook beside the main bar.

"My name is James Wilson," I said, and smiled. "Tough morning, huh! Would you folks like a Bloody Mary or screwdriver to perk you up? I'll make it."

They both shook their heads. "Water, perhaps?"

"Yes, water would be nice." I looted the fridge under the bar and brought them each bottles of water and took one for myself. French bottled water, no less. Evian. I opened the cap and sipped. It tasted okay.

The wife jumped right in. "So who do you work for, Mr. Wilson?"

"Call me Jim. I'm a civil servant." I produced my bogus passport and State Department ID. The lady merely glanced at the stuff and handed it back.

"And how about you," I asked. "Are you retired or still working?"

"I'm a college professor, and Ricardo is a capitalist."

"Really!" I said. Addressing myself to Ricardo, I said, "You are the very first person I've ever met who was willing to wear the 'capitalist' label. Most folks just call themselves businessmen."

"I'm an investor," Silva said with no warmth. "Some would call me a venture capitalist. I invest in start-ups run by great people with great ideas."

"Tough racket, I've heard," was my response. "I suppose in his own way Yegan Korjev is a venture capitalist too. Have you known him long?"

"Years."

"Un-huh. Is this your first cruise aboard Korjev's yacht?"

"No. This is our third cruise. We did one last year and one the year before. Yegan called me up and said he'd love to see us both. Ava and I looked at the calendar, she took some leave, and here we are, damn it."

"Really," I responded.

"We were going to Corfu," Ava said, jumping right in. "Yegan said he had to get back to Russia for urgent business, and we certainly understand that." Her husband nodded. She got busy telling me about past vacations ruined by unexpected trouble with an investment. I sympathized. Making big money is apparently a lot more hassle than I thought it would be, but I didn't make that remark.

I addressed Ricardo. "Have you ever done business with Yegan Korjev in the past?"

He simply stared. His wife spit out, "I don't think our private business is any of yours."

I did a soft back-pedal, which is hard to do sitting down. "As I said, I'm just a civil servant. Last night Yegan Korjev was shot in the master bedroom in an apparent murder attempt. We're doing a little preliminary investigation—attempted murder is a very bad crime, as you know, whether it happens in the States or in international waters. Everyone aboard this ship is going to get a hard look by law enforcement —that's inevitable."

They apparently had heard about Korjev's narrow escape from the grim reaper and had stopped weeping about his injuries and near demise.

In any event, they had no questions. Ricardo Silva's short answer to me was, "We make all our SEC filings. Read 'em."

"Thank you for your time," I said, and sent them back to the lounge with the others.

The two Englishmen willingly gave me the information they knew I had from their passports, and that was about it. Oh, they were pleasant and polite about it, but they knew nothing about Korjev's businesses and were simply social guests. They were vague on when they received their invitations to this cruise, although they did remember they had joined her in Monaco. Asked why they thought they had been invited, one said he didn't know Korjev's thinking, and the other said he couldn't imagine.

The German couple were retired investors, I was told. They had met Korjev somewhere in prior years—they couldn't remember just where or when—and he had graciously invited them to spend a few weeks cruising. They hoped he made a full recovery from the attempt on his life, which was tragic. They ventured the opinion that the man who shot Korjev was deranged.

The last guest couple were from Vienna, one of the greatest cities of Europe, in my opinion. Korjev's son knew their son, so that is why they were invited, they thought. Really, though, they hadn't asked. Do you ask your host why she invited you to dinner?

Maybe the FBI could get more out of the Silvas if they wanted to try. The Brits we would have to leave to the tender mercies of Scotland Yard. Whether the German or Austrian couple would ever answer a question when they got home was beyond my power of prediction.

After I finished with the four couples, I walked past them through the lounge. They were in earnest, whispered conversations with their spouses or significant others. I let it go at that: I had no lever to pry them open with. I suspected their attorneys were going to get calls as soon as they got home, wherever that was.

I went through the ship looking in every compartment, ensuring we had scoffed up every computer. The people who had searched the crew and passengers assured me that we had every cellphone. I had them go back and pull all the cushions from the stuffed chairs and couches and strip all the beds. They found two more phones. A couple of Marines were loading laptops and desktops into large padded bags for transport by helicopter to *Hornet* when Jake Grafton came to watch.

"Gonna be a problem if they drop a bag in the water," I suggested.

"They'll try not to do that," he deadpanned. "Next chopper, let's get on it and go see how Korjev is doing. He should be out of surgery by now."

"What about this scow?"

"The *Catherine*? When we leave, the captain will take her on to Sevastopol. The passengers can get off in Istanbul."

"Might be hard to catch a flight from Sevastopol."

"I suppose," Grafton said.

"And the dead man?"

"Captain Olga's problem. We have enough of our own."

When we were back aboard the *Hornet*, Grafton went off the Flag Ops Center to do a post-op debrief of the strike on *Catherine the Great* with the admiral and his chief of staff. A Marine colonel and the senior SEAL were there, along with Lieutenant Wilt the Stilt. I sat in one corner and listened, but no one asked me anything. The computers we stole were flying off the ship that evening via an Osprey to NAS Sigonella, Sicily, where the Air Force would have a transport waiting to take them on to the States. They would be in the grubby hands of the National Security Agency (NSA) within twenty hours.

After the post-op debrief, we visited the medical spaces. The doctors told Grafton Yegan Korjev was coming out from under anesthesia and that he could have a few minutes. The admiral went in alone. He was back out in less than ten minutes. He didn't look happy. I don't know what, if anything, Korjev told him, but in that length of time it couldn't have been much.

What he said to me was, "Be a couple of days before he can be moved. Let's go get some dinner, then I want a briefing on what the passengers told you."

"I can do the briefing right now. They didn't tell me anything."

"You must be losing your touch."

"It's only hot young women who want to unburden their souls to me," I explained. "The youngest passenger was a gay guy from Birmingham who was fifty-two and looked every day of sixty-five. The rest were older than dirt." I told him about the whispered conversations and worried looks.

Grafton merely grunted.

The menu in the wardroom was curry. Rice and beef tips, or perhaps it was lamb, with lots of yellow curry sauce and a few vegetables for color. I asked, but the Navy didn't have any beans handy. Normally I am not a curry fan, but I ate it because I was hungry.

After coffee, I said good-night to Grafton and went up on deck for an evening stroll. I checked in every quadrant; *Catherine the Great* was no longer in sight. The wind was freshening and some of the stars were obscured. *Hornet* seemed to be pitching and rolling with more vigor than she had earlier. Below decks, a helicopter outfit was showing a movie in their ready room. I slipped into a seat in back. The flick couldn't have been very good because I went to sleep. Afterwards, a woman Marine shook me awake and suggested I go roost in my own bunk.

I stopped by sick bay to see how Korjev was doing. Jake Grafton was in his room with the door closed, the corpsman said. The Marine sentry in front of the door looked at me with cold eyes. Bill Leitz was sitting at a little table in the reception area in front of a computer. I headed for my waiting bunk. After I stretched out the background noise of a ship at sea kept me awake for at least thirty seconds.

"I know absolutely nothing about a branch bank in Estonia," Yegan Korjev said with conviction in his voice. "I have never used such a bank, have never been to Estonia, nor do I know anyone who has ever banked there." He spoke with a Russian accent, but the English was excellent, quite understandable. English, the *lingua franca* of the modern age. A businessman who did business around the world must know it.

Jake Grafton settled back in his chair and looked at the man in the bed. He was about ten years younger than the admiral, balding, carrying thirty pounds he didn't need, with IVs in both arms. A catheter dripped into a bottle in a bracket under the bed. Grafton could hear the drip, drip, drip. Korjev's left side was covered in bandages and there was a sling for his left arm—the doctors said the bullet to his shoulder had torn the muscle. The head of the bed was propped up at a thirty-degree angle.

Jake decided to change tactics.

"Tell me about Capri."

"There is nothing to tell."

"Mr. Korjev, three of my officers were murdered in a house overlooking the harbor, and another, together with an American naval officer, were both the victims of attempted murder on the quay, in full view of your yacht. Your captain says you were on the bridge with binoculars. What did you see?"

Korjev looked around again at the small room he was in. The metal walls, the light fixtures, the gentle motion of the room, the swaying of the IV bottles on their hooks: there was no doubt he was on a ship. "The last thing I remember," he said, "was shooting through the door at that piece of dog dung named Pavlychev. He had shot me and we traded shots through the stateroom door. I remember that." He looked at the bandages and grimaced. "Apparently he shot me twice."

He shook his head and grimaced again. "The rest is just a blur. I was bleeding, the girls were screaming, then... I must have slept, because I heard the pounding on the door. It's very..." he searched for a word. "...vague. I remember the pistol in my hand and standing, opening the door, and then nothing. I woke up here. In this room. A captive of the Americans."

"Before all that. Two nights before. The yacht was in Capri and you were on the bridge. What did you see?"

"Why do you want to know?"

Ahh, Jake thought. We get down to it. Why? He couldn't say that billions of dollars were flowing from Russia through Estonia and on out into the world, and that a man in the SVR fingered you. Pointed at you as the man responsible—not in words, but in context. No, Jake couldn't say that. What he could do was wonder at the accuracy of Janos Ilin's finger, which had done the pointing.

What he said to Korjev was, "Because three Americans were murdered, shot, and there must have been a reason. I am not accusing you of sending a man to kill them, but the possibility that you might have is in my mind. Because a man on the quay opened fire with a submachine gun equipped with a suppressor at two other Americans. They dove into the harbor, unhurt. The man with the gun ran. All this must be explained."

"Why do you ask me?"

"Because you saw the man on the quay, gave orders to your captain to get underway, and set a course for Sebastopol in the Crimea. That was a drastic change of plans. Your guests thought the yacht was going to Corfu. Your captain thought the yacht was going to Corfu. No, Sebastopol! Now! Right now!"

Korvjev watched Grafton's face and didn't reply.

"Messages were sent to Russia. Messages were received from Russia. They are on the computers that were in the radio room on the yacht, and we have the computers. In a few days, I will have a translation of every message. This is your chance to explain the sudden decision to sail to the Crimea."

"By what right do you ask me anything?"

"Pavlychev spent the early morning hours before you were shot on the encrypted radio circuit. Two hours, at least. Then he went to your stateroom, knocked on the door, and shot you. Why?"

Korjev inspected the overhead and the IV bottles.

"You are lucky to be alive."

"Ah yes. Lucky. That is so true. In Russia today every man is lucky to be alive, to eat, lucky to hope to be alive tomorrow."

Grafton decided to press. "If we hadn't stopped that yacht and brought you to the medical facilities aboard this ship, you would probably be dead by now. Or you would soon be dead when *Catherine the Great* reached Sebastopol."

"What do you want?" Korjev asked, searching the admiral's face.

"I want you to talk to me, to answer my questions. I want you to think about the people in Russia who want you dead. I want you to think about what you owe them. I want you to think about whether you wish to keep living."

Yegan Korjev finally nodded. "I will think about it, Admiral. But now I am tired. I want to sleep."

"Later, then." Grafton rose and left the room, closing the door behind him.

He found Bill Leitz at a little table outside hunkered over the computer. Leitz made eye contact with Grafton and nodded. Grafton went on out of sick bay and proceeded to the Flag Ops Center.

Grafton found the admiral and his chief of staff, a captain, waiting there. After the enlisted men and women left and the door was locked, the admiral asked, "Any luck?"

"No."

"So what do you want to do with Korjev?"

"I don't know." Grafton flung himself into a chair and rubbed his head. He was tired and needed a break. "The bottom line is that a man on that yacht tried to kill him, and that man didn't get that idea out of thin air. Someone told him to do it. Korjev knows that. He knows that if we put him ashore, he'll probably be killed. He needs to cogitate upon that. We'll have to give him time."

The two naval officers nodded.

"Go get some sleep," the admiral said to the CIA director.

Jake Grafton shook both their hands and left the compartment.

Lying in his private stateroom, listening to the ship's tiny creeks and groans as it rode the back of the sea, Grafton reviewed his prior contacts through the years with Janos Ilin, a high officer in the SVR. Ilin's loyalty was to Mother Russia, not the dictator who happened to be on top of the Kremlin heap at the moment. At least that had been the case in the past. Whether it was now...

Then there was Yegan Korjev. Ilin's hint hadn't really been necessary. Grafton would have suspected Korjev regardless. Might have taken a little while to get there, but he would have eventually concluded that Korjev was a man who needed to be investigated.

Yegan Korjev had found a way for Russia to evade the American and European sanctions on their activities in the separatist Ukrainian states of Donetsk and Luhansk, and the breakaway states in Georgia. He created The International Settlements Bank in Tskhinvali in South Ossetia, on Stalin Street. He was the guiding force in opening the Center for International Settlements in Moscow. Using these banks, Russia sent critical goods, such as fuel and food, to the separatist states. The collected money financed the operation, all as a way to circumvent international sanctions that might have a severely crippling effect on Russia if Europe or America tightened the screw.

The CIA thought hundreds of millions of dollars had flowed through these banks, easing the financial pain of cash-starved Russia. At stake was Russia's vision of itself, its desire to be a regional and international power. The sad fact, if one were sitting in the Kremlin looking out, was that the money to pay for this vision of Russia's future was not in the treasury. Nor, indeed, was it in the country. America, the UK, Europe, China, Japan, Korea, even that miserable sinkhole Vietnam, were staggering in fits and starts toward a world economy that enriched all these countries with international trade. Russia was not a part of it.

Enter Yegan Korjev.

So Jake Grafton had thought Ilin's naming Korjev as the man making the money river flow through the good offices of the Bank of Scandinavia in Estonia was plausible. Probable. Now, he was not so sure.

Korjev needs to stew a while, he thought. Someone in Russia wants him dead. Let him think about that, remember the bullets, and watch the IVs drip. And listen to the dripping of the urine from the catheter.

Another possibility was that Yegan Korjev was a pawn that the Kremlin was willing to sacrifice to divert the Americans and protect the monetary river. *I need to keep that possibility firmly in mind*, Grafton thought.

On the other hand, someone wanted the money river discovered. The fate of Audra Rogers was Exhibit A.

All these thoughts were swirling in his head when sleep claimed him.

Hany Khalidi, the Palestinian, owned a pawn shop in South Boston. Like so many immigrants who had come to America in the last two centuries, he settled in an area populated by people who spoke his language, liked the food he liked, and worshipped the same way he did. The mosque was just down the street, the grocery store on the next corner. His wife and two daughters lived with him upstairs over the pawn shop. He rarely left the neighborhood.

Khalidi was rich. His business was loaning money at exorbitant rates. The Prophet, May He Rest in Peace, had frowned on interest for loans, so Hany Khalidi didn't loan money *per se* to fellow Muslims... although he certainly took in the items they didn't need when they needed to pawn them, and he did charge them a little interest. In America, one had to do that to survive. He was a pragmatist and comfortable with his decision; he was known in the neighborhood as the man to see when the wolf was at the door. He was a respected member of the community, and he liked that.

He did loan money, however, to nonbelievers, and he charged them dearly for it. One of his customers was Sal "Big Tuna" Pizzoli, who was a money lender himself. Unknown to Sal, Khalidi kept a book in which he recorded the dates, amounts, and identity of his clients.

Today his shop was empty, so he was sitting on a stool behind the counter examining the book. The women were cooking in the kitchen above, and the smell of something spicy was drifting down the stairs.

Two men in abayas and black and white keffiahs entered the shop. Khalidi looked up from his book as the door opened, but he recognized neither man. They closed the door, came over to the counter, and began looking at the rings and knick-knacks displayed there. As he looked at one of the men, the other pulled a silenced submachine gun from under his robe, pointed it at Khalidi, and pulled the trigger. The gutteral snarl filled the shop, as did the sound of broken glass and bullets thudding into solid pieces of the building.

When the gunman's weapon was empty, Hany Khalidi lay behind the counter in a sea of glass.

The other man removed a pistol from his pocket, screwed a silencer on to the barrel, and stepped behind the counter. Khalidi was surely dead, with at least eight bullet holes in his body, one in the neck and one under his left eye. Still, the gunman aimed and fired one shot into the center of Khalidi's forehead.

Calls came down the stairs. Perhaps the women had heard the noise.

The two men put their weapons under their robes and walked out of the shop.

When her father didn't answer her calls, one of Khalidi's daughters came down the stairs and found him.

# Chapter Eleven

After breakfast I went to Sick Bay to check on Korjev. The Marine sentry in front of his door didn't say anything, but the doctor told me the Russian was resting comfortably after taking a pain pill in the wee hours. His vital signs were good.

I told the doctor about my scuffle a few days ago in Sweden and the fact my right hand was still sore. A corpsman x-rayed it, I waited a bit, then the doctor called me in and showed me the x-ray. "See this line on this bone behind the middle knuckle? Green-twig fracture. Avoid heavy lifting."

"I always try to do that."

"If you must slug someone, use your elbow or aim at soft tissue. I always use a kidney punch myself."

"I'll try to remember."

"Want some pills?"

"Doesn't hurt that bad." Actually, I didn't want to get addicted to anything—drugs, tobacco, booze, sex, money, anything, excepting of course breathing, eating, and sleeping. Maybe I should take vows and become a monk.

Grafton was hanging out in the Flag Ops spaces, reading and writing messages to the folks back in the good old U.S. of A. After all, he was the director of a big important government agency even when he was taking a Mediterranean cruise.

On the aft end of the flight deck some Marines were having fun shooting at tin cars they tossed into the ship's wake. The ship wasn't going very fast, so the cans didn't get sucked under immediately.

The jarheads knew a sucker when they saw one; I was invited to try my hand with an assault rifle. The sergeant in charge praised my marksmanship, which led to an invitation to wager a little money on my skill. When we quit, I owed him eight and a half bucks. I gave him ten euros and told him to have a beer on me his next time in port.

At noon, the ship went to flight quarters. The sailors and Marines had big important things to do. I went to lunch.

Later that afternoon I sat in Sick Bay in front of a laptop computer that was recording Grafton's conversation with Korjev. The two of them were in the little hospital room, and the sentry was at the door. I was wearing a set of earphones so that I could hear the conversation in real time.

Before I began my stint on the computer, I had listened to Grafton's conversation last night. After I had had a few moments to think about it, I said to the admiral, "This guy says he doesn't know shit. What are you going to do with him?"

Jake Grafton shrugged. "I don't know. That's up to him."

"If he doesn't want to defect and spill what he knows, if anything, seems to me your options are to throw him overboard or give him a free chopper ride to the beach."

"That's about it," Grafton agreed.

"Or you could put him on a chopper and let him rappel down onto *Catherine the Great*."

"What's your take on all this, Tommy?" Grafton asked.

That comment startled me. Grafton was the brains and I was the muscle. Or the action hero, depending on your point of view. After another moment to exercise my limited IQ, I said, "We don't have any hard evidence that Yegan Korjev did anything except leave Capri without paying his harbor bill. Maybe he didn't even do that, but left a credit card with the harbormaster."

Jake Grafton ran his hand through his thinning hair.

"Admiral, we don't know *anything*. We don't know if he was involved in the Estonia gig, the money river, nor do we know why the Russians sent all that money all over Europe and America."

"That's right."

"We don't know jack shit," I said, summing up.

Grafton grunted.

That inspired me to keep talking. "Someone wants Korjev dead. Maybe because they can make him a sacrificial goat, or perhaps because he does know something, in fact, knows too much. That Pavlychev dude was supposed to kill him. Someone told him to do it. Yet he didn't get it done. That failure couldn't be fake: nobody gets into a shootout to wound the supposed victim and get himself killed. That failure may be our first break."

Grafton gathered himself. "Tommy, you seem to think that some one person issues all the orders. That's probably not the case. Think multiple people with multiple agendas. That's usually the way the world works. Look at America."

I couldn't argue with that.

So here I sat, with the earphones on and Grafton in with Yegan Korjev.

"How are you feeling this afternoon?" Grafton.

"Sore."

"The doctors tell me you will probably make a complete recovery. Your lung is recovering nicely, your shoulder will heal, there is no sign of infection... All in all, you are indeed fortunate."

"Ah, yes." Korjev. "Fortunate. Lucky. What do you Americans say, 'Shit-house luck?'"

"That's the phrase."

"So what ship is this?"

"USS *Hornet*, a helicopter assault ship. She carries a Marine Expeditionary Unit, an MEU. American taxpayers paid for *Hornet*."

"Why is this ship in the Mediterranean?"

"She is here to support our allies and help keep the peace in this corner of the world."

"Did the thought ever occur to you that this ship, and others like it, may be part of the problem?"

"That depends upon your viewpoint," Jake Grafton replied. "One person's problem is another person's solution."

"Russia's viewpoint is the only viewpoint that matters in Russia. The Kremlin is the center of the Russian universe. You Americans think it is Washington, the French know it is Paris, the British London, the Israelis Jerusalem... Those cities are their mountaintops from which they view the world."

"And that gets us where?"

Yegan Korjev shrugged, then winced. "You figure it out."

Grafton took his time answering. "Billions of dollars of fake money—oh, some of it might be real, but certainly not even a large fraction—flowed to the West through that tiny branch bank in Tallinn. Not to buy goods or services: I reject that. Money as acid, to corrode the ties that cement people together."

"I can tell you nothing," Korjev said with a grimace, "that you don't already know. Go think about what you know and stop bothering me."

"I want you to think about this," Jake Grafton said. "I suspect you know more than you have told me, a lot more. Unless you are willing to share some truth, not nebulous geopolitical fog, your future is uncertain. I don't know whether or not you care. Perhaps you are ready to die. Someone has already tried to help you on your way—and you know who that is, not I. Perhaps this someone would still like to ease you into eternity."

Grafton paused, watching the expression on Korjev's face, which was stony. "The United States Navy will see that you have medical care to get on your feet, but our hospitality is not bottomless. You must decide where you go from here."

Grafton rose from his chair, opened the door and passed through, leaving the door open behind him. A doctor and corpsman entered. Jake heard the doctor say, "Good afternoon, sir. It's time for you to get up, walk a little bit. Would you like to go to the head?"

That evening I transcribed Grafton's two interviews with Korjev, which didn't take long. The admiral had loaned Grafton a small office in the flag spaces with a desk, two chairs and plenty of plugs for our computers. I had finished the transcript and was listening to the interviews again while I read along, ensuring I got every word correctly, when Grafton entered the space. He dropped into the one empty chair.

When I finished my chore and printed off the transcript, I handed it to him. He gave me a multipage message.

The folks in Langley were getting some results. The first was a report on the passengers who had been aboard *Catherine the Great*. The first mini-bio was of Ava Silva, age seventy-two, professor at NYU. She had studied under Saul Alinsky and was one of his disciples. She was considered the most radical member of NYU's faculty. A list of her publications was attached.

I put down the message to consult my memory. Alinsky's *Rules for Radicals*, published in 1971, was the bible for the radical left. I remembered reading it for a political science course in college, and hadn't been impressed. Dedicated to Lucifer, the book championed political ammorality. The electorate were sheep, Alinsky believed, to be herded, lied to, and manipulated so that the radical few could "change the world from what it is to what they believe it should be"…if I recall correctly.

The book was a crackpot vision of mankind and civilization, in my opinion, right down there in the sewer with *Mein Kampf* by Adolph Hitler, whose tactics for taking over a democratic state Alinsky had used as for model. Although Alinsky made his bows to the values of democracy, he urged political action by whatever means to achieve the radicals' goals. The question, he said, was always, "Does this particular end justify this particular means?" That was the question he put to the person trying to decide if he was justified in lying, manipulating, cheating, and slandering to get what he and his fellow believers wanted. Of course, the answer was and is always yes. *Yes, yes, yes.* Folks, let's welcome Lenin, Hitler, Stalin, Chairman Mao, and Fidel Castro to the stage.

Lucifer... Satan. The Devil.

I read on. Ava's mate, Ricardo Silva, was a capitalist all right, a principal in a hedge fund with a personal fortune estimated as $800 million. His hedge fund managed over fifty billion in assets. Through various shell charities, he had helped fund the Central American migrant caravans that rode up through Mexico to the U. S. border. He was a good friend and business associate of the late Anton Hunt, a multi-billionaire radical whom I had had a minor role in sending on his way to reside with Lucifer just last year. Ah, yes, Mr. Hunt. *Adios*, asshole.

Brian Smith was a British solicitor from Birmingham, known for politics and views somewhere to the left of Lenin and Chairman Mao. He firmly believed that Western civilization was rotten to the core and must be destroyed so that a socialist dictatorship could rise from the ashes to save mankind.

Geoff MacDonald, Smith's lover, was also a radical, one whose advocacy of a violent revolution had been too much even for the dons at Oxford. They quietly sent him on his way after questions were asked in Parliament about just where the permissible outer boundaries of free speech were in academia.

The German couple were avowed Communists, as were the couple from Eastern Europe. The implosion of Communism and the old Soviet Union had not caused them a moment of doubt or introspection. Like all fanatics, their faith in their worldview was absolute.

After the summaries were five photos without captions. I studied them. In the best one, shot obviously with a telephoto lens in late afternoon, Korjev and the late Anton Hunt were conferring around a table with mountains in the background. I suspected the photo was shot in Davos, Switzerland. There were four other photos, all apparently snapped at the same time as the first, which showed armed guards around the two men and only partial faces.

I tossed the message on the desk. Jake Grafton couldn't sit still. He was wandering aimlessly around the little office, looking at everything and seeing nothing.

*He's working himself up to something,* I thought.

Finally, he flung himself down in the chair, stretched out and stared at his shoes. After a minute of that, he looked at me without turning his head.

"Korjev knows things we want to know," he said.

"No doubt," I agreed, and looked again at the best photo of our favorite Russian with Anton Hunt, God rot his soul.

"We're taking him to the States," Grafton said.

"Have you gotten White House approval? A blessing, a drop or two of holy water?"

"No."

"Discussed this with the National Security Adviser? The Director of National Intelligence? Anyone?"

"No."

My eyebrows rose a mite. I've had a lot of practice controlling my face, but this was the biggest leap I had seen Grafton make in our peripatetic professional association.

"The Navy's encrypted messages are read all over the earth," Grafton explained. "One suspects the CIA's are too. I would rather leave the listeners in the dark for a while."

"The powers that be may have your ass for this, Admiral."

"If they want it, they can have it. That's always been the case." He snatched up the message about *Catherine*'s passengers and the transcript I had prepared, opened the door and strode out.

Later that night we went to see Yegan Korjev in Sick Bay. He was sitting in a chair watching the ship's television, some movie about a superhero who wore a mask and skin-tight costume. He was unshaven, with his few strands of gray hair sticking out at weird angles, wearing a hospital gown.

Grafton sent the Marine sentry out of the room and closed the door behind him.

"Mr. Korjev, I have decided to take you to the United States. The doctors say you are physically capable of making the trip. We leave early in the morning."

Korjev eyed Grafton from under bushy eyebrows. "Do I have a choice?"

"Yes. You can go under your own power, or we can sedate you and take you in a strait jacket strapped to a gurney. If you go sedated, you sleep the whole way. Which would you prefer?"

"This is a kidnapping," he growled.

Grafton shrugged. "Someday you can sue me, if you're still alive."

"When we get there, what am I going to do in the great United States?"

"You're going to do a brain dump. You're going to tell me everything you've learned or experienced since you got out of diapers."

# Chapter Twelve

In the Flag Ops spaces, Grafton wrote messages that set up the airplane shuttles that would take us and Korjev back to the States. While he waited for the logistics train to prepare, he read classified summaries from the CIA staff. The story of the money train was metastasizing in America.

Editors and enemies of the administration had realized the possibilities of the corrosive effects of billions of dollars of Russian money flooding through the economy and were trying desperately to find out who ended up with sizable chunks of it. They had plenty of help from sympathetic leaks from law enforcement agencies and anyone else who thought they knew something. Telling tales on rich people, regardless of the truth, became the sport of the hour.

President Vaughn Conyers was an obvious target. A billionaire developer prior to his successful run for the presidency, he had built an empire that contained, one reporter estimated, 546 separate companies. It stood to reason that one or more of them had somehow received financial nourishment from this money gusher—intentionally or unintentionally didn't matter. His political enemies thought they might have found a weapon with which to destroy him.

Newspaper articles and the usual network shows with liberal and radical commentators who told half-truths and untruths as if they were derived from the Gospel flooded America. The truth, Grafton sensed, mattered not at all to these talking heads. Saul Alinsky, he reflected, would have approved.

At Grafton's order, two unarmed Force Recon Marines were with Yegan Korjev day and night to ensure he didn't commit suicide or injure himself. An armed sentry stood guard outside the door. No one except medical personnel, Grafton, and me were admitted to Korjev's presence.

Despite the fact that he had offered Korjev a choice on how he was going to make the trip to the United States, Grafton decided the issue. Korjev was going sedated, although he was not told. Two days after his last interview with Grafton, an anesthetic was added to an IV mixture and the Russian billionaire went quietly to sleep. He was strapped to a gurney, covered with Navy blankets, and taken to the flight deck. The gurney was wheeled into a V-22 Osprey and strapped down. Grafton led the little procession of company employees that took seats aboard the aircraft. In addition to the director, there was Bill Leitz, Armanti Hall, Doc Gordon, and me. A hard locker containing the computer we had used to record and transcribe Grafton's interviews was also loaded aboard and strapped down. A doctor and *Hornet*'s only anesthesiologist accompanied the gurney.

The Osprey took us to NAS Sigonella in Sicily, where an Air Force C-5M Super Galaxy was waiting, one normally based in Germany and used for the transport of combat wounded from the Middle Eastern wars back to state-side hospitals. A doctor, nurse, and anesthesiologist were aboard the huge transport, so *Hornet*'s medicos rode the Osprey back to the ship.

When Ricardo and Ava Silva came out of the immigration and customs facilities at Kennedy Airport in New York, their limo was waiting by the curb. Their uniformed chauffeur had met them at the door and loaded their luggage.

Ricardo knew he had a huge problem. Just how big, he and Ava had tried to decide on the long plane rides home, which they suffered through in First Class with free champagne and gourmet delicacies. Ava had recognized the oldest pirate who boarded the *Catherine* from his photos in the newspapers, which she had seen from time to time. She knew he was Jake Grafton, director of the CIA.

The CIA had confiscated Ricardo's laptop. Stolen it. He spent the hours over Europe and the Atlantic reviewing what was in the memory of the device, and his thoughts weren't good. Oh sure, he had a good password, actually two layers of passwords, but it wouldn't take professionals more than a few minutes to crack those with the aid of powerful computers.

Then they would be into his emails and investment records. The computer was two years old... actually twenty-six months, so there were twenty-six months-worth of emails in the hard drive, twenty-six months of research on possible investments. His investor accounts and investments records were on the servers at his office, which the Feds could only get with a search warrant. Yet with just the laptop, they would read all those emails, the ones he had sent and the ones he had received.

He was trying to figure out how he was going to handle this crisis as he rode with unseeing eyes through the great city, over the Triborough Bridge, and on toward the millionaires' village of Westchester.

Since the CIA had stolen his computer, he doubted if prosecutors could introduce the contents of the hard drive as evidence in a trial. He would have to ask his lawyers about that.

He weighed his options. One would be to go to the FBI and tell them everything he knew. What was the phrase—"turn state's evidence"? Rat out all those people from whom he had received Russian money and to whom he had passed it on. And tell the prosecutors where he had invested it.

There was a lot of money. He had handled about ten billion dollars for Korjev, and a serious fraction of that amount had wound up in his funds' investor accounts. Yet if he ratted out the money river, he would lose all that money and probably more—perhaps everything he had, everything he had worked a lifetime to acquire. The real people who invested money with him would hear of his troubles and want to pull their money out of his funds. Oh, he had reams of contracts that limited their ability to do that because the money was invested in illiquid assets, but after all, paper was only paper, and the investors had lawyers, schools of legal sharks who would tie him up in courts all over the nation until he ran out of cash to pay his attorneys—or the Second Coming, whichever happened first.

And there was the IRS, the tax termites. They would be all over him like stink on a skunk. Tax fraud would be the charge, a thousand counts. Perhaps mail fraud, wire fraud. The prosecutors would slap charges on the indictment until it was as thick as a telephone book.

Perhaps he should warn the people up and down the line to batten down the hatches, the Feds were coming. The problem with that course of action was that while it might protect his co-conspirators, it wouldn't shield him from anything. And no doubt some of the people he warned would rat him out to save themselves.

He thought about going to his senior senator, Harlan Westfall, who also happened to be the Senate Minority Leader. He had contributed lustily to the great one's campaigns in the past, bundled contributions, and the senator had said dozens of times to call if he had anything he wanted to discuss. The senator sat on the government oversight committee and would undoubtedly take a dim view of the CIA stealing computers from American citizens, here or abroad. But could the senator deflect the CIA's attention? Just what, precisely, could the senator, any senator, do to protect him from man-eating bureaucrats?

As they rode north toward Westchester, Ava flipped on the television in the limo. The very first thing that popped up was a commentator on CNBC telling her listeners about the money river that flowed through Estonia from Russia.

As the Super Galaxy flew west chasing the sun through an endless day, Jake Grafton spent hours thinking about Saul Alinsky. His *Rules for Radicals* had enormously influenced leftist politicians for several generations, whether they actually read his screed or not. Two prominent politicians who had read and approved of Alinsky's writings were former president Barry Sotero—who had actually worked for Alinsky's organizations in Chicago during his community-organizer days and taught seminars on Alinsky tactics—and former presidential candidate Cynthia Hinton, who wrote her senior thesis at Wellesley on Alinsky. She even interviewed him.

Sotero was fond of paraphrasing Alinsky. His wife was once quoted as saying that her husband said, "All of us are driven by the simple belief that *the world as it is* just won't do—that we have an obligation to fight for *the world as it should be.*"

"The world as it should be..." That Alinsky phrase sounded benign enough, until one realized that Alinsky advocated ammoral means to get there: lying, cheating, election fraud, and character assassination, all of which were the antithesis of the underlying philosophy of democratic, representative government.

As Grafton well knew, the world that Alinsky and his disciples envisioned, *the world as it should be*, was a socialist dictatorship that jettisoned the right of the governed to choose their rulers. The ruled were to be manipulated by radical visionaries for their own benefit. This prescription had been used with catastrophic effect by revolutionaries during the 20th century. Alinsky merely defined their methods. In effect, he updated Machiavelli's 16th Century advice to the prince. And, appropriately enough, dedicated his efforts to the Devil.

And yet, Grafton mused, it was certainly possible to overstate Alinsky's influence. All he did was dress up and present for public consumption a justification of methods used since the dawn of human history by political and religious fanatics to gain and retain power. Fanatics know to an absolute certainty that their view of the world is correct and that their enemies are not merely misguided, but evil. One must fight the devil with any tools at hand. Any tactics are justified. Unfortunately, today, the political scene in America had radicalized many on both the left and right who had never read or even heard of Saul Alinsky. How can one who knows the truth in the depths of his soul compromise with evil?

Grafton suspected Alinsky had nothing to teach the men in the Kremlin. Russia has always been a totalitarian society. The Czars, Communists, and the men who now ruled instinctively understood how to seize and maintain power by censoring the press, silencing their enemies, discrediting them, and if necessary, crushing them using the apparatus of the state. The men in the Kremlin and their predecessors had been doing that for a thousand years. Alinsky's contribution had been to justify these tactics for American radicals.

Grafton tried to think of something else and get a little sleep, but he failed. He wandered up to the flight deck and watched the crew shepherd the plane toward the afternoon sun. The endless sky, the eternal clouds, the occasional glimpses of dark ocean far below—it had a calming effect. The pilot invited him to sit in the copilot seat, so he did. He asked a few questions of the Air Force crew, smiled, shook hands, and went aft to his seat. Finally he managed to drift off to sleep.

The Super Galaxy eventually returned to earth at Joint Base Andrews on the southeastern side of Washington, D.C., as the sun was setting. Grafton left us there. The Air Force refueled the monster, then another crew flew us to Hill AFB in Utah, where we were loaded into a large helicopter in the wee hours of a dark morning.

The sun was just peeping above the eastern horizon when the twin-rotor chopper settled into a pasture in central Utah. Guys wearing jeans and jackets were waiting with two vans. After a quarter-hour drive over dirt roads, we arrived at a CIA safe house in the middle of the emptiest spot on the American map. I asked where we were. Somewhere between the Canyonlands and the San Rafael Swell. The nearest town was forty miles away, I was told, and didn't have a stoplight.

Korjev's gurney was wheeled into a locked hospital room, the medicos checked his vital signs once again, changed the dressings on his wounds, wired him up to a monitor, and he was left to wake up naturally from his drug-induced sleep. Armanti, Doc, and I were introduced to the safe house staff and the resident medical team. I called Grafton at home on an encrypted landline to tell him we had arrived.

We sat down to a breakfast of bacon, sausage, eggs, potatoes, and toast. The three of us were jet lagged to the max. I had had almost no sleep on the planes and helicopter and didn't have much appetite. Armanti and Doc ate like they hadn't seen food in a year. I had a drink, took a laxative, and crashed in a two-man bunkroom, hoping to feel better when I awoke.

Jake Grafton was escorted to Reem Kiddus' office at nine o'clock that morning. He had with him the transcript of his conversations with Yegan Korjev, the message giving the particulars of Korjev's passengers on his yacht, and the photos of Korjev and the late Anton Hunt.

Kiddus was in a better mood than Grafton expected. The admiral had watched some of the morning news shows, which reported breathlessly on the rumors circulating inside the Beltway about recipients of Russian largess. He had read the front-page stories in both the *Washington Times* and the *Washington Post*. He hadn't yet been to Langley to look at the pile of paper on his desk awaiting his arrival.

"You seem happy," he told Kiddus.

The chief of staff smiled. "Breaking news. The former CFO of the Hinton Foundation says the Foundation was the recipient of at least ten million dollars of Russian money. I don't know how he got that figure, since Putin probably didn't send a check, but that's the number he gave reporters ten minutes ago. Gonna be a bad day for Democrats."

"Oh, their day will come," Grafton said flatly. "One suspects the Kremlin sent gifts to everyone. Wouldn't surprise me to hear that your checking or savings account has several more thousand dollars than you can recall depositing. When was the last time you balanced your account statements?"

Kiddus frowned.

Grafton continued, "Vaughn Conyers is about as vulnerable as a man could possibly be. Forty plus years of doing business all over the world? Hundreds of companies, probably a thousand or more accounts?"

Kiddus sighed.

"Got some things I want you to see," Grafton said. He handed Kiddus the documents.

When Reem Kiddus laid the documents on his desk, Jake broke the news: Yegan Korjev was in a CIA safe house in the United States. The chief of staff turned pale.

"Reem, we must find out what the hell went on in Russia. Until we know that, you are just running around dodging bullets."

"You think Korjev knows the big picture?"

"We'll find out. At the least, he knows who he talked to in Moscow, what they wanted done, what he did, what they hope to accomplish. We need to get that out of him any way we can."

"If you use drugs, we can't prosecute."

Grafton snorted. "He'll never be prosecuted. Not a snowball's chance in hell. I suspect that when we empty him out, we will find most of what he knows is inadmissible hearsay. But we need a road map."

"Where are you holding him?"

"You don't want to know that, the president doesn't, and you certainly don't want the White House staff to know. People can't leak what they don't know."

Kiddus started to speak, but Grafton held up his hand. "If there's any blowback on this that you can't handle, you can blame me, an out-of-control spook. You're going to have enough troubles to keep you busy."

"Well," the chief of staff said. "What's done is done. What's your take on all this... crap?"

"It isn't about money," Jake Grafton said heavily. "It's about politics. I think the Kremlin is out to destabilize the United States government and the governments of Europe. That was Yegan Korjev's big hint. The Kremlin wants us at each other's throats. I brought Korjev to America so we can learn everything he knows. Everything he even suspects."

"Abe, Ricardo Silva. Thanks for returning my call."

Abe was Abraham Cohen, the senior partner at the firm Silva used for his personal matters. Cohen was a Jew, but he was also a diehard Democrat, even though many prominent Democrats considered Israel the aggressor in the Middle East and supported the Muslims, who loudly, publicly, and repeatedly declared their desire to kill all Jews. Silva had always wondered about that irony, but had never asked his Jewish friends why they thought as they did. He merely assumed they didn't give a damn about their fellow Jewish believers. Ricardo Silva didn't condemn them for that: after all, he didn't give a damn about Israel either.

Today, without getting into the details of the mess in which he found himself, he laid out the bare facts of CIA officers boarding a yacht on the high seas and confiscating his laptop computer. "They had no warrant," he told his attorney. "They stole the computer. They'll get into the memory of that thing and read my emails, plus some records that may be problematic for me. Can they pass that information on to law enforcement or prosecutors?"

"No," Cohen said. "Information obtained illegally cannot be used in court, nor can it be used as a basis of investigation. The judges call that 'fruit of the poisoned tree.' Just the fact that the government stole your computer with confidential information on it, assuming the information is germane to whatever crimes they are investigating, would probably prevent a successful prosecution."

After that telephone conversation, Ricardo Silva felt better. He would just stonewall the bastards if they came around. Refuse to talk to investigators, FBI agents, anyone, and if they subpoenaed him into court or before a Grand Jury, take the Fifth Amendment. That wouldn't do his business any good, but he could publicly proclaim his innocence and they couldn't charge him. Any unpleasantness would eventually blow over.

The Utah safe house—it's a vast, sprawling ranch, actually—got its television signal from a satellite. When I staggered out into the common area in mid-afternoon, Armanti was there watching Fox News. I flopped down on the couch.

"Get any sleep?" I asked.

"Some." He gestured at the television. "Man, you won't believe what's happening in Washington. The politicians are going nuts. The Democrats are certain they've got a scandal that will force the president out of office, and the Republicans are certain the scandal will shatter what's left of the Democrat party. Both groups are ready to take to the barricades and start burning tires."

"Is Korjev awake?"

"The nurse went by a little bit ago. She's says he's fine but groggy."

"That phrase describes me too," I said. "Any coffee around here?"

Armanti gestured toward the kitchen and changed channels, apparently hoping the news might be better on another network.

I got a cup of joe and dumped my dirty clothes, which were all of them, in a washing machine with some detergent. Then I went outside. The air was clear as glass, the temp in the 80s. The sun felt good.

The house was the center of a ranch complex. A garage with vehicles sat fifty yards to the south. There were several sheds and a barn with associated corrals. Four horses were visible cropping grass. I walked that way to see what I could see.

In the barn was a guy who looked like a real, honest-to-God cowboy, with cowboy boots that had never seen polish, ratty, stained jeans, a western shirt that had once been nice, and a battered Stetson. And he was doing a cowboy chore: shoveling manure out of the stalls and installing new straw.

I leaned against frame of the big open door. "Hey there," I said.

"Hey."

"I'm Tommy Carmellini."

"Alvie Johnson."

I looked at the empty stalls and sipped coffee.

Alvie eyed the holstered pistol under my left armpit and asked, "You wear that all the time?"

"Except when I'm in the shower."

"Ever shoot anybody with that?"

"It's just a fashion accessory, strictly for social purposes."

"Don't see many guns around here," Alvie said, and threw another shovel-full in a wheelbarrow. "We bring our rifles out here in the fall and get a deer apiece, but we have to take them home afterward. Guy who runs the place—have you met him, Mac Kelly?" I nodded. "Mac says he doesn't want us banging away at stuff, making noise. Likes it quiet and serene."

Alvie leaned on his shovel handle. "Gonna be here long?"

"Damn if I know."

"So who is that guy you brought with you?"

I finished the now-cold coffee before I spoke. "You a full-time employee?"

"Yep." He went back to shoveling. "Got out of the army and the company recruited me to work here. Grew up over in Hanksville."

"Un-huh."

"Been here a year in September."

"You've been around long enough to know not to ask questions."

"Pretty dull here," he said in way of explanation, not apology.

"Peaceful," I said, turning for a gander at the local flora, rolling terrain, and distant mountains on the horizon. I turned around and walked into the barn, leaned on the top of a stall gate.

Alvie leaned on the gate of the stall he was cleaning and got out his round can of Skoal. He placed a pinch between his gum and lower lip, spit, and sighed. He had all day, so he chinned with me.

During his hitch in the army, Alvie was an infantryman with the 4th Infantry Division and had been deployed in Afghanistan. Here at the "ranch," as he called it, he was the junior man on a five-man crew, hence the shoveling. The men lived in the bunkhouse and got every other week off while another five-man crew took over. Got paid well, ate well, and were earning a government retirement.

They spent their days looking after the 500 or so cattle that roamed the 80,000-acre spread—only a few thousand deeded acres and the rest leased BLM land—patrolled the ranch perimeter in pickups and on ATVs, kept up the fences, and cleaned out water holes. The senior man on his crew was a guy named Butch, a retired Marine.

"We call him Gunny," Alvie said, "but not to his face. He wants to be called Butch." He leaned forward a little and lowered his voice, as if to confide a secret. "I don't think he ever made it all the way up to gunnery sergeant. He's all Marine, though. I think he wishes he was still in."

"You got any cameras or sensors on the perimeter fence?"

"Naw. We're way the hell out here in the middle of Utah. Ain't nothin' out here but Mormons and Mexicans, and they're sparse. Afghanistan was more thickly settled, what I saw of it. This is a dry country. Gotta irrigate to raise hay. Cattle gotta scratch hard for a living." He shrugged. "So do the people."

"Tell me about your horses," I said. "If I get feeling frisky I might want to straddle one and go look at a cow."

Alvie shifted his gaze through the door to the nags in the adjacent corral or paddock, whatever they called it. "They don't get ridden enough. Unless you know horses, I suggest you ride an ATV out to see the cows."

We visited some more and he told me about the gasoline-drinking mounts that never bite you, kick you, step on your feet, or shit all over a stall. Progress is wonderful, isn't it? We march on.

I finally parted company with Alvie and walked down to the bunk-house, visited the vehicle garage and looked at the workbench, the storage sheds, inspected the big tank that held propane for the main house and powered the generator. Some of the sheds and the bunkhouse were new, the rest looked like they had been around for decades. Some repair work had been done. I looked the main house over carefully. Contractors had expanded it in the recent past. Some of the paint didn't match.

All in all, a nice facility.

# Chapter Thirteen

Jake Grafton arrived late that afternoon on a two-rotor helicopter, perhaps the same one that brought us from Hill. Armanti Hall and I had finished dinner and were sitting with Mac Kelly in rockers on the porch when Grafton and another fellow got out of a van that had picked them up from the pasture where the chopper dropped them. As the van drove away, they came walking up the gentle incline toward the house carrying overnight bags. "Hello, Tommy, Armanti, Mr. Kelly."

"Evenin', Admiral."

He gestured to the guy behind him, "Bob Tregaskis. Bob's an interrogator who speaks Russian, one of his five languages."

We arose, shook hands with Bob while Grafton pumped Kelly's hand, and Grafton said, "You guys go in. Let me talk to Tommy."

When we were alone he asked, "How's security here?"

"Nonexistent. Armanti, Doc, and I have the only guns in reach, as far as I know. Mac says he has some assault rifles and ammo locked in a closet. He has the key. Kelly used to run a dude ranch in Wyoming before the company hired him to run this place. He did a hitch in the Navy when he was a kid. He says the sign on the padlocked gate at the hard road says this is a dude ranch. The gate is two miles from where we are standing and I suspect everyone who works here has a key to the padlock. On the ranch are four pickups, a van, and a flatbed truck. Two women live in the house, both maids who keep the place clean, and they get weekends off. The cook is retired Navy, a Filipino, now a naturalized citizen: he lives here and comes and goes as he pleases. Those are their cars over there." I pointed. "Kelly's is the green Chevy pickup. He has an elderly mother in Hanksville, forty miles from here: he says he took this job so he can keep an eye on her. He visits her at least once a week."

I paused for air, then continued, "The doctor and nurse live near town and come here only when summoned: They are both former army officers and I'm sure they have security clearances up the wazoo. Five ranch hands live in the bunkhouse, and they are just that, ranch hands. Two crews of five each, and they rotate so each crew can spend every other week at home, wherever that is. Their private rides are at the bunkhouse, which is a quarter mile over that little rise to the east, just out of sight of this house. They're well paid, drive newer pickups. The ranch has never had any dude vacationers, and no doubt the locals know too much."

"We've only had this facility for eighteen months or so," Grafton explained. "The idea was to keep it low-profile."

"My advice is to get some snake-eaters out here to set up a security perimeter, and have them camp out."

"Are the recorders in the house operable?"

"I checked them out this afternoon. The equipment seems to be working fine."

"I want you to record everything said in Korjev's presence. Everything."

"I can do that."

"I'll see about a security detail."

"Okay."

"Let's go inside."

I have no idea about how one is supposed to start an interrogation of a POW or enemy agent, but Jake Grafton began with an apology after he introduced Bob Tregaskis, whom he said was a colleague. "I'm sorry that we sedated you for your journey, but I thought it would be more comfortable. Glad to see you are awake now."

That was a crock. He ordered Yegan Korjev sedated so he couldn't injure himself, commit suicide, or hurt any of us during the long plane rides. No doubt Korjev knew that too.

The Russian didn't want to talk about that. "Where are we?" he asked.

"Utah."

"And where is Utah?"

"In the middle of the United States."

"I have never been to the United States before."

I wondered if the bastard was lying. The conversation went downhill from there. They chattered away for an hour or so with the professional interrogator, Tregaskis, listening and keeping his own counsel. He didn't utter a peep. The yacht, Korjev's early life, the world situation, how one makes money in Russia, the religious fanaticism of the holy warriors—they covered the world from pole to pole.

I was seriously bored listening to this treacle when Grafton asked, "Have you given any thought to how you are going to live the rest of your life? That assassination attempt aboard your yacht seemed like a serious message to me."

"I am waiting for you to make me an offer."

I heard Grafton make a noise. That hard-ass wasn't given to chuckling, but it sounded as if he tried.

"What we can do for you depends on what you can do for us," Grafton said. "We can't make you an offer until we know what you have to sell. We won't pay much for low-grade bullshit or fiction. Truth is the gold standard, truth we can check."

Silence. Apparently Korjev was thinking. After twenty or thirty seconds he said, "I think Putin wants me dead."

"Somebody does," Grafton agreed. "You're fortunate that Pavlychev wasn't a very good assassin. Maybe he hadn't murdered anyone before and it was a sort of spur-of-the moment thing. Anyway, he tried and botched it. You killed the hell out of him. Maybe the next people the Kremlin sends will be better tradesmen, know their business better."

"Maybe," Korjev said. "And if they kill me you won't ever learn what I know."

"And you'll be dead. Forever. I want you to think about that. Dead forever, or alive with a future that we can give you."

I heard the scrapping of chairs. "Are you hungry?" Grafton asked.

"A little food," Korjev said. "And some tea. Hot. Please."

"I'll have the nurse come in and help you to a chair. We'll have some food for you in a few minutes."

I heard the door opening, then Jake Grafton came around to the cubbyhole where I sat. The interrogator/translator walked on by without a glance. I gave Grafton a thumbs-up. He walked on, toward the kitchen.

The nurse went in to see Korjev. Nothing important was said. She was strictly business. The translator or Grafton needed to talk to her, tell her to soften her shell, improve her bedside manner. Korjev was in no condition to make a pass at her and he needed some friends. I made sure the computer was catching every sound and took off the headset.

The interrogation started for real the next morning after breakfast. Grafton talked to the doctor and the nurse, found out what Korjev's medical condition was—"Stable, with no infections. He will make a complete recovery."—and how he slept.

"Fitfully," he was told by the nurse. "He was awake for three hours during the night, and asked for a sleeping pill, which I gave him. The doctor had ordered it in case he needed it."

Grafton sat down by me with a headset so he could listen and sent Tregaskis into the patient's room alone.

"Good morning, Mr. Korjev."

"Good morning."

"I'm Bob Tregaskis. We met last night."

"I remember."

"How do you feel? Did you sleep well?"

Korjev grunted.

"Admiral Grafton asked me to talk to you this morning. Is that okay with you?"

"I presume this conversation is being recorded."

"Yes, it is."

My eyebrows went up when I heard that. Tregaskis was playing it straight, no doubt on orders from Jake Grafton, whose face didn't register any emotion when he heard that comment. On the other hand, Grafton had the best poker face I have yet encountered: I wouldn't risk a matchstick in a game with him.

Bob Tregaskis continued: "If I had said no, you would have thought I was lying. So I told you the truth. Truth is the standard we will use. For you and also for Admiral Grafton and me. We won't lie to you. You will get the truth as we believe it to be. And that is what we want from you."

Korjev grunted again.

"This morning I wish to discuss the political dynamics inside the Kremlin, to the extent that you know them," Tregaskis said. "This will give us a chance to explore the ground rules. I wish to know what you know of your personal knowledge, what you know by rumor or secondhand knowledge and believe to be true, and what you speculate might be true. When you give me a fact or opinion, please label it one of those: personal knowledge, hearsay, or speculation. Will you help me with that?"

"Yes."

"If you don't want to answer a question, just say so. What we can do for you will be determined by what you can do for us, but evasion or lying will be a waste of your time and mine, and ultimately do neither of us any good."

He paused, and I heard no audible response. Maybe Korjev was nodding. Or frowning.

"When did you first meet Vladimir Putin?"

Away they went. Korjev and Putin were colleagues in the old KGB. They attended KGB training courses together, became social friends, political friends, professional friends. Korjev actually became talkative, reliving the old days, volunteering anecdotes, assignments, personal facts of their relationship. To hear him tell it, they became good friends.

Tregaskis eventually steered the conversation around to the immediate past. Putin was in the driver's seat in Russia, but he had rivals in the Kremlin. Some wanted him out; some had different agendas, some just disagreed on how to get to where Putin and his colleagues wanted to go. They differed on every policy choice imaginable: NATO, America, the Middle East, Europe, the export of oil and natural gas, the Ukraine, the Crimea, and Russia's relationship with China. Sometimes the lieutenants were on one side, sometimes the other. Putin got high marks from Korjev for keeping the team pulling together.

The interrogator was careful to always get a label on Korjev's musings and stories: personal knowledge, hearsay, or speculation. It sounded to me as if the doings in the Kremlin were the subject of as much popular discussion in the upper echelons in Russia as the melodrama of the royals were in Britain. Who said this, who did that, who got snubbed at a party, who was screwing or stroking whom, who was on the rise and who was on the way out. Who is gaining power, who is losing it. It reminded me of American morning talk show hosts gossiping about the personalities in the White House.

Grafton seemed at ease listening to all this background, which he did with his eyes closed most of the time. No doubt he wanted to know about the money river just as much as I did, but he had more faith in the roundabout approach. I was ready to get to the heart of the matter.

Tregaskis moved the conversation on to how Korjev survived the collapse of Communism in 1991 and the transformation of the Soviet Union into Republics. He started by quitting his job at the KGB and using his connections to buy state-owned assets. Suddenly the whole damned country was for sale. Factories, military equipment, airplanes, airlines, banks, everything. You signed promissory notes and you were the new owner, a capitalist. You paid off the bureaucrats and became one of those blood-suckers that Karl Marx hated. The law was whatever you could pay for. You owned the means of production and profited by the labor of the proletariat. Marx probably rolled over in his grave.

I was appalled. Even the Chinese and Vietnamese Communists understood that the key to political power was ensuring that prosperity spread, that education and hard work paid off for a great many people. The Russians had only two kinds of people: billionaires who owned everything, and everyone else, the working poor. No wonder Russia was finding itself left behind in a world of free enterprise and rising prosperity.

It was obvious Yegan Korjev was smart, ruthless, and had connections. He got filthy rich. He acquired arms factories because in our unstable world, guns would always be valuable, and he bought or founded banks because he believed, like Willie Sutton, that that was where the money was.

Tregaskis developed the banking theme and asked about Korjev's banking exploits in the last five or six years, specifically the settlement banks. Who told him what they wanted done or suggested how to do it? He named names. None of the names were Putin.

"Did you believe the president had given his permission?"

"Yes. That is my personal belief. This is what I thought Putin wanted me to do. Find a way for Russia to facilitate the purchase of goods and services by the break-away provinces in Ukraine and Georgia."

"So you did it."

"Of course. I owed Vladimir Vladimirovich too much to refuse. And I thought he was right. Russia needs friends, a buffer between itself and the West. Facilitating honest trade with these provinces full of Russian patriots, in a way that evaded the sanctions of Russia's enemies, was the patriotic thing to do, the right thing to do. So I did it. I have no regrets, nothing to apologize for."

Apparently he felt that statement insufficient, so he added, "I am a Russian. I am a patriot."

"Too bad someone in Russia wants you dead," Grafton murmured.

I looked at my watch. They had been at it for over two hours. In a few minutes, Korjev announced he was tired. Tregaskis ended the interview, said they would talk later, after lunch. He came out of the room and the doctor went in. I went to the restroom while Tregaskis and Grafton conferred.

The afternoon session was when Tregaskis mined the richest ore. Yegan Korjev admitted, or stated, that the Kremlin was looking for a way to destabilize the West, Europe and America, which were punishing Russia with sanctions for helping the ethnic Russians in Georgia and Ukraine—and, incidentally, for grabbing the Crimea. Korjev didn't know where the idea of flooding the West with phony money came from, but he heard it about four years ago from Putin's Number Two at an all-night drinking session.

The more Korjev thought about it, the better he liked the idea. It took several months to set up the operation. The cooperation of a foreign bank would be required, and they settled on the Bank of Scandinavia— the Tallinn branch was just a few hundred kilometers over the Russian border. It was convenient: Russians could appear in person at the branch on little notice, open accounts, sign checks, whatever the bankers required. And people in Stockholm high up in the bank were quite willing to go along. The more money that went through the Tallinn branch, the more money the bank made. Even without bribery, the bank officials understood that the greater the quantity of money that went through the bank, the larger the bank's profits and the larger their bonuses. But a little graft under the table, just gifts really, helped cement the deal. The powers that be in Stockholm soon decided that allowing Russians to open online accounts would encourage more people to deposit money in their bank.

When the money river became a raging torrent, it was necessary to actually bribe the nervous Swedes, who were convinced that they were witnessing a money laundering operation. They weren't. They were watching money being created, but they didn't know that.

Friends had to be recruited in Europe and America to spread the wealth around. It was essential that when the storm broke, the maximum number of people would have dirty hands.

"So you recruited people like Ricardo Silva."

"Yes. Ricardo ran a hedge fund. We sent him money that he could label as investments or profits and report to his supervising ministry, and that in turn would cause more people to invest in his fund. And he could use the shell companies that sent him money to transfer money back to Russia. Of course the people in the Kremlin wanted theirs, and they insisted that some of the money be used to counteract the Western sanctions. That led to even more money flowing outward through the Tallinn branch bank."

I took off my headset and stared at Grafton, who kept his headset on. The friggin' Russians were out to destroy the American and European banking systems! And when the poop ultimately hit the fan, they wanted to bring down governments and tip the big economies into recession. All so they could play their games around the Black Sea and in the middle east. According to Korjev. This was hearsay and personal knowledge, plus some speculation to connect all the dots.

I put the headset back on.

Tregaskis got into the names of the people who helped spread the money where it would do the most good in Europe and the United States. Korjev had only a few names, but those were key personnel in the scheme.

"They had to know the shape of the scam," Tregaskis remarked.

Korjev agreed that they did. They were carefully briefed, usually by SVR officers.

"Why did they do it?"

Here Korjev balked. "There are probably as many reasons as there were people recruited. They all got a cut of the money, but for some of them the payoff would be to see people or companies they hated humiliated or criminally convicted of financial crimes. Disclosure of their greed or stupidity would ruin them."

"And disclosure was always Moscow's game plan, wasn't it?"

"I don't know that of my personal knowledge, but I suspect so," Korjev said in his flavorful, accented English. "That much money... the secret could not be kept indefinitely. People are people."

"Why now?"

"I didn't make that decision. It came, I suspect, from the Kremlin. The political conditions in Europe and America are ripe. The liberals and conservatives hate each other; each considers the other subhuman. They are ready for war to the death. Given weapons, they will destroy each other. It is in Russia's best interest that they do so. Why not now?"

"Why the shoot-out in Capri?"

"I don't know."

"Why were you targeted for assassination?"

"I don't know," Korjev said slowly. "Perhaps someone wants a sacrificial goat. Perhaps they have convinced my friends that I am a thief or traitor. I just don't know."

Why not now? I mused that question as I stood on the porch of the ranch house looking at the distant mountains to the east, which still had snow on the peaks. The La Sals, Mac Kelly said. I wished I were there.

The guys had the television on in the little living room. More on the money river flowing from Russia through Estonia. People in the FBI were

leaking—that was obvious—and the news was that over fifty shell companies had been identified that received cash from somewhere. They had
no assets and the money was gone from the companies' bank accounts.
The question of the evening was: Where is the money?

Also watching television that evening was an attorney with a dozen-
lawyer firm in Connecticut, Stone, Muren, and Fumero. Adam Townsend
was a junior partner specializing in non-profit law. For the last three
years he had been a busy man. He was donating money to colleges and
universities in the Northeastern United States on behalf of an anonymous
donor, the widow of an Oklahoma oil man who had left her about two
billion dollars in liquid investments and interests in hundreds of Sooner
Trend wells.

Townsend knew her name, of course, although he had never met the
lady. She was in her late seventies. Watching the news, hearing about the
combination of Russian money and untraceable funds flowing around
in the United States, made something click in his head. Even though it
was eight in the evening in Connecticut, he told his wife he was going to
the office. He jumped in his car, drove the ten minutes to the office,
unlocked the door, and turned on lights.

He dove into the files. In April three years ago, he had had an
appointment with an Oklahoma attorney. The Tulsa widow wanted to
donate roughly a billion dollars to twelve institutions of higher learning
in the Northeast, and do it in such a way that no one would ever know
where the money came from.

"She does not wish to have her name on buildings or be touted in
fundraising efforts," the Oklahoma attorney told him. He was with a
two-man firm with an office in a Tulsa suburb. Jerry Kunze was his
name, the Kunze of Kunze and Gadd. Tall, wearing a gray wool suit, a
gorgeous tie, Lucchese alligator boots, and a hand-wrought silver belt
buckle under the small overhang of a sagging tummy, his sartorial

splendor had impressed Townsend. A lawyer couldn't get away with dressing like that in Connecticut unless he represented rich defendants accused of murdering their wives or mistresses or screwing teenage babysitters.

The two lawyers discussed how the donations would be handled: the widow would send checks to Townsend's firm to deposit in the trust account, and when the check cleared, Townsend would donate the money to a recipient university, get a receipt, and send it to Tulsa. The school would never be told the source of the funds, so the identity of the donor would never leak, nor could the recipient go after the donor for another donation.

They went to lunch, then returned to the office to discuss how much money each institution would actually receive.

Townsend had kept every scrap of paper. He had the widow sign documents acknowledging her intent to fund gifts to the schools, copies of checks, letters back and forth to the Tulsa attorney... copies of letters from the presidents of the recipient schools gushing with gratitude, the originals of which he had forwarded along to the widow.

Still... Adam Townsend felt a chill. He had donated $1,095,000,000 to the designated schools, the largest gift of four hundred million going to a big private university here in Connecticut. The smallest gift on the list was a fifty million donation to a very liberal private women's college in New Hampshire.

Rummaging through a file, he found a letterhead for the Tulsa lawyer. He picked up the telephone on his desk and called the office. Got an answering machine. "Adam Townsend, Jerry. Please call me in the morning."

He sat there with the files, one for each of the institutional recipients, thinking, as he had for the thousandth time, how wonderful it was that some wealthy people were willing to share their money with institutions that educated young men and women who, without help, might never be able to afford a college education. Yet the worm of worry gnawed at him.

He had never met the oil widow. He had never been to Tulsa. Hell, he had never been to Oklahoma. Oil wells and farms, flat as a pancake...

why in the world would anyone go to Oklahoma? In fact, as he thought about it, he had never checked out that Tulsa attorney, Jerry Kunze, online. He turned on his computer and googled the name.

The computer found twenty-two men named Jerry Kunze. One was a racecar driver, several were farmers, one had just passed away at the age of 82... He spent several minutes reading about them. Nope, not one of them was a lawyer in or near Tulsa. He typed in the Martindale-Hubbell website which contained listings for every lawyer in America, went to the Oklahoma section, then typed in Jerry Kunze. Nothing. He looked at the firm's name on the stationary and typed that in. Nothing.

He typed in the widow's name to the Google search engine. Yes, there she was. He read her bio. Oklahoma oil money, a deceased husband, grown children... She was a philanthropist, thank God. Yet her charities of choice were Oklahoma hospitals. There was a cancer ward at a hospital in Oklahoma City named after her late husband.

Who the hell was the lawyer? That Jerry Kunze?

Adam Townsend knew he would have to contact the donor lady. He rummaged through the file. He had neither her telephone number nor her address. Back to the computer. Yes, there was an address, a law firm. It certainly wasn't the Kunze and Gadd firm.

He would have to call them in the morning, but he already knew what the lawyers would say: she hadn't donated a dime to any charity or college outside the state of Oklahoma.

Townsend sat stupefied, staring at the ceiling. A billion dollars in *real* money: the checks all cleared his firm's trust account. Jesus Christ! *A billion dollars*!

At the same time that Adam Townsend was trying to grasp the implications of being a conduit for a billion dollars from God knows where, a group of politicians were meeting in Washington. Two senators, three Congressmen, and two Congresswomen, informally known by the media as the "Dump Conyers" gang.

They routinely made announcements about impeaching the president, worked the corridors of Congress seeking allies, gave interviews about his many sins, and fought against every proposal he made simply because *he* made it. They opposed the president because their political supporters in their states and congressional districts—all urban—hated the president, hated his style, hated his money, hated the way he wore his hair, and hated the fact that he had an extraordinarily beautiful wife. And, by the way, they also hated his politics. If they had their way, they would stop the wheels of government dead until Conyers resigned, was impeached, or assassinated. Pure, unadulterated, unreasoning hatred is a beautiful thing, and it filled their hard little political hearts.

Tonight, alone without aides in an office routinely swept for listening devices, they told each other what they had found out from their various sources and allies in the bureaucracies. Three of them had friends in Justice and two had friends in the FBI. One had a source in the White House. All had reporters they had groomed through the years by feeding them scoops their editors saw fit to print.

Senator Westfall from New York, the Senate Minority Leader, was the group's impromptu head. He was often said that the Devil had a higher approval rating in New York City than Vaughn Conyers did. Wags noted that both the Devil and Conyers hailed from New York, but Westfall wasn't the kind of man who had a sense of humor—not where politics were concerned. He was a true believer in a world without borders, a world government, and unlimited and unchecked immigration: he had even advocated allowing everyone to vote regardless of immigration status or felony convictions. He advocated sending absentee ballots to the prisons.

His listeners tonight were his political soulmates, united in opposition to the president. On a deeper level, they thought Conyers' America was an anathema: obsolete, racist, something from a dead past that should be buried and forgotten.

Tonight, these politicians were in a good mood. An FBI agent had whispered that Russian money had been invested in a hedge fund, and some of that money had gone into a hotel/resort complex that Conyers had started a year before he ran for president. "He couldn't have built that thing without the two hundred and seventy million the hedge fund brought to the table."

Someone asked how the FBI knew that Russian money was invested in the hotel. "Money is money," the Speaker of the House, Judy Mucci, answered. "Russian bucks went into the hedge fund and hedge fund money went into Conyers' hotel. That investment is making Conyers money *now*. We can use this. This is the Russian connection that idiot special counsel spent two years searching for and never found. Here it is!"

"Did Conyers know this was dirty money?"

"Who cares?" Mucci was curt. "We'll slather him with this and some of it will stick. You work the cloakroom and aisles every day—you know that we can get votes if we can just make something dirty stick to the bastard. This is it."

"My friends in Justice think the FBI is being too careful. They say the bureau has money trails and names."

Westfall was in no mood to wait for anything. "The FBI needs to sweat these people, threaten them with prosecution, Justice needs to drag them in front of Grand Juries, and get on with the program. If they work these crooks right, they'll get the stories we need. We need to make this happen, people."

He got nods all around the table. This little group had been searching for a crisis to weaponize; this one seemed rife with possibilities.

"We've got to get our reporters involved," one of the women representatives said. "Feed them some facts and spin it the way we want it spun, so they can make some impact."

Her listeners nodded their concurrence. A news story, even a false one, had life. Once a story was out there, it became a gravitational force field that changed the political landscape, warping space and time like a black hole. This was a rule for radicals right out of Saul Alinsky's playbook. The Hinton campaign had commissioned a fictitious dossier on Vaughn Conyers for the last election based on this same principle.

"We must seize the initiative," Senator Westfall said, clenching his fist and shaking it, "and never let it go."

They began discussing journalists: who could they use, who had credibility, who didn't. That some journalists had surrendered their professional reputations to their past ambitions bothered them not a whit. In war there are casualties; it's sad but inevitable.

# Chapter Fourteen

The interrogation of Yegan Korjev at the ranch in Utah settled into a routine. Either Grafton or Tregaskis questioned him, guided the discussion, and the one who wasn't on duty manned the computer that recorded the conversation. Sometimes I was there with them, but I skipped hours of it. Those two wanted details, but I ran out of juice occasionally and took to wandering off to watch the spectacle unfold on television.

And what a show it was. The political circus ran from MSNBC and CNN on the left, to ABC, CBS, and NBC, which made pretensions of objectivity, somewhere in the middle, to Fox on the right. I surfed the networks, switching channels every half hour or so to see how the story was shaping up. Badly, I decided.

Meanwhile Jake Grafton's snake-eaters arrived. Actually they were Marines, a force recon platoon. The officer in charge had a tête-à-tête with the admiral, then the jarheads disappeared into the brush, never to be seen again. Marines are into dirt and sweat, so presumably they were having a blast doing a big campout. I was delighted they were doing it and I wasn't. I had good food, a comfortable bed, a shower, clean clothes, access to a ceramic convenience, and all the toilet paper I could ever want. Doc and Armanti were obviously enjoying the amenities too, both mellowing somewhat. Yet, unlike me, they weren't listening to the filth coming from our Russian.

Korjev was gaining strength and taking little walks inside the building. He often sat at the table outside the hospital room beside the computer for his sessions with the interrogators. He was talking freely, holding nothing back, or so it appeared to me. What Grafton thought he didn't tell me.

The ten guests that were aboard *Catherine* when we snatched Korjev were discussed one by one. Inevitably, the people distributing money, the legmen, would go as far as it was safe for them to go until they decided they had had enough. Every person or entity to whom they gave money increased their risk. Free money was not a secret that could be kept indefinitely; the legmen were advised to give off an odor of corruption, which guaranteed that recipients would keep their lips sealed, at least for a while. Still, people whispered, and new people had to be constantly recruited. Korjev's yacht guests were a relatively new batch, he said. Korjev had been briefing them, instructing them on how to avoid detection by the law and evade, deflect, or defeat investigations by suspicious law enforcement agencies. His KGB training and experience proved invaluable.

Some of the Russian's revelations shook me to the core. His lieutenants had been busy boys. The problem was the amount of money that they wished to distribute. The recipients could only absorb so much, no matter how greedy they were, without a fire alarm sounding. For example, he had five attorneys in various places in the United States distributing money to colleges and universities, hospitals, and charities. None of the five knew about the others. It was classic spycraft. If one agent were discovered, he knew nothing of the others, so he could tell nothing.

It seemed that research for every disease and a whole host of other humanitarian causes were getting anonymous money, large donations from shell outfits or organizations, private persons if donations were not too large. The beauty of the scheme was that all these charities were being infected with fake money. When the bubble ultimately burst and the money trails were uncovered, the charities would probably writhe and squirm and press the authorities for non-disclosure to the public, for fear that future, real donations would be curtailed. The donees were being slowly poisoned, and the poison would spread to the bureaucracies, law enforcement agencies, and prosecutors—some of whom had received Russian money themselves.

The Russian agents donated to politicians of every stripe. If one were in public office, or even running for office, regardless of party or prospects, he or she got a check. Most donations were small, in obedience of legal limits on donations, but some politicos were pigs and got wads of cash under the table. Candidates for president, Congress, governorships, attorney general, statehouse offices, county offices, district attorneys, state legislators, city councilmen, of whatever race or sex—all were fed with fake Russian cash via political action committees, corporations, and private donors. Politicians always had their hands out. Many of them desperately wanted plane rides to campaign stops, vacation spas, or funds for "fact-finding" missions to tourist destinations. The greedier they were, the more they got. Yegan Korjev named names. He didn't know them all, of course, but he remembered and named the more prominent politicians, as well as some of the more spectacular hogs. His favorite was an Alabama politician who realized that he had stumbled upon the mother lode... but I digress.

The corruption campaign wasn't limited to the United States. Great Britain, Germany, France, Italy, Greece, Turkey, Spain... they were all targets. The interrogators tried to wring the highlights from Korjev on those countries too, but they concentrated on America.

Jake Grafton spent hours on the scrambled satellite phone to Langley. I thought he was talking to his deputy, Jack Norris, his department heads, and my sweetie Sarah Houston, who was trying to follow the money trail. I knew he had a couple of conversations with Robert Levy, the director of the FBI, and probably got little comfort there. His sessions with Reem Kiddus at the White House left him in a black mood. I knew because I could listen to his side of the conversations and watch how he reacted to whatever he was being told.

When Grafton wasn't on the phone, sitting in on interrogations, or asking the Russian questions himself, he was moody. Days passed, Yegan Korjev talked and talked, and Jake Grafton became more and more withdrawn.

In Washington, the leaks continued. Senator Westfall was on television at least twice a day, and stories began appearing that contained dollops of truth larded with buckets of fiction. These were dutifully reported and commented upon by the networks, each of which spun the stories according to their political slant. I surfed the channels, as did my colleagues, and we agreed that none of the networks had yet tumbled to the fact that the river of money was manufactured money, Monopoly money, created from thin cyberspace.

On a Friday afternoon, Richard Philbrick, Atlanta investment genius, decided this was the day he needed to grab the money and run. His accountant and office manager had left at noon to play golf. The banks were still open, so he could transfer the money to that account he had opened two years ago in the Cayman Islands, and on Monday he could arrange to have it transferred to Argentina, where Philbrick had long ago decided to retire. Learn to Tango, find a young dolly, buy a ranch on the pampas. He already had his airline tickets—first class, one way—to Buenos Aires.

The stories on television had him worried. Washington was heating up, Russian money had been spread around, and no doubt the FBI and SEC were bestirring themselves.

He turned on his computer, ignored the hundred or so emails that were waiting unread, and went to the first bank site. Got out his secret notebook that he kept locked in a safe, and began typing the account number and password. This account contained about fifty million dollars.

The bank's server took a moment to process the password and let him into the account. That's when Richard Philbrick's life changed forever. The account contained just a few thousand dollars!

He stared at the screen, unable to believe his eyes. $2,312.32. That was the balance.

Where had all that money gone?

He pushed the icon to transfers... Fifty-one million dollars had been transferred this morning from this account.

He said a curse word as he stared at the screen, letting it sink in.

His accountant and office manager—the bastards had cleaned out the account this morning!

He switched to another bank's website, a bank in Florida, did the drill about account number and secret password, and voila! He was in.

He leaned back in his chair and swore viciously. This account too contained merely enough money to keep it open. A transfer this morning...

Three more accounts... all empty... and Richard Philbrick gave up.

It was over! He was finished! He had been robbed.

He went over the events of the morning, how either the accountant or office manager had been with him every minute discussing some facet of the business. He had trouble breaking away to the restroom. Those *bastards*! While one was smoozing him, making sure he stayed off the computer, the other was transferring the money, cleaning out the firm's accounts.

He sat frozen, unable to envision the future that stretched before him as a fugitive with no money. His fellow thieves had double-crossed him, precisely what he intended to do to them. And there was nothing he could do about it. He stared into the abyss.

*My God, what am I going to do?*

The ringing telephone eventually brought him out of his trance. He didn't answer it, of course. Still, it rang a while, stopped, perhaps the caller left a message, then after a moment, began ringing again.

Philbrick looked around at his office one last time. Unconsciously, he put his notebook with account numbers and passwords in his pocket. His suitcase, ten grand in cash, and his passport and airline tickets were in his car in the garage. He wandered out of the suite. Didn't turn off the lights or even his computer. Pulled the door shut behind him, didn't check to see if it locked.

Still in a trance, he waited for the elevator and entered when it stopped. Pushed the button for the parking garage.

*My God, what am I going to do?*

What?

*God damn those two thieves!*

When the elevator opened in the second parking level, which was below ground, he walked toward his car. There were some other people getting out of cars. Men and women.

He ignored them, walked over to his sports car, and unlocked the door with an audible click.

One of the women nearby said hello.

He reached for the car door.

"Richard Philbrick? I'm with the FBI." The woman was holding up a fold and Philbrick got a glimpse of a badge. Other people were surrounding him, and he saw at least one pistol pointed at him.

"You are under arrest, Mr. Philbrick. Put your hands on the top of the car and spread your legs."

I took a tour around the ranch house. I wasn't about to go traipsing off into the brush to have an up-close and personal encounter with armed Marines, so I stayed close. I went down to the barn to commune with the horses, who ignored me. My favorite cowboy, Alvie Johnson, was there, shoveling manure and savoring a wad of Skoal.

"Looks like you have a lifetime occupation," I said.

"It goes in one end and out the other," he admitted.

"I thought this was your week off?"

"Well, the wife of some guy on the other crew got into a car wreck, so he decided to stay home with her this week. I volunteered to stay. Extra money. I'm saving up for a new pickup. Got it all picked out."

I wished my life was as uncluttered and simple as Alvie Johnson's. Maybe I should give him my pistol and take over the shovel.

"Gunny ran into some Marines out in the brush," Alvie informed me, keeping his voice low because this was probably a government secret. "It was like old home week."

"I'll bet."

"Guess they're out there now, keeping an eye on the place."

"Hmm."

He was brimming with curiosity but wasn't going to ask me again who was in the house or what was going on. And I wasn't about to tell him. "Gunny and the rest of your crew are home now?"

"Yep. Doing the shopping and chores around their places, you know."

And, I thought, running off at the mouth about Marines. Our profile here wasn't low enough.

"Our boss this week is a guy named Elijah. Eli Gertner."

"So how are the horses today?"

"Fine. Wanna ride one?"

"Why not? Got a real bronco that will throw me off?"

"Yep. You don't want to get on him. I sure as hell don't. The one you want is that gray gelding there." Alvie pointed. "He used to be in a riding stable. Probably ought to go to a dog food factory, but he's gentle enough."

So we hazed the gray in, got him accoutered, lunged him for ten minutes on a lead rope, and your trusty correspondent climbed aboard.

The horse just stood there. I whacked him in the ribs with my heels and made giddy-up noises until he got underway. I rode him around enough to ensure he had the idea of me riding and him doing the walking. Then I moseyed off, staying on the dirt road all the way to the main gate at the hard road.

I liked to mosey and look at the country, smell the sage, watch the puffy clouds and think cowboy thoughts. Just me and my horse and the whole world to ride in. "I should have been a cowboy, just like Gene and Roy..." When we reached the gate at the hard road, we turned back toward the barn. The damn horse began to trot, jolting me viciously up and down. I pulled on the reins and shouted "Whoa," but he ignored me. Then he broke into a gallop; I hung on for dear life.

The two of us roared up to the barn, where my charger slammed on the brakes. I almost went over his head. When motion stopped I bailed off.

Alvie was standing there watching. After he squirted a little brown juice between his lips, he asked, "Nice ride?"

"Going out, yes. Coming back, no."

"He sure likes the home place," Alvie said philosophically. "Thing is, you can never be sure what a horse is thinking. If they think. Sometimes you get a nasty surprise. Guess you sign up for whatever is coming when you climb aboard."

All of which got me thinking. How much of what Yegan Korjev was telling us was true? Was that attempted assassination aboard *Catherine the Great* real, or only well-orchestrated theater? The blood was real enough, but Korjev could have gunned the supposed gunman, and a pal could have shot him twice, carefully, then waited for the inevitable interception of the yacht by the suspicious Americans, who had been alerted by Janos Ilin about the supposed moneyman. The body and his wounds would be proof of his bona fides.

I massaged my rump and plopped into a rocker on the porch to think about it. Grafton must have already had these thoughts, I decided. I went inside to make myself a sandwich for a late lunch.

Sal "Big Tuna" Pizzolli came home after a busy day at his restaurant. His office was a cubbyhole behind the kitchen, and it was there he met customers. The restaurant wouldn't close until midnight, but he rarely stayed that late.

He had visited his mistress during the afternoon, gone back to the restaurant accompanied by his two bodyguards, and they were with him now as parked the car in his garage. They parked right beside him. On the wall the security monitor blinked green, indicating all was well within. Pizzolli punched in the code to disarm it. One of the guards went into the empty house to check it out while the other lowered the garage door.

The man who lowered the door preceded Big Tuna into the house. They walked in through the kitchen, which opened into a large family room that was Big Tuna's lair, complete with three flat screen televisions and a monster couch that he often used to bed a whore or two.

There were three men waiting with drawn guns. The first of Pizzolli's guards was already lying on the floor with a hole in his head. Before the guard with Pizzolli could get his pistol from its holster, he too was shot in the head from behind. The shot came from a fourth man who had been waiting beside the big refrigerator. This pistol wasn't silenced. As it boomed, blood and brains flew out from the victim's forehead and the body smacked into the floor.

The man behind him Pizzoli jabbed him in the back with the gun. "Move. On in."

Pizzolli almost didn't understand the words because the accent was so heavy.

He was trying to figure out why the light in the alarm had been green. Then the thought occurred to him that the alarm had been disabled. That damned kid who came by yesterday on his monthly visit to check all the window and door sensors and check the camera monitors!

He didn't have time to dwell on that.

"We are friends of the Palestinian," one of them said, and Pizzolli recognized the accent. Russian.

Another lifted a burlap bag from the couch and emptied the contents on the floor. Two heads rolled out. Big Tuna recognized the faces. They were the hitters he had sent to do the Palestinian.

That fucking raghead didn't just get his money from the Russians—he got it from the Russian mafia.

"There is a safe. Open it."

The Big Tuna took a deep breath and exhaled. The man who first spoke shot him in the right leg with a silenced pistol. Big Tuna fell and grabbed his leg. Blood seeped out between his fingers.

"You're gonna kill me anyway," he said through clenched teeth. "Do it and be damned."

The man smiled. He had some kind of gray metal fillings in his teeth. "Ah, but the question is—How long you suffer before you die? We have all night. Open the safe."

Sal Pizzolli opened the safe.

After dinner I had a few minutes with Grafton on the porch. "Are you sure we haven't been set up with Korjev? Do you believe him?"

He took his time answering. "I am not sure of anything. Tracing the money will prove if he told the truth... about the money we can trace. Mixing some truth with fiction is the best way to sell a lie. We'll see what we will see."

"All we're doing is questioning this guy," I remarked.

Grafton set his rocker in motion. "Do you boil eggs for breakfast?"

"Sometimes," I admitted. Probably should have kept my trap shut.

"You put water in a pan, add the eggs, turn on the heat, and wait for the water to boil, right?"

I nodded.

"You can stand there looking into the pan telling the water to hurry up and boil, but it doesn't matter whether you do or not. It will boil when it's hot enough, and not a moment before."

I changed the subject. "The hands who work here are probably shooting off their mouths back home about Marines at the ranch. If someone still wants Korjev dead..."

The admiral rocked back and forth. The damned guy had no nerves.

"Or somebody may want you dead," I said.

"If the Russians try to kill Korjev, again," Grafton asked, "will you be more inclined to believe his story?"

"I suppose," I admitted.

"The people in the Kremlin may suppose so too."

Adam Townsend had an appointment with the president of the Connecticut university that he had donated $400 million to on behalf of the Oklahoma oil widow. They met in the president's office, a wonderful, large room with a desk, original art, a Persian rug, and big windows. The president greeted him warmly, with a wide smile. Part of his job was to raise money for the university, and he was compensated accordingly. Townsend had given a big chunk on behalf of an anonymous donor; perhaps he would do the trick again. After the usual greetings, Townsend got down to it.

The money from the anonymous donor had, perhaps, come from Russian sources, Townsend said. He personally suspected that it had. The supposed donor existed, but her attorneys denied she had ever given this university a dime.

The president took the revelation with poor grace. He lost his temper, then began berating Townsend for being so naive as to let himself be used.

Adam Townsend couldn't resist making a few remarks. "My firm charged the donor only for my time. We thought we had a client who wished to preserve her anonymity, and so we told you. *You* didn't ask for more. We've both been had. And your university is *four hundred million* dollars richer."

"You don't know that that was Russian money."

"I said I didn't. I said I *suspect* it was. You read newspapers and watch television. Hundreds of *billions* of dollars went through that bank in Estonia. Your university might have gotten some of it."

"And might not. *You* don't know."

"No sir, I don't. I am informing you because I feel I am ethically bound to do so. Even if you wanted to return the money, I have no idea to whom you would return it. That's the nub of it."

The president calmed down. Townsend decided that the prospect of disgorging the funds was what had the president worried. If he did have to direct the school's endowment treasurer to write a check, he would have to tell the board of trustees why he wanted to return the funds, and he certainly didn't want to do that.

After talking it over with Townsend, the president reached a decision. "We'll continue with business as usual until someone with a better right to the funds than we have demands them."

After Townsend left, the president called the university's lead attorney and made an appointment to see him.

No one was going to demand the funds be returned, the president decided. The money would be put to good use. He would talk to the attorney, but unless and until someone squawked, the less said about the donation the better.

# Chapter Fifteen

The pot began to boil the next morning. Senator Harlan Westfall's favorite reporter had written a story alleging that the FBI was investigating a Toad Hall Capital Management investment in president Vaughn Conyer's new hotel in Houston. According to the story, a "high-placed official with knowledge of the investigation" said agents were trying to establish if Toad Hall had received Russian money, and if Russian money had gone into the hotel. Another source that the reporter said refused to be identified said the amount involved was about $270 million.

The newspaper that printed this story was known for its well-placed sources in the bureaucracies, so it had some level of credibility.

That Saturday morning, Senator Westfall, still in his pajamas, read the story in the kitchen of his Washington townhouse as he waited for his coffee to drip through. He chuckled. This would put some pressure on the White House. Westfall's FBI source had told him that Ricardo Silva had been on Yegan Korjev's yacht in the Mediterranean when it was stopped by the Navy, and the senator had slipped that fact to the reporter.

Westfall was personally acquainted with Silva, a resident of the great state of New York who had donated generously to his campaign through the years. Yet the senator had no compunction about throwing Silva to the wolves. After all, the financier would never learn how the reporter got his name.

The reporter quoted *his* source as saying that Ricardo Silva was being investigated and that the public records of Silva Capital's business dealings were being examined, although subpoenas had yet to procured. The fact that Silva Capital had indeed invested in Toad Hall Capital Management, and that Toad Hall had in turn invested in the Conyers hotel project two years ago, was a matter of public record; anyone trying to verify the story would learn that when they read the SEC filings.

Westfall laughed out loud. The story was a classic smear, and yet nothing in it was libelous. Silva could and probably would hotly deny that he had received Russian money. The White House could brand the story fake news. The Silva Capital/Toad Hall paper trail was made to look sleazy, as if everyone involved had something to hide. All the story really said was that the secretive FBI was investigating.

After his first sip of delicious coffee, Harlan Westfall turned on the small television set on the kitchen counter to see how the networks were handling the paper's story.

The immaculately coiffed and made-up talking head holding forth on his favorite network, the Life Network, was reporting another story. She said that the former chief financial officer of the Hinton Foundation—the so-called charity of former president Willy Hinton and his wife, who was also Conyers' unsuccessful antagonist in the last presidential election—had alleged that the foundation received at least twenty-five million dollars in donations from Russian individuals or entities controlled by the Russians. They even showed a short clip of reporters questioning the guy on a sidewalk somewhere. He looked honest and harassed. His wife clung to his arm. He said that he had resigned from the Hinton Foundation when he realized what was going on. He said he had already talked to the FBI and investigators from the New York attorney general's office.

Harland Westfall swore aloud. His cell phone rang. He looked at the caller ID. The Speaker of the House, Judy Mucci. He took the call. "They're sliming the Hintons again," Mucci wailed. "It's even on CNN. What should we do? My God, what can we do?"

"I'll call the New York AG. That nincompoop needs to back off."

"*Somebody* needs to talk to him," Judy Mucci agreed.

"Damn that bastard," Westfall swore. The bastard he was referring to was, of course, the president of the United States. Westfall thought that Conyers had to be behind the former CFO's public statements, and would never believe he wasn't, even if he received the sworn affidavits of three angels—which were hard to find in Washington, D.C. Westfall knew how the game was played, or at least he thought he did, because that was how *he* played the game.

When the Speaker hung up, Westfall called the attorney general of the state of New York. The guy answered because, of course, he was always available to Harlan Westfall.

"Have you seen the stuff on television?" Westfall demanded. "The former CFO of the Hinton Foundation talking about his conversations with investigators from *your* office?"

"I just got out of bed, Senator, and am just turning on the television—"

"He says the Russians gave the Hinton Foundation twenty-five million dollars."

"Well—"

"Listen, and listen good. New York is Hinton country. Sure, the Hintons are greedy bastards, but they are *our* bastards. More than half the people in America voted for that goddamn cunt in the last election. We can't afford to lose a single one of those votes. She would have been elected if it weren't for the damned electoral college. Who gives a good goddamn what the shit-kickers in Wyoming and North Dakota think?

You better figure out a way to defuse the impact of his interviews with your people. Got that?"

"Senator, we—"

"You want to be the governor of New York when your turn comes, don't you? We need some loyalty here. Don't fuck this up, you silly shit."

And with that, Harlan Westfall hung up.

The Silva Capital/Toad Hall story hit Ricardo Silva like a hammer. He knew it was coming because the reporter who wrote the story called his office yesterday afternoon. Silva's executive assistant took the call, listened to what he had to say, and declined to comment. Then he called Ricardo Silva with the news.

Neither Ricardo nor Ava had slept more than an hour or two, waiting to see what the morning would bring. As the sun rose in Westchester, they found the networks had the story and were going all out. Would this be the crime that toppled President Conyers?

Silva's phone began ringing incessantly. An unlisted number. Ava seemed calmer, more self-assured. She had wanted a socialist revolution in America all her adult life and had worked for it. Now, with the help of Russian fake money spread far and wide, the whole rotten establishment was going to shatter and crumble.

Yet neither Ricardo nor Ava had thought that when the crisis came, they would be front and center in the crosshairs of the media. "We've been living in a fool's paradise," Ricardo muttered. "When the CIA kidnapped Korjev..." They hadn't factored that in when working with the Russian.

"What is he telling the CIA?" Ricardo demanded of the modern art that decorated his home office. "What has he *told* them?" he demanded of the commentator, his flapping mouth filling the large flat television screen on the wall. The talking head didn't answer.

"Yegan needs to die," Ava Silva said flatly.

Ricardo wasn't going to argue the point. The news that the Toad Hall people had invested money in a Conyers' hotel-resort had blindsided him. No one had any proof that he knew that Silva Capital had ever taken a dime of Russian money, although of course he did. Yet it was being smeared because he and Ava were on that goddamn yacht when the CIA snatched Korjev.

The irony was that if Yegan Korjev told the CIA interrogators the real reason the Silvas were on the yacht, there was little the CIA or FBI could do. The United States Constitution protected them: fruit of the poisoned tree and all that. This damned rumor, however, was dynamite that could ultimately kill Silva Capital. Guilty until proven innocent— wasn't that the Alinsky credo?

"We need to get someone to do the job, and we need to find out where Korjev is."

So they had two major problems. Most people who suddenly, fervently wish an enemy's death are stumped by the problem of causing that death, since most people don't want to spend the rest of their lives in prison. Nor do most people have the contacts to discover the CIA's most tightly held secrets. Yet most people aren't worth hundreds of millions of dollars, which Ricardo Silva certainly was.

Among the investors of Silva Capital were some who didn't want the facts or amounts of their investment bandied about. They ran enterprises that were legal, and some—the most profitable—that weren't. Silva knew three such men. One was into prostitution and gambling, another reputedly ran the rackets on Philly's north side, and another was rumored to have made a fortune in political graft. The last had never been caught, not even arrested or prosecuted. Silva kept their names and telephone numbers in a little address book which he kept locked in his office safe. He opened the safe and got the book. The names and telephone numbers were in code, a progression he had memorized many years ago. He picked up his cell phone and started with the man he thought most likely to be able to help.

Meanwhile, Ava Silva was thinking about some of the young men and women she had met in her political science courses through the years.

She had made it a point to keep track of the most promising ones. She stood at a French door and looked across the lawn with unseeing eyes as she thought about faces and names.

Ah yes... There was that girl, very progressive, who married a young man rumored to be a CIA agent. What was her name?

I was eating breakfast on the porch of the Utah farmhouse when Jake Grafton came out after an hour on the satellite phone. He motioned with his head as he walked out into the yard, so I abandoned my plate and followed him. The sun was just peeping over the eastern horizon. I don't know how long Grafton had been up, or if he had even been to bed. He wasn't getting much sleep these days.

"The pot is really cooking now," he murmured as we walked down toward the barn. There was a big rock that was perfect for sitting on, so he parked his butt.

"Remember the Silvas?"

"When I get my yacht they'll be my first guests."

"They're talking about killing Korjev. Ricardo apparently got pissed when Senator Westland leaked that story about Toad Hall Capital investing in Conyers' resort, with money they got from Silva. The implication is that Silva is a conduit for Russian money."

"Is he?"

"Korjev says he is." Grafton sighed. "Silva will never admit it, though. An admission like that would destroy him, and one suspects he knows that."

"How do you know all this?" I confess, I always feel silly asking Grafton where he gets his information. "God whispering in your ear again?"

Jake Grafton made a noise, somewhere between a chuckle and a snort. "Sarah has turned their phones and computers into listening devices. The Silvas, Westfall, some of the others."

I should have known. Grafton was always two jumps ahead. When John Kerry was negotiating the Iran treaty in Switzerland, Sarah was tasked to figure out a way to listen in to private conversations. She found the Israelis had already been there with a program that captured target cell phones and computers and turned them into microphones. Every sound these devices picked up was transmitted over the hotel's wifi onto the internet, right to the Mossad's recorders. Sarah improved on the program and had used it before.

"Ricardo is talking to some mobsters about a hit on Korjev, as soon as he can find out where he is. Ava is talking to some former students, trying to find someone who is ideologically pure or can be bribed big time to tell her about this safe house."

He scratched himself and smiled at me. "Get out those rifles and ammo and get ready. We may have visitors, sooner rather than later. I'll talk to the Marines."

"They're probably bored silly."

He nodded in agreement. "This will be like tossing meat to a pack of hungry lions. But you get out those rifles and load 'em up, just in case."

"How much longer are you going to dink around with Korjev?"

"I am going to give him the juice tonight. Don't plan on any sleep."

The juice he was talking about was a truth drug, a pharmaceutical cocktail that the chemists had spent years perfecting. With a shot of that in your veins, you were going to tell everything you knew. Everything.

"Took you long enough to get around to it," I remarked.

He gave me the eye. Yeah, I was smarting off again, which he didn't like. "I wanted to admire the paint job before we looked under the hood," he said in way of explanation.

Ricardo Silva called his office and told them he wasn't coming in. "We're besieged," his office manager told him. "There are at least two television crews on the street. Look on your television."

Silva looked. Yep, there was his building behind a talking head, who was reporting that Silva and his wife were on a yacht in the Med with a Russian banker when it was stopped by the U.S. Navy, and that Yegan Korjev was taken off at the request of the Italian government. Then they ran a clip of an Italian official who told of the murders of three Americans in Capri, and Korjev's yacht's hasty departure from that port. Yes, the Italian government wanted to question Yegan Korjev.

"Why?" the reporter asked.

"We investigate. I cannot comment on an ongoing investigation." The same old crap, Silva thought. He was being set up for a perp walk.

He hung up his telephone—he had used the landline as a precaution—and saw Ava standing in the doorway.

"Reporters are outside the gate. They have lights rigged and trucks."

The two went to the window. The gate was forty yards down the drive, a big, wrought iron thing, twelve-feet high. Through it, they could see a mob of people out on the street, which was actually a county road.

"Call the sheriff," Ricardo told his wife.

"I already have. They are sending an officer."

Back to the television. On another network, the Silvas saw their house. The reporter was breathless, going on about Yegan Korjev, *the Russian banker*, his yacht, the interception at sea at the request of the Italian government. Silva turned off the idiot box and sat at his desk, trying to decide what to do.

That goddamn Anton Hunt had got Ricardo and Ava into this. And Hunt was dead, had been dead for seven months. Fell off that building in New York. If there was a hell, Ricardo hoped that Anton Hunt was in it.

Hunt! Perhaps there was some way to blame him for this. At least, send the press off in another direction. Yes, the press would love Hunt, the leftist billionaire financier who had given money to every liberal politician in the nation and funded progressive causes. If his name came into this, some politicians would start sweating.

Perhaps that was the way he should go. Sic the press on the politicians.

Silva went to his bedroom, shaved, and dressed while he thought about trying to turn the press onto the politicians. Before he did anything, he would discuss the move with Ava.

The hard truth was that Silva Capital couldn't survive if it stayed in the spotlight. Sooner or later the press would learn of the infusions of Russian cash into his hedge fund. When that happened... he could lose *everything*. Perhaps Senator Westfall or the governor could help him keep the New York attorney general off his back, but if the Justice Department or FBI got involved...

It was time to take to the lifeboats. This ship had sprung a big leak. It was every man for himself.

He talked the situation over with Ava. "Call Westfall," she advised. "We need political cover. We need him on our side."

He picked up his cell phone, then put it down. No, he would use the landline. The damned reporters might be intercepting cell phone calls. That was illegal as hell, but the bastards would do anything for a really big story.

What he learned was that Senator Harlan Westfall was too busy to take his call. The aide apologized.

"He's pushing you over the side," Ava said.

"Maybe."

"You must talk to the press. Let's figure out what you are going to say."

Reverend Dr. Zachariah Weston, the president of the Wright Bible College in Nevada, Arkansas, was having a bad morning. Six months ago a foundation had donated ten million dollars to the college, an unsolicited gift that could be used for any purpose. Of course the college's attorneys had checked on the foundation, which had an office in Dallas, but they hadn't gotten far. The principals of the foundation were supposedly professional men, bankers, oil men and such, and committed Christians. The director of the foundation assured the attorneys that the check was good.

Dr. Weston had taken their report under advisement and put the check in the bank. The small bible college was tuition-driven and had been struggling for years; it could certainly use the money. That day six months ago ten million bucks had looked like manna from heaven.

This morning, as he watched the television circus, Zach Weston was having second thoughts. What if the ten million was Russian money? He called the college attorneys and asked them to dig deeper into that foundation.

An hour later they called back. The foundation office had been closed. The Texas authorities said they had never heard of it.

It was the tone of the television commentators that worried Weston. The college had accepted an unsolicited gift. What was the harm in that? They had done their due diligence. The bank the check was written on had honored it in the routine course of business. Still, the commentators today were hinting, implying, that Russian money from that branch bank in Estonia was somehow dirty, tainted. They were after President Conyers because of a Russian investment in one of his real estate companies, and they were after the Hinton Foundation for accepting a donation. Accepting a donation—that is just what he did on behalf of the college.

What would the college trustees think?

He turned off the sound on his television and called the chairman of the board. "Have you been watching television?"

"Of course?"

"I'm worried about that ten-million-dollar donation we got in December," Weston said. "Remember that?"

"Biggest gift the college ever received—of course I remember it. I've been thinking about it too."

"Marshall, we may have a problem on our hands. The foundation that donated the money has closed its doors, and the Texas Secretary of State says she never heard of it."

"But you checked when we got the money, didn't you?"

"Our attorneys did. This morning I asked them to check again. I just got off the phone with them."

"Uh-oh."

"You see the problem. If we sit tight and it comes out that we accepted Russian money, dirty money, we are going to have a huge problem. The press is after the president and the Hintons."

They discussed it, and the chairman said he would call the other trustees, have a conference call and get back to Dr. Weston. When the call ended, Weston turned the volume back up on his television and surfed the channels. The Speaker of the House was calling for another investigation into Conyers' finances, and said that if indeed the Russians had invested in his businesses, the House would bring a bill of impeachment.

It was noon in Utah and I was making a sandwich in the kitchen when I saw Ricardo Silva on television. He was standing outside the driveway gate to his house in Westchester, an 18-room McMansion that resembled a French chateau. He looked reasonably calm, all things considered.

Yes, he said, he and his wife had been guests on Yegan Korjev's yacht in the Mediterranean when the U.S. Navy, which had removed Korjev from the yacht, stopped it. He hadn't protested.

"Why not?" the reporter asked.

"During the night someone tried to kill him," Silva said. "Apparently Korjev killed the assassin, but he was in a coma when the Navy arrived."

This was a big revelation, and the three reporters spent fifteen minutes getting every detail from Ricardo Silva, who hadn't actually seen the shootings, he said. He and his wife had been asleep.

Finally a reporter asked the question Silva had been waiting for. "Why were you and your wife on that yacht?"

"We were invited by Yegan Korjev. We had been introduced to him about three years ago by Anton Hunt."

"Hunt the financier?"

"Yes. It was merely a social thing. Ava and I needed a break, so when Korjev invited us, we accepted and joined the yacht in Naples."

"Why did Anton Hunt introduce you to Korjev?"

"We were at a meeting in Switzerland, and of course we knew Anton, and he introduced us."

"Did you ever discuss money with Mr. Korjev?"

Here Silva smiled. "Gentlemen, I run a hedge fund. I discuss investments with almost everyone I meet who is also in the business. Of course Mr. Korjev and I discussed the world economy, business conditions in America, Brazil, Europe, Russia, the Middle East... I can't even remember all the subjects that we touched upon."

"And Mr. Hunt?"

"He and I both ran hedge funds," Silva said with another smile. "We talked at least weekly, about many things." So now the recently departed Anton Hunt, who had tried and failed to fix the 2016 presidential election—Jake Grafton and I knew that, although the general public certainly didn't—was linked to Korjev and Russian money.

I went to find Grafton and learned that he was napping.

After I ate my sandwich and Doc and Armanti had gobbled theirs, we got busy cleaning the assault rifles. Disassembled them, swabbed out the barrels, and used solvent on every part, then reassembled them and oiled them lightly. Began loading cartridges into magazines.

Anton Hunt.

We took our new toys outside and went off to find the Marines. Jake Grafton had given me directions, so we commandeered a pickup and went looking. Found them too.

They were happy to watch us bang away at some tin cans I had rescued from the garbage.

Then the jarheads emptied a magazine apiece. They were better shots than we were.

It was a pleasant two hours.

As we put away our rifles, I took the officer in charge, a Marine captain, aside and told him that Grafton thought we might have company in a few days. Or anytime.

"It will be a shooting matter," I said. "The target is our guest in the house."

"Any ideas on who or how many?"

"No. Maybe they'll come through the gate, maybe by helicopter, maybe overland, day or night, I don't know. Maybe they'll try to bomb the house or burn it down. When I know more, if I learn more, I'll come give you a heads up. Just be on your toes."

"We're always on our toes," the captain said curtly.

"Semper Fi, Mac," I told him and mounted the passenger seat of the pickup. Doc was behind the wheel and got us rolling.

"Tommy, you owe me four dollars and eighty cents," Armanti said from the back seat, "and you owe Doc seven bucks even."

"You guys were cheating," I said. "I don't know how, but you must have been to beat me. I'm not paying a cent."

The evening news was full of politicians running their mouths. They were promising hell fire and damnation, and prosecutions, for anyone who took dirty Russian money. It was quite a spectacle. Near the end of the newscast, the network we were watching aired an interview with the president of a bible college in Arkansas, a Dr. Zachariah Weston, with a reporter from an Arkansas television station. The college had accepted a ten-million-dollar donation in December from a Texas foundation that had since disappeared. The president had no further information beyond that, but there was a possibility the money was tainted somehow.

"From Russia?"

"We have no way of knowing. We did our due diligence and the donation appeared legitimate when we accepted it. Now, in light of the news we see on television, we are not so sure."

"Is the college going to return the money?" The reporter asked. Proof, if any were needed, that some reporters are not too bright.

"To whom?" the president asked.

The whole interview lasted less than sixty seconds. Back in the network studio, the host said, "If a small bible college in Arkansas received a questionable donation, perhaps of Russian money—although there is no proof that the money came from that source—I wonder if other institutions of higher learning also received questionable donations. The American Association of Colleges and Universities reported that 2018 was a great year for donations to their members. We'll follow up on this story."

There was another Russian money story that day, although the press didn't label it as such. The Southside Mall filed for bankruptcy. Zeke Rossen had finally faced the hard truth that the changing shopping habits of the American public made huge malls like his obsolete.

He was reluctant to tell his attorney about the Russian money, which was undoubtedly invested in his mall, but he had to list the owners. He gave the lawyer the address of the nominal investor and sheepishly admitted how crooked the whole deal was.

The attorney didn't seem impressed. "The nice thing about bankruptcy," he told Rossen, "is that it is like the last rites of the Church. Are you a Catholic?"

"No."

"Well, a priest gives the dying person absolution for all his sins, and voila, he zips off to heaven clean as a whistle for whatever comes next. Bankruptcy is like that. The owners of your mall, including yourself, are going to get wiped out, the secured creditors will get first priority, and the unsecured creditors will get what's left, if anything. Even the IRS will have to take what there is to get, which is damned little. It's kinda like you get your virginity back. You walk away naked and clean."

Zeke Rossen started laughing. He had sweated blood since the Russian money story broke, and now it didn't mean a thing. The bogeyman was dead.

"Life's pretty crazy," he told the lawyer, who agreed with him.

# Chapter Sixteen

After supper the doctor gave Yegan Korjev a sedative. The Russian didn't know it. It was a drug in his coffee, and he went quietly to sleep. Jake Grafton and I were in the room when the doctor administered an injection of the truth serum. Now to wait.

"The sedative will wear off in about an hour," the doctor said. "The patient will be in a state of semi-consciousness. He can be questioned and he will answer. When the serum wears off, he won't remember anything."

Grafton grunted and went back to the kitchen for another cup of coffee. Tregakis and I fiddled with the recording equipment. There had been some discussion about whether the questions should be asked in Russian. If so, presumably Korjev would answer in Russian. Grafton had put a question to Tregaskis: "Does he know English well enough to answer in English? I want a recording, if we can get it, in English."

Tregaskis thought so, but then he shrugged. "We'll see," he said.

These are the kind of experts I like, the ones who hedge their bets.

An hour later, Grafton and Tregaskis were in the room with Korjev, and I was manning the recorder. The nurse had been sent home. The doctor was in the living room with Doc and Armanti, on call. Mac Kelley and the staff were cleaning up the kitchen and planning future meals.

Grafton started out. "Yegan, can you hear me?"

A muffled yes.

"What is your name?"

"Yegan Ivanovich Korjev."

"Where are you?"

"In Utah. America."

So they were off. I listened as carefully as I could. Grafton spent some time on Korjev's early life, then asked him about Putin, where they had met, how well he knew him. The answers were precisely the same as he had given for the last four days. Korjev's voice was strong, his answers coherent. Then, abruptly, Grafton switched subjects.

"Tell me about Anton Hunt. When did you first meet him?"

"Anton Hunt? I don't know him."

"He was an American hedge fund operator. Did you meet him in Switzerland?"

"Yes."

"Where?"

"At Davos."

"Did Hunt suggest flooding America with Russian money?"

"No."

"The money that went through the branch bank in Estonia? Tell me about that."

Thirty minutes later Grafton came out of the room with a fierce scowl on his face. Tregaskis was asking the questions. Grafton listened for a minute, then said, "He's lying."

"How can that be?" I asked. "The drug..."

"Get the doctor."

I went to fetch him. Grafton faced him. "I want you to sedate him again, put him under. I think he's had an antidote to the truth drug."

"How..." The doctor was mystified.

"I don't know. We'll help you strip him, then I want him x-rayed. Head to toe. They can't have known when we would give him the drug, so it must be in a time-release capsule of some sort, under his skin. I want to find it."

This time the sedative was an injection. With Armati's help, Grafton and I stripped the comatose man and began inspecting every square inch of the Russian's skin. We finally found it on an x-ray, buried under his hair.

"Cut it out," Grafton told the doctor.

"Now?"

"He's sedated. Use a scalpel. Cut the damn thing out of him and stitch him up. Let's get at it."

The thing was about a half-inch long and a quarter inch in diameter. It looked for all the world like a suppository. The covering looked like some kind of permeable material that allowed the drug to seep out over time.

Grafton was visibly frustrated. He sat in the living room thinking about things while Korjev slept. I asked, "How did you know the truth drug wasn't working?"

"Every answer," Grafton said, "was precisely what he said during four days of interrogation. That's impossible. You know he's been lying and I know it. Yet he sticks to the story. There had to be a reason. Nobody can talk for four days and tell nothing but the truth. Nobody. Humans aren't built that way. Little falsehoods inevitably creep in during long interrogations. We put ourselves in the best light, we paper over things we don't know for a fact, we make assumptions, we just tell lies because we are human. In there tonight, he was merely rehashing the story that he's spent four days telling us."

"So what is the truth?"

"I'll know it when I hear it. You will too."

"Maybe," I said.

"The truth will have a lot of Anton Hunt in it," Grafton said flatly. "Korjev didn't meet him three years ago at Davos. He met him at least five years ago and we have the photos to prove it. Wouldn't surprise me to learn that he met Hunt ten years ago."

"That assassination attempt aboard his yacht, *Catherine the Great*?"

"Fake," was Jake Grafton's verdict. "There was a shootout in the owner's suite, and a body is lying right there when we arrive. It supposedly happened hours before. And the captain and crew did nothing? I don't believe it. Korjev was the moneyman, he owned the yacht! He paid their salaries. He gets shot and is down there bleeding and the scene is undisturbed when we get there?"

"Hmm," I said.

"And that helicopter. It sat right there on deck until we arrived. After the owner got shot they didn't bandage him up, load him in it and chopper off to a Greek doctor. Explain that."

I frowned. "That bothered me too."

"Remember how fast Korjev pulled the anchor and steamed out of Capri? He said he knew nothing of the murders of our agents in the observatory. Yet as soon as someone shoots at someone on the quay, and misses by the way, Korjev orders the captain to get the yacht underway. Explain that."

"He panicked."

"You've watched him for four days. Does he strike you as the kind of man who panics?"

"No."

"Me either. It's too damn pat. It was a play put on for our benefit. Korjev took a couple of bullets, which did him no serious harm, lost some blood... did you see how much blood was in that stateroom?"

"A lot."

"Too damned much. Must have been a pint or two."

"The dead man. What about him?"

"Oh, he was dead, all right. Someone shot him. But we have no idea who. Bet it wasn't Korjev. That poor fool was probably the most surprised man in town when the pistol was turned in his direction and someone plugged him four times. By the way, at least three of those bullets that hit him should have been fatal. He was flat on the deck when the last two were fired—I'll bet my pension on that. Almost no blood around the entry wounds. And the crew of that yacht left him lying there for us to see. Thoughtful of them."

He sighed.

"They didn't know we were going to stop that yacht."

"No, they didn't. But they played for it, acted suspiciously. We obliged them."

"What about Janos Ilin's tip? He put the finger on Korjev."

"That he did. Korjev may indeed be the man who arranged the river of money. That's possible. Ilin may have believed that. Or he may have been fed a lie in the hope he would pass it on. If the latter is the case, Ilin's days are numbered: he's going to be dead soon. However, the most likely scenario is that Ilin was given the name and told to pass it on, which he did."

"What about the computers we took off that ship?"

"Sarah says they are full of treacle. Nothing important."

"Even Silva's?"

"His and his wife's are the only ones that have something to tell us. One suspects the Silvas were pawns to be sacrificed. The irony is those two didn't know it. Ricardo did indeed get Russian money and was spreading it around. And putting some of it to work in his hedge fund."

"So what do you want from Korjev?"

"Names. American names." Grafton stretched in the chair and put his hands in his pockets. "Here's the way I suspect it went down. Some American came up with the idea for this op, perhaps Anton Hunt, and took it to Korjev, who took it to Putin. The key was having Americans who could and would salt the money around to eventually cause a major political meltdown. The other side of the coin could be true: Putin thought it up and took it to some Americans who liked the idea a lot. Whichever way it went down, the people involved *here* wanted America to collapse, to fail. They wanted to drive a stake through the heart of representative democracy by showing the whole establishment is rotten from top to bottom. After Hunt died, I think the Kremlin kept going. The opportunity to cause a stupendous political crisis in the United States, to make America turn inward and surrender their foreign policy influence in Europe and the Middle East, was just too good to pass up. That's what I think happened, and Korjev knows. Damn it, he *knows*! He knows the names. Those are what I want from him."

"The FBI will eventually get them," I ventured.

"The damage is being done *now*." He gestured at the television, which was off. "We can't wait three or four years for the FBI to do pretty little investigations all tied up with bows to pass to Justice to take to Grand Juries."

"Already congressmen and senators are talking about impeaching the president."

Grafton frowned. "With the country divided down the middle into two warring camps, removal of a president from office for political reasons might touch off a civil war. Wouldn't the guys in the Kremlin love that?"

He cleared his throat and rubbed his forehead. "Is there any bourbon around this dump?"

"Yes," I said.

"Pour three fingers over ice, and I'll take it to bed. We'll sweat that son of a bitch tomorrow and get the truth out of him."

"We'll know it when we hear it," I said dubiously.

"You're goddamn right," the admiral said, and pushed himself upright. I went to get the whiskey bottle.

When the admiral tottered off to bed, I sat there looking out the window. I had a MP-5 right beside me and a Beretta under my armpit. What we were going to get out of Korjev was the truth *as he believed it to be.* That was an important qualifier.

No doubt Jake Grafton knew that. Hell, he knew everything.

I was up early, just as the day was getting gray. I turned on the television. After all, it was two hours later on the east coast. Sure enough, the politicians were fulminating. Greed, lies, treason—all were being talked about. At the bottom of the screen, the news ticker rolled by. Two more colleges had reported questionable donations in the last two years, for amounts in the tens of millions of dollars.

Then came the bombshell: one of the Federal Reserve governors opined that all the money that flowed through the branch of the Bank of Scandinavia in Estonia was fake money. Not counterfeit, which implies printing fake bills, but fake money, with nothing to back it up. It disappeared into the world's financial system and thereby became real money. "Created money," was her phrase.

The host jumped right on that. "But isn't creating money what the Fed does?"

"Yes, but—"

I killed the savage beast and got busy fixing myself a couple of eggs. Ah yes, the Fed creates American dollars, but the rotten evil Russians aren't supposed to. Create American dollars, that is. They can create all the damn rubles they want, if they want, but not American dollars. Those swine.

I watched the water heat up in the pot with my two eggs. Yep, Grafton was right. Watching didn't make the water boil faster.

I was sipping coffee and finishing my eggs when Grafton came in. "It's on the news," I said. "Some Fed governor says the Russian money was 'created.' Not in Washington, but somewhere in the bowels of the evil empire."

The admiral grunted at me, poured himself a mug of coffee and said, "Let's get the doc, check on our patient, and get after it."

"Think that antidote to the truth serum is out of Korjev's system?"

"We'll find out."

We were walking across the living room when I heard a plane. Sounded like a turboprop, low. It flew right over the house washing us with a crescendo of noise.

"Outside," Grafton roared. "Shoot it down."

I grabbed my MP-5 and raced out the front door. Something like a shower was raining down. I knew what it was by the smell. *Kerosene.*

The plane was pulling up steeply, the pilot using the rudder to push the nose over, a cropduster turn. I was right by the house, so after he made the turn, he was coming right toward me. I flipped the rifle's selector switch to full automatic and went down on one knee to get steady. I began shooting when he was about a hundred yards out, leading him.

I had no idea how much to lead him, and I didn't have tracer bullets to help me get it right. I swung a little ahead to a lot as he came over me. It was actually a pretty easy shot, with almost no deflection. The gun hammered and the sound of his engine rose. It was a Pawnee or some such, a single-seat ag plane. I could see the kerosene spewing from pipes under his wings. I held the trigger down.

He was right above me when my magazine went dry. The extra mags were in the house. Shit!

But I had scored. The engine was screaming now, the sound of tortured metal. I closed my eyes and lowered my head as the kerosene came down like a shower. When I looked again, the plane was just above the ground, the left wing down, over a hundred yards away. Then it kissed the ground, skipped once, then hit the dirt, raising a great cloud, and slid to a stop. Miraculously, there was no fire. Silence.

I dropped the empty MP-5 and ran toward the wreck, which was about two hundred or so yards away now.

I was scared silly. Kerosene, which was jet fuel, plus a hot engine— the whole wreck could go up like a firecracker. But it didn't. The plane was on the ground and the left wing was partially broken off. The ends of the prop were bent back along the fuselage, so the prop had been still turning when it hit. The smell of kerosene was pungent.

I was about thirty yards away when the pilot got the canopy open and came scrambling out of the cockpit. I jerked the Beretta from my shoulder holster.

The guy ran directly away from the airplane. Then he saw me, holding the pistol in both hands, pointing it at him. He stopped, raised his hands. "No," he said loudly. He couldn't stop his feet, which kept moving him away from the plane in tiny steps.

Behind me I could hear shouting. People were bailing out of the house as fast as they could. That damn kerosene ran down from my hair into my eyes.

"No!" the guy said, almost a prayer. He skittered a few more steps away from the airplane, still holding his hands up.

The kerosene was making my eyes burn.

I shot him.

The bullet didn't knock him down. Hit him in the stomach, I think, and he bent over some, screaming, "No, no, no..."

My vision was blurry. I blinked mightily and shot him again. This time he went over backwards into the dirt.

I walked toward him wiping my eyes.

His eyes tracked me, so he wasn't dead.

I felt his pockets. Got his phone and wallet.

Jake Grafton was beside me. "That asshole Silva," I said. "You said he was hunting for an assassin."

"None of the conspirators figured on us grabbing Korjev," Grafton replied. "The Russians double-crossed them."

The slick, slimy kerosene stank to high heaven. I was slightly nauseated.

We left the pilot lying on the ground and walked back toward the house. Mac Kelly, the doctor, Doc Gordon, Armanti Hall, and the Filipino cook were all in the yard watching as we approached. Doc and Armanti had their MP-5s in hand.

"You guys get some hoses," Grafton said, "wash down a corridor between the house and that wreck. If that thing catches fire, the whole house could go."

He had just finished the sentence when the plane lit off. Whumpf! We ran for the hoses. When I looked up I saw that a ribbon of fire had reached the pilot lying on the ground and he was burning. He raised one hand, then was engulfed in fire.

Two hours later we were sure we had saved the house. The Marines had come to help and Alvie Johnson, my favorite cowboy, had fired up the backhoe and bulldozed a strip to keep the fire from spreading. I made a mental note to send him some Skoal.

The plane burned fiercely after the flames reached and ignited the flares the pilot had with him in the cockpit, flares he was going to throw out to ignite the kerosene he had sprayed on the house.

"I know that plane," Alvie Johnson said as he stood watching the wreck being consumed. "Outta some place near Salt Lake. The guy flew it down to the Hanksville airport occasionally, kept a few drums of fuel there just for his use. Ain't no terminal there, no fuel for sale, none of that. Just the drums for this guy. I saw him there a couple of times, and he kinda ignored us clod-hoppers standing around watching."

When the fire finally burned out most of the airplane had been reduced to ashes and the pilot cremated.

I looked at the guy's wallet and got his name and address. His phone was locked with a password, so I didn't fool with it. Sarah and her minions could crack that thing like an egg and get all the nourishment from it.

"Somebody in the company leaked," I said to Grafton, who didn't reply.

I went to the bedroom, stripped and got into the shower. Getting that crap out of my hair was almost a career. When I was in clean duds, I took the stuff stinking of kerosene to the garbage and threw it in.

Armanti Hall had a few words after dinner. "Kinda sorry you shot that guy, Tommy."

I wasn't in the mood, but he continued. "Been my experience that it's better to shoot people after they tell you everything you want to know, rather than before."

"I'll try to keep that in mind."

"I, for one, would like to know just who sent that murderous son of a bitch," Armanti said, quite superfluously.

"Yeah."

"By the way," he said to me, "You still stink."

"You don't smell so hot yourself. Maybe you need to get that beard and hair shaved off so you'll look like the dickhead you are."

"One of the things I like about you, Tommy, is that you're so subtle."

"That's enough, you two," Jake Grafton said firmly.

Our interrogation of Yegan Korjev was almost anti-climatic. He was partially sedated; we administered the truth serum again, and an hour later Grafton began asking questions.

Yes, Anton Hunt had approached Korjev six years ago with the idea of subverting his political enemies in America with funny money. Korjev took it to his pal in the Kremlin, and after they had worried the bone, got an approval. The whole operation took a year or so to set up.

Needless to say, Hunt had his list of recipients to poison with funny money and the Kremlin had theirs, and they didn't coincide. So the Russians took it upon themselves to spread the wealth to people and institutions on their list, without bothering to inform Hunt. Hunt's death last year didn't make any difference. The operation was three years along.

Hunt's son, another committed radical progressive, took over in his stead, but it didn't matter—the Russians didn't need them anymore. The operation suffered from mission creep—the list of recipients kept expanding. It was just a matter of time until the whole thing exploded, but the recent tensions in Syria and the Black Sea, plus European and U.S. sanctions, made the Kremlin decide to not wait for nature to take its course. They arranged for the kidnapping so as to expose the branch bank, then set up Korjev in his yacht. Korjev had invited key players in the scheme for the foreign authorities to get interested in when the smelly stuff hit the fan. In effect, Russia double-crossed its foreign agents and allies.

Under the influence of the drug, Korjev named names, at least twenty Americans who were direct recipients of Estonian transfers, people Hunt had designated, with instructions to pass the money on. No doubt some of the money stuck to some of them, but that really didn't matter, since they were all expendable as far as the Kremlin was concerned. The whole idea was to stir up massive finger-pointing and recriminations, ruin reputations, cause the Americans to turn on each other. If another American civil war broke out, that was fine with the men in the Kremlin. And Korjev gave us names of Kremlin agents, who had been busy donating money to Hunt's friends.

As I listened to all this, I took solace from the fact that I had made a small contribution to help Anton Hunt start his journey to hell.

After an hour, Grafton had all he wanted. He came out of the room, closed the door, and pointed his boney finger at me. "Come along, Tommy."

On the porch the odor of kerosene was still rank. The plane had burned itself out. There wasn't much left, just a lump where the motor had been.

Grafton plopped down on the edge of the porch and I sat beside him. He leaned over, picked up a pebble and tossed it. Then another.

"You could give those names and a summary to the FBI," I suggested. He picked up another pebble, inspected it and chucked it into the yard.

"Or you could leak it to your favorite reporter," I added.

More pebbles.

The sun was sinking toward the mountains on the far western horizon. All in all, it had been one hell of a day. The setting sun, the stink of kerosene, the wisping smoke off the ashes of that airplane...

"Is Korjev telling the truth now?" I asked.

Grafton looked as if he had taken a punch. He tossed another pebble. "He's telling part of it, anyway."

"Can a man lie under the influence of the truth drugs?"

"It's been done," Jake Grafton said.

"I don't understand what the Russians have to hide," I said. "We know they sent the money through Estonia. We suspect it was funny money. They're blaming it on a dead man. The people who received it don't know beans about how or why. What is the big secret?"

"That's just it," Grafton said. "At this point, what do they have to hide?"

"Perhaps nothing," I suggested.

"Nothing if we buy the story as presented. They've worked really hard to sell it to us."

"Do you buy it?"

Jake Grafton took his time answering. "It could be true. The problem is that they've worked really hard to sell it to us, and that bothers me."

"So what are we going to do?" I asked.

"We're going to put the fear of God in the people Korjev named. His accusations aren't enough. We need to make them talk. Make them run screaming for the nearest FBI office."

"Too bad we don't have a Hannibal Lecter."

"You listened to those names. They're rich people, important people: sanctimonious, self-righteous assholes willing to light the fuses to blow up America. The FBI will go knock on their doors hat in hand, they'll lawyer up and won't say peep, and meanwhile the political circus will play on until America comes apart at the seams, just as the Kremlin intended."

"I'll sign on for fear. How are we going to do it?"

# Chapter Seventeen

Desert View, Utah, was a bedroom suburb south of Salt Lake City. The pilot of the ag plane who tried to immolate us was a dude named Paul Hockersmith, who lived in Desert View. Or did until yesterday. His place of business was, of course, at the airport. I stopped there first, but his cubbyhole office at the end of a row of tee-hangars was locked up. I peeked in through the dirty window and saw one room with a littered desk and what appeared to be a toilet and a closet.

The airport didn't look prosperous. Hockersmith's office didn't look prosperous. I went back to the airport manager at the FBO, who had told me where to find Hockersmith's office. "He isn't there," I said, and leaned on the counter. The coffee pot in the corner was plugged in. "Got any coffee?"

"Help yourself. Only cream is that damn powder." This guy was wearing an old green Air Force flight jacket.

"I drink it black," I said, and toggled some into a styrofoam cup. It looked like it had been in that pot since Christmas. I took a deep breath and sipped it. Ye Gods.

"You were an Air Force pilot, huh?" I said.

"Yep. Twenty-two years. Flew Phantoms. F-4s. After they retired them I mostly flew desks."

"Hockersmith, was he a military pilot?"

"Naw. Civilian. Ag pilot. Doesn't fly much. Not much spraying around here, and what there is that new company at the big airport ten miles north gets."

"Got any idea when he might be back?" I tried another sip of that black stuff.

"No. He goes away for three or four days at a time. Haven't seen him for a couple of days."

"Well, maybe I'll just try his cell phone. Do you have that number?"

The old guy eyed me shrewdly. "You're with the government, aren't you?"

I let my surprise register. "Does it show?"

"You're packing heat. I know the bulge. You with the DEA?"

"They been out here?"

"Twice. Last time about three weeks ago."

"Huh."

"Bet you've already got his cell number?"

I grinned at him. "As a matter of fact, I do. You're pretty sharp."

"I ain't accusing Paul of nothin', you understand. But I never could figure how a guy, a pro pilot, who does as little ag work as he does, even keeps eatin'. Drives a nice ride, too. His work car is that pickup parked by his office. Only two years old."

"Maybe he married money," I said. "That's what I intend to do."

"Good luck with that."

We chatted another minute or so, I took the battery acid he called coffee with me, and when I was out of sight of the FBO poured it into the grass. It would kill the grass there, as if a dog peed on it.

I typed Hockersmith's home address into my phone and drove over. It was a decent, middle-class, three-bedroom, two-bath house in a tract development with a lawn full of weeds that had never seen a sprinkler.

A kid's trike lay on its side near the porch. There was a driveway and a one-car garage, where I figured the family car lived.

I could hear a dog barking as I walked up the crumbling sidewalk to the porch, climbed the two steps, and knocked. In a minute I could hear a woman's voice, talking to the dog. She opened the door about half way. The screen door was closed and, I suspect, latched.

"Yes."

"Hi. My name is Jim Wilson." I had my ID fold in my hand, but she merely glanced at it. "I'm with the FAA. Is Mr. Hockersmith around?"

"No, he isn't." She didn't relax or make any indication she might open the screen door. The dog was right at her knee, and he was a big one. Wasn't growling, though he looked like he would welcome the opportunity to take a nice hunk out of me.

"Do you know when he'll be home?" I put the ID back in my jacket pocket, taking my time.

"Maybe in a day or two."

"I see. Well, Mrs. Hockersmith, he didn't answer the last letter we sent him, so they sent me around to see him. If he would just call us at the phone number on the letterhead?" This wasn't as big a leap of faith as one might suspect. If the DEA was interested in this guy, the FAA probably was too. Flying drugs around was a bad crime.

She didn't deny he got letters from the FAA. Just said, "I'll tell him."

"I'd really appreciate that. I really would. You have a nice day."

I turned and went down the sidewalk toward the street. I heard her close the door behind me.

Jake Grafton and Yegan Korjev went for a walk. Korjev was up and about, had his IVs out, and was dressed in some old clothes that Mac Kelly had that fit well enough for a farm.

Jake kicked a few pebbles as he walked along with his hands in his pockets. "Where do you want to go from here?" he asked Korjev.

The Russian eyed him. "What are my choices?"

"I think you've told us about everything you want us to know, so where do you want to go?"

"That *I* want you to know?"

"You heard me. The drugs we gave you can be defeated by hypnosis. They hypnotized you in Russia before this caper went down. I give you and the SVR an A grade. You can tell Putin that."

"And you don't believe me?"

"I believe that you haven't told me the whole story."

The Russian walked along with long glances at the La Sal Mountains to the east and the Henry Mountains to the south. "What do you believe?" he asked.

"I think that Anton Hunt approached you five or six years ago. He was a revolutionary who wanted to bring down the United States government. You took the proposal to Putin, and he and his aides thought this was a good, cheap way to cause the American government some serious grief, tie it up in knots, make it focus inward. So Putin gave his approval."

"We didn't fool you."

"You almost did."

"Ilin said you wouldn't believe it."

"Putin didn't really care if you fooled me or not. He just wanted to give Conyers' enemies some ammunition to shoot. They're running around chasing their tails."

"So you are done with me." It wasn't a question, but a statement.

"Yes. You can go home if you wish. We'll give you transit papers and put you on a plane. Or you can go wherever. Your choice."

"Russia is my country. I'd like to go to Moscow."

"I'll make some telephone calls."

Yegan Korjev saw a boulder the size of a table, looked for snakes and didn't see any, and sat on it. "America is a beautiful country," he said. "I had no idea."

Jake Grafton stood looking around, as if he were seeing it for the first time. The blue sky, puffy clouds, the distant mountains. *Yes*, he thought, *a beautiful country.* He smiled at Korjev.

What was the secret that Korjev and Putin had worked so hard to protect?

As he and the Russian walked back to the safe house, Jake realized that the secret could only be one thing: the identity of the person who proposed the funny money operation. It could have been Hunt, but if it had been, why work so hard to pin it on him?

Yet if it wasn't Anton Hunt, who was it?

I had dinner at a chain steakhouse and drifted out to the airport again after dark. There was a light on a pole that illuminated the self-service fuel dispenser, but the FBO office was dark and there was no light down at the tee-hangars where Hockersmith had his office. I parked behind the tee-hangars, put on surgical gloves, and tackled the pickup first. Got the door open and climbed inside.

It was normal messy, I suspect, with bugs smashed on the windshield, dust on nearly every square inch and dirt on the floor carpets. Little notes here and there, a few gas station receipts, nothing interesting. There was a nine-millimeter pistol and a box of shells in the center console between the driver's and passenger's seats. It was loaded.

I had enough guns, so I left it there.

I locked up the pickup and attacked the office door. Had it in about two minutes. Once inside, I turned on the light and got busy on Hockersmith's desk. He wasn't a neat-nik. What I really wanted, of course, was a note in his handwriting with a phone number and a few words that said, "Use kerosene and flares." But I would take a lot less.

I got a lot less. Got exactly nothing except for a few telephone numbers to pass on to Sarah Houston.

I was regretting shooting the guy. He knew damn well who had paid him to murder us, and after a session with Armanti Hall, he would have been delighted to share that information. After all, he had been standing there with his damned hands up when I drilled him. That had not been one of my better moments.

I finally gave up on the desk and checked out the closet. In addition to some miscellaneous junk, it held toilet paper, an open box of red mechanic's rags, two cases of aviation oil, and a half-empty box of road flares. So we were right: there had been flares in that cockpit. They had burned with an amazingly intense heat when the fire got to them.

Looking at the flares, my distress at shooting the bastard as he held up his hands dissipated, never to return.

Senator Harland Westfall was having another terrible day. The man who thought of himself as the prophet of the new Democratic party was also the brain behind the Dump Conyers movement in the House and Senate. The Speaker had to get the votes in the House of Representatives to impeach, but Westfall had to get the votes in the Senate to convict the bastard in order to throw him out of the White House—a much bigger order. Today wasn't going well. The news on the Russian money scandal—now the "Russian Fake Money" scandal—was like Chinese water torture: another story every hour, drip, drip, drip.

It seemed to Westfall that the FBI had every agent in the country digging into bank records and questioning people who sent or received fake money. Some people told the FBI to go pound sand, but a lot of them were trying to talk their way out of trouble. It's human nature. You can tell a person he doesn't have to say a word, but that's counter-intuitive—that isn't the way the world works. We all know that. From childhood on, you must tell the truth or think up a good lie when you are accused of something nasty, from eating all the cookies, screwing your girlfriend in the family car, or driving at a hundred miles an hour while your sweetie sucks your dick. Man, you gotta have a story! Silence isn't an option.

Unfortunately for Harlan Westfall, while he had plenty of greasy, slimy things on Conyers and Republicans, who apparently were awash in Russian funny money, the Democrats were awash in it too. Today it was Westfall's turn. Over a million dollars in Russian money went into his reelection coffers, and to make matters worse, his campaign manager had spent the damn money, so he didn't have it to refund. That is, if he even knew who to refund the money to—which he didn't. It had been donated by a bunch of PACs, foundations, shit like that that no one could ever really find. No real addresses, no real tangible people to grill and skewer, no phone numbers. Just the money the campaign manager had blown on ads to tell the good people of New York how great a job Westfall was doing bringing the great Satan, Conyers, to account—so great a job that he needed another term in the Senate. The bastard manager had damn near financed a landslide with fake Russian money. Westfall got seventy percent of the vote, and in some precincts in Brooklyn and the Bronx, over ninety percent. Severe overkill, like a nuclear blast. Now Westfall was paying the price. The smart move would be to give the money to a charity to cleanse himself, purify himself before the public, but it was gone. Damn.

Right now on the phone, Westfall was downplaying the amount of funny money his campaign received to a reporter. "Out of over twenty-four million contributed, only a million was Russian money," he said, "About four percent, actually less than four percent."

"Why do you think the Russians wanted to help you, Senator?"

Westfall almost smashed the phone on the desk. "I don't think the Russians wanted to do anything except slime me, attempt to derail our representative government, ruin my reputation."

"Why you?"

Ah, here was a question Westfall could hit out of the ballpark, a slow floater right across the middle of the plate. Yet he watched it go by without swinging. Everyone was getting slimed; that was his best defense. The money meant nothing. He said that to the reporter.

"So this money that was invested in Conyers' resort—how would you characterize that?"

"I don't know if he solicited it or not. The FBI is investigating. So is Congress. If the president is corrupt, he will answer for his crimes."

The reporter tried to push him into defending himself and condemning the president, but Westfall stopped without digging his own hole deeper. He hung up the phone and shouted a common obscenity.

His phone beeped. The receptionist. "Another reporter, sir, on the Hinton Foundation scandal." Yep, the FBI was busy there too. The former CFO said the foundation had received $25 million; now the figure was up to $42 million. One network was doing bongs for every million of Russian money that had gone to the Hintons. Cynthia was trying to repair the political damage, but Willy had reportedly jetted off to a private island in the Caribbean where, allegedly, underage prostitutes serviced old hulks. Westfall wished he were there too.

"No," he told the receptionist. "I will not comment upon the Hintons' problems. I know absolutely nothing except that I have full faith in their honesty and moral character."

"Yes, sir. And your accountant wants you to call him. There's a fifteen-thousand dollar deposit in your investment account that seems odd."

"My investment account?" This was trouble. The campaign account he could defend, but his personal accounts? Uh-oh. Still, only fifteen thousand, chicken feed. "I'll call him."

So he did. "No, Senator. It's fifteen thousand a month for the last twenty-two months."

"For the love of Christ, how in hell did you miss deposits that big?"

"Senator, the deposits were bank transfers. They looked normal to me. I even put them on your income tax returns. Didn't you read the things?"

Hell, no. He had signed them, his wife had signed them, and the secretary sent them off to the IRS, the State of New York, and the City of New York. Did this pinhead really think he had nothing better to do than sit in his office reading forms he didn't understand, the federal return three-quarters of an inch thick? He snarled at the accountant, "I pay you to fill in the blanks, keep me out of trouble. That's what you are supposed to be doing."

"I'm trying, Senator. I'm trying. Apparently someone else is doing their best to boil you in oil."

A half hour later, he got another telephone call on his private line, this one from a secret friend in one of the agencies. The man didn't give his name, but Harlan Westfall recognized the voice. "The Russian is talking, Senator. He's naming names."

Westfall cradled the receiver and sat looking at the wall. No two ways about it, the fucking Russians had double-crossed them. Anton Hunt was such an ass. And he, Harlan Westfall, had been a fool.

Jesse Hughes lived in a four-room flat in Ellicott City, Maryland, which is just west of Baltimore. His was the third floor of an old house that had been converted to flats and condo-ized. He was the guy who had spoken to Paul Hockersmith on his cell phone five times in the two days before his death. Maybe he had paid Hockersmith to burn up the safe house with the Russian in it, or maybe he was financing a flight from Mexico to the U.S. with a load of drugs.

Sarah had given me and Armanti some information about Hughes. He was a retired civil servant, supposedly now a part-time financial consultant for one of the big hedge funds. Had a business degree from the University of Maryland. Was gay but looked straight. His partner was very effeminate and stayed home with the pooch, a lapdog that liked to bark. They didn't own a car; used Uber if it was too far to walk.

"So as far as we know, no one knows Hockersmith is dead," I said to Sarah.

"As far as we know."

"He might have run off to Mexico or Argentina."

"Might have."

"Or he might have been arrested by the DEA or FBI and is ratting out people."

"That's a possibility too," she admitted.

"We can work with that."

After we got back to Washington, Armanti and I drove out to Ellicott City to scope out Hughes' pad. We had no idea what he looked like, nor had we seen a photo of the love interest. Just to be on the safe side, we called Bill Leitz, who was following us with a van decked out to monitor bugs.

"You ready?"

"Born ready."

"Let me test these out." I got the bugs out of my pocket one by one and whispered into them. They were the latest hot thing, so small they rested on the head of a pin, ridiculously easy to plant. Just jab the pin into a piece of stuffed furniture or a drape, even a carpet in a spot where it wouldn't be trod upon too much, and let the tech gods do the rest.

We were in a little bar on the corner sipping soft drinks when we saw the partner come along from the park with a little yapper on a leash. At least, we saw a very effeminate guy with a very small dog. Armanti nudged me.

He went into the building, and in a moment the lights on the third floor of the building came on. We ordered coffee.

Hughes was supposedly about six feet and an inch, weighed about two hundred, and was balding. After a bit, a guy who answered that description came by carrying a rolled-up umbrella and a brief case. He turned in at the building across the street.

We sat and watched to see if anyone else was interested in Mr. Hughes. Apparently not. I called Sarah. "Do you have his cell phone tapped?"

"Yep."

"We're going over now. Shouldn't take over fifteen minutes, if that. Listen up."

So we paid our bill and walked across the street. Pushed the button above the mailbox to buzz the third floor.

"Who is it?"

"FBI, Mr. Hughes. If we might have a word."

A long moment of silence. Then the click and Armanti pulled the door open. He looked at me and I looked at him.

No elevator. We hiked up to the third floor and knocked.

Hughes opened the door. He was trying to manage his face. "Mr. Jesse Hughes? I'm agent Wilson and this is agent Brown." We offered our credentials, which were great CIA fakes, even better than the real ones. The badges were works of art.

He merely glanced at them. "What do you want?"

I kept the puss deadpan. "Well, it might be better to talk to you in your home with the door closed, or you can come downtown with us, if you like."

He opened the door. We entered and the dog yapped. The lover was wearing a dressing gown and had shaved legs. After he closed the door I asked, "And this is...?"

"Joe Leschetizky."

Armanti dropped to a seat on the couch and whipped out a notebook. He said, all business, "You are going to have to spell that for me, please."

Hughes did. So he was rattled, already on the defensive. The dog kept barking. The apartment was severely hip, as modern as the day after tomorrow, with art on the walls that would have baffled Picasso and uncomfortable chairs of many different primary colors. If you liked this sort of thing, this is the sort of thing you would like.

I sank into a purple chair. Hughes took a chair which was some shade of red.

"We could probably do without the dog," I said gently, almost allowing myself to smile. Joe L. floated up from his chair, which was blue, and sashayed out of the room, murmuring to the dog, which followed him. He closed the door.

"Mr. Hughes, we find ourselves in a very difficult position. Do you know a man named Paul Hockersmith?"

He had to think about that. "Hockersmith?"

"Yes. Paul Hockersmith." I spelled the last name for him.

He decided he wasn't going to know Mr. Hockersmith.

"He says he knows you, Mr. Hughes. He's in protective custody. Apparently someone is trying to assassinate him."

Hughes eyes grew noticeably bigger and rounder.

"Do you know any reason why anyone would want to kill Mr. Hockersmith?"

This question conveniently ignored the fact that he had just said he didn't know the man. He remembered, but barely, just in time. "Why no... but I don't recall ever meeting Mr... Hockersmith, you say?"

"Right. Paul Hockersmith."

He tried to look mystified and succeeded in looking just plain scared.

"Well, if you have never met the man," I said, and stood. Armanti rose and seemed to expand as he did so. Hall was an ugly-looking bastard. I could see Hughes giving him the eye. Armanti adjusted his shoulder holster. Hughes saw that, sure enough.

I held out a card and he tore his eyes from Armanti. "Thank you for your time tonight, Mr. Hughes. Obviously, your name came up in our interviews with Mr. Hockersmith, who does say he knows you. If you think of anything else you want to tell us, that's my card. Give me a ring anytime and leave a message. I'll get back to you as soon as I can."

He took the card.

"What is Hockersmith saying about me?"

I smiled and shrugged. "We can't talk about ongoing investigations, Mr. Hughes. But we are worried about possible assassins. If you see or hear anything that makes you suspicious, please call. We can't help unless we know you need help."

And with that we made our exit. Trooped down the stairs and headed for the bar across the street. "Got four planted," Armanti told me.

We perched on two stools at the end of the bar. I could watch the door to the apartment house by looking in the mirror.

"Been a long day," Armanti said to the bartender. "What do you have on draft?"

He ordered a Guinness. I said I'd take the same. Armanti called Bill Leitz to see if the bugs were working. He nodded at me. Yes.

We were sipping stout and relaxing when my phone rang. The caller ID said it was Sarah.

"He's on the phone to a man named Kevin Edwards, one of the twenty. He's almost hysterical. Edwards is trying to calm him down. Here's Edwards' address." She read it to me and I copied it down.

"Call me back when they get done," I said.

Twenty minutes slipped by. When the phone rang, Sarah had some information. "Edwards is a big wheel in a hedge fund." She named it. "Your friend in Utah named him as one of the twenty."

We finished our Guinness and walked to where we parked our car. We set off for New York City with Bill Leitz following in the van. We crashed at a small hotel that specialized in housing government employees on per diem, a tired old hotel with tiny elevators and tiny rooms. The next morning, we went to find Kevin Edwards. He lived in the fifties, between Park and Madison. After we had another conversation with Bill Leitz and tested another half dozen bugs, we rang Edwards' button in the lobby.

"Yes." A man's voice. So we caught him at home.

"FBI, Mr. Edwards. May we have a few minutes of your time?"

There were three cameras mounted high in the lobby, no doubt taping Hall and me for future reference, or posterity, if anyone ever cared to check.

Six minutes later we were seated in Edwards' living room. We displayed our credentials. Edwards actually looked at mine. He was in his fifties, pretty buff, wearing work-out clothes that showed off his biceps and shoulders. Flat stomach. About five-feet eight or nine inches. Armanti Hall could have broken him in half with one hand.

"Your name came up, Mr. Edwards, in the interrogation of a Mr. Paul Hockersmith."

"I don't believe I know the man. Does he live here in New York?"

"Utah."

"I don't know anyone in Utah." He frowned. "I don't think I have ever been there, even."

"He mentioned your name. And that of a Mr. Jesse Hughes. We have talked with Mr. Hughes, and he said he didn't know Mr. Hockersmith either."

"Well, I don't, so I can't help you." Edwards stood. I didn't.

"Here's why we are here, Mr. Edwards." I lowered my voice a notch and watched his eyes. I didn't want him watching Hall jab pins into the furniture. "We believe assassins are targeting Mr. Hockersmith, Mr. Hughes, and you. I can't tell you where this information comes from, but we believe it to be credible. If I were you, I would take reasonable precautions. Do you have a bodyguard?"

"No." He was still standing, but trying to decide if he wanted to sit. His eyes were riveted upon me.

"You might think about employing one or more. If an assassination attempt comes, it won't be half-hearted. It will happen extremely fast." I snapped my fingers.

Now Armanti and I stood and walked toward the door. "Look both ways before you cross the street," Hall told the guy. I bit my lip to keep from smiling. I checked Edwards' eyes again. He didn't think that was funny. He was scared, obviously.

"Good day, Mr. Edwards." We pulled the door shut behind us.

In the elevator I said to Hall, "You ass. Watch both ways... Shit."

"Six more bugs."

"Onward and upward."

"I'm ready to go get some breakfast," he said. We hailed a taxi on the street and gave the hackie the address of our favorite bagel joint. My phone rang before we got there. Sarah again. "Edwards is on the landline. He's calling Senator Westfall, but I can only hear his half of the conversation."

"Well, how about that?" I said.

# Chapter Eighteen

When he was on the truth serum, Yegan Korjev fingered Ava Silva as the Kremlin's minister-without-portfolio in the fake money sting targeted against Democrats. She had plenty of help, of course, from committed progressives who knew that Democrats were just Republicans who didn't belong to a church or golf club. The progressive revolution would not, could not, succeed unless and until both the Democrats and Republicans were consigned to the dustbin of history.

Ava's disciples had been the ones who flooded the Hinton Foundation with cash, gave money to most of the Democratic candidates for the House and Senate, including Harlan Westfall, and got prominent Democrats tied up in inexplicable, embarrassing conflicts of interest. One of their best stunts was to get the Democrat senator from Massachusetts, the former Indian and Harvard professor who wanted to be president, entrapped as a slum lord in downtown Boston by buying buildings at tax sales, in bankruptcy court, and in mortgage foreclosure proceedings in the name of a corporation they had created for her. They had done the same thing to the mayor of Detroit, but on a lesser scale. The Boston strike was a masterpiece.

When the *Boston Globe* got wind of it two days ago, the senator owned twelve and a half million dollars-worth of rat and cockroach-infested tenements, forty percent of which had been condemned.

This morning the story broke and Ava Silva was savoring the triumph. She was in her office at the university reading the story on the *Globe*'s website when her telephone rang. She checked the caller ID. Her maid. "Yes, Juanita."

"Ah, Senora, some men are here." There followed some words that Ava didn't get, followed by some she did. "...Gas company. Should I let them in?"

Ava had no doubt these were indeed gas company employees checking the lines for leaks. "Oh, of course."

Doc Gordon and I were waiting at the door when the Mexican maid returned. "Senora says all right."

We were admitted with our testing devices, so we sampled the air in the basement, the kitchen, and around the three gas-log fireplaces... and left bugs all over. The whole job took twenty minutes. We thanked Juanita and went out the door to our borrowed power company ride.

As Doc piloted us down the drive, I checked our list again. Next stop, Ava's Number One lieutenant, an economist, Langwith Chandler, who worked for the largest private bank in America. Fortunately, he lived just three miles from the Silva's humble cottage.

I looked back at Bill Leitz, who was wearing earphones and manning the tech console. He gave me a thumbs up.

Two minutes later I got a call from Sarah. "Ava is on the phone to Langwith Chandler. Apparently he's at home today, about to do a telephone call-in interview with CNBC."

"We'll try to stay out from underfoot," I told her.

And by golly we did. Admitted to check for gas leaks, I actually got into Chandler's office while he was on the air with the financial gurus. He ignored me. I waved the wand around, checked the readings, and inserted two pins with bugs on them in the stuffed chairs.

We had done five dwellings by noon. Three of them were simple two or three-room flats whose building superintendent gave us the key. We went in, checked for leaks, and got out of each place as quickly as our professional chores would allow. In the last place we hit, the tenant was there, an emaciated stringbean in his thirties who was obviously on heroin. He had needle tracks in his arms. He typed on his computer while we checked his digs, and damn if we didn't find his stove was leaking. Got him into the kitchen, showed him the reading, and called the power company on the spot. We had our bugs all in place when the real gas men turned up, so we faded.

In the van, Armanti said, "He ain't ever gonna live to see the revolution, not with that habit of his."

"Only if it happens quickly," I said judiciously. "Like this week, or maybe the next."

"How many millions did this dude handle?"

"Over half a billion, Sarah thinks."

"He's probably got enough shit stashed away to keep New York pain-free for a decade."

The addict was the last of Ava's local contacts, so we broke for lunch. After, we took the van back to the power company. We reclaimed our car and Armanti Hall and I set forth upon the highways to visit some more of Ava's friends with Bill Leitz following in the company van. Two days later, we jumped a plane for California.

If you are going to plot revolution and dictatorship, California is the place to do it. In the first place, everyone there thinks they are part of the intellectual elite and should therefore be on the dictatorship committee. Second, everyone from San Diego to the Oregon border hates someone with a pure and perfect passion. I should know: I grew up there.

One of Ava Silva's acolytes was a professor at Berkeley, Justin Alschwede, who had been busy using Russian money to slime and destroy prominent Democrats around the state. He lived with three girlfriends in a rooftop condo, just far enough from campus to be affordable. The girls didn't work... just hung out and provided Justin with all the sex he could stand in return for food and pot.

There didn't seem to be much point in bugging the place, so we didn't try. Justin didn't have a landline and we were monitoring his cell phone calls.

Yet as Armanti and I talked about Justin's situation, we wondered if perhaps we could do something more, some little thing to make his life more exciting.

I soon found out that he liked to have lunch at a food court at the student union on campus, so I rendezvoused with him there. Got in line just behind him, followed him with my tray and sat down right beside him. He had thinning hair and a scraggly goatee. What was left of his hair was held together with a rubber band in a pony-tail. "Hope you don't mind," I mumbled.

He looked down his nose at me as if I were a Republican. I put my hand on his arm. "Don't get up, and don't look around. I'm taking a desperate chance talking to you like this, so don't give me away, for Christ's sake."

His eyes bulged. He ran his eyes right and left as far as he could without turning his head.

"It's that big black man with all the hair standing against the wall. Is he looking at us?"

"Yes," Professor Justin whispered. "He's staring."

"Don't look at him. Eat your meal." The guy had some kind of kale and quinoa salad in a disposable dish. It looked awful. "Use your fork," I directed. "We're just talking normally. Ignore that black man."

Justin took a bite as directed. As he chewed kale he asked, "Who is he?"

"He's a hired killer. The Democrats know what you've been up to; they've hired this guy to pop you. You've made some serious enemies in Sacramento and Washington."

He stared at me. "Who are you? How do you know all this?"

"I'm a friend. They tried to hire me, but I refused." I shrugged and attacked my salad, which was green spinach with bacon bits, onions, some boiled egg crumbles, and two kinds of peppers. "It's not that I have any qualms about killing, you understand—sometimes it is necessary—but I refuse to terminate people I agree with politically."

The asshole's head bobbed when he heard this. Yeah, man, never do the seekers of wisdom and truth.

I shot Armanti a glance. He was planted right against that wall, glowering at us.

"Professor, you and I both know how the Democrats have enslaved people of color, kept them in poverty and on drugs, just so they could capture their votes on election day. They're evil." I made eye contact and looked deep into his brown ones. "*Evil*," I whispered.

I sighed and forked some salad. It was actually pretty good, but I had to cut off my interview and get out of there before Justin and I became new best friends.

"They want you dead," I told him just loud enough for him to hear. "Take precautions. Watch who is around you. Always leave yourself an escape route. Don't trust anyone." I patted him on the arm.

"Keep up the good work, and stay alive."

I rose and walked out, leaving the bulk of my salad on the table. Since I gave him a life-saving tip, maybe Justin Alschwede would bus my lunch when he finished his.

When Jake Grafton's cell rang, he checked the caller ID. The phone didn't recognize the caller, but it was a Washington area code, so he answered it.

"Mr. Grafton, this is the president."

"Yes, sir. I recognize your voice."

"What have you learned from that Russian, Korjev?"

"Sir, this is an unsecure line. Perhaps I should—"

"Goddamn it, I am tired of sitting in the dark like a damned mushroom waiting for people to feed me shit. What have you learned?"

Grafton was in the safe house boiling two eggs for breakfast, so he turned the stove off and went outside where there would be no curious ears. As he brought the president up to speed on the questioning of Yegan Korjev, he watched the sun peep over the La Sal mountains. The sky was absolutely clear. The day was going to be fantastic.

"Mr. President, I have been using the secure satellite phone to talk to Reem Kiddus, to keep him informed. Hasn't he been briefing you?"

"He has, but I want it firsthand. And I want to ask the sixty-four dollar question: What do you think?"

"I think the possibilities of political paralysis in America looked irresistible to the boys in the Kremlin. They could see a lot of upside and not much downside."

"How in hell are we going to save America?"

"We need to get these people who distributed the money talking. I don't care a fig about prosecutions, or about all the warnings the FBI and cops have to give. We can't wait two or three years while the wheels of justice grind along. We're going to get it in their own words, one way or another."

"When?"

"As soon as possible."

"Washington is going critical, becoming a self-sustaining chain reaction," Vaughn Conyers said. "If this goes on for any length of time, in my judgment, the United States Constitution is going to be torn up. We're heading for a collapse of representative government. The choice will ultimately boil down to a dictatorship of the right or the left."

Jake prayed no one was recording this conversation.

"That's after the civil war," Conyers continued. "The whole concept of the 'loyal opposition' is going up the flue. Both sides hate each other. They are working their way up to wanting the other side dead."

Jake Grafton made a noise.

Conyers continued, almost thinking aloud. "This morning some columnist said maybe it's time to tear America down and start all over again. That's terrible thinking. What he's really saying is that the Constitution is inadequate. I reject that. The Constitution is a political compromise, and ripping it up isn't going to fill in the political divide between conservatives and liberals. I didn't sign up to be the last president of the United States."

Jake realized that Vaughn Conyers needed someone to talk to. The president continued, "When a nationally syndicated columnist who usually has good sense writes something like that, that will be read all over the United States, Jake, we have big troubles. Now I know how Lincoln felt when the southern states seceded from the union. We're on the edge of the abyss and no one can see the bottom, but a bunch of people are working themselves up to jumping."

"Yes, sir."

"I want you to keep me informed. Call me at any hour of the day or night at this number. Your phone captured it."

"Yes, sir. I will."

"If I can't answer, leave a message. I'll call you back when I can." The president hung up.

The gentle breeze smelled of early summer. Jake Grafton took one good whiff and went back into the house. He had to get back to Washington. He got the fire going under the eggs and made several telephone calls to arrange transportation.

When Mac Kelley came in, Grafton said, "I'm leaving. Korjev will be going with me. The Marines will stay."

They discussed logistics for a moment, then Grafton ate his eggs and went to pack his duffel. Two hours later, Alvie Johnson gave them a ride to the helicopter landing site.

"If you see that Tommy guy again, tell him I said hi."

"I'll do that."

"I'm sorry he killed that pilot," the cowboy said, "but if Tommy hadn't shot the airplane down he would have burned up the house and everyone in it."

"That's true."

"He's not going to be in trouble for killing that guy, is he?"

"No. He's just got to live with it. Anytime you make a life or death judgment, you must live with it. Goes with the territory."

Alvie just nodded. He, Jake Grafton, and Yegan Korjev sat in the cab of the pickup talking about nothing much until the helicopter came. Alvie carried Grafton's bag over and shoved it through the door. Korjev carried the stuff he had been given in a pillowcase. After Korjev was aboard, Grafton shook Alvie's hand and climbed into the thing. The helicopter still had the engines running and the rotor turning.

When the helicopter had disappeared to the northwest in the direction of Capitol Reef, Alvie got his can of Skoal from his hip pocket, put a pinch in his mouth, then got into the pickup and headed back to the barn. He wondered who the other guy was, but he hadn't asked. He finally understood that it was possible to know too much. He had shit to shovel, and he was happy with that.

Abraham Goldman was a banker. He had an office on the twenty-first floor of his bank building in downtown San Francisco, on top of one of the hills. Armanti and I were wearing ties with our sports coats when we presented our fake credentials to the receptionist and asked to speak to Mr. Goldman, the CEO and chairman of the board.

I heard her whisper into the phone, "Federal officers, Mr. Goldman."

We were directed to an elevator that took us straight to the top. A receptionist was waiting to meet us, not sitting behind a desk doing her nails, but standing there waiting when we came strolling out of the elevator door. She showed us in to a corner office with lots of windows and closed the door behind us.

"Took you long enough," the man behind the desk said. He was in his seventies, with his coat and tie off and his sleeves rolled up. Little guy, wispy white hair. He had three televisions in his office, and they were all on different networks. This guy was a news junkie.

"I called you three days ago," he said. "What is your problem?"

I glanced at Armanti and found he was looking at me with his eyebrows up.

I took a chair in front of the desk and Armanti sank into the one beside it. I suspected that Goldman thought we were really important people, like FBI agents or bank examiners, maybe IRS agents, someone with some stroke.

"We came as soon as we could, Mr. Goldman," I said apologetically.

Goldman gestured toward the televisions. "Goddamn country is coming apart. Some senator just advocated tearing up the United States Constitution. On a nationwide television show. Can you believe it?"

"Some people can't contain their enthusiasm," I remarked.

"I know that I am partially responsible for this crisis," Abraham Goldman said, "and I want to take full responsibility for my part in it. I want to confess. I want this off my conscience. I bitterly regret agreeing to have anything to do with this."

I noticed that Armanti had two of the bugs out and stabbed them into the chairs. He also had his cellphone in his hand, and I thought he was recording the conversation. He held the phone in his lap, below Goldman's level of vision.

"Who first approached you, Mr. Goldman?"

It took him a moment to collect himself. He licked his lips and began: "Michael Hunt, Anton's son. About three years or so ago. I don't remember the exact date. We were at a conference in Jackson Hole."

"What did he want you to do?"

"Help spread some fake Russian money around to embarrass California politicians. He was quite upfront about it." And away Mr. Goldman went, telling us everything about the operation.

He talked on and on, getting this mess off his chest, with only a few prompts from me. I hoped Bill Leitz in the van was getting all this on the bugs. Armanti was checking his phone every few minutes. I had no idea how big the memory in that phone was, how much of this he could record.

Goldman was obviously near a nervous breakdown. His hands shook, his lips quivered, he had trouble speaking in complete sentences.

I had my little notebook out and was jotting down some of the more important points. About how Goldman spread hundreds of millions of dollars to every contractor and politician involved with Caltrans, the ill-starred commuter train that was grossly over-budget. He had a list of people and companies he had passed money to, most of them having no idea where the money came from or what it was for. He offered the list and I took it. The total was $463 million. He had even signed the thing. I studied it, folded it, and put it inside my jacket pocket.

His distress was painful to watch. Finally I had had enough.

"Mr. Goldman, let's take a break here. We are indeed federal officers, but I doubt if we are from the agency you were expecting. Who did you think we work for?"

He stared. Finally he got it out. "FBI."

"Actually we are from the CIA, the Central Intelligence Agency. My name is Tommy Carmellini and my colleague is Armanti Hall. We are here because Russian money was involved. We had good reason to believe you helped spread it around, which is why we called on you today."

He hid his face behind one hand. I watched for a moment, then realized Abraham Goldman was probably weeping.

"You didn't come to arrest me." It wasn't a question, but a statement.

"We have no powers of arrest. We are trying to determine who the Russians used to pump over two hundred billion in fake money into the American economy and how those people spread it around." I certainly didn't know that that much moola had come to America, but I wasn't ready to split hairs. I gestured toward the televisions on the wall. "You see that the money is causing a crisis that is threatening America."

"Yes."

"Knowing who we really are, do you wish to continue your statement?"

"Yes. I want you to record it and get someone to type it up, and I want to sign it. I want this off my chest. America is a great country—oh, hell, it has its problems, but that is called life. My father fought on Guadalcanal and my brother was killed in Vietnam. I wonder what they would have thought if they knew what I did. I'll take whatever punishment the government feels appropriate."

"We can do a video," I said, "with your permission, and go through it from end to end. Would you be agreeable to that?"

"Yes."

"I can make some phone calls and set it up. Now. But I want you to think this through, Mr. Goldman. You may want to discuss this with your attorney before you do it. From what you've told me, it seems that you are open to lawsuits from some of these people or companies you sent money to. I am sure Hunt intended that your name would never come out. Now you are talking about putting it out there for the world to hear."

"No damned lawyers. I shouldn't have done it, and I'll take what's coming."

"Before I make the telephone call, Mr. Goldman, I'd like to shake your hand if you are willing."

I rose and went around the desk and he shook my hand. He had tears glistening on his cheeks. Armanti Hall was right behind me.

I reached Jake Grafton in a plane on his way to Washington. "I thought you were supposed to have your cell phone off on those things."

"Yeah. What is it, Tommy?"

I told him about Mr. Goldman and my videotape idea. "He's willing. He wants to confess and liked my idea."

"I'll make some arrangements and call you back. Where are you exactly?"

I told him the name of the bank and the address.

"'Bye." And he was gone.

I turned to Mr. Goldman. "That was my boss, the director of the Central Intelligence Agency, Jacob L. Grafton."

"I've heard the name."

"He liked the videotape idea, if you are willing. Maybe we can undo some of the damage that money has caused."

Grafton called back fifteen minutes later and asked to talk to Mr. Goldman. I could only hear Goldman's end of it. They were still on the telephone a half hour later when the receptionist knocked, then entered.

"There is a cameraman and reporter here, Mr. Goldman." He held the phone away from his head and said, "Send them in."

The banker finished his talk with Grafton while the television people set up lights and a camera. Finally he handed my cellphone back. Grafton was still on the thing.

"Let the TV people do the interview, Tommy, but you can ask questions from off camera. Get the whole story out. They'll run the thing tonight. Let's see if we can kill some snakes with the truth."

"Yes, sir."

So we did it. I never did get to ask Grafton who he knew at WSFC, and he never mentioned it, but his circle of acquaintances and old shipmates all over the country never ceased to amaze me.

Mr. Goldman went to the little restroom beside his office before we began. When he came out I could see he had washed his face. Then he put on his tie and jacket and seated himself behind his desk. When the camera started rolling he started talking.

Every now and then I asked a pointed question from off camera. I made damn sure that Michael Hunt's name was mentioned three times. Two hours passed before the reporter looked at me with raised eyebrows. Goldman was visibly wilting. I nodded, and the cameraman turned off his equipment and killed the lights.

"Seven o'clock tonight," the reporter said as she was leaving. She made it a point to shake hands with Mr. Goldman.

I looked at the battery level in my cellphone. A little left. I called Jake Grafton again. He was back in Washington, probably Langley.

"Seven o'clock Pacific on WSFC," I said. "Two hours' worth."

"Good job, Tommy."

"What do you want me and Armanti to do? We can't just leave Mr. Goldman. The shit is going to hit the fan when this thing airs."

"Check out of your hotel and take him to his home. Stay with him. Keep him safe."

"Yes, sir."

"I'll have some people relieve you tomorrow. Until then, he doesn't talk to anyone but his immediate family. No FBI, no calls from New York, none of his colleagues at the bank, no reporters, no one."

"Got it."

"After it airs, call me and tell me how Mr. Goldman is doing."

"Wilco."

"Until then."

# Chapter Nineteen

Jake Grafton came back from Utah to a CIA headquarters in ferment. Monitoring the cell phones and listening devices that Carmellini had planted took dozens of people and large rooms full of equipment. Sarah Houston was in charge of that effort, which looked like organized chaos. They had talked three or four times a day while he was in Utah, but still, there was no substitute for actually seeing what was happening where the rubber met the road.

Grafton had a problem: Someone had leaked the fact that Yegan Korjev was in Utah. The assassination attempt had followed almost as soon as it could be arranged, so the leak had happened early, within hours of the decision being made that the Russian would be interrogated in Utah.

The real question, he thought, was how far the information had spread. Was it a whisper that one of the conspirators had taken for action, or had it been disseminated widely among the people in the know? He suspected he would soon find out. The people in the conspiracy to spread the fake money far and wide obviously intended to rock the American system of government, not just the existing government, but the system, to its foundations. Vladimir Putin had plenty of help. But Putin was in Russia and they were here, with everything staked on the outcome. The conspirators would be ruined if their roles became public. It would soon become war to the knife, and the knife to the hilt, if it wasn't already.

Sarah Houston was not one for mincing words. "I need more people, Admiral."

Grafton didn't hesitate. "Draft them from every office in the building. If we don't defuse this Russian money crisis, this agency is going to disintegrate along with the rest of the federal government. These people are going to be unemployed very soon."

She nodded.

"Oh, by the way, here are a couple more telephone numbers I want monitored. Every conversation, everything these phones overhear. And you are going to have to be the one to do it. No one else."

Jake Grafton decided that this evening might be a good time to try out his new, personal access to the president, so he gave him a call. "Jake Grafton, Mr. President. I am told that WSFC in San Francisco is going to run a two-hour confession from the chairman of the First Bank of the United States at ten o'clock our time this evening. No doubt it will be simulcast on the web."

"I'll watch."

"The president of WSFC tells me the network refused to carry it sight unseen. If they think it is newsworthy, they'll break into existing programing and run the thing nationwide. That's the best we could get."

"What will happen after they air it?"

"For Abe Goldman, personal catharsis at a hell of a price. He will probably have to go bankrupt and his bank may fail. But this thing is going to be a wake-up call for a lot of people who thought they could subvert the government and remain anonymous."

"Tomorrow will be even more exciting than today," Vaughn Conyers said bitterly.

"One suspects so. But I think we are coming to a crisis. We'll weather it or we won't."

"I'll watch. Thanks for the call." The president hung up.

Jake was ten minutes into watching the broadcast of Abraham Goldman's confession on his office computer when the network WSFC belonged to started carrying it. The program appeared on his office television, which had been tuned to the right channel, just in case. A note at the bottom of the screen stated that the program had been recorded "earlier today."

The first notification that Goldman's statement had hit some raw nerves was a telephone call from one of California's senators, a woman politically joined at the hip with Harland Westfall, one who was obviously just now on the verge of a meltdown. "Grafton, I called WSFC about this *filth* they are airing this very minute, and the program manager said to call your agency. Are you responsible for this... this... *venom* from a deranged mind?"

"I am not deranged, Madam."

"Don't fuck with me, little man. I am not a madam! I am *Senator* Konchina to you! That bank is the largest in California! You just put the California economy on the chopping block. I want your resignation to be tomorrow morning's headline or your agency will never get another dollar from the intelligence committee. Do you understand?"

"Is that a promise?"

"You are goddamn right—"

"Making promises you can't keep is a bad habit, Senator." Grafton hung up on her.

His next call—the calls were filtered by the executive assistant on duty, since the receptionist had gone home for the evening—was from a journalist Grafton had known for years, Jack Yocke (pronounced Yock-key). "Good evening, Admiral."

"As I live and breathe."

"The reason I am calling, Admiral, is that I just got a telephone call from Senator Konchina's chief of staff. She and I have this little thing going. Anyway, she says the senator is bouncing off the walls because you are behind this confession of the chairman of the First Bank of the United States that is airing right now."

"I'm watching it," Jake said. "You can probably hear the soundtrack in the background. This is the first time I've seen it."

"Did you have anything to do with this?"

"Jack, you know I don't answer questions from the press, especially open-ended questions like that. You need to call the CIA public affairs office or the White House Press office tomorrow. Maybe one of those will have a statement. Or maybe they won't."

"Admiral, the senator is going public with her accusations that you set up this 'manure dump' by Abe Goldman. I need something for the website. Would 'No Comment' be fair?"

"I suppose. By the way, what are you up to professionally these days?"

"I have an hour show on Sunday evening for Fox that you obviously haven't been watching," the reporter said. "Maybe that will grow into something."

"How are your ratings?"

"Middling. We're selling pillows, cooking gadgets, and silver wafers. Silver is the investment you need for the coming depression."

"Jack, you and I have always had a good working relationship in the past. You have played fair and haven't cheated on the ground rules. If in the future there is a story that you could help tell, I'll give you a call at this number, if you wish."

"Anytime, Admiral, day or night. Except Sunday night when I'm on camera."

"Thanks, Jack."

Abe Goldman's confession left Jake Grafton shaken. He hadn't realized how detailed it was. The sources of the money, shell corporations, transfers, dates, telephone conversations with fellow conspirators... all those details gave it the power of authenticity that would make it extremely difficult for anyone to call Abe Goldman a liar and make it stick.

He went to the basement where Sarah Houston had set up shop. "Let me see everything you have on Senator Westfall."

He knew that Westfall and the late Anton Hunt had been political soulmates, and now he learned that the younger Hunt, Michael, was equally in Westfall's orbit. Or Westfall was in his. From the comments the two made to each other, they had made exhaustive plans to distribute the Russian largess. They kept referring to those plans. But what were they? Where were they?

Could he somehow convince Westfall he had the plans? Or should he try to get them?

He flipped through the transcripts, which were not prepared by stenographers listening to raw audio, but by computers that converted sounds to print. Consequently there were typos, missed words, unrecognizable phrases, and the like. But the gist was usually there. If necessary, a real human could listen to the conversation in question and see if a better transcript could be prepared.

Half the senators in Westfall's party were apparently in on some portion of the secret. It was a miracle that such a secret had been kept so long. No wonder the Russians had been ready to spin the wheel—if they didn't, it would have come out piecemeal.

Grafton moved over to the transcripts of Ava Silva's calls. She was getting more and more worried as the days passed and she talked to her confederates, some of whom repeated the assassin rumors that Carmellini had helped spread. At first she discounted those rumors, but lately she had ceased to do so. She even warned several of her fellow conspirators to be careful, to watch for strangers, to take reasonable precautions.

Which begged the question: What were reasonable precautions against a determined assassin?

As he rose to leave, he saw Sarah Houston watching him under lowered eyebrows, frowning. She was wearing a headset that was plugged into a computer. "Do you know who those last two phones belong to that you wanted monitored?"

"Conyers and Kiddus."

"You'll put us both in prison."

Grafton went back to his office and stirred through the telephone messages that had accumulated this evening. He called for his driver and went to the parking lot to meet him.

Abe Goldman watched the first hour or so of his confession, then his wife turned off the television. She was petite, like him. She looked at Goldman and said, "Enough. You and I are going to bed."

"I had to do it, Rachel. I had to confess."

"I know. You did the right thing. But it's time for bed. These men will sit here and make sure we get a good night's sleep."

"We will," Armanti Hall said.

Goldman was all used up. I helped him walk into the bedroom and sit on the edge of the bed. His wife said she would take it from there, so I left and closed the door.

The telephone was off the hook.

What do you say or do when you have just blown up the existence you spent all your life building? Sure, he did the crimes, but still... after all, this is *America*! You lawyer up, deny everything, take the Fifth, string it out as long as humanly possible with delays and appeals, and finally, if heaven forbid you are convicted, when the sentencing comes you throw yourself on the mercy of the court. You do the remorse thing; talk about your charities, tell the judge you are now in tight with Jesus or Jehovah, have friends testify about your wonderful warm heart and have your doctor testify about your infirmities.

Goldman didn't do that. He stood tall to take the bullet.

I really liked the guy.

Out in the living room Armanti Hall was standing looking out a window at the night skyline of San Francisco. You could see the First Bank tower on the top of a hill, standing all lit up against the dark sky.

"Maybe we shouldn't be standing in front of this window—" I said, just as a hole appeared in a pane of glass in the middle. A tiny shower of bits flew inward. The bullet had passed between us. We hit the deck anyway.

"Gonna be a long night," Armanti said.

I stretched out on the floor. "Think we ought to call the cops?" I asked.

"It'll be an hour before they get here. That dude will be asleep in Oakland by then."

We settled the matter by finding the liquor cabinet and pouring ourselves stiff ones.

Although he was exhausted, Jake Grafton had the driver take him to the Lincoln Memorial. He left the car and walked up the stairs, stood at Lincoln's feet, and, finally, turned and looked back toward the Washington Monument. Then he left the memorial and walked the hundred yards to the wall, the Vietnam Memorial, with its 58,000 names.

That was a strange place. If you closed your eyes and fingered the engraved names, you could see them through the mists of time, see those young men from your youth, those young Americans who went forth to fight because they were told this was America's battle. Those faces, precisely like the faces of the men who fought at Shiloh and Gettysburg, in the smoke of the Wilderness, on the Marne, at Normandy, Guadalcanal, and a thousand other places...

It was one in the morning when Jake Grafton found the car and driver and asked to go to Arlington Cemetery. When the Civil War dead were being brought to Washington, they were interred in Robert E. Lee's lawn, at the Custis-Lee Mansion at Arlington. American soldiers, sailors, Marines, and airmen have been interred there ever since.

On an early summer night, Jake Grafton could feel their presence.

It was after two when the driver dropped him at his building in Roslyn and he let himself into his condo with a key.

"Jake, is that you?" Callie's voice.

"I'm home."

The next morning every network on the planet was playing short snippets of Abe Goldman's confession, so Harland Westfall, Franky Konchina, and the Speaker of the House put their heads together to see what might be done. They decided that they needed to nudge the media off the Goldman story, the Russian fake money story, the attempted bribery of almost every public official in the nation and half the prominent businesses. The Speaker introduced a bill in the House to impeach President Conyers for unspecified "high crimes and misdemeanors." She announced it in the rotunda of the Capitol. One of the high crimes was the investment of Russian money in the president's resort he had developed in Florida.

While she was regaling the press with recitations of Conyers' crimes, a national newspaper broke the story that the Speaker and her husband had made over eight million dollars from assorted lobbyists in Washington and Sacramento, money that didn't look as if it were Russian money, although it might have been. The payments, according to the story, were apparently bribes for political favors, including securing government contracts for the Speaker's spouse, who was a construction contractor.

When she had finished with her announcement of the impeachment bill, one of the reporters asked her about the bribery story, which she had not yet read or been briefed upon.

Still, the Speaker denounced that story as fake, a smear, although she had just smeared the president with Russian money herself. That irony was not lost on her.

Humiliated and enraged, the Speaker stalked off to Harlan Westfall's office to unburden herself with an epic rant; Westfall's office computer captured every syllable.

The question presented itself, so a pundit finally asked it: If you had an unlimited source of free money and knew some politicians who were a bit less than honest, how much would you spend to get the kind of government you richly deserved, that you knew your fellow Americans richly deserved? How much would you spend to soothe the appetites of the savage politicians and improve the world for all mankind?

# Chapter Twenty

The political scene was a cornucopia that kept on giving if you were in the news business. The press had yet to tumble to the fact that Ava Silva and Senator Westfall had been busy giving money to their political enemies in a way that would create problems for them. Meanwhile, Ava and her disciples were doing the same to their so-called friends. If your goal is to topple the establishment, screw everybody. Saul Alinsky never said that, but he should have.

Of course, the Russians had helped. They had agents, or friends, or, usually, damn fools who didn't know where the money was coming from or care, who gave people money in ways that would ruin them if the receipt of the funds ever came to light. And now the light was beginning to shine.

The morning newspaper was a catalogue of greed and stupidity, Jake Grafton decided. He had the kitchen television on while he slurped coffee, scrutinized headlines, and read snippets of stories. His cell phone was still off. The instant he turned it on, people in his agency and across the spectrum of government would be after him.

The amazing thing, he thought, was that all the politicians were pointing fingers at their ideological enemies, in public, in print, on camera. Their opponents were evil, greedy men and women without scruples, lying hypocrites who said one thing to the voters and did something else in their private lives. Even if a politician had been slimed himself, he seemed to think it perfectly logical to accuse his ideological enemies of the same kind of odious behavior that he himself had been accused of.

When Callie came into the kitchen in her robe, he kissed her and poured her some coffee. She sat down beside him at the counter and took her first experimental morning sip. For the first time that morning, Jake Grafton actually became aware of his surroundings. The sun peeping up over Washington threw the bright colors of the kitchen in stark relief. He realized that Callie had put a planter with three little flowers in the windowsill.

"What are those?" He gestured at the flowers.

"Violets. I have always loved them."

He smiled and kissed her. "I missed you, lady."

"I missed you too, husband of mine." She sighed and gestured at the television and newspaper. "Where is all this going, Jake?"

"They hate each other, the mutual hatred society."

"People used to be able to disagree about politics."

"We've lost that somewhere along the way," her husband said thoughtfully.

She glanced at the clock. "The driver will be here for you in thirty minutes."

He stood. There was just time to shower and shave. "When this is over, I'm retiring."

"Do you mean that?"

"Honest Injun. Cross my heart." He smiled and touched her hair. "I want to spend my days with you. And I want to get the airplane out of the hangar, get it inspected, and go flying." Jake owned a Cessna 170B that he hadn't flown in two years. The tires were probably flat and mice were converting it into condominiums.

"Oh, Jake, I wish you would really retire," Callie said, searching his eyes. "I want some us time."

He kissed her, then headed for the bedroom and master bath.

The driver and bodyguard were waiting at the curb when Jake walked out of his building. Typical morning traffic, a pleasant morning, the sidewalk area in shadow from a building across the street, and the men were smiling at him.

He heard the whack as the bullet hit him, the sickening thunk of a bullet traveling at over two-thousand feet-per-second finding flesh. The impact staggered him; then he was falling, the world was spinning... the concrete sidewalk hit him in the face and the world went black.

"Holy fuck," the bodyguard screamed as he crouched, pulled his pistol and looked wildly around for the shooter. The driver was already lying on top of the admiral, trying to ensure the shooter didn't put another bullet into him.

"Over there," a bystander shouted, and pointed at the parking garage across the street.

The bodyguard checked, didn't see anyone, then set about saving the life of the man he was supposed to protect. He pulled him over to the shelter of the car and told the driver to call 911. Shots fired, man down.

Grafton was still breathing, thank God, but his pulse was erratic. A chest wound. A big hole in his back. He was bleeding onto the concrete. Bright red blood.

The guard had spent eight years in the army, done three tours in Afghanistan. He had seen his share of gunshot wounds. This one looked really bad. He had that horrible feeling that this guy wasn't going to make it.

In less than a minute, the guard heard the distant wail of sirens.

At five-thirty in the morning my cell phone woke me. I was asleep on Abraham Goldman's living room couch. The damn thing wouldn't stop buzzing, and of course I couldn't find it. After a search, I found it had slipped down between the cushions. The buzzing had stopped by then.

The call had been from Sarah Houston. I headed for the kitchen to make some coffee and pushed the buttons to call her back.

"Hey, kiddo."

"Tommy, Jake Grafton has been shot outside his condo in Roslyn on his way to work this morning. An ambulance took him to the hospital. He's in surgery now."

I was wide awake. "Tell me about it."

"A sniper, apparently, in that garage across the street. I think you had better come back to Washington."

"There's a leak in the company, Sarah. That sprayer in Utah knew where to find the Russian. Now this."

"I'm looking. You come back. Better call the EAs and make sure Goldman has some guards."

"I'm on it."

I put the phone in my pocket and stood looking around. I was a bit baffled to find I was in the kitchen. What did I come in here for?

*Jake Grafton shot.*

Damnation! I went to find Armanti. After I woke him up and dropped the bomb, I called Langley. The two people I knew best were Grafton's executive assistants, Anastasia Roberts—actually Dr. Roberts, since she had a PhD in foreign policy or something like that—and Max Hurley, intelligence analysist. Roberts went to the University of Chicago to teach a couple years ago, lasted two semesters, then asked Grafton if she could come back to the company. She was freaky smart, like Sarah Houston. Say what you will, smart women are the most fun to be around.

Hurley wasn't in Roberts' class, but he had a severely logical mind and a photographic memory. He was skinny and liked to run marathons. He was the one who answered the phone this morning.

"Max, this is Tommy. I just heard about the boss."

"He's critical, Tommy. May not make it. His wife is at the hospital."

"I think I should probably come back to Washington, but I'm sitting here in San Francisco with Armanti Hall guarding Abe Goldman. We need some more bodies out here."

"Got three guys on the way. They actually left last night. 'Tasia and I think you should get back here, too. I'll have the travel office see what they can do to get you a reservation on a plane."

"I'm on my way to the airport now."

I briefed Armanti on the situation, called an Uber, and went outside on the curb to wait for it. A television reporter and her crew were setting up on the sidewalk. *Welcome to your new life, Mr. Goldman.* The reporter was eyeing me as a possible victim for the morning news when the Uber pulled up. I hopped in and he rolled away before the cameraman could get a shot.

I stopped by the hotel to rescue my stuff and pay my bill, and then rode out to the airport. Sure enough, I had a reservation, and only had to wait an hour to board. Since I was a federal officer I kept the pistol with me, but I had to have a word with the captain. Even though I had slept in my clothes and hadn't shaved, they gave me a seat in first class.

Jake Grafton. Man, the adventures I had with that guy! A sniper! The fact is, I was crabby and depressed. If Grafton died, I was quitting the company. I wasn't cut out to be a cog in a vast bureaucratic machine. I knew it and Grafton knew it, which was why we got along.

The Frisco plane landed at Dulles, which is fifteen miles west of the Washington beltway. Used to be Dulles International was way the hell out in the sticks, but now it was just way the hell out in the 'burbs, sur-rounded by tech companies no one ever heard of. Dulles was a miserable place, far too small for the number of humans that used it, and it seemed that I had been through that airport a couple of hundred times. The mood I was in, if I never saw the place again in this life that would suit me fine. I retrieved my bag from the carousel and went outside to wait in the taxi line. A Muslim in a sheet with a fat wife wearing a scarf and face rag tried to cut in front of me, but I used my elbows and growled at the SOB, "Wait for your turn, Ahab."

"I beg your pardon," he said in perfect British English.

I had left my pickup in the lot at Langley, so I told the taxi driver to drop me there. On the way I called Sarah. "How is he?"

"In the ICU." She named the hospital. "I'm sitting here with Mrs. Grafton."

"See you in a bit."

The cabbie apparently thought he was going to make a funny about dropping me at the Langley gate, but after he looked at my face he decided against it.

Forty-five minutes after I found my truck in the Langley lot I was walking into the hospital.

They were in the ICU waiting room. I sat down beside Mrs. Grafton. She and Sarah filled me in. A single shot had struck the admiral as he walked across the sidewalk to the waiting car. The doctor thought the bullet was a hunting round, an expansion bullet, due to the massive internal damage. "Someone wanted him really dead," Sarah said, "and he should have been. Perhaps a .270 or .30-06. The doctor says it's touch and go, gives him a fifty-fifty chance."

I asked Callie, "Have you been in to see him?"

"They let me hold his hand for a moment when he came out of surgery. More for my benefit than his, since he was still heavily sedated. He never knew I was there." Once again, I was impressed with how tough Callie Grafton really was. The ultimate warrior had found a warrior mate.

"Let's go to the cafeteria and get some dinner," I suggested.

Over meatloaf, mashed potatoes, and vegetables I asked Mrs. Grafton, "Do you have any idea who did this?"

She shook her head.

I looked at Sarah. "How is the phone number project coming?" She knew the one I meant, finding the leak who had told someone that Korjev was being held at a safe house in Utah.

"They're working on it at the office."

"It is someone who knew about the safe house. That really cuts down the possibilities. That information is pretty tightly held."

Mrs. Grafton was working on a salad, pretending she didn't hear us talking shop.

We were all nursing styrofoam cups of coffee when Jack Norris, the agency vice-director, came into the cafeteria, looked around, saw us, and came walking over. "There's one of the possibilities now," Sarah muttered.

"Callie," he said, extending his hand. "I have been trying to get away all day. How is he?"

Mrs. Grafton went into that, the shooting, the operation, the admiral's critical condition, the fact he hadn't yet awakened.

"It sounds like a miracle that he's still alive," Norris said.

Callie nodded slowly. "It's in God's hands," she said.

Apparently Norris thought that was a good place to change the direction of the conversation, because he looked at me and said, "I hear you had some excitement last night in San Francisco."

"Yes, sir. We got Goldman home and someone put a bullet through his window, probably a pistol bullet or a twenty-two. We didn't hear the report. It came through the glass and just missed me and Hall."

"Did you find the bullet?"

"Didn't look. Didn't call the cops either. I figured Mr. and Mrs. Goldman had had more than enough for one day."

Norris frowned. By reputation he was a "by-the-book" guy. If so, he had endured a lot of heartburn working for Jake Grafton, who rarely even looked at the book, much less went by it. That thought reminded me that Norris was now running the company, until such time as Grafton could get back to work.

He hovered over Mrs. Grafton a while, held her hand, looked into her eyes, then said his goodbyes. Told me to stop in and see him in the morning. I said, "Yes, sir," but I doubt if he heard it. He was already on his way out.

I watched him go. "Yeah," I said to Sarah, "he is indeed a possibility."

"I think that you know far too much," Sarah said, "and at this stage of the game, so do I."

Callie was watching our faces. "Be careful out there," she said.

I leaned over and kissed her on the cheek.

We had taken our second cups of coffee to the ICU waiting room and checked in again with the nurse, who just shook her head. We were sitting in the little room telling stories about Jake Grafton when the Graftons' daughter, Amy Carol, arrived. She and Callie went into a clinch.

A few minutes later Sarah and I left. In the doorway of the hospital, Sarah asked, "Your place or mine?"

"Neither. A hotel tonight, I think. We'll put it on the company credit card."

She followed me out of the parking lot; we found a hotel near the beltway. The bar was still open, so we stopped in there for a drink before we went up to our room. I was drinking bourbon and she was sipping wine when she said, "I wasn't kidding. Norris is a real possibility."

"I know that. I've been thinking about him."

"If it is Norris, he'll want us off the case as soon as possible, before we decide it might be him."

"That's why we're in a hotel," I said.

"You think he might send someone after us?"

"The Silvas were looking for an assassin to kill Korjev. Then there was the telephone trail from the ag pilot to Harlan Westfall. Someone sent that ag pilot to the safe house in Utah. If organized crime was involved, we will probably never be able to make the connections to prove them in court. Yet I keep coming back to the fact that only a handful of company employees knew that Yegan Korjev was at the safe house in Utah. That was the critical piece of information."

I thought about it some more. "Last night, Abe Goldman confessed on national television. Somebody's getting really worried, or a bunch of somebodies are. This morning, Jake Grafton was shot. It's got to be cause and effect. Anything is possible."

Up in the room Sarah and I began listing possibilities. Jack Norris was at the head of the list, just above Max Hurley and Anastasia Roberts, who knew everything there was to know about the company, its activities and its secrets. There was the department head in charge of safe houses, Albert "Kid" Baisi. Of course Baisi's staffers knew all about the safe house or ranch since they had helped design, supervise, and fund the construction, but they probably didn't know that Korjev was being sent there. After all, the company ran a bunch of safe houses all over the planet; the number was constantly changing.

Norris, Hurley, Roberts, Baisi... who else? Well, Sarah and me, of course, and Armanti Hall and Doc Gordon, plus the staff of the ranch, Mac Kelly, and the doctor and nurse. The maids, doubtful. The cowboys? Naw. I also scratched Sarah and myself from the list.

"Nanya Friend," Sarah suggested. Of course. She was the head of the Russian department, spoke the language, and had a PhD in Russian studies from... I forget. I didn't know Nanya well, but I liked her... at a distance. Some people think that because women are plumbed for kids they have better personalities and more scruples than men, but I am not one of them. I have found women just as petty, conniving, brilliant, mean, and vengeful as men.

I knew Max Hurley and Anastasia Roberts well. We had worked in the same office for years. Traitors?—I didn't believe it. Hall or Gordon? Man, we had been shot at together. And calling an ag plane down on your own head spraying jet fuel? You would have to show me. Kelley, the doctor, or nurse? Possible, but not probable.

In truth, too many people at the company knew about the safe house and Korjev... we were only guessing. The leaker might be someone we didn't even know.

But if it was someone we did know, we were left with Kid Baisi, Nanya Friend, and Jack Norris. I tried to envision Friend huddled over a rifle ready to murder her boss, and found it difficult. I also couldn't see her haggling over the job with a thug. Baisi was an okay guy as far as I knew—yet certainly cold-blooded enough to give someone the chop, if he had a reason.

My thoughts congealed on Jack Norris. I confess, I had never liked him. I sorta hoped it was him. I wondered if he did his own shooting or had it done for him.

The next morning we were up at the crack of dawn, checked out of the hotel, and took Sarah's car to her place. It was a typical apartment house, with a parking lot that wrapped around the thing, plus trees and other apartment houses sprawled all over. The best place for a sniper was on a nearby roof, so I cruised slowly into the lot, looking.

If there was a sniper, he had either been up all night waiting for Sarah and me, or he was a really early bird, out to get two worms. Grafton was predictable; we certainly weren't.

I parked right under the overhang in front of the main entrance in the No Parking Fire Zone. Sarah used her code on the door and we went inside.

She fired up her computer for me, then headed for the shower. I logged onto Facebook. Typed in Kid Baisi. The jerk wasn't on Facebook! Where were you during the tech revolution, Daddy?

My telephone dinged. I had a text message... from Callie Grafton. Her husband was awake in the ICU. I wrote back, thanking her for the information.

Nanya Friend was on Facebook. She was a grandmother, and a proud one. Lots of photos of her grandbabies... and son and daughter. She also had a dog that got photographed a lot. No man in her life that I could see. Wrong. A husband named Rod. Athletic, fit, with a good grin.

Jack Norris was also on Facebook. He had a wife named Nora... Nora Norris. Ugh. Two kids... no wait, three. They lived someplace rural, with a lawn and barn and tractor and... horses. I wondered which of them had the money. Career civil servants don't earn that kind of bucks. I got into the old photos of Jack. He was a diligent Facebooker. No doubt Zuckerberg knew everything there was to know about him and had sold the information to every ad company on the planet.

And there it was, the photo that froze me. Jack posing with a dead deer, one whose demise he had presumably just caused. He wore a camo outfit and a big grin, and held a scoped bolt-action rifle in his hands.

I looked up Nora Norris. Photos of her on horses, with dogs, with the kids, at a birthday party... Maybe that was New Year's.

That rifle...

Senator Harlan Westfall had a breakfast meeting at the Willard Hotel with Cheney G. Kopp, who was the chairman of the board of Life Network, which was an ally of liberal causes across the spectrum. After they ordered, they discussed the news and issues of the day, from Russian funny money to Abe Goldman's confession to the possible impeachment of Vaughn Conyers.

Westfall had his phone on the tablecloth beside his coffee cup. He checked the battery charge again. The damn battery seemed to be losing juice quickly these days. The phone probably needed a new battery, he thought. He abandoned the phone and captured Kopp's eyes. "Cheney, I thought you and I had an understanding."

Kopp raised an eyebrow and took another sip of the superb coffee. "About what?"

"That your people were going to ignore news stories that made us look bad." The 'us' that Westfall was referring to were, of course, the liberals.

"We do, to the extent we can."

"Last night and this morning the news people on Life are beating the hell out of that Goldman story. Can't they lighten up on that a little?"

"Harlan, we're in the advertising business. We sell ads to corporate America to run on our shows. They look at our demographics and decide if the people they will reach are worth the cost of the ads. News shows are a different animal than talk shows, which have the personalities people like to follow, the talent. If a story is being covered nationwide as news, then we must give it some air time. Have to, to maintain our credibility and those demographics the advertisers want. If our audience just up and changes the channel on us, we're screwed. You see that?"

The senator said, "It's the amount of coverage and emphasis on each story that I am interested in."

"That's left up to the producer of each show. They try to juggle the day's events, keeping our liberal slant yet not losing the audience. Actually, they try to expand it if possible. The size of the audience determines their paycheck."

"Maybe they need more guidance. This Russian money thing, the upcoming impeachment..."

Their breakfasts came, so they stopped talking while the food was served and their coffee cups refilled from a thermos pot on the table.

When they were again alone, Cheney Kopp said, "Harland, I just run the damn company. I can't and don't call the news show producers and tell them what to run, how long to make the segments, and I certainly don't edit the anchors' remarks. There aren't that many hours in the day."

"I am not asking you to do that, Cheney. I just want you to understand that we have reached a critical moment in the life of our country. What people think about the events of the next few weeks that will determine our future will be, in some small part, determined by how television handles the news. I want you, your producers and news anchors to keep that firmly in mind."

The two men ate breakfast while discussing the nuances of television news. Then Kopp asked a question that had been on his mind for months. "Harland, you, Judy Mucci, Franky Konchina, Cynthia Hinton, Barry Soetoro, all you heavy-hitter Democrats used to be for clamping down on illegal immigration. We've got days of footage of speeches you people made assuring the voters you were against illegal immigration, railing against the parasites from south of the border who soak up welfare, food stamps, and Medicaid money. Then you changed. All of you, like flipping a switch. Now you're not only against controlling it, you're for it. What happened?"

Harland Westfall frowned. He wouldn't discuss this subject unless it were with a liberal Democrat he trusted completely. He didn't know if he would put Cheney Kopp in that category, but he needed the man. Trust him and find out. If Kopp ever quoted Westfall, the senator could deny the conversation ever took place.

"What happened," Westfall said, "was a political earthquake. Vaughn Conyers won the 2016 election. He captured the white middle class. *Captured* is the wrong word. He *seized* it. Baldly put, the future of the Democratic party is with blacks and Hispanics. We need every Hispanic vote we can get, and we need to expand the franchise to get them, as California is doing. Citizens, illegals, felons, welfare people, we need them all. If we don't get them, you've seen the last Democrat in the White House."

"That's why you were against the wall?"

"That's it. It would cut illegal immigration to a trickle, and we can't live with that."

Cheney Kopp pushed his plate back. He stared at Westfall from under his bushy eyebrows. "What if you lose the blacks and Hispanics? Blexit? What if they start voting Republican?"

Westfall frowned again. "That would be disaster. We can't let that happen. We'll do anything we have to do to prevent it. A black voting for a Republican is betraying his race. Ditto the Latinos. That's the message we must get across. That's the message *we need your help* getting across."

"Harlan, I want you to understand exactly where Life is coming from. My personal politics don't enter into it. I get paid to run a business and I do it to the very best of my ability. We want young, hip, educated audiences who spend every dime they can get their hands on. That's the demographic the ad agencies pay the most for. As it happens, those young, hip, educated people are liberal... but if that ever changes, Life will also change. Life Network is a for-profit business."

"It will never change," Harlan Westfall said, a pronouncement he certainly hoped was true.

"Change is the one constant," Kopp said, reaching for his wallet to pay the tab. "Once upon a time, the Democratic Party was the fervent defender of human slavery in America. All those nasty Confederates were Democrats."

"Young educated people won't change their political outlook in our lifetime," Westfall insisted. He wished he hadn't discussed immigration with Cheney Kopp.

The network mogul plopped his credit card down on top of the bill folder. He eyed the senator and said, "Young black people abandon the Democrats because the big cities, which the Democrats rule, are cesspools of hopelessness, welfare, and crime. Blacks are the victims, the road-kill, of one-party politics. If young white Americans abandon the Democrats, it will be because of illegal immigration. To the extent that you and Judy Mucci succeed in opening the borders to vast numbers of uneducated, unskilled people that these young, hip, educated white workers will have to pay more taxes to support—to that extent, you will have helped kill liberalism. Destroying your political opposition and making America into a one-party nation will lead to tyranny and eviscerate democracy."

Kopp handed the bill folder and his credit card to the waiter. "Liberalism did America a lot of good," he said. "Social Security, racial justice, human rights, clean air, clean water... If liberalism dies, I, for one, will cry at the funeral. Yet if the Democrats succeed in transforming America into a one-party state, I'll be out there with a rifle beside the Republicans manning the barricades."

# Chapter Twenty-One

Sarah and I each drove our own vehicles out to Langley, which was routine for us. Neither of us knew when we would be done for the day, and sitting around twiddling thumbs waiting for the other didn't make much sense. We parked side by side in the CIA lot.

As we walked for the door, I said to Sarah, "That phone that belonged to Paul Hockersmith, the ag pilot who wanted to be an assassin. We need everything you can get out of it as soon as you can."

"Do you think the same person tried to hire Korjev's murder, and perhaps Grafton?"

I stopped and stood with her watching the usual morning crowd heading for the entrance. "That's too big a leap. Let's concentrate on Korjev. The telephone trail leads to Senator Westfall, but one doubts if he had anything to fear from Korjev. The Silvas certainly did. And I just can't see Westfall getting into a conspiracy to murder anyone with those clowns on the telephone trail."

"He's evil enough," Sarah said. She had been reading his transcripts.

"Evil, but not stupid. I think Jesse Hughes probably talked to Hockersmith about drugs—he wanted to buy some. Hughes and Edwards, perhaps the same subject. We drop around and Kevin Edwards called Westfall, his senator, perhaps because he was scared and wanted some handholding. That's one possible explanation."

Sarah stood amid the cars thinking it over. "Paul Hockersmith smuggled drugs for a living. Whoever hired him knew that. They knew if the money was right Hockersmith was stupid enough to push everything out onto the come line. You think it's on the cell phone?"

"I am hoping it is. We need you to put names and addresses to Hockersmith's telephone numbers. One of them may be our man, the guy who convinced Hockersmith to try to permanently silence Korjev. It may be the same guy who decided Jake Grafton would be better off dead, or it may not."

"What's the case for thinking it might be the same person?"

"Whoever wanted Korjev dead knew where to find him, and that information had to come from inside the company. That same someone knew Jake Grafton was on the job and obviously feared him. There could be more than one someone, but it doesn't feel right: life doesn't work that way."

"I'll give that telephone a good look as soon as I can."

"Thanks."

We were admitted through the door and Sarah went her way while I went mine. My way led to the executive suite and the EA's office, where I shared a desk with a guy who had immigrated from Poland back when he was young and now spent his days poring over news from the Vatican and Warsaw. I don't know that it takes all kinds to make a world, but we certainly have all kinds.

About nine o'clock I went to Jack Norris' office and talked to his receptionist, gave her my name and said that last night the great one said he wanted to see me this morning. She said she'd call me. I wandered off for coffee, then stood around the pot with the other EAs talking about Jake Grafton.

At 9:35 I was admitted to Norris' office. "Tommy, I want you to write a report, everything you can remember about the interrogation of Yegan Korjev and the attempted assassination at the Utah ranch. Justice is making noises."

"Yes, sir. When do you want this report?"

"Everything you can remember. Tomorrow?"

"Got it," I said, and made my departure.

I stuck my hands in my pockets and kick-started the brain as I walked along. I wasn't stupid enough to actually believe Norris' BS... Justice didn't know diddlysquat about the interrogation of Korjev, the antics of Paul Hockersmith, nor that I potted him. Norris wanted me busy and out of the way. I wondered why.

I went down to Sarah's office in the basement, the boiler room with a dozen people monitoring telephone calls and eavesdropping, reading transcriptions, making spread sheets of telephone numbers. I was in there taking it in when I saw Sarah answer the telephone. She looked at me as she talked. It was a short conversation.

She came over to the door where I stood. "That was Norris. He wants me upstairs for a report on where we are."

"He's going to shut you down," I said.

She eyed me. I explained about my report.

"Why don't you and I blow this joint and go over to your house and get on the internet. We need to know a lot more about Norris, fast."

"Like what?"

"We need to find a connection between Norris and Paul Hockersmith, the Utah ag pilot, if there is one. Without that we can't prove anything."

"If it was Norris. It might be someone else."

"My gut says Norris."

"Let me get my purse."

"And Hockersmith's cell phone. Then go upstairs and get your marching orders. He'll figure we're busy for a day or two and leave us alone. I'll meet you by the Starbucks on the main floor."

When she came down, we got coffees, then walked straight out of the building. "You were right. He wanted me to stop the phone project and write a report."

We got in our vehicles and disappeared. We rendezvoused at the lock shop I co-owned just outside the district in Maryland. Willy "The Wire" Varner was drinking coffee, eating doughnuts, and reading the newspaper when we walked in. Willy is my co-owner. Actually, I put up the money for the shop and he does all the work. Every now and then he gives me a twenty as my share of the profits. If I eat at McDonald's or Chick-fil-A I can get two lunches out of that twenty.

Sarah sat down at the computer and logged on while Willy attacked me. "Says here Jake Grafton got hisself shot yesterday morning. How come I read about this in the paper and you haven't tol' me?"

"Man, I called everybody I know when it happened. Must have missed you."

"He dead or alive this morning?"

"Alive, barely."

"How's his wife takin' all this?" Truly, one of the reasons I like Willy is because he gets right to the real nub of things fast.

"We saw her at the hospital last night. She's one tough cookie, but she looked like road kill."

"I'll bet. When's he gonna retire?"

"I don't know. I'll ask him sometime."

"Ought to be soon or he ain't gonna collect a damn penny of his pension. Too many people don't like him." He waved the front page of the paper. The political news was grim. Willy instinctively understood one of the Washington truths—this town was about power, and the director of the CIA had it. When things were going well he had enemies. When things were going badly, such as now, he had more enemies, worse ones. Most of them didn't shoot at him, thank God, but if he got run over by a garbage truck they weren't going to cry at the funeral.

We batted things around a bit, then Willy went out to the van and took off to rekey the door locks for a woman who had thrown her spouse out of the house. I dug Hockersmith's cell phone from Sarah's purse and turned it on. It needed a password. "What's the password?" I asked Sarah, who had figured this out days ago.

"Six Zero One Nine Quebec. That was his airplane's registration number."

Even though Sarah was scary smart, she was dynamite in bed. I kid you not.

I typed the password in and... "It's only five digits. I need one more."

"Add a zero."

Voila!

Sure enough, Hockersmith had five calls from Jesse Hughes in the two days before I shot him down. I looked at the other telephone numbers, all from area code 801, which was the Salt Lake City area. Sarah had worked on them with the company database, and if she couldn't pull them up they were probably local numbers; bill collectors or telemarketers or even, God forbid, Hockersmith's wife.

I checked his contact list. I was hoping for at least a senator, or even a congressman, but just 801 area codes.

So who was Jesse Hughes?

Sarah and I talked. She got on the internet. Facebook bios are a great place to start, then Wikipedia. Then you can do a search of the guy's criminal history, real estate holdings, county tax records, and if you do this stuff at the graduate level, you can search data bases that you need a password or government access to view. And, of course, there are commercial services that say they can find anyone if you are willing to pay their fee.

Finally she said, "Hughes is a retired civil servant. Retired two years ago from the Justice Department."

"He's a lawyer?"

"No. He was an investigator. Whether civil or criminal or both, I don't know."

I saw a glimmer of light. "Check Jack Norris' bio on the company website. Didn't he spend a few years on a drug task force in Mexico?"

Mexican drugs were in the FBI's bailiwick, but now and then the politicians wanted every federal agency to send representatives to 'liaise.' CIA, Justice, Homeland, everybody.

Three minutes. "Yes, he did. Then a department head, now assistant director."

She made eye contact and shrugged. "It's possible."

"Possible, not probable."

"How are we going to find out?"

"Go see Jesse Hughes and ask. He lives in Ellicott City."

We locked up the shop and set forth in my pickup, which is a fine ride. We went around the beltway and up U.S. Route 29 to Ellicott City on the Patapsco River. It's an old town in the river gorge, probably because there was a mill there once upon a time before automobiles were revealed to our ancestors, before farms became "raw land." Now the flats above the river gorge are subdivisions of tract houses.

We parked across the street from Hughes' building and looked at the old wreck. Big trees laden with leaves cast the house and the little twisty two-lane street in shadow. Traffic was terrible, as usual.

"How are we going to do this?" Sarah asked.

"I've been thinking about that. Go in and scare the shit out of them, I suppose."

"Tommy, Jesse Hughes could go to prison for the rest of his natural life if he admits that he arranged a murder for Jack Norris. If he denies he knows Norris, what then?"

"Money. You know he did it for money. We're investigating the money."

"So he starts lying. His mother's older sister kicked the bucket." She pounded the dashboard. "We've got absolutely nothing to sting him with."

"Suggest something."

"Call him. Tell him Jack Norris has been arrested."

"He'll ask who I am."

"Norris told you to call to tell him to clear out. The FBI is after him. He'd better save himself."

She and I thought about it as cars and trucks whizzed by. "It might work," I admitted. "What's his number?"

She had that memorized too. If men didn't have that Y chromosome, women wouldn't need us at all.

I called the number. It rang and rang, then eventually the answering machine picked up. I hung up.

I tried again fifteen minutes later. Still no answer.

"Maybe they aren't home," I suggested.

"Let's go knock on the door," Sarah Houston said.

Well, why not?

I dug in the center console for the lock picking set, pocketed it, then we got out and I locked up the truck. When we got a break in traffic we jaywalked.

We hiked up to the third floor and knocked, but there was no answer. We knocked repeatedly.

Then I heard the dog yapping inside.

I got out the picks and got busy on the lock.

Took a little more than a minute, then the lock released. I opened the door and stepped inside.

The dog came running.

Jesse was lying on the floor in the main room, near the door. His lover was lying in the door to the kitchen. Both had been shot.

Sarah made a noise behind me. "Take the dog for a walk while I look around," I told her.

She picked the damned thing up and went out, pulling the door shut behind her.

I am certainly no expert, but I've seen a few corpses. These guys had been dead for some hours: at least three or four would be my guess. Putting the back of a wrist on an arm gave you a sense of how much they had cooled off, which was a lot. Both appeared to have been shot once in the chest, probably a heart shot, then shot again in the head in a *coup de grace* to make sure. Maybe early this morning.

I looked in the kitchen. Breakfast stuff still on the table... toast sticking up from the toaster... Coffee pot still on. A bowl of cereal with milk in it.

I took one last look. The heads were intact, so he had probably used a low-power bullet, perhaps 9mm, probably suppressed.

I stopped to examine the door. It had been locked when I opened it with the picks, so Hughes had opened it, the guy had come in, shot them both, then pulled the door shut behind him on the way out and it locked. I made sure the door would not lock behind me. Went down the stairs to the sidewalk. Sarah was standing there with the dog.

"It's peed," she said.

I took the pooch and carried it back upstairs, opened the door and put it in, then punched the button so the door would lock, pulled it shut and wiped the knob. Stood there trying to decide if I'd touched anything inside. Naw, I am not that stupid.

Went down, collected Sarah, and we walked back to the truck.

"They've been dead since this morning."

"Who did it?"

"Three guesses."

I handed Sarah my phone. "Dial Nine One One."

She did so and passed the thing to me. I squeaked off the address in Ellicott City in my best falsetto. "Better hurry," I added. "I think they're dead." Then I pushed the button to kill the thing. I started the truck, got into traffic, and headed for I-70.

Two miles along she said, "Pull over."

I did. She unfastened her seat belt, opened the door, leaned out, and puked. After a bit she spit a few more times, then sat up and took a deep breath. "Okay," she said as she pulled the door shut, "let's go."

★

Robert Levy, director of the FBI, was ushered into Senator Harlan Westfall's office. He found that Senator Franky Konchina and the Speaker of the House, Judy Mucci, were there. The aide who did the ushering closed the door behind the nation's chief law enforcement officer. He nodded at everyone, didn't bother shaking hands, and dropped into a seat on the couch.

Westfall skipped the social pleasantries. "Who shot Jake Grafton?"

"Damn if I know," Levy said. "We've got a dozen scientists working on that parking garage, and so far they have come up with zilch. Not even a booger that we can mine for DNA."

Konchina spoke up. "This morning's *Post* said that there are security cameras in that garage."

"Reporters," Levy said, sneering. "There ought to be a bounty on them. There is a security camera system, but someone cut the cable feed last Wednesday."

"Can't you check the last video and see who did it?"

"The video goes off-site to an office building where the eleven parking garages owned by that company are monitored. The recording system is a closed loop, so video is only retained for twenty-four hours, then recorded over. Eleven parking garages, samples of six cameras a garage, that's a lot of server memory."

"Why wasn't the camera system fixed?" the Speaker, Judy Mucci, asked.

Levy looked at the Speaker as if she were senile, which many people had long suspected was the case. "The ten-bucks-an-hour parking people aren't qualified to fix the system. They called the security company that installed the system, and they scheduled a repair tech out there a week from this coming Thursday."

"So you're fucked," Westfall said.

Levy was patient. "We are interviewing everyone who keeps a car in that garage, everyone we can find. The shooting took place at 7:30 on a workday morning, and someone must have seen the bastard. Given time and good police work, we'll find someone who did."

"Yesterday a Congressman accused me of doing the shooting," Westfall said.

Konchina said, "Harlan, you can't—"

"And the Conyers' impeachment bill," Westfall said. "A Republican congressman said yesterday that if it passes the Democrats are inviting civil war. And he, for one, is for it. He's got a list of Democrats he'd like to shoot."

"Why don't you arrest him?" Konchina asked Levy. "This country is awash in guns. These Republican racists own arsenals. If the damned crackers start shooting then the whole country will descend into anarchy. This place will look like Damascus."

Levy took his time answering. "Congressmen and senators can say anything they wish in their chambers or on the floor of their house. They can't be held criminally or civilly liable. Surely you know that?" Levy thought Konchina was another ditz, although he only said that in the sacred precincts of the executive suite of the Hoover building. This was more proof.

"These bastards are pouring gasoline on a raging fire," Westfall told the FBI director. "Surely something can be done. Something *must* be done!"

"If he carries a rifle into the Capitol Building, the federal police will arrest him." Levy smote the arm of the couch. "You people are just as bad," he roared. "You think you have a crisis that you can play to sweep into power. Toss out the president, tear up the Constitution, throw him out over some fucking made-up shit that is happening to half the people in this town. Fake Russian money! *Bull fucking shit*! You are *idiots*! This country is split right down the goddamn middle, and it will be tomorrow too."

He pointed a finger at Westfall. "I seem to recall reading that you got some of this Putin money." Now at the Speaker. "And you." The finger went to Konchina. "And you." The finger came down. "Wouldn't surprise me to find that *I* am a recipient of some funny Russian money. God, *I hope so*. I could sure as hell use a vacation and a new car. I'll call my bank when I get back to the office to see if the Russian tooth fairy remembered me."

Levy maneuvered himself upright, said, "Thanks for wasting my time," and marched out.

Sarah used her cell phone to get Jack Norris' address, then typed it into the map feature. It was a horse property, sure enough, west of Middleburg, with a separate garage, a barn, and a storage shed. Decent wooden fences behind the barn where four horses cropped grass. A blue Honda sports car stood in front of the house, which looked to be about eight or ten rooms. The thing was brick and had two chimneys.

Sarah kept busy with her phone. Two grown daughters and a grown son. One daughter was married and living in California, another was going through drug rehab for the third or fourth time, and the son was going to be a senior this fall at the University of Tennessee on an athletic scholarship.

"What's he athletic of?"

"Football."

"Where is he now?"

"I don't know."

"And the spouse?"

"The little wife..." Sarah murmured as she worked that phone. "Dental tech," she said after a moment.

We were well past the farm, if that is what they called it, and were at a crossroads festooned with stop signs in every direction. There was a real, genuine, honest-to-God country store on one corner. It was after two in the afternoon and we were hungry. I pulled in.

As we munched sandwiches, pickles and chips, and sucked down soft drinks in the cab of my ride, Sarah asked, "How sure are you that Norris is our guy?"

"That he shot Grafton and those two in Ellicott City?" I sipped some diet Sprite. "Just a gut feeling. No evidence at all. That little act this morning... He wanted me to drop whatever I was doing for Grafton and spin my wheels. Justice doesn't get reports from the CIA, for Pete's sake. I was appalled that he couldn't come up with a better excuse."

"If he had just shot two men an hour before," Sarah suggested, "maybe he wasn't thinking clearly yet."

I reached for a pickle. It was crunchy. "That house back there. Jack and Nora did really well swinging that place on the salaries of a dental tech and company spook. How long have they owned it?"

Sarah licked her fingers and picked up her phone. "That I can check."

Two minutes later she said, "They bought it seven years ago. The tax assessment is for fifty-five acres, eight and a half million."

I got the last bite of my sandwich down, then said, "About the time he was knocking around Mexico."

"Uh-huh," she said. "About then."

"You want another potato chip?"

"You finish them."

"Maybe one of them inherited money."

"Maybe so..."

She called Callie Grafton. Jake was awake now and she had seen him for five minutes this morning and at noon. She was on her way home for a nap. The doctor was hopeful.

# Chapter Twenty-Two

When we cruised by the Norris estate again the blue Honda was gone. I pulled into the drive and stopped in front of the house. "Let's see if anyone is home," I said.

We got out of the truck and I made sure my sport coat was covering my shoulder holster. We went up to the door and rang the bell. Could hear it dinging in the house.

There was a surveillance camera at each end of the porch. I suspected that the feed was accessible on Jack's and Nora's phones, if they took the time to look.

I rang the bell a couple more times, then we walked around the house. No one in the back yard, which had a little herb garden and some tomato plants. There was also a camera arranged to face the back door.

"What do you think?" Sarah asked.

"I'm wondering if that rifle I saw on Facebook is in the house."

"Want to look?"

"Yes."

I tried the back door, just in case. And sure enough, the knob turned in my hand. Unlocked. I held it open for Sarah.

We were in a mud room. Boots on a little shelf, sweaters and jackets on pegs. Three or four hats. We went on through into the kitchen, which was comfortably messy. They weren't ready for a *House Beautiful* photographer, but the place was cozy. Family dining around a kitchen table.

We strolled on, bedrooms, baths, a formal dining room, a family room with a huge television, and finally, a den, a family office with a computer. Sarah Houston sat down in front of it and made herself at home.

In the den was a gun cabinet with a glass door locked with a flimsy furniture lock. I looked. There was only one scoped bolt-action rifle in there, and it wore a wooden stock. Two shotguns and a little .22 single-shot. There was also an antique muzzle-loader that was missing most of its finish, one perfect for civil war re-enactments.

I went back to the bedrooms and looked under the beds and in the closets. No more long guns. The attic was accessed by a covered hatch in a hall ceiling, and I looked around for a chair or ladder. Nothing. They had painted the hatch cover and the ceiling at the same time, and the paint didn't look chipped or flaked.

I headed for the basement. No gun safe. No guns.

Out to the barn. I was working quickly now, because I didn't want Mrs. Norris to come busting in on our party. The loft had some loose hay on the floor, and there was no way to be sure what was under it unless I moved all of it with a hay fork. I looked the hay over and decided it looked undisturbed. There were square bales of it stacked against one wall. He could have a rifle wedged behind one, but which one?

The shed had a farm tractor, a lawn tractor, spray equipment, an ATV... basically an excellent sampling of stuff from Tractor Supply, "the stuff you need out here." But no guns.

If he didn't have another rifle in his car or truck, that one in the den was it. I trooped back to the den and checked the security cameras. There was one in here, but not in the kitchen. I used my picks on the gun cabinet lock and pulled out the rifle. Looked through the scope out the window at a distant tree. Caliber was .270 Winchester.

Then I took it into the kitchen. The action was empty. I popped out the bolt and looked through the barrel. With modern powders one shot isn't going to get a barrel very dirty. The few crumbs I saw could have been dust. I smelled the muzzle. Well, maybe.

Then I took the caps off the scope adjustment turrets. Used a quarter in my pocket to rotate the vertical adjustment upward to the stop, and the sideways adjustment all the way to the right. Put the caps back on, inserted the bolt, wiped the gun with my handkerchief, and put the gun back in the gun cabinet.

Sarah was still on the computer. "Any luck?" I asked.

"The main password is right here on the keyboard in ink. I think his wife uses the computer too. She's got a lot of emails on here. Then he has some secret files that are double-password protected, and I can't get into those."

"Turn it off. Let's get out of here."

We went outside the way we came in, through the back door. Went around and climbed in the truck. "Let's explore," I said. Sarah opened a gate, I drove through, and she closed it behind me while I put the truck in four-wheel drive. Off through the pasture we went, up a wooded hill right to the top, then along it. I found a big rock on the ridge and parked behind it.

I opened the rear door of the cab and lifted the seat. There was an old blanket rolled up in there. I unrolled it and got out my old Winchester Model 94. There was a box of shells there, caliber .30-30, and I loaded it. Put the rest of the shells in my pocket. Threw the sports coat in the back seat.

"Let's climb up on top of the rock."

"What's your plan?"

"Jack Norris knows we're here—those security cameras. If he's innocent, he calls the police. If he's a killer, he doesn't want us talking to the cops because he isn't sure what we know. That's the way I figure it."

"Okay."

"That rifle in the gun cabinet may not have been the one he used to pot Grafton, but perhaps it is. He had to get to work quickly yesterday morning after he made that shot, if he did, and he was at work all day. Then this morning he did Jesse Hughes and friend—if he threw a rifle away he was pressed for time to get to a place where it would never be recovered, like a big river. If he has another rifle in the trunk of his car we have problems. I'm hoping there's only the one."

"I hope so too," Sarah said with conviction.

"With only two shotguns and a .22, this guy isn't a gun collector," I added, arguing the case, trying to convince myself.

"If he's guilty, he's going to try to kill us," she said.

"Yep," I agreed. "He's got no other choice."

General Leighton Freidenrich was Chairman of the Joint Chiefs of Staff. An Army general, he considered it part of his duty, an unenjoyable part, to talk to politicians. The fact that he was good at stroking huge, fragile egos was one reason—some said the only reason—he was selected as chairman.

This afternoon he was making the rounds in the senate office building trying to drum up support for the next military appropriation bill. Although the service chiefs were tasked with the job by the Department of Defense, the senators always wanted to personally hear the chairman's take on the issues, which meant they wanted his opinion on how to divide up the largess since he was supposed to be above the parochial scrum by each branch "as they rooted at the trough," according to Senator Westfall, in whose office Freidenrich now sat.

The general didn't personally like Westfall, whom he thought a bombastic ideologue, but you would have never known it from watching his face and demeanor. There are a lot of people to like, Freidenrich once told his wife, although not many inside the beltway. As Harry Truman once said, if you want a friend in Washington, get a dog.

"Senator," the general said, "you know we military men are all gentlemen by acts of Congress, and we don't root. We grab." He said that with a smile and Westfall chuckled.

Then the senator lowered his voice. "General, there has been some talk on the floor of Congress about a civil war if the president is impeached. I know we are speculating about an event that may never happen, but what is the chiefs' mood about that possibility?"

The smile disappeared from the soldier's face. "We haven't discussed that, sir. I am at a loss about what to say."

Westfall looked uncomfortable, as if he hated to be even discussing this topic. "But what is your personal feeling on this matter, general?"

"Sir, I serve my country. I obey orders and I obey the law."

Westfall wanted more. "You see the problem. If the senate votes to remove the president and an armed insurrection takes place, perhaps right here in Washington, what will be the military's role?"

General Freidenrich wondered if Westfall was taping this conversation, which was improper, he thought.

"Senator, my answer must be that the uniformed services will obey the law and obey lawful orders from their superiors. From George Washington to the present day, that's been the case. This *is* America!"

No fool, Westfall saw that he wasn't going to get any more out of this general. He changed the subject to the Navy's request for another aircraft carrier.

From the top of the rock we could see the road, house, and barn. The horses were still eating grass. In one end and out the other. Somehow it was comforting to think of Jack Norris in the barn shoveling horse shit at least once a day.

It was just a few minutes after four o'clock. The summer sun was still high in the sky. I gave the pistol to Sarah and set out with the rifle to check out the ridge. I certainly didn't want Norris surprising us from behind. He knew the terrain well, I assumed, as well as all the neighbors.

I also assumed he was busy as blazes at Langley, and couldn't, or wouldn't get here before six, at the earliest.

That's the problem with ambushes. They rested on a shaky pile of assumptions, and any one could be wrong. Life is like that, I suppose.

The ridge was a long one that ran off both ends of the property, wooded, brushy. In some places, the summer brush was so thick you couldn't see ten feet. I jumped a deer that left in a pounding hurry—I caught a glimpse of a white tail going away. It took a moment for my heart to slow down after that surprise. Heard some squirrels in the leaves, saw a couple in the trees.

Why was I wasting my life in the CIA?

I worked my way along the back fence, which was on the west side of the ridge, and came back along the ridge toward the big rock. Sarah was sitting on the rock watching the house. I made some noise to be sure she heard me coming along.

When I got to the foot of the rock I asked, "Are we still alone?"

"Yes."

"After this, if we don't go to jail, I was thinking about you and me in Idaho," I told her. "Find a real job, buy a cabin, settle in."

"I thought you were interested in a post-spook career in burglary."

"I'm rethinking that."

It was six o'clock and I was rubbing my hands over the old lever-action Winchester when the fact that something was wrong finally soaked into my pea-sized brain. I looked at the rifle, really looked. The rear-sight elevation wedge was gone!

The main sight housing was in a dovetail groove in the barrel, and the actual sight was on a flexible steel spring that was held in position by a wedge with notches. The wedge was gone, so the rear sight was lying flat on the barrel.

Oh, man. Without that wedge, the bullet would go low, very low, probably right into the dirt a hundred feet from me. I seemed to recall that I had the wedge set on the second notch, which put the bullet three inches high at a hundred yards, but it had been three or four years since I shot this thing.

Maybe I should shoot it right now and see where the bullet goes.

Even as that thought crossed my small mind, a car pulled up in front of the Norris house. Jack Norris climbed out. At least, I thought it was him, but at four hundred or so yards, I couldn't be sure.

I went over to Sarah and showed her the sight. "We're in trouble," I said.

"You've been in trouble since you got out of diapers," she shot back.

"Get over there behind a tree and stay there," I told her. "I'm going to have to get this guy to come up here. Maybe we can do something."

"Like die," she said.

Women are such pessimists. At least she did trot over to a tree and got behind it, just to the south of the big rock.

I hunkered down behind a bush and kept an eye on the guy in the yard. He went into the house. Must be Norris or the guy who was servicing his wife.

Three minutes later he came out with the scoped rifle. Stood looking around. Walked toward the gate looking at the ground. No doubt my pickup tracks were plain, right through the gate and out across the pasture toward the ridge.

He thought so too. He stood there looking up toward the ridge. Rested the rifle on the gate and used the scope to look. I eased down out of sight.

I wondered if the wedge for the rear sight was in the blanket in the truck. I slipped over, keeping low, and opened the rear door. Got busy rummaging in the blanket on the rear seat, then eased the seat up and looked underneath. Didn't see the damn wedge, which was about the thickness of a dime and an inch long.

Well, I was just going to have to pretend it was there. Fake it. I threw the rifle to my shoulder and pointed it where it felt right. Ah me... The sights of his rifle were screwed up and he didn't know it. Mine were screwed up and I did know.

I got down on my belly and crawled back to my bush. Looked for Norris and didn't see him.

Where...?

There he was, getting an ATV from the shed. I listened and heard the murmur of the engine, almost inaudible at this distance. He straddled the thing, held his rifle with his left hand, and used his right to steer and feed gas. When he got to the gate he opened it. One of the horses thought this would be a good time to check out the grass in the front lawn. Norris shooed it back, moved the ATV into the pasture, and closed the gate.

I was proud of him for remembering to close the gate. *After you murder Sarah and me, you don't want to be chasing horses all over the county.*

He started the ATV up the hill, along the tracks of the pickup.

My cell phone buzzed. Who...?

It was Jake Grafton. I answered it.

"Tommy..." His voice was weak. "Where are you?"

"Out at Jack Norris' place. I think the bastard shot you. He's chasing Sarah and me with a rifle as we speak. Call you back later." I broke the connection and turned the phone completely off, so it wouldn't ring when I was getting ready to pot Norris, or he was getting ready to pot me, as the case might be.

Vaughn Conyers and Callie Grafton were sitting beside Jake Grafton's bed. "He says that Jack Norris shot me, and he's chasing them with a rifle right now."

The president frowned. "Shouldn't we...?"

"If Jack Norris is after Tommy Carmellini, he's going to be dead pretty quick," the admiral whispered.

"Do you think Norris shot you?"

"I don't know what to think," Grafton said, and closed his eyes. He was amazed at how little energy he had. He just wanted to sleep, and fought against it.

"When Tommy gets back, I'll call you," he told the president. "Thanks for coming."

Conyers stood, shook Callie's hand, and left.

She leaned over and kissed her husband. "Get well, husband of mine. We've got a lot of living left to do."

"Amen to that," he whispered, and went promptly to sleep.

There Jack Norris came, riding slowly up the hill toward the tree line. Obviously he didn't think I had a rifle or he wouldn't be doing that.

The thought was in my mind that I wanted him to shoot first. If he shot first, then I could claim self-defense. Really, it was stupid, but that's how my mind was working just then. Maybe I was still in shock from learning that my rifle had no rear sight. Some days it doesn't pay to get out of bed.

Then the thought crossed my devious little mind that perhaps he had a pal coming up the ridge from the other side. I crawled away and went over to a tree on the downslope of the western side and stood listening. All I could hear was that damn ATV burbling along.

Well, if Norris had a pal, he was going to get a free shot. I could only look in one direction at a time. I got low and crawled the last twenty feet to my bush beside the big rock.

He was only a hundred or so yards away.

Screw the first shot. I poked the old Winchester out around the roots and put the front sight on the ATV. With no rear sight, this was very iffy. I held the rifle tightly, cocked the hammer, and squeezed the trigger.

The report surprised me. It surprised the hell out of Jack Norris. He bailed off that ATV like the Luftwaffe was after him and sprawled out in the dirt, pointed more or less my way.

I worked the lever and lay on my back a bit, wondering where that bullet went.

After about a minute I turned over and peeked around the base of the bush. He was crawling my way. Still about a hundred yards out. The ATV was crawling off without him. He ignored it—he had other problems.

I ooched backwards, he saw something moving, and shot at it. I heard the bullet whiz by to my left.

I dove behind the big rock, climbed a little until I saw him. He saw me at the same time. I managed to get off the first shot, then I pushed myself backwards out of sight. Another bullet whizzed by. Damn things were supersonic, so there was that little sonic crack.

"Going to kill you, Carmellini," he shouted.

I didn't need to waste air on a reply. I ran along the ridge for twenty yards or so, found a nice tree that gave me a view of where he lay, and poked the Winchester out. I tried to guess if the bullets were going high or low.

Low, I decided. I lowered the rear of the rifle a smidgen and waited.

Saw his head bob up for a moment, then it was gone.

The next time, I told myself.

There! I fired.

Saw the dirt fly up on the rise between him and me. Needed a bit more front sight elevation.

Bang. A bullet slammed into the tree beside me, maybe three feet over my head. I wondered if Norris knew how badly he was missing. I hoped not. I worked the lever, chambered another round. Then I dug into my pocket and shoved two shells into the magazine.

That done, I boogied. Went down the ridge another fifty feet and eased my head around a tree, wondering where he had gone. Didn't see him.

I lay perfectly still, as if I were already a corpse. If he didn't see movement, he wouldn't know where I was. That was my thinking, if you can call it that. Truth was, I was scared. Really scared. This bastard wanted to kill me, and after he got it done he would try to kill Sarah.

Then I heard him, some distance away. I rolled over. I thought he was working around to my right, trying to keep his distance.

I carefully turned until I was pointed that way. Had the old .30-30 cocked and ready.

Time seemed to drag. I could hear squirrels playing and a jet running high. Somewhere, maybe a mile away, a car horn honking.

Then I saw him out of the corner of my eye. He was about fifty feet to my right, stepping around a tree with the rifle up. I was pointed the wrong way. I was dead.

"Hi." Sarah's voice.

He spun towards her, and the pistol in her hand went off. He was knocked backwards.

I scrambled up and ran toward him.

Sarah just walked up, holding the pistol in both hands.

"Goodbye, Mr. Norris," she said, and shot him four times as fast as she could pull the trigger.

I took another step closer and looked. He was extremely dead.

I took the pistol from her hand and put it in my shoulder holster.

"Let's go call the law," I said, put my arm around her shoulders and steered her toward the truck. We left Jack Norris and his .270 lying there in the leaves.

# Chapter Twenty-Three

Senator Harlan Westfall got a ride to New York from Michael Hunt. He met the financier, son of the late Anton Hunt, in the private jet terminal at Reagan National Airport. They walked across the ramp together and went up the stairs into Hunt's Gulfstream. The copilot followed them up the ladder and toggled the switch to raise it, sealing the plane, while the petite flight attendant seated the two gentlemen in the cabin. They were the only passengers.

"Do you have a charger I could use for my phone?" Senator Westfall asked the flight attendant. "Can't keep the battery charged up," he explained to his host.

Yes, indeed, the lady had a charger and plugged it in to the senator's armrest. He plugged in the cell phone. She also took their orders for drinks, and as they taxied for take-off, she brought each man a tumbler of twenty-five-year-old single-malt Scotch.

"Really appreciate the ride, Michael," the senator said.

"Glad I could do it," Michael Hunt said. He was no spring chicken, a man in his sixties, but he had inherited the political proclivities of his father as well as his physical characteristics. Like Anton, who fell off an office building in New York just last year, Michael was dedicated to the new world order, a world without borders, and was willing to use his pocketbook to get what he wanted, regardless of what other people thought or wanted.

"You see how it's going," Westfall said as the plane took the runway and accelerated for takeoff. "Your father's plan is working. Russian money has had a corrosive effect on our enemies. It's really amazing."

Hunt nodded. "Dad would have been shocked at how the Russians also used it on our friends," he said. "They are truly perfidious bastards."

Westfall always enjoyed the way these executive jets maneuvered so effortlessly. The late evening sun was still above the horizon, firing the haze so badly that the city was almost invisible as the little jet climbed for altitude.

"We screwed the Republicans and the Russians screwed us," Westfall said. "Perhaps it was inevitable. Yet we can still make something out of this mess. Conyers is in deep and serious trouble. Judy Mucci thinks the House will impeach him, and God willing, the Senate will fry him. It'll be close, but I think it can be done."

They discussed personalities as the jet leveled off at altitude and flew northeast: which senators would vote to remove Conyers from office and which ones wouldn't. It was actually a short flight, so one drink was about all the flight attendant ever managed to serve before the jet began its descent into Teterboro. They discussed ways to pressure recalcitrant senators.

"We've got to get this done," Westfall said, and Michael Hunt agreed. It was dark when the plane parked at the Jet Center in Teterboro and Hunt and Westfall transferred to a helicopter for the ride across the Hudson to Manhattan. A million lights below them, the city spread out in all its glory. The view was sublime.

It was nearly eleven o'clock when the county sheriff and FBI agents told Sarah Houston and me that we could go home. They were reluctant to let us go, but the 9mm pistol Jack Norris had on him was the clincher, that and the silencer in his trouser pocket. The law waited until the ballistics report came in on the pistol, which was one Norris had purchased several years ago. It had indeed fired the bullets that killed Jesse Hughes and Joe Leschetizky.

We drove back to Sarah's place in my pickup. The Model 94 .30-30 was wrapped up in my blanket and back under the rear seat. Since I hadn't managed to shoot anyone with the rifle, the law enforcers let me keep it, and when I was wrapping it up, the wedge for the rear sight fell out of the blanket. They kept the 9mm Beretta, however, which was government-issue. I'd have to fill out a report for the company, but as long as Grafton didn't croak on me, I doubted if I would have to pay for it.

As we rode along Sarah checked in with Callie Grafton. The admiral was awake, so Sarah gave Callie a summary of our day to pass along. "There is no doubt, Mrs. Grafton. Jack Norris shot your husband."

I thought Sarah overstated the case. Unless they found the intact bullet that had passed through Grafton's body, there was no way to be absolutely certain Norris' .270 was the guilty gun. Still, it probably was and the law dogs all knew it. I wasn't going to keep looking.

They had kept us separate from Nora Norris, who came home about seven and found the law there with a flock of scientists. Later, an ambulance crew removed her husband's body. The Norris son, the football player, came home about nine and didn't say much, the sheriff said. I didn't see him either, but I felt sorry for him. How would you like to come home after a movie and find your dad had murdered two people, tried to kill several others, and now was dead?

Sarah and I were famished, so we dropped in to a late-night bar I knew about and had drinks and dinner while listening to jazz. She said to me, "I'll expect that report for Justice on my desk tomorrow." We had a chuckle about that. Then she wanted to know if I were really serious about Idaho.

"Yes. Very soon."

We talked and talked about Idaho. The music was Dave Brubeck, Kenny G., and Thelonious Monk. Yeah.

When we saw Jake Grafton, he had IVs in each arm, an oxygen cannula taped to his nose, a catheter in his dick, and drains in the surgical incisions. His wife hadn't yet come to the hospital that morning, which was just as well. "She needs the sleep," Grafton whispered. He was wired to a computer which sat beside the bed and displayed all his vital signs on a monitor. It was mesmerizing watching his heart beat, his blood pressure, oxygen saturation level, and whatever else they had. Grafton saw me looking at the thing and whispered, "I like to watch it. When the squiggles stop I'm dead."

"You'll be the first to know," I agreed.

We were telling him about the shoot-out with Jack Norris when a doctor and nurse came in. Two orderlies were right behind. They fussed over him, rearranged him in the bed, checked the catheter, examined the IVs, asked how he was doing, and told us not to stay very long.

I followed the doctor into the hallway. One of the company's covert operators was sitting in a chair beside the door, a guy named Harry Franklin. I knew Harry fairly well from adventures we shared in the Middle East. He was armed and competent.

I followed the doctor to the nurse's station and said, "I'm one of Admiral Grafton's executive assistants, Doctor."

The doctor made an instant decision to tell me everything. "He should have died right there on that sidewalk where he was shot. Massive trauma, massive blood loss, shock, call it what you will. It's a miracle. He's lost part of a lung, yet I feel an incredible optimism. I think he's actually going to survive and make an excellent recovery."

"When?"

"It's going to take time. And he'll never get back to where he was before he was shot. Maybe a seventy or eighty percent recovery. But he'll be back doing normal things, walking, driving, working, making decisions. And that will be flat miraculous. Man, they come in here in all kinds of conditions, and Mr. Grafton is about the worst I've seen to actually survive surgery and start back. When I first saw him I thought he'd die on the table."

"Thank you, Doctor."

"Don't stay too long. He will tire very quickly; rest is the best medicine."

I went back into the room. The medical personnel were gone and Sarah Houston was bent over the bed listening to Jake Grafton whisper. She kept mumbling, "Yes."

He saw me, tried a smile, then Sarah grasped my arm and we left the room. Mrs. Grafton had texted Sarah that she was on her way, but we didn't wait for her. "The boss wants Norris' home computer," she told me, and we headed for the parking lot.

When we whipped into the entrance to Norris' drive, we found saw four cars there, one of which was the football player's blue sports car. None of the others looked official.

"Think we should wait?" Sarah asked.

"If we do then the FBI will get around to asking for the thing, if they haven't already."

"Mrs. Norris and the son haven't seen us, have they?"

"No, but they probably heard our names." I wasn't hopeful.

Thank heavens I wore a tie this morning. I checked that it was on straight, Sarah made sure she was properly put together, and we got out of her little BMW and climbed to the porch.

The kid answered the bell. He was a muscled-up, athletic specimen who could have played linebacker in better days. Today he looked as if he had been in a serious car wreck, and I didn't blame him. I wondered about Jack Norris' brains, if he had really had any.

Before we could say anything, the kid opened the door and let us in. "Mom's in the kitchen," he said, and beat it.

So we went that way.

It was easy to see which one was Nora Norris. She was in even worse shape than her son. Four women friends were gathered around the middle island, and they were all talking softly among themselves.

Sarah and I waited until Mrs. Norris noticed us, then Sarah went over, offered a hand and condolences. I could see them whispering but couldn't hear what was being said.

In a moment, Mrs. Norris led Sarah toward the den. I followed. The desktop computer was sitting right there, still.

"Can you remember the passwords, Mrs. Norris?" Sarah asked.

"The main one is on the keyboard. I can never remember passwords."

"We'll bring the computer back as soon as possible, Mrs. Norris. Would you like a receipt?"

She shook her head no and walked away, back toward the bedroom and master bath.

"Unplug the box and let's get out of here," Sarah whispered to me.

We did. Three minutes later we were in the car going down the drive.

"What did you tell her?" I asked my partner in crime.

"That the company had to check Mr. Norris' computer to see if it held any classified material. She bought it. I never even told her my name." She shuddered. "I feel slimy."

"Your explanation is almost true," I shot back, "which is a rarity in the spook business. And I wish to remind you that you'd feel a lot worse if you were shot up like Jake Grafton."

"I know."

"Or dead. But I don't suppose the dead feel anything."

The new acting director, Nanya Friend, called me into her office and asked for a complete briefing on what happened yesterday. I gave it to her straight. The color drained from her face as she listened.

But she was tough as Callie Grafton. With that behind her, she wanted a complete briefing on the Russian fake money fiasco. An hour later she was still asking questions.

"So where do you go from here?" she asked.

"After lunch I'm going back to the hospital to wait for Jake Grafton to wake up. Then I'm going to find out what Sarah Houston and I are going to do. If you want, you might come along."

Nanya Friend took a deep breath and stirred through the phone message chits on her desk with a finger. "I'd better try to keep this agency functioning," she said. "Give the director my warmest wishes."

"I will," I assured her, and headed for the hallway.

Senator Harland Westfall heard the news about Jack Norris, assistant director of the CIA, from his secret FBI friend, who had called him early that morning at home. That dumb bastard Norris apparently shot Jake Grafton, the director, his boss, in an attempt to derail the Russian money investigation. Then he killed the man who hired an ag pilot to kill Yegan Korjev. When Tommy Carmellini and a CIA female techie showed up at his house yesterday evening, he tried to kill them, and got killed himself. And by the way, Jake Grafton was alive and guarded around the clock. The doctor thought he would eventually make an excellent recovery.

On the positive side, the impeachment of Vaughn Conyers seemed to be progressing nicely. The liberal media was sounding the trumpets about Russian money invested in Conyers' projects. As one talk show host told her audience, "He's dirty and you know it. This is a good excuse to get rid of the bastard. Let's do it. No apologies, no second guessing, let's just do it."

One commentator noted that that rant sounded like a buildup to a lynching, but the liberal media ignored that crack.

Westfall, the Senate Minority Leader, and Judy Mucci, Speaker of the House, couldn't afford to ignore shots like that, which drew blood. Even if they successfully hung Conyers and left him twisting slowly in the wind, they had to govern afterwards; they had to get a Democrat elected to the White House in the next election, win back the Senate, and keep the House. It was a tall order and required strategic planning. The liberal mouths on television didn't help their cause. The problem was toning them down without bruising huge, extremely fragile egos.

One way was to phone them, so Mucci and Westfall divided the list and made the calls. "We appreciate your enthusiasm, but for God's sake, show a little restraint. Talk about due process and a fair hearing, then after we hang the son of a bitch you can laugh."

"We've got to impeach and convict him," Mucci told Westfall at a conference in his office. "Letting Conyers stand in front of cameras ranting to stadiums full of cheering people is a good way for us to lose the next election, and you know it. We've got to get him off that podium."

One of those huge, extremely fragile egos belonged to the "Squaw," as Westfall referred to the former Indian and college professor who was running for president in the next election. He didn't call her that to her face of course, or where anyone but his immediate staff could hear, but Westfall found her self-righteous speeches a bit much. Still, there was a chance, a very small chance, but a chance nonetheless, that she might actually get herself elected to the presidency, so Westfall always took her calls.

"Harlan, I've just been talking to Dr. Barber." Michael J. Barber was, as everyone knew, the president of the university where the squaw used to teach, the richest, most prestigious private university in the nation. "There's a damned bible college in Arkansas that claims they got some Russian money, so Barber has had his own staff checking. He says there are gifts to the endowment fund from at least four foundations in the last two years that look very suspicious. They total one hundred sixty-four million dollars."

"Why do they look suspicious?" Westfall asked.

"The staff was checking the W-9s they provided. It seems those foundations no longer exist, if they ever did. The IRS never heard of them."

Westfall didn't know what W-9s were, but assumed, correctly, that they were some obscure IRS form. To keep the squaw talking, he said, "Sorry to hear that."

"Harlan, I've been publicly hammering Conyers about accepting Russian money. Now it's *my* university! Do you see the spot this puts me in?"

"Liz, I don't know what to say. Our friends didn't do this!"

"Well, by God, somebody did. They did it to make me look like a fool and a hypocrite. If the university goes public with this—and Barber says the board insists upon it—I can't unsay all the things I've said. I can't denounce *the university*. The networks will have a field day at my expense." She blithely ignored the fact that she could have refused to comment until all the facts were known. The squaw and her allies didn't operate that way.

"I'm sorry—"

"*Sorry?* This whole scam has been a debacle from end to end, a damned nigger tar baby, and now we're stuck to it."

She hung up. Hung up on Harlan Westfall!

As he sat there with the dead receiver in his hand, Harlan Westfall said to himself, but not aloud, *You can't use the N-word, Liz.*

The news that the director of the CIA had been shot in an assassination attempt was front-page news for two whole days, then the story flared again when Jack Norris, the assistant director, was killed in a shoot-out. The police refused to speculate, but someone in the FBI did, so the press linked the stories together on the front pages for another two days. Then the political news and finger-pointing drove the CIA's troubles into the back pages.

A prominent nationally syndicated columnist said that it was obvious things weren't going well with the spooks in Langley, yet he had no facts. He wanted a congressional investigation, but Congress' attention was elsewhere. The progressives had decided this was the time to slay the dragon in the White House, a quest that made all other matters momentarily irrelevant.

That week the House of Representatives passed a Bill of Impeachment against the president, Vaughn Conyers. It was political theater that filled the television news channels, devoured train-loads of printer's ink, and gave radio talk-show hosts their best audiences in years. Advertisers were horrified to see how much they would have to pay to sell their products over the airwaves during this time of national crisis. There hadn't been a circus like this in America in a generation, not since Willy Hinton was impeached in the House for perjuring himself before a grand jury and obstructing justice (and every Democrat in the Senate had refused to convict him and remove him from office).

In the midst of all this, FBI special agent Dylan Litzenberg came home late one evening; he was working twelve hours a day supervising a task force of agents attempting to discover how Russian money had been routed and squeezed through the nation's banks, and where that money ended up.

His live-in girlfriend, Rhonda Sides, was also putting in twelve-hour days at CIA headquarters at Langley. They had a pact that neither would discuss their work, which was confidential or classified, at home. Sometimes this led to long silences, but usually they discussed the news of the day, gossip about mutual acquaintances, what they had heard from their families, and where they should go on their next vacation.

One evening, however, Rhonda decided she needed a wee bit of sympathy, and said, "I am so sick of listening to those intercepts."

Dylan Litzenberg raised his eyebrows but held his tongue. He was intensely curious but was afraid to ask a single question.

"There's just so much of it," Rhonda said as she poured herself a glass of wine. By God, after the day she had had, she deserved a glass of wine!

Litzenberg poured himself a vodka on the rocks and added a twist as he tried to decide how to squeeze a little more from Rhonda. He raised the glass and took a sip as he studied her face. She looked exhausted.

"Must be listening to a lot of people," he said casually.

Then Rhonda did what she had told herself she would never do, which was reveal company secrets to people without clearances. "They're listening to everyone who's anyone. Half of Washington. You'd be amazed. They're using cell phones and computers as listening devices, then the transcripts must be spot-checked." She snorted. She took her wine and headed for the bedroom to change out of her work clothes.

Dylan Litzenberg stood frozen. He had just glimpsed white-hot fire through a partially open furnace door, a door that had immediately closed. The director and assistant director of the CIA had been shot: the director was in critical condition and the assistant director was dead. The Congress was becoming a self-sustaining chain reaction.

He felt slightly nauseous. He had talked to Westfall on the phone just last week. Maybe the spooks already had him by the balls. What if the spooks were listening to Harlan Westfall? What if the spooks had overheard him leaking FBI information to Westfall? *What if they had it in a computer?*

Dylan Litzenberg was ambitious. He didn't want to spend the rest of his career in Waco or Boise doing background checks or chasing bank stick-up artists through trailer parks. He knew how one got promoted in the FBI: by making friends with powerful people, like the big weenies in the Hoover Building or in Congress… people like the Senate Minority Leader.

If the CIA were listening to anyone in Washington, they were certainly listening to Westfall, who was the driving force in the Senate behind the attempt to remove President Conyers.

One thing was certain: he had to warn Westfall, and telephoning him wouldn't get it done. Nor texting. Nor emails. No, he was going to have to deliver a written note.

While Rhonda was in the shower he sat down to write it. Litzenberg was so nervous his hands shook. He took a healthy swig of vodka and began.

At CIA headquarters in Langley, Sarah Houston and her colleagues sorted through hundreds of transcripts of cell phone and computer-captured conversations. The more interesting ones were set aside, the audio put on a master thumb drive and checked against the written transcript.

Sarah gave Jack Norris' home computer to her brightest protégé to crack. Sarah just didn't have the time.

The Bill of Impeachment passed the House of Representatives on a Friday, and on Monday, Jake Grafton was moved from the ICU to a regular hospital room, a single. He sat up in bed with a box of conversation transcripts and read them when he felt like it. Callie helped him sort them, then they both read the piles.

On Tuesday Harlan Westfall went dark. Sarah didn't find out about it until late that evening, when she told me. "Westfall's stopped using his cell phone. Doesn't use his office or home landline, and his computer is disconnected from his office Wifi. In fact, I think it's unplugged."

"He's wise to what's going on," I said.

"He was worried about his cell phone battery life," she remarked, "but he's shut off everything. There's a leak somewhere."

"Here."

"Probably." She was gloomy. The fact that the massive eavesdropping campaign against Americans was illegal meant that the more people who knew about it, the more difficult the secret was to keep. She had pointed that out repeatedly to Jake Grafton, who had used the capability sparingly and only as necessary, usually overseas. Never like it was being used now, to monitor the conversations of over two dozen Americans... twenty-nine, to be exact.

I began to fret. If Harlan Westfall knew we were listening, he might pass it on. Sarah gave me Westfall's transcripts and I dug in. What a slime-ball!

On Wednesday morning, I read the conversation that Westfall had had on his cellphone before the Norris shooting. The man didn't identify himself and Westfall didn't call him by name, but the man knew all about the FBI's investigation of the money trail, and he was tattling to Westfall, who already knew more than the FBI would ever learn.

I decided it could be, and went back to the beginning of the surveillance of Westfall to see if I could find another conversation with this guy. I found two that I thought had to be him, talking about the money trail. I was convinced this guy was an FBI agent. I got one of Sarah's minions to help me find the conversations in the computer archives so I could listen to the raw audio.

I discussed it with Sarah. "Westfall has a source in the FBI. He might have gotten a tip from him that we're eavesdropping, although I have no clue how the agency found out."

She puffed out her cheeks and tapped one with a pencil eraser. "One of the women on this project lives with an FBI agent. I heard her talking to a co-worker."

"Which woman?"

"Rhonda Sides."

Maybe she was the leak, maybe she wasn't. It was something to know.

Something began nagging at me. "Do you think Westfall had anything to do with the Korjev attempt, or Jack Norris?"

"I've seen no indication," she said.

Friday afternoon, Jake Grafton called Sarah and asked her to bring me and the latest intercepts to the hospital. A CIA security man was on duty in the hallway, one I didn't know. We found Jack Yocke and Callie in the room with the admiral.

I thought Grafton looked better. The color in his face was back, he had fewer IVs in him, and he had shaved within the last day or two. The cannula was still taped in place. His voice was stronger than it had been the last two times I saw him, and they had his bed cranked up a bit so he could read. He had his glasses on.

"You must be perking along pretty well," I told him. "The glint is back in your eye, and you look mean as ever."

He snorted, then said to me, "Get more chairs." Yep, there were only two in the room.

When that was attended to, he told me to close the door, and I did.

He shot the breeze a bit with Yocke, sizing him up. I knew what he was doing. Grafton was going to sell the reporter something that he probably wouldn't want, but he was going to buy it anyway.

After a few moments of idle chatter, Grafton said to Yocke, "I am going to tell you a story off the record, then make a proposal. We won't do any negotiating. If you agree to my proposal, you get to use the story. If you don't, you can never tell a soul about this conversation or anything you learned."

Yocke's eyes left Grafton and he looked around from face to face. His gaze ended up where it had began, on the admiral. Yocke shrugged. "I'm willing to listen."

"With the proviso as stated. You must listen to the whole story. If you don't like the deal your lips are eternally sealed."

"Your choice of words implies that I'm going to be dead. Assuming you don't mean to kill me if I don't like your proposal, I will keep it to myself."

Grafton nodded once. "Good," he said. "Tommy?"

That was my cue. Grafton wasn't strong enough to talk for an hour, so I was supposed to set the stage. I began with the senator's visit to the director's office to ask for our help rescuing a kidnapped kid in Tallinn, Estonia. I finished with our capture of Yegan Korjev and the interrogation in Utah. "Someone sent an assassin to try to murder Korjev, and we think we know who that was. That will all become apparent," I said.

"Sarah," Jake Grafton said.

Sarah cleared her throat. "Admiral Grafton asked me if I could use some secret programs we have developed through the years to turn various cell phones, laptop computers, and desktops into listening devices. He gave me the names and in some cases, telephone numbers.

"We have intercepted and recorded a bit over a hundred hours of conversations, so far, and—"

"Americans?" Yocke demanded.

"Yes."

"Jesus H. Christ!" Jack Yocke exclaimed. "Isn't that illegal?"

"Yes."

"Felonies?"

"Yes."

"I don't want to hear this. Christ, I could be prosecuted as a co-conspirator." He closed his eyes and stuck his fingers in his ears.

I laughed. He must have heard me, because he pulled his fingers out of his head, opened his eyes and looked at me sourly. "You asshole," he said.

"You ball-less bastard," I shot back, and leaned toward him. "Your country is awash with fake Russian money, reputations are being ruined, we are seeing the worst political crisis of our lifetime, Jake Grafton is lying there in that bed with a hole in him that damn near killed him, and you are worried about putting your shriveled little weenie on the line. Reporters can print things obtained illegally, and you know that. Remember the Pentagon Papers? Kiss my ass."

"That's enough, Tommy," Grafton said. He waited until Yocke shifted his gaze from me to him. "Our deal was you listen to all of it, then decide."

"I can tell you now I don't like it." Yocke was defiant, petulant. Personally, I always thought the guy lacked guts. He wanted to be at the top of his profession without doing any sweating or bleeding to get there.

"You can tell me that when we're done too," Grafton said. "Your decision."

Yocke shrugged, then nodded.

"Callie, give him the transcripts in the order that we arranged them." To Yocke he said, "We will start with Senate Minority Leader Harland Westfall and House Speaker Judy Mucci. Then we will move on to other players. These are merely computer-generated transcripts of oral conversations, and we have the conversations in digital form if you want to listen to the raw audio."

He nodded and Callie handed him the first pile.

I stood, and Sarah did too. Jake Grafton winked at me.

We went to the cafeteria for a cup of coffee.

"What do you think?" Sarah asked me.

"I think Yocke's crazy if he doesn't go for it. This is the story of the century; it will make his career. Shows, books, he's being handed the gold ring. Grafton may go to prison, but Yocke will come out smelling like a rose."

We had coffee, decided that an early dinner would sit well, so we went back through the cafeteria line with trays and plates.

Sitting at a table eating, we talked about Idaho. Maybe a cabin in the woods, near a town where we could get jobs. I knew a guy whose family were fishing and hunting outfitters—maybe something along those lines would keep me occupied.

"I could always do computer consulting," Sarah said tentatively.

"When you aren't hiking, fishing, camping, skiing, all that important stuff?"

She smiled. "We can give it a try, Tommy, but I think you're going to miss the action. Teaching some guy to fly-fish isn't the same as bugging an embassy in the middle of the night or rappelling down a rope with the SEALs to snatch a Russian mogul."

"I'm really tired of shooting people, Sarah."

# Chapter Twenty-Four

**I**t really bothers me that Harlan Westfall got a tip about our eaves-dropping," Sarah said.

"People are people," I responded. "If you can figure out how to stop wagging tongues your fortune is made."

She rested her elbow on the table and used her hand as a chin rest. "Westfall knew about the fake Russian money scramble," she mused. "He knew that Anton Hunt organized it, he knew how and why and when, and now he and his friends have everything on the table betting they can use Russian money to drive a stake through Vaughn Conyers' heart."

"Uh-huh."

"The Russians just want America tied up in knots. Sending fake money over here cost them pennies. It was a classic KGB operation."

She was right, of course.

"If we tumbled to it, the Russians could deny everything, and even if we proved they did it, so what? Westfall and friends, however, have more at stake."

I stared at her. When Grafton sailed off into the sunset, Sarah Houston should be the next director of the CIA.

"Let's go back upstairs," I said.

The security man was still outside Grafton's room, and the door was closed. The door across the hallway was standing open. I looked in. The room was empty.

I went to the desk where the wings came together, where the elevators were. The nurse on duty was a man. "403. Grafton. I want him moved to another room. That room right across the hallway, 404, is open. That will do nicely."

The guy looked at me. "I can't just shuffle patients around willy-nilly on your say-so. Who the hell are you, anyway?"

I opened my sports coat so he could see the gun under my armpit. "I'm the meanest son of a bitch you ever met. I was in Grafton's room, 403, a half hour ago and saw a rat, a big sewer rat. 404 won't cost the government a dime more than 403. If you don't move the admiral right fucking now, I'm going to call a reporter and my lawyer."

"So you're CIA?"

"No, Clara Barton. I'm with Murder Incorporated. Come on, let's move the bed and all that equipment."

Yocke was still reading. We left him at it and the nurse, Sarah, Callie and I moved the bed and computer monitor and IV trees. Then I hustled Yocke across the hallway and brought the chairs over.

When I was finished, I carefully closed the door to 403 and had the security man sit in front of it, just where he had been sitting. Looking right, he could see along the hall to the nurse's station and the elevator doors. To his left, he could see all the way down the hallway to the end, where there was a door to the emergency stairwell. That fire door, I knew, was rigged so that it only opened from the hallway side. Once a person was in the stairwell, he was going to the bottom unless he was a fireman or had the keys to the floors.

I went into the new room to see how Grafton and Yocke were getting along.

Yocke had apparently finished his assigned reading. The pile of papers was on a chair beside him. "It's dynamite," he was saying, "and you knew I'd have to take it when you called me."

Grafton didn't acknowledge that. "Tomorrow Sarah can give you audio on the transcripts you want to use. Take the transcripts—these are just copies—and use them to put this together into a narrative, then run it as soon as possible. However, you cannot say how you got this, who you got it from, how it was obtained, any of that. Is that understood?"

"A little bird gave it to me."

Grafton wiggled a finger at Yocke. "Nobody at all gave you anything unless you're under oath in a courtroom and the judge orders you to answer the question. Then and only then can you give my name, and only to keep from going to jail on contempt charges."

I couldn't resist. "If you are really ambitious, Jack, you could give the judge the finger and go to jail standing up for the First Amendment. The network would have you out by Labor Day and you'd be a rock star. The female anchors would be bopping you off-camera."

"Or on," Sarah said brightly.

Callie Grafton didn't say a word.

Sarah, Jack Yocke, and Callie Grafton left a half hour later. Since I'd made such a horse's ass out of myself over the admiral's room, I thought I had better wait to meet the villains, if they came. If they didn't come, all would be well. Since I couldn't stay awake all night I called a couple of colleagues, Willis Coffee and Travis Clay. I had known and worked with them for years. Willis agreed to relieve me at midnight. "Bring a shotgun," I said.

Saturday morning Nanya Friend went to the office. Running the CIA was a seven-days-a-week job. She was up to her eyeballs in reports and phone calls from senators, the White House, and the FBI when Grafton's senior executive assistant brought her a court document that had been served upon the gate guards. It was a cease and desist order signed by a federal district judge. Friend told the receptionist to hold the telephone calls and settled down to read it.

Upon information received, Senator Harlan Westfall alleged that the Central Intelligence Agency was monitoring his telephone calls and had installed listening devices in his computers. He went on for a page or so, leading up to the allegation that all this was grossly illegal. The judge had found that an injunction would probably be granted if the allegations were proven at a hearing, but considering their sensational nature and the fact that there would be no legal way for the said agency to monitor the said senator, a cease and desist order should be immediately issued. And it was. The thing was stapled to the back of the document. A date two weeks in the future was set for a hearing in United States District Court.

Friend called Sarah Houston and asked her to come to her office. When she arrived, Nanya showed her the court order.

Sarah read it carefully and handed it back. "So what do you want me to do, Ms. Friend?"

Nanya Friend knew Jake Grafton, and she knew the admiral was playing a dangerous game. She also thought Jake Grafton knew the risks he was taking. She turned the question around. "What do you suggest?"

"We've made transcripts of every word Westfall has uttered as well as every word uttered in his presence since we got the bugs in. Every word. The admiral wants those transcripts. He already has a stack of them."

"What about this court order?"

"We're obeying the court order," Sarah Houston said. "Westfall has already gone dark. We're not hearing anything from Westfall unless someone else whom we are monitoring calls him. I think you should pass this document to Admiral Grafton. He's still the director of this agency." Sarah Houston stopped right there. She was unwilling to tell Ms. Friend about Grafton's deal with Jack Yocke. Grafton could tell Friend whatever he wanted her to know, Sarah thought. Two weeks! America would die whimpering or explode into civil war long before anyone had to face a federal judge.

Friend was not stupid and knew that she was not getting the whole picture. The silence shrieked. Friend broke it with the comment, "That he is."

"An assassination attempt was made on a Russian under interrogation at a safe house," Sarah said. "The assistant director of this agency shot the director, almost killing him, and murdered two people—this has gone way beyond court orders and nice little statutes. It's gone way beyond poisonous politics and impeachment of the president. We're into murder and treason."

"Treason?"

"Treason," Sarah said flatly. "A conspiracy to bring down the government is treason."

Friend decided she didn't want to touch that comment. She said, "Levy said you shot Jack Norris."

Sarah's head bobbed. "That I did. Shot him dead. I put five bullets into him. He was trying to kill me and Tommy Carmellini with the rifle he used to shoot Jake Grafton." She made a gesture, dismissing the whole subject, then asked, "How did Westfall find out he was being monitored?"

Friend's eyes narrowed and she scrutinized the younger woman. "Obviously someone told him. Any idea who?"

Sarah Houston considered her answer. "Jack Norris is the most likely source. We think he initiated the attempted hit in Utah. But perhaps he didn't tell Westfall that he was being monitored by the agency. The timing isn't quite right. We're mining the telephone numbers of people who talked to Westfall. We should know something soon."

"Try to do that," the acting director said. "I'm going to the hospital this afternoon to see Admiral Grafton. I'll show him this. Meanwhile I have to talk to Robert Levy again. The FBI is getting a tremendous amount of heat. Levy thinks this agency, and Admiral Grafton, know a lot more than we are sharing."

"We certainly do," Sarah shot back. "I hope we know enough."

Harlan Westfall was on the verge of a nervous breakdown. He kept reviewing the conversations he had had with his political allies over the last week. But that wasn't enough time. Ten days. No, two weeks, or three. Maybe more. The FBI agent didn't know.

Jake Grafton. That... that... Who would have believed that an agency of the federal government would monitor him, the Senate Minority Leader?

No wonder the battery in his cellphone wouldn't hold a charge: it never rested. It had been constantly on, transmitting everything it heard. Westfall had stopped his car on the Chain Bridge over the Potomac, and as motorists behind him honked and shouted, got out of the car and threw the cellphone over the railing into the river.

He felt better without it. Felt clean. The only consolation was that that asshole Grafton would never be able to use recordings he and his agency had obtained illegally. Feloniously. No judge in America would allow that crap into his courtroom.

The IT people were going over all the computers in his office at the Senate Office Building and at his condo. Apparently all were infected by a virus that turned them into listening devices. Outrageous. That Grafton! He had to go, if he didn't die. Maybe he would die. He certainly deserved to go to the graveyard. A coffin would be the perfect place for him!

The CIA had gotten too damn big and evil for its britches. He would introduce a bill in the Senate to kill the agency, to split up its functions. Perhaps Congress should fire all the seventeen thousand maggots at Langley. No pensions. Just fire the sons of bitches. Even the Republicans would be outraged when they understood what Grafton's CIA had done. And the people at Langley who knew about this, who helped do it, they should be prosecuted. Levy at the FBI would love to hammer them. Perhaps we need another special prosecutor.

He sat in his office thinking about that as the tech people checked the office for bugs.

Harlan Westfall would get even. Grafton would rue the day he strapped on Harlan Westfall.

Then his thoughts turned to Vaughn Conyers. He was probably behind this. He probably told Grafton to do it. *We'll take that son of a bitch down!*

As he thought about Vaugh Conyers, Harlan Westfall wished he had recordings of everything that bastard said in the Oval Office for the last two years. Everything! The irony of that wish didn't cross his mind.

No one came to shoot Jake Grafton at the hospital Friday night or Saturday morning. I relieved Travis Clay, who had relieved Willis Coffee. The agency security guys also had a man on duty.

Nanya Friend came to the hospital Saturday afternoon and stayed for an hour and left. After she left I went in to see Grafton. All the other patients up and down the hallway had their television babysitter on, but Grafton didn't.

He looked tired. "Hey, Admiral."

"Hey, Tommy."

"Would you like your television on? Washington is trying to incinerate itself. The impeachment, Russian money, accusations right and left, shouts of treason. America is tearing itself apart."

He looked sad. "This is the end game. Both sides are trying to destroy the other."

"Putin," I said. "This is what he wanted."

"Oh, no doubt he's enjoying the show, but this mess is American-made. We did it to ourselves."

"Barry Sotero. He and Anton Hunt. This is right down their alley."

"It wasn't Barry," Grafton said softly. He couldn't speak much above a whisper. "And it wasn't Hunt. Neither is smart or subtle enough for this maneuver."

"So who?"

He told me.

I didn't believe it. "Got any proof?"

"None. And we need to get some. I want you to get whatever you need to wire this room for sound and video. Put a computer across the hallway to capture every whisper or fart."

I thought he had lost his mind, but I played along. "When?"

"Now. The other guys can watch for assassins. I doubt we'll have any this evening or tomorrow, but I want that stuff installed, checked, and in perfect working order by tomorrow night."

"When Yocke broadcasts?"

"Yes."

I was at a loss for words. Finally I said, "You going to watch Yocke on your TV?"

"Wouldn't miss it. Now go to Langley and get what you need."

"You're sure?"

"Go, Tommy. It's the only solution that makes sense."

So I left him lying there, took the elevator to the ground floor and walked across the parking lot to my truck. A light rain was falling from a gray sky. The puddles weren't very deep, but I stomped in them anyway. The poor devil had lost his marbles. The job had been too much. He should have retired last year.

I felt sorry for Callie.

Jack Yocke's Sunday evening show originated in a studio at the local Fox station in Washington. With over ten hours of audio to be edited down to a one-hour show, complete with streamers along the bottom of the screen for those who couldn't quite hear what was being said, Yocke had a huge task getting ready for his Sunday night broadcast. His producer and an unpaid intern helped sort the material and offered suggestions. Commercials would eat up part of his hour: Yocke knew he was just scratching the surface with the audio intercepts that he would have time to air. And Grafton had only given him intercepted conversations in which Senate Minority Leader Harlan Westfall and House Speaker Judy Mucci participated.

At first Yocke was tempted to limit the conversations to the attack on Conyers via impeachment, but he realized that story could wait for a few weeks. After tonight he might not have a television show. "We'll go with the hottest stuff first," he told his producer and intern.

"This stuff sizzles," the producer said. He was a thirty-something skinny guy with lumberjack facial hair and a ponytail. "How sure are you that this stuff is real?"

That was certainly a valid question. If Yocke was the victim of a *War of the Worlds* fiction production, his career would be as dead as King Tut. The damage to the network would be incalculable.

"Absolutely certain."

"Where'd you get this stuff?"

"From an unimpeachable source."

When the producer took a potty break Saturday evening, he decided to visit the executive suite. Even if Yocke were willing to risk his career, the producer wasn't. Twenty minutes after the producer returned to the studio, Yocke was summoned to the executive offices.

The manager of the local station didn't pretend he didn't know what was going on. "Tell me about these telephone recordings you are going to use tomorrow night." He was in his fifties and had begun, like Yocke, on a newspaper before making the leap to television. His name was Stu Metz.

So Yocke told how he visited CIA Director Jake Grafton in his hospital room on Friday and was given this material by Grafton, on the condition that he not reveal his source. "Is it genuine?"

"Of course. We compared tapes of Westfall and Mucci and the voice prints match up perfectly."

"Did the CIA have warrants for telephone taps?" Metz asked.

"No."

"So these recordings are illegal."

"Yes."

"Your deal with Grafton—can you ever reveal your source?"

"Under oath in a courtroom to avoid a contempt citation."

Metz frowned. "What if he denies it?"

"He won't. I've known him for years and he's given me my biggest stories. Jake Grafton plays straight and fair, and he's one of the few in this town who does."

"I want to see the show when you get it finished. Then we'll decide if we are going to run it."

"It's your network."

"I just work here," Stu Metz said. "And I want to keep this job. I like it. I've got a mortgage and two car payments to make every month. However, I do know the guys who own a controlling interest in this network's parent. They believe in cutting-edge journalism, but they are not interested in committing suicide delivering it. We're in business to make a profit, not to provide full employment for the Washington legal profession."

"I understand. I'd better get back at it. I'll call you tomorrow when I have the show in the can."

Jack Yocke's intern, Gabriella Saba, was a young woman in her first year of grad school at George Washington University. She was shocked at the vitriol pouring forth from the computer. Mucci and Westfall! Who would have believed it? When she went home at nine on Saturday night, she told her boyfriend about the show.

He was a bit farther left on the political scale that Gabriella, and so on Sunday morning after she had left for work, he called a buddy whose wife worked for Judy Mucci and told him about the show. "The congresswoman's in it, Gabby says."

"And these are telephone taps?"

"That's what Gabby said."

"Where did they come from?"

"She didn't know. Yocke refused to say. My guess would be FBI."

"Holy... Thanks for calling." And the buddy hung up.

At eleven on Sunday morning, Judy Mucci called Stu Metz. "I hear you have some illegal wiretaps one of your people is going to use on a show tonight."

"Where'd you hear that?"

"That's beside the point. Is it true?"

"I'm not a lawyer. I'm a journalist."

"I give you fair warning, Metz. If you run anything obtained illegally that features my voice, I'll sue your damned network until hell won't have it."

"The courthouse is open Monday through Friday from nine to five," Stu Metz told her.

Then Metz called his boss in New York and told him about Yocke's show and the speaker's threat.

"What's Yocke got that's so hot?"

"I haven't heard it yet."

"Have Yocke call me."

Jack Yocke did call New York, and at four that afternoon, after he finished taping his show, he and Stu Metz sat down to watch it. At the same time, it was running in the executive suite in New York.

When the show finished, Metz and Yocke sat in silence, awaiting the verdict from on high. Yocke was nervous. Metz chewed a fingernail, then stuck a stick of gum into his mouth and munched that. Finally, the phone rang.

"Stu, Jack?"

"Yessir."

"I just got off the phone with Harlan Westfall, who called just as the show ended. Was he infuriated! I can see why. That bastard is in *big* trouble. So is that senile nincompoop Mucci. Those two deserve each other."

Silence. Then a chuckle came over the desk loudspeaker. The chuckle grew to a laugh.

"Yocke, you did a good job. Run that thing. Don't change a word."

The connection broke. Stu Metz reached for Yocke's hand, shook it, and they went to dinner.

# Chapter Twenty-Five

Saturday night Sarah and I ate with Armanti Hall and some of the guys in the hospital cafeteria. The food was wholesome and good, yet the prices were very low. Apparently, Band-Aid and iodine sales in the rooms upstairs were subsiding the food service.

I had finished installing audio and video recorders in Grafton's hospital room earlier, so we sat across the hall and watched the nurse maneuver the bedpan. No one said a word. All of us have a bedpan in our future if we live long enough.

When we finished dinner, we lingered over coffee while Callie visited with her husband upstairs. No one had much to say. I thought I was the only one there who had an inkling about what Grafton planned, what he thought would happen, and I had been around long enough to know that keeping your mouth shut is usually the best policy.

We made our arrangements about who was going to be on watch tonight, then Sarah and I drove home. The rain had stopped and the night was just black and wet.

Sunday was a day of waiting. Sarah went back to Langley and brought Grafton another cardboard box full of intercept transcripts and another thumb drive that contained the raw audio. The hospital staff had Grafton sitting up in bed by then. The admiral and his wife dug into the box after lunch.

When Callie told him he had to take a nap, he grumped a bit, she lowered the top of the bed, and he dropped right off to sleep.

She came out in the hall to visit with Sarah and me.

There was a rapt audience in the hospital for the Jack Yocke show that Sunday evening. We sent out for pizza and ate it in the hour leading up to the show.

I had to hand it to him. Yocke knew how to do it. He started the story with the money flowing through the branch of the Bank of Scandinavia in Tallinn, Estonia, and went on from there. It was obvious to me that he had received a detailed brief from Jake Grafton, had paid attention, and taken notes. Then he got into the telephone conversations we had taped. I loved Westfall's conversation with Cheney Kopp, the Chairman of the Board and CEO of the Life Network. I was tempted to call Senator Westfall to see if he was watching—after all, we knew his telephone number—but I refrained. He would be down for quite a while, so I didn't have to rush to kick him.

I must say, Speaker Mucci sounded more shrill and elderly on the television than I remembered her. Perhaps Yocke tweeked the tweeter to give her a little more squeak at the high end of the register. Still, it was her, no doubt, even if she did sound like the Wicked Witch of the West.

Yocke made the point that the money was created by Russia and transferred so that the Democrats could slime their enemies with it. Westfall's comment that the Russians had double-crossed them was brilliant.

Grafton had even given Yocke some audio of Yegan Korsev whaling the tar out of Anton Hunt, may he rest in peace. Still, I thought Yocke went kinda easy on Hunt, probably because corpses can no longer defend themselves. He had snippets of Westfall's conversation with Michael Hunt, the scion of the Hunt clan, talking about the New World Order.

The best parts of the Yocke show, in my opinion, were Westfall's conversations with the "squaw." The conversation where she used the N-word made me break out in laughter. And I almost lost it when I heard Westfall refer to former presidential candidate Cynthia Hinton with the c-word.

When he signed off, Jack Yocke promised more next week.

We cheered and went into Grafton's room and did a victory stomp. The admiral turned off the television. A nurse hustled in and told us to tone it down or leave. She was nice about it, but hospitals are like libraries.

After five minutes or so Grafton gave me the sign, so I suggested we let him get some sleep. The other guys left, and I sat down on the chair across the corridor from his room. Armanti Hall had decided to do this hospital gig up right, and was wearing blue surgical scrubs and pushing a room-cleaning cart with a shotgun in it. He stationed himself at the opposite end of the corridor from the nurses' station. Sarah and Callie Grafton went into the old room where we had all our equipment, along with Doc Gordon. We settled down to wait.

I had argued that our guy might not come tonight. Grafton dismissed that statement with a wiggle of his finger. "He wants to know how much I know and how much I intend to spill. He'll be here."

I was too keyed up to sit, and walked up and down the corridor end-lessly. I was standing beside the nurses' station when I heard the elevator coming up. I grabbed a patient's chart and busied myself over it while the nurse on duty, the guy I had called Clara Barton, frowned at me.

The elevator door opened and Vaughn Conyers, president of the United States, walked out with four Secret Service agents. The muscle looked me and the nurse over as the president marched down the corridor for Grafton's room.

Conyers didn't seem surprised to find that Grafton had moved across the hallway. Maybe he had forgotten which side he was on. The security man, Billy Franks, was sitting in the chair, and he smiled and pointed at the admiral's room. The Secret Service dudes dropped off, and Conyers opened Grafton's door, went in, and pulled it shut behind him.

I adjusted the ear piece in my right ear. "Good evening, Admiral."

"Good evening, Mr. President."

"Mind if I sit down?" The scraping of the chair legs on the linoleum, or whatever that floor covering was.

The Secret Service guys looked hyped. They were playing with their ear pieces, scrutinizing Billy and Armanti at the end of the corridor, no doubt picking spots where they could drill us both if we even twitched. One of them muttered into his lapel mike. "We're here." I heard it distinctly through my earpiece, so I suppose the frequency of their little radio system was close enough to ours for us to capture the bleed-through. The systems were no more than ten feet away.

One of the agents glanced at me and the male nurse at the nurses' station from time to time. I put the chart back and took another to study.

"Admiral... May I call you Jake?"

"Please do, sir."

"How are you getting along?"

"Better."

"When are they going to let you out of here?"

"It'll be a few weeks. I start hiking up and down the hall tomorrow, then physical therapy in a few days. That will take a few weeks, then maybe I can go home and do the therapy as an out-patient."

"Sorry this happened to you," Conyers said. No shit, I thought.

Two of the Secret Service guys had arranged themselves on either side of Billy Franks. The other two were strolling the corridor, one toward me and one toward Armanti.

"So am I," Jake Grafton said.

"I watched the Jack Yocke show tonight. Reem passed to me the fact that you called and suggested we watch it."

"Yocke did well with the material," Grafton said.

"Obviously you leaked that information to him—"

"'Leak' isn't exactly the right word. I called Yocke and he came here, sat right where you're sitting, and I briefed him. Let him read the telephone transcripts, listen to raw audio, then asked him to put that show together. He agreed to do it."

Conyers didn't say anything for a moment. He seemed to be arranging his thoughts.

"How much more are you going to tell him?"

"I haven't decided. I thought you and I could talk about that."

"Why me?" the president said.

"Mr. President," Grafton said, his voice soft. He was exhausted and using all the juice he had left to carry this conversation. "The Russians went to a lot of trouble to get this thing rolling along. Two hundred billion fake dollars, Monopoly money someone called it, tossed into the air like confetti, just so the Americans could humiliate themselves scrambling for it. And we did.

"Then they went to a lot more trouble to make sure all this was going to become public, that we couldn't sweep it under the rug, that the whole stinking mess would see the light of day and the flies would swarm. That didn't just happen; the Russians made it happen."

A moment of silence. Maybe Conyers was nodding. The four bodyguards were in their relative positions, and one of them keyed his lapel radio. To my amazement, I again heard his transmission.

"We're in place and ready."

Jake Grafton was saying, "They set up Yegan Korjev, cast him to play the hero's part. We kidnapped him, interrogated him, used drugs on him, all to get him to tell us the 'truth,' whatever in hell that is. The Russians had taken the trouble to hypnotize him to make sure his story stayed consistent under drugs. I doubt that at this point Yegan Korjev even knows what the truth is."

*Ready for what?* I was only half listening to Grafton and staring at the four Secret Service dudes. They didn't look as if they had submachine guns on them, but no doubt they were carrying pistols and were damn good with them.

"What is the truth?" The president asked that, and I thought it a good question. If I could figure that one out I could get a PhD in philosophy from any university in the country.

"Why don't you tell me, Mr. President."

I heard a faint snort.

One of the Secret Service agents was reaching under his jacket, fingering his pistol. I pulled mine out, took the safety off, and held it down under the counter.

"There's going to be a lot of speculation by the Democrats and their media allies that you are the one who set this up with the Russians," Jake Grafton told the president.

"You know I didn't."

"That isn't the point. The point is that you will be accused, tried and convicted by the left-wing media. Those women on *The View* will savage you. Half the country will believe them."

"If you know I didn't do it, who do you think did?"

"Cynthia Hinton," Jake Grafton said. "There's no one else. Anton Hunt didn't have the brains or stature for this caper. Cynthia even went to the Russians for a fake dossier on you that she could use to keep you from being elected. When that didn't work, the Deep State had you investigated by a special prosecutor. Anything to make it more difficult to get your program through Congress. Anything to make it more difficult for you to get reelected."

"*We're ready*," the Secret Service guy said again into his lapel mike. I almost peed my pants. What was he ready for? Our bugs *must* be picking up the bleed-over from his transmissions. I really didn't consciously think about it—I just assumed it was so.

"She went to the Russians seven years ago," Conyers said, "after Sotero made her Secretary of State. The Russians used funny money to make their donations to the Hinton Foundation after she approved their application to buy ten percent of America's uranium production."

"And she figured out the funny money scam," Jake Grafton prompted.

"She did," the president acknowledged. "She realized that she could screw her political enemies with dirty money. The name of her game is power."

"And the Russians realized that they could screw both sides of the political divide with dirty money," Grafton prompted.

"That's it."

"So why don't you want this to come out?"

"We have to live on this planet with the Russians. Either live with them or kill them, and killing them isn't a viable option. And regardless of what she's done, Cynthia Hinton is an icon for a lot of Democrats, mostly women. She got the Democrat nomination and ran for president of the United States. And now we accuse her of treasonous acts that we can't prove? Absolutely not. She'll come out looking like a saint and we'll look like evil trolls who live under a bridge and eat children."

"Where do you want this investigation to go from here, Mr. President?"

"I don't want you accusing Cynthia Hinton of anything," Vaughn Conyers said. "I wish I could turn off Robert Levy, but you know I can't. The FBI is going to blunder about in the china shop breaking dishes regardless of what we do. What they won't do is find Cynthia Hinton's fingerprints on anything they can get into court. Not even if they look under every rock from here to Moscow."

Jake Grafton seemed to agree with that. In my mind's eye I could see him nodding. Then he said, "What I think we can do is give Jack Yocke enough wiretap conversations to defuse some of this political madness. The politicians are in it to their eyes, and if the public sees that, this whole kerfuffle will die a natural death."

"This impeachment thing might too," the president said.

I heard the chair scrape. He must be rising.

"*Do it*," somebody said over the Secret Service net.

The agent standing on Billy Franks' left drew his pistol and shot Billy right in the neck. The sound reverberated down that corridor as if a cannon had been fired. Billy went sprawling over to his right. The agent pulled Billy's pistol and went charging into the room that held the president and Jake Grafton.

Armanti and I opened fire at the same time—towards each other. We hadn't thought this out very well. I hit the guy who was looking my way, he went down, and two blasts of Number Four buckshot swept the other two off their feet. Buckshot pattered around me like hail. Something smacked me in the left thigh, not too hard. I stayed upright and ran toward the hospital room as shots rang out, muffled. The bastard was in there gunning the president and Jake Grafton.

Two of the agents in the hallway were still thrashing around when Armanti and I reached them. Armanti blew one's head apart with the shotgun and I put a .45 slug into the other's chest.

Going through the door of Grafton's room, I couldn't believe my eyes. The would-be assassin was lying on the floor motionless, still holding his gun in his hand. I kicked the gun away. His eyes were focused on infinity.

Jake Grafton had a gun in his hand and was half-turned in the bed, despite the IVs. The president was standing on the other side of the bed looking shocked. Armanti Hall came into the room behind me.

Jake Grafton handed Conyers the pistol. "Here," he said, and the president took the weapon. "You are now the first American president to shoot an assassin."

# Chapter Twenty-Six

The attempted assassination of the president of the United States was front-page news worldwide. Radio talk shows and television talking heads got the facts out quickly, helped by the audio and video recordings from the CIA director's hospital room. Apparently the assassins weren't aware of this equipment, which even captured the agents' back and forth on their private radio network.

The fact that the agent who tried to shoot the president and Jake Grafton with the pistol he took from CIA security officer Billy Franks indicated, FBI Director Robert Levy said, that the conspirators intended to rig the scene so that the blame would fall on CIA personnel.

The identity and political leanings of the deceased assassin were hot items. His name was Vincent Matthews. His life was examined from birth to death: it included a failed marriage and a large influx of cash into his girlfriend's bank account the week prior to his demise. The FBI said that after Matthews shot officer Franks and took his pistol, he strode into the hospital room, and the president, alerted by the sound of gunshots in the hallway, grabbed a pistol from CIA director Jake Grafton's bed and shot him. One shot, right through the heart, and that was it for

Mr. Matthews. The entire sequence, captured on audio, from first shot to last took eight seconds. The pistol Conyers had used was the one Callie Grafton had brought to the hospital and tucked into the bed where her husband could reach it, if necessary.

Two of the other Secret Service officers died at the scene. The one survivor was critically wounded and would have permanent injuries. He wasn't talking to law enforcement agents. The investigation in the weeks that followed found that all four men had received several million dollars each in untraceable funds. Russian money? No one knew.

The audio of the conversation between the president and CIA director before the assassin started shooting was immediately classified Top Secret and withheld from the press. The media squawked about it, but the president stood firm. The conversation stayed classified. The video, if there was one, was never produced.

Although Jack Yocke's show was overshadowed by the assassination news, eventually the media got around to the political slant and remembered Yocke's show the Sunday night before the assassination attempt. The following Sunday evening he put on another show using more wiretapped conversations. Attorneys for the House Speaker and Senate Minority Leader went to court that week demanding injunctions to keep Yocke off the air with recordings he obtained illegally. They didn't get them. Their remedy, the court said, was to sue whoever taped their conversations for damages. Of course, if a law had been violated, then the Justice Department could prosecute if it chose. But the media's right to broadcast even stolen material was protected by the First Amendment. Of course, if the material the media used was untrue, a suit for damages would lie.

Two days after the second Yocke show aired, Judy Mucci resigned as Speaker of the House and announced she would not run for re-election to her house seat. Four days later Senator Harland Westfall was found sitting in his car in his garage, dead of carbon monoxide poisoning. The automobile's engine had died during the night, probably due to the lack of oxygen in the garage.

Yocke did only the two shows using material that he obtained from Jake Grafton, although he never once told anyone where it came from. That detail got lost somehow in the nationwide search for the people behind the attempted assassination of the president. Eight million dollars, a voice on the radio, three bodies, and a severely injured fourth man got barrels of printer's ink and hundreds of hours of air time.

Robert Levy's FBI pulled out all the stops. The FBI's previous involvement with the Russian dossier and the failed attempts of senior agency officials to smear the president had placed the agency under a huge spotlight. The public would be satisfied with nothing less than a trial and conviction of the people responsible for the assassination attempt. Senators and Congressmen stated flatly that the future of the agency was at stake.

About a month after the assassination attempt, the Russian banking system collapsed. I read about it one morning in the *Washington Times*. It seems every computer in every bank in Russia wiped itself clean overnight, paralyzing the entire banking system.

I drank my coffee, ate my omelet, and went to physical therapy. It turned out that the bullet I took in the leg required an operation, which meant hospital time and therapy afterwards. After therapy, I dropped by my fitness center and got on the treadmill. The television was still riding the Conyers' attempted assassination story pretty hard, but the banking collapse in the evil empire got some minutes. The expert of the network I was watching thought computer hacking and malware was probably the cause, but no one had any facts. Oddly, the Russians weren't yet accusing anyone. I had my candidate, and it was the woman I slept with. Screwing the Russians was right down Sarah Houston's alley. The CIA was going to miss her.

I had lunch with Jake Grafton, who was at home those days, walking with a cane. The physical therapist visited him there three times a week.

He and Callie looked glad to see me. Our first subject was our wounds, which were healing. I was fortunate that the guy who shot me didn't hit anything I really needed to keep the machine running, and I was lucky enough to get shot in a hospital with doctors and an operating room just paces away.

"So you're leaving the agency this Friday?" Grafton asked as we finished lunch, which was soup and home-made chicken-salad.

"That's Sarah's last day too," I told him. "We'll get our stuff packed and put in storage, then we're off to Idaho."

"I went out with a flight instructor this past weekend," Grafton said. "He says there is no reason I can't resume flying whenever I think I can get in and out of the plane and gas it and so on. I called the guys at the airport where I keep my plane and they've started an annual inspection on it. Now all I need is a letter from my doctor that says I am not likely to die at the controls, in his opinion."

Callie brought us coffee and heard the flying comment. She winked at me. "With me as his ground crew, he'd be ready to fly right now if the plane was."

"Are you retiring, Admiral?" I asked.

"I'm on terminal leave now," he said. "I don't know when the White House will announce it. Probably not until they get someone else lined up to take the job."

"Nanya Friend?"

"That was my recommendation, but you know how it is."

"This Russian banking system collapse. Would you know anything about that?"

He smiled and sipped his coffee.

"So who bought the president's murder, and tried to buy yours?"

He shrugged. "You'll have to ask Robert Levy that question, but I doubt if he knows. The bureau is trying to trace the money. They are really motivated. Unless they can do that or someone confesses, it's hopeless. That wounded Secret Service agent is brain damaged and isn't saying anything to anyone."

"There's a book in his future."

"There's a wheelchair there for sure," Grafton said sourly, "and maybe some bullets. The poor bastard may commit suicide by shooting himself three times in the back of his head."

"You said Cynthia Hinton was behind the money river, and so did Vaughn Conyers."

"That's one possibility," Grafton said, weighing his words. "You could probably find another hundred or so candidates in the Deep State. Some of those people thought Conyers was the devil incarnate."

"What about the other voice on the Secret Service tactical net? The guy who said, 'Do it?'"

"That's a possible lead, if they can ever match that voice. But that guy didn't pay eight million dollars for a couple of hits. Whoever did probably wasn't within ten miles of that hospital."

"Ah, but he'll know who paid him."

Grafton merely smiled.

"Admiral, they are still talking and writing books about the JFK assassination, which happened in 1963. What is that? Fifty-six years ago? They'll be talking and writing books about Conyers' attempted murder for a hundred years unless the government charges someone and proves they did it to an absolute certainty."

Grafton shifted positions in his chair. "Assassinating a president is the worst crime anyone can commit. Trying to do it is just as bad. The government will pull out all the stops. They'll investigate until they have gathered all the evidence that can be found, down to the last iota. They'll never quit, and there is no statute of limitations. Whoever tried to arrange Conyers' murder will be living in dread for the rest of his life."

"What I don't want," I explained, "is to have some half-wit theorize that Jake Grafton and Tommy Carmellini tried to whack the president."

Jake Grafton chuckled. "In fifty or sixty years," he said, "some guy might write a book about us doing just that. I'll be long gone, so I won't care, and you can sue him for defamation of character and fund your retirement."

I laughed. "In fifty years I'll be too old to care," I said. "Seriously, was Conyers right to tell you to lay off Cynthia?"

Jake Grafton scrutinized my face. "We could never get enough admissible evidence to indict her, much less convict her," he said. "Conyers was right about that. The Russians will *never* talk. If we had named her as a suspect in the money shuffle she would have become a martyr. On the other hand, if we don't do anything then the whispers will eventually destroy her politically, like Chinese water torture, drop by drop."

"At heart, you're a really mean bastard," I said appreciatively. "But why do I think Cynthia might have panicked and paid to have you and Conyers murdered?"

He got the funniest look on his face. "Because she was afraid of us," he replied. "That's what a guilty conscience will do."

I smiled. "The old attack pilot." I said. "I like that."

Jake Grafton grunted.

I decided to leave it there. I shifted my attention to Callie. "When are you coming to Idaho?"

"This fall, during some good weather," she said. "Jake doesn't want to fly on instruments any more. Keep us advised of where you are, and of your telephone numbers."

I finished my coffee, we talked about inconsequential things, then I shook hands and said goodbye. And walked out of the Graftons' lives.

That summer afternoon I limped out the door to his building and stood looking across the street at the parking garage that Jack Norris used as a sniper's perch when he gunned the admiral. I wasn't even wearing a windbreaker, much less a pistol. Maybe it would be better this way.

It was an October day, with clear skies and temps in the high 50s, a little wind stirring what remained of the fall foliage. Sarah and I sat in the pickup near the upwind end of a 2,800-foot-long grass runway, which ran a little uphill to where we sat.

We got out, leaned against the side of the truck, and watched a flight of geese making their way south with the mountains behind them. Finally I heard it, a tiny buzzing, very pleasant, growing slowly.

Sarah saw it first: a little high-wing airplane to the southeast, just above the mountain ridge. As we watched, she dropped lower and came flying toward us; the engine noise grew from a burble to a growl. She flew right over the truck with the engine singing, then swung out on a downwind leg. The pilot pulled the power and I realized that he had lowered flaps.

She came around and lined up on the runway, settling, then gently kissed the earth in a three-point landing, the tailwheel arriving at the same time as the mains. No bounce.

With the engine at idle she rolled up to us; the pilot stopped the left main wheel and spun the tail around with a blast of power. The spinning prop baptized us with dust and noise.

The engine died and the prop waggled to a stop. In the silence, I could hear the click as the pilot's door opened... there was Jake Grafton, smiling at me. "Hello, Tommy."

I couldn't contain myself. I jumped up and down on one foot, then the other, pumping air with both fists and shouting as Sarah laughed and Mrs. Grafton waved from the right seat. Life was moving on...

*The End*